Woman Missing

WOMAN
MISSING

KAELIN WENNERBERG

JOFFE BOOKS

Joffe Books, London

www.joffebooks.com

First published in Great Britain in 2025

Cover art by Nick Castle

ISBN: 978-1-80573-217-4

This book is dedicated to my father, Michael.
Raising four girls couldn't have been easy but you did it perfectly.
I love you.

CHAPTER ONE

June 18th, 2004
2:02 a.m.

I can do this. I don't have a choice. I have to do this.

Every time I make the decision to drive home drunk, these thoughts invade my mind. I know it's not safe and not right, but I do it anyways. I've done it more times than I can count. I know the quickest route from my favorite bar by heart. Six miles — I've done the math. The logical part of my brain begs me not to, but I usually listen to the stupid side instead. The side that insists it's not a big deal.

I've done it so many times, I think I'm in complete control. If anything, I'm more alert than when I drive sober. When I'm sober, I'll talk on the phone, eat, or even check my hair in the mirror. When I'm wasted, I scope out the road for people, other cars, and, most importantly, police cars. I've been taking this route home for the past year, and I've yet to see one. It's safe, and that soothes my conscience. That, and for a majority of my life, my conscience has had so many other things to worry about that this seems like child's play. I'm not hurting anyone by doing it. Just driving home. That's the thing about my life; I am always in control.

Except for the pouring rain, this Friday is no exception. A security guard has just escorted me out the door. I stand outside the back parking lot of the bar for a couple moments as I search inside my purse for the keys to my 1992 Toyota Cressida. After locating them, I jump inside and quickly close the door. I turn the key in the ignition, blasting the heat to warm up my soaked body. Wearing a gray tank top and jean shorts seemed like a good idea when I left home. I smile, remembering how when I was little my mother would always chase me around trying to get me into my jacket. Old habits really do die hard.

I switch on the radio, watching as other vehicles leave the parking lot and waiting until nearly all of them have gone. Some people are walking home. Some nights, depending on how intoxicated I am, I will offer rides to some of them. Not tonight. The liquor has turned my usually kind nature sour.

Opening the sun visor, I flip the mirror open. The rain has caused my mascara to run, and my hair is sticking to the sides of my face. I look an utter fright. Not that it matters. I had only come out in hopes of seeing my ex-boyfriend Mikey. We always visited this bar on Saturday nights, and I knew he'd be here.

I spotted Mikey, but he ignored me any time I attempted to speak to him. I don't blame him. Our relationship ended this morning. I slept with one of his buddies yesterday, and the guy confessed. Mikey called me and ended the relationship then and there before giving me any time to explain myself. A stupid part of me thought we could reconcile if I came out tonight.

Every relationship I've had in my twenty-two years has ended the same way. I've yet to find a man who can hold my attention for more than a couple months. Mikey made it to three months. I liked — and still do like — him. We were good friends before he asked me out. I almost didn't accept because I didn't want to ruin our friendship, but word around town was that he was a gentleman. I thought maybe, for the first time, I could fall in love. I want to fall in love, but there just always seems to be a part of me that can't. A part that doesn't want to go through the heartbreak I saw my parents go through. Heartbroken people make rash, dangerous decisions.

Liquor is the only thing in my life that doesn't end in disappointment. My family tells me I'll end up just like my mother if I keep on drinking. They don't understand that I am in control of my life, unlike my alcoholic, pill-addicted mother.

Once I've partly warmed up, I put my car into drive and start on my way home. It's raining so hard that even with my wipers going full speed, I can hardly see the road.

My eyes begin to water. Fuck. I always cry when I drink gin. I should've known to stick to vodka or beer. My breakup with Mikey intensified my usual weekend theatrics, resulting in me ordering a lot more gin and tonics than usual. I just wanted to drown my despair.

Have I missed my turn? My clouded vision along with the constant downpour of rain is a bad mix. Every street looks the same — each one with an assortment of cars lining it. I am close to blacking out.

I roll my window down and poke my head out, attempting to get a better view. Rain dribbles down my hair. As I search for the nearest street sign, my phone begins buzzing. I reach for the passenger seat, searching for where I may have thrown my purse when getting into the car. *Am I so drunk that I accidentally dropped it into the footwell?*

I reach down to grab it, taking my eyes away from the road for a mere second — or is it longer? I feel around in my purse, my phone grazing past my fingers. I look back at the road.

Too late. Something big hits the hood and the windshield with a horrible thud, and then it is gone.

3

I ram my foot on the brakes. I want to get out and check, but my legs decline to move. Instead, I scan the road for the thing I collided with. My windshield is cobwebbed with cracks, making it impossible to see anything outside.

I put my head out the window again. Lying on the pavement barely four yards from my Toyota's now-steaming dented hood is a man. I let out a horrified scream. *Oh no, no, no.* A part of me wants to back up and flee the scene. Drive away and get as far from here as possible.

Stopped in the street, rain pelting the shattered windshield, I hear the music playing. It's a melancholy jazz song with a slow beat. "I'll Never Smile Again" by Tommy Dorsey. The song turns my stomach. If the collision hasn't already killed this man, if I run away, he might die. He could have loved ones who will never smile or laugh again.

Be brave, Maxine. My mother's words ring in my ear. They always come back to me when I'm stuck, not sure what I should or shouldn't do.

As I contemplate, my car's engine stutters and dies. I can still make a run for it. That's what I've done before, after each of the two incidents in my life where something horrendous occurred. I simply ran off, not wanting to face the reality of the situation.

I'm hyperventilating. I thought I'd never see another dead body again. Not after last time. What if this person I just hit isn't dead? If he's alive, things can't go that badly for me. I have the chance to save him, not just stand there like I did the last time.

Be brave, Maxine.

After getting my breathing under control, I open the door and step out. Although it's chilly, the air feels thick, hard to breathe in. Shivers crawl up my spine like spiders. I rest my hand against the side of my sedan as I walk toward the unmoving body. Once I make it to the end of my hood and no longer have its support,

I might fall to my knees. Images flash through my mind. I might throw up all the gin and tonics I slurped down tonight.

Although the rain has drained most of it down the road, there are traces of blood on the pavement and on the hood of my car. I kneel once I'm close to the man and slowly reach out to touch his shoulder. I give him a gentle shake, praying he'll say something, anything.

After a couple moments of trying, I twist his body around so he's lying on his side facing me instead of on his back. His face is bloodied, and his nose looks broken. His eyes are closed. I press my ear close to his mouth, trying to hear any breathing. It's hard to tell with the rain coming down. I feel for a pulse. It's faint, but it's there.

I assure him I'll be back and run to my car, to find my phone. I dial 911 and frantically explain what happened. When I hang up, I realize how slurred my words must have sounded. I know when the ambulance and police show up, I must do a better job enunciating.

As I wait for the ambulance, I grab a couple napkins and run back to the man's body. I press the napkins to his bloodied face. I wipe away blood flowing from his broken nose and busted lip. It's the only area I can find blood coming out of. It should relieve me, but it doesn't because now I'm wondering if he has internal bleeding.

When the napkins become soggy, I toss them to the side and stare at the man wishing he'd just wake up. Then, after a couple minutes pass and the rain begins to lighten, finally the man coughs and spits out blood. Some lands on my face, and my heart is beating so rapidly I don't wipe it away. He begins to shake, and he reaches toward me. As a reflex I pull out of his grasp. Then he opens his eyes.

I don't mean to back away, but the expression in his eyes frightens me. His eyes follow my movement with a look of hatred. I don't blame him; I would feel the same.

The man tries to speak. Most of his words are mumbled, and I can tell he's aching from the pain as he struggles to speak. I wish he would stop; I know whatever he wants to say to the woman who just hit him can't be anything positive.

I hear a siren nearing us. *Thank God.* As I look toward the sound, a hand grasps my arm. I look down, terrified.

The man is well built and ruggedly handsome, even with his face covered in blood. He's freshly shaven, with thin lips and a large nose.

"They're—" The man coughs up more blood. "They're going to make you pay for this."

"W-what?" I ask, shaking.

His eyes are wild with anger. Just as an ambulance and police car close in, I pry my arm from his powerful grasp, falling from my kneeling position to my ass. I scoot away, wrapping my arms around my body. I'm overrun with fear. I'm going to vomit any moment now.

They're going to make you pay for this.

What did he mean by that? Who are "they"?

The police officers and EMT workers run over to us, but I feel unable to move or breathe. The man lets out an exasperated breath before closing his eyes once again. He goes still.

For the first time in a long time, I realize I am not in control of my life anymore.

CHAPTER TWO

October 9th, 2009
8:57 p.m.

It's been five years and four months since I killed a man. Or, as the state of Wyoming puts it, since I committed aggravated vehicular homicide. Thanks to my criminal defense lawyer, I've been spared more time behind bars.

When the accident first happened, I knew I was screwed; I couldn't afford a good lawyer and would be stuck with one appointed by the court. Out of fear I used my one phone call to call my dad. He showed mercy on my drunken mistake and hired a criminal defense lawyer to represent me. He couldn't afford him, but they were old buddies and my dad, who ran his own construction company, paid him by replacing the roof on the man's enormous house.

I didn't deserve or expect this saving grace, but I got it. To this day I still don't understand why my father did this for me. Since I turned eighteen, we haven't been close. Hell, after my mom died when I was a child, we haven't been close. I always knew he thought of me as the child of the crazy woman he never should have married. The woman who forever tainted the name of Masterson.

While in jail I often thought of the man's last words to me: *They're going to make you pay for this.*

I managed to push his words from my mind and instead channeled my energy into working on a plea deal with my lawyer. He assured me that if I were to plead guilty, the sentence would be much lighter than if it went to trial. That was fine by me — I knew I was guilty and deserved the consequences coming my way.

After I pled guilty, the judge sentenced me to eight years in prison with the possibility of parole. I was sent to Wyoming Women's Center, a prison located over a hundred miles from my hometown of Mendex, Wyoming. I did my best to blend in and do my job. In the end I got released on parole three years before the end of my sentence, thanks to my remorse and good behavior.

During those four, nearly five years locked up, I endured a lot of loneliness. I knew it was what I deserved. I had taken a man's life. Taken a son away from his mother and father. If he still had parents, that is — I never found out if he did or not. I didn't get to learn much information about him. His name was George Dawson, and he was in his early thirties. Never married, no kids, and worked at a lumber mill.

I, unlike so many in town, forgave myself for my mistake. It took most of my time in prison to expel all the guilt, but if I wanted a chance at a normal life out in the real world, I would have to. My mother's tearful words telling me to be brave rang in my ears. I was brave that night; I did the right thing. It helped with my path to self-forgiveness.

I may have left behind the guilt, but I'm still sorry for what I did. Sorry for all the pain I've caused. Sorry for the Dawson family. I never received any hate mail from them in prison. However, I did receive a lot from other people in town. Most I didn't even know. I understood their anger. I had been the epitome of selfishness.

In a sort of fucked-up way, I think it was good I went to prison. These nearly five years have utterly transformed me.

Now it's been six months since I was released from prison. I went to a halfway house for two months after getting released on parole. It didn't take long for me to gain employment at a local family restaurant managed by my aunt. Thanks to my dad letting me move into a small rental home he's fixing up to sell, I wasn't stuck in the halfway house. He gave me six months to stay and save for my own place. Eventually, I'll need to find a way to save up enough money to pay him for the work he did for my defense lawyer. All in all, I'll be in debt until my forties. I don't go out much anymore — too much stigma attached to me. For someone with my history, living in a small Wyoming town has far more downsides than up.

The only place I venture out to is my work. My aunt, Almeida, is one of the few who isn't ashamed to share a family name with me. She believes all of this is my mother's fault. The twisted love she gave me, driving me to get ice cream when she was completely plastered. The crimes she committed when she was off her meds and blackout drunk on tequila. So much so that it was normalized in my mind to drive in that state. I don't like to play the blame game. I knew very well what I was doing that night and the many nights prior was reckless, but I did it anyways. I let Aunt Almeida take pity on me. So far, she's been quite fair to me at work.

However, everyone else mostly avoids me. After work, I walk home to sit on my couch, clean, or work out. Now that I'm twenty-seven, my metabolism has slowed down, and if I don't keep up with vigorous exercise, I'll gain weight.

Having decent looks and a slim figure means I fared better in prison than I might have otherwise. The male guards showed me kindness, and the lesbian inmates would offer me old vodka they had snuck in. I drank for years while incarcerated but eventually swore it off. I knew if there was any chance for me to heal and be a better person, I had to stop. If not for me, then for my family. Alcohol is the main reason my life went downhill the way it did.

I try not to think of liquor, but every night, in my lonely one-bedroom apartment, the craving gets worse. One of the only rules my father and Aunt Almeida had for me to have a roof over my head and a place to earn income was that I drink no alcohol and attend weekly AA meetings, both of which have been difficult to manage. I never understood the control liquor had on me until I was forced to give it up.

Once 9 p.m. hits on a slow Wednesday night at the restaurant, I begin performing my closing tasks. What takes most girls an hour to do I can complete in half that time. I became efficient in prison. In twenty minutes, I have already finished vacuuming the carpet area, mopping the tile area, and refilling salt and pepper shakers. Another five and I've bleached all the booths, chairs, and tables.

As I'm refilling the ketchup and mustard bottles, the door chimes. I sigh, annoyed that someone is coming in this close to closing. It's not that I have anywhere special to be; it just means my walk home will be colder.

I put on a fake smile and walk to the front of the restaurant. Thankfully there is only one man standing by the hostess stand. My fake smile slips. I know him.

His name is Red Adkins. We went to high school together. He was one of the popular football jocks, and friends with one of my crushes in high school. The last time I saw him, we were in another boy's room at a party, and I was plastered. I blink three times, trying to erase those memories.

"Hi, sir," I say as cheerfully as I can manage.

I hope Red doesn't remember me. I catch a whiff of alcohol on his breath. His eyes are glassy and bloodshot. After high school he got a girl from our graduating class pregnant and married her that year. Last I heard, they got divorced after only two years of marriage.

Red takes an overly long look at me. He's swaying as he stares.

"Max Masterson, I haven't seen you in years," he mumbles.

I offer another awkward smile. "Eating tonight, Red?"

"No, I just wanted a shake. Heard they're tasty here. Speaking of tasty—" Red moves closer to me.

I take a step back, trying to remain calm.

"What flavor, Red?" I ask.

Red licks his lips. "Hey, didn't you just get out of prison? Bet you haven't had a good dicking down in a while."

I scrunch my face in disgust. Where does he get off talking to me like this? I haven't had sex in many years, but even I'd never have sex with this man. Not only due to his state and weak pickup lines, but because of the secret we share.

"I'm not interested, Red," I say bluntly.

Red's creepy grin changes into a scowl.

"You think anyone else will want you after what you did?"

Ouch. He's not wrong, but I'd rather be alone the rest of my life than spend a night in bed with him. Red and I are the only ones in the restaurant lobby area besides the fry cook, Tayen. I can't risk being rude to him — I don't know what this drunken mess of a man is capable of.

"Leave, please."

Red takes another step closer to me. Just as he's about to speak, I hear Tayen approaching from behind me. For this very reason, he generally stays until the last waitress leaves. He's a tall Native American, nearing three hundred pounds and sporting a goatee. The other waitresses mistake his kindness as creepiness, but not me.

"Is there a problem here, Max?" he asks.

Red glances at Tayen, then turns his attention back at me, smirking.

"No problem. Catch you later, Max." He turns and leaves the restaurant.

I take a deep sigh of relief. "Thank you."

"Don't listen to assholes like that."

Too bad I already do listen to assholes like that. None that have frightened me to this degree. Just ones who glare or leer at me. Or whisper my name as I work.

"Finished already, Max?" He looks around at the tidy restaurant.

I nod, trying not to seem too cocky. I'm happy Tayen didn't want to discuss that interaction any further.

"Prison really made you a damn good worker."

I like Tayen, unlike most people I've met since getting out of prison. I suspect he's done some time behind bars too. It's the only thing that makes his kindness toward me make sense.

"I have a to-go order for someone coming in. Should be here any minute. If you could give it to him, that would be great."

"Didn't we stop taking to-go orders half an hour ago?"

"Yeah, but he's a buddy and I owe him a favor."

"A favor, huh?"

Tayen leans in closer to me and whispers, "Yeah. Between us, I get my weed from him. I was a little short on funds, so I offered him a couple burgers."

Just thinking of weed makes me jealous. Since I can't drink, I wish I could get my hands on anything else that could calm my nerves. Anything that can quiet my never-ending thoughts about how everyone views me now. How they either glare or gasp at the sight of me.

"You already got the weed, right? I'm not going to be your middleman." I try to keep my voice light and not too serious.

"Come on, I wouldn't do that to you." He nudges my arm.

Although it's only a momentary touch, I can't help but wish it lasted longer. It's not that I'm attracted to Tayen, but I haven't been touched by anyone in a long time. Apart from the regular old men who come in. They like to touch the girls' lower backs, keeping their hands lingering there a couple seconds. Being celibate has become the second-hardest thing to adjust to after drinking.

His touch brings up memories of my last boyfriend. Mikey Connolly. He was one of the last men to touch me before I went to prison. He's the only man I've dated who I waited to sleep with. I suspect that's where our connection stemmed from. We spent the first month of our relationship talking about each other's interests, going on dates, and hanging out with his friends. He stayed over frequently, and we'd cuddle all night. I liked him, but didn't like the idea of getting too close to someone.

Tayen hands me two bags full of food for his weed man. I put some napkins and plastic forks in the bag along with ketchup and mustard sachets. Once I have tied them both up, I hear the door chime again. I grab the bags and, taking a deep breath, walk toward the entrance of the restaurant.

I prepare myself to be faced with some stoner type. The kind of drug dealer that wears a beanie and an oversized long-sleeved T-shirt underneath another oversized short-sleeved shirt sporting some anime character. But the person who walks in is not a stoner. He's average height with pale skin and attractive features. I know him immediately. His curly dark auburn hair, cut just below his ears, is a dead giveaway. It's Mikey, my ex-boyfriend.

CHAPTER THREE

October 9th, 2009
9:42 p.m.

He's changed since the last time I saw him. He's gained twenty or so pounds, and his skin is no longer tanned from working long hours outdoors. He has a somewhat pudgy belly and larger arms. He's also grown a short beard that's the same shade as his hair. He used to wear simple clothing, like old, ripped jeans and tacky shirts with funny images. Now he's wearing a thick bomber jacket, a navy-blue button-up shirt underneath with dark blue jeans, and leather lace-up dress shoes.

We stare at each other for a couple moments. I hope he won't recognize me, but by the way his eyes widen, I know he does. I haven't changed much besides some weight loss. I have the same honey-colored hair, although now it's midway down my back instead of shoulder-length. I barely wear any makeup, unlike back in the day when I'd be coated in it.

I want to save the awkward encounter, so I try to keep my facial expression neutral. Like with most people around town I know, I'll pretend I don't recognize him and hope he chooses not to acknowledge knowing me. We didn't leave things on the greatest terms.

"Are you here for the to-go order?" I ask.

Mikey furrows his brows in confusion. "Max Masterson. Hey. It's me, Mikey."

Damn, he really is going to go this route. The awkward *Hey, last time I saw you, you'd just run someone over in your car.* Maybe he wants to bask in my failure. Get revenge. Mikey never seemed the type to make someone endure that, but it's been over five years. Maybe he's become a bitterer person. I think back on all our good times, wanting to give him the benefit of the doubt.

"Mikey Connolly?" I excitedly say, putting on a shocked expression.

Mikey smiles, looking relieved that I remember who he is. I don't know how he doesn't realize I had recognized him immediately. I never told him, but out of the handful of boyfriends I had, he was my favorite. He was the one I felt comfortable talking to.

"I can't believe Tayen didn't tell me you were working here. How the hell are you?"

I gulp and shrug. "Oh, you know, same old, same old."

"I never really got to tell you how sorry I was, you know? For what happened."

It's rare people tell me that they're sorry. I feel the same discomfort as when they glare or gawk at me. I don't deserve pity. What happened to me is a direct result of the dumb, reckless shit I did. It's also a punishment for all my other past wrongdoings. Like cheating on Mikey.

"Don't be sorry, I was . . . I was a shitty person. I deserve everything that happened to me."

Mikey looks away and puts his hands in his pockets. What I said must've struck a chord with him.

"You weren't a shitty person. Just young. All of us drove drunk. Hell, that night I did too."

15

I appreciate his kindness. His words could've really helped back in the early days after I was convicted. On visiting days, I always hoped he would appear. He never did. For a short while, I anticipated receiving a letter from him. That, too, never happened.

"Everything happens for a reason," I say, the same corny thing I've been thinking for years.

"Well, between us, I have no hard feelings."

I crack a smile. A real one. It's the first time I have in a while. Mikey always had a knack for getting a genuine smile out of me. I remember the first time we met, at one of the local bars. I knocked back two shots of tequila with ease, and he introduced himself, telling me how most men couldn't pull off a feat like that.

"Would you want to get coffee sometime?" I blurt out, grimacing at how desperate that must sound.

That's when Mikey loses his smile. Shit, I said something wrong. How stupid of me to think he'd want to have coffee with the girl who broke his heart and killed an innocent man. He removes his hands from his pockets and raises his left hand. That's when I catch sight of the gold ring on his finger.

"I mean, personally I would love that, but the wife . . . she might not—"

"No, of course she wouldn't. I didn't know you got married," I interrupt, shaking my head in embarrassment.

That explains why he's got more than one burger. Another indicator I should have caught on to. *For God's sake, Max, it's been five fucking years.* People don't stay single that long.

"It's okay, maybe I can talk to the wife. I'm sure she'd understand."

"Yeah, I'm sure having coffee with your ex-girlfriend who's a felon would be just peachy with her," I say sarcastically.

Mikey begins laughing. His laugh is still so cute. It's loud and genuine. Mikey never did fake a laugh.

"Now that you put it like that."

We're silent for a couple moments, and I realize this is the end of our encounter. I'm happy to see Mikey's in a good place. I don't want him to go but know it's for the best. I had my chance with him, but it's gone now. He'll be the one that got away. Every girl has one. The good guy they completely fluffed it with.

"Are you closing up for the night?" Mikey asks.

"Yeah, you were my last customer."

"It's kind of dark out. I can walk you to your car."

I feel my cheeks flush again. "I don't drive."

Mikey raises his eyebrows. He's silent for a couple moments, putting the pieces together on why I don't drive. It's my choice not to drive. That, and lack of funds.

"I can give you a ride."

Mikey really isn't letting up on this kindness act. It must be pity. I don't need anyone's pity. All the pain I'm dealing with is my own fault. Although someone pitying me instead of hating my guts is a breath of fresh air.

"It's fine. I don't want your wife's food getting cold."

"She'll be fine. She's doing what she usually does on Friday nights. Engrossed in some shitty reality television show."

"Mikey, you don't need to feel pity for me."

"It's not that. I just . . . I've missed you, Max."

I roll my eyes and sigh. "Okay, give me a couple minutes to lock up."

Mikey winks at me before turning around and walking out. Once he's gone, I say my goodbyes to Tayen and finish wiping down the surfaces. I take my time, hoping Mikey will give up on his nice deed. It's not that I don't want to spend time with him — I miss having company. I just don't want to add fraternizing with a married man to my list of reasons why everyone in this place hates me.

Before clocking out, I check myself in the break room mirror. Seeing my hair is tousled from working nine hours, I grab a nearby brush and run it through a couple times. In my younger days, I spent hours in front of a mirror perfecting my appearance. Now I spend five to ten minutes, just long enough to look presentable and clean.

Before heading out, I grab an old solid-black zip-up jacket. It's too short and adds little to no warmth to my chilly walks home. I'm grateful it hasn't snowed yet this year, though it's been chilly and windy lately. Once it does snow, I know I'll have to purchase more winter clothing.

Mikey's still waiting for me when I get outside. His hands are nestled in the pockets of his jacket.

"If you're walking home every night, you should really bring a better coat than that." Mikey chuckles as I begin shivering.

"It's a good thing I have you, then, huh?" I joke, attempting to hide how this is one of the few jackets I own.

We begin walking to the back parking lot. As we walk, the wind blows, and I get a whiff of Mikey. Cedar. The same scent he wore back when we were dating.

The sky is already dark. Just four months ago, when I first started working here, the sun would just now be setting.

The sidewalk between the restaurant and the road is lined with Thuja conifers, only fifteen feet high. They gave the restaurant a natural vibe but didn't fully hide the brick building from the road. During the summer months, in between the trees there will be hydrangeas with beautiful lilac and pink flowers.

Years ago, when Mikey and I had started dating, he had picked me a couple of these flowers. At the time I had wondered why he couldn't just buy me a bouquet of flowers from a shop, but now as a woman who hasn't had a date in five years, I would do anything to be given even one flower.

As if reading my thoughts, Mikey says, "Wasn't one of our first dates here?"

I smile and nod. I stare at Mikey's open hand, wishing I could hold it like we had done in this exact spot so many years ago. I still remember the warmth of his calloused hand as it held mine. Whoever he married is one lucky girl.

"Who did you end up marrying, Mikey?" I ask, my curiosity getting the best of me.

"Adrienne Fettler."

Mikey doesn't even have to ask if I remember her. He knows I do. Adrienne and I were never friends. She had been good friends with Mikey and his crowd when I entered the picture and he and I started dating. From the very beginning I knew she despised me and warned Mikey that I was a barfly. She had been right. It's confusing, though — Mikey told me at the time that he didn't find her attractive in the slightest.

"How long have you two been together?"

"Four years, I think. A, uh, year after you and I broke up, we started dating. Not long after that, she got knocked up."

Mikey sounds almost embarrassed telling me this. Like getting married and having a child is a bad thing. He's two years older than me, so doing all those things seems to be in the right time frame for his age. And I can't blame Adrienne for warning Mikey of my reputation all those years ago — she had the right gut feeling about me. She didn't jump in right away to snatch Mikey up, either. She can't be that bad.

"That's great. You guys have a boy or girl?" I ask, doing my best to put on my cheery voice.

"Little boy. Paxton. He's two and a half now. Pain in the ass, but I love the hell out of him."

Now that part Mikey sounds happy to explain.

Before I can respond, Mikey stops in his tracks, briefly grabbing ahold of my arm to stop me. I open my mouth to ask him what's wrong, but then I spot them. Across the dark street, standing underneath a flickering streetlight, is the figure of someone. They're standing completely still, facing us. They are hidden by a baseball cap, but I can tell they're watching us. Staring at us.

CHAPTER FOUR

October 9th, 2009
9:56 p.m.

"Um, who's that?" I ask, desperate to grasp Mikey's hand.

"I have no idea. Just keep walking. My Jeep's in the front of the parking lot straight ahead."

I look toward the empty lot, spotting a black Jeep Commander. If I weren't too focused on the creep under the streetlight, I'd ask Mikey how he could afford such a nice ride. Last I knew he had worked as a roofer for a construction company. Maybe he finally started his own company; I had always supported him in starting one. He had the skill and knowledge.

While I wait for Mikey to unlock the Jeep, I keep my eyes on the figure. Almost like I'm expecting him to start sprinting toward us like in a horror movie. Once we get in, Mikey locks the doors and starts the Jeep. We both stare at each other, unsure what to say. Soon the overhead light shuts off, and that's when we both start laughing.

"What the hell happened to Mendex while I was gone?" I ask.

Mendex, Wyoming, isn't exactly a touristy town. It's not even one of those cute little towns that get a rush of visitors during the summer. Most of the six thousand people that live in Mendex were born and raised here and never left. The scenery is its only saving grace. The town is located on a flat terrain, but there are plenty of lakes nearby, and an abundance of wheat fields, and the Grand Tetons are just within eyeshot. In the summer everything turns green and flowers grow.

Of the three gas stations in Mendex, the one on the outskirts of town receives the most patronage. Generally, hikers passing through only stop to fuel up and then they leave right away to explore the forest. But even if it's a two-bit town, it's never been known as a hotbed of crime.

"Mendex got shittier. The cops are a bunch of morons, and the mayor is too busy stuffing his own pocket to solve any problems."

Once Mikey reverses the Jeep, the person under the lamp turns around and walks off down an alleyway. Disappearing into the darkness.

"I should follow that asshole," Mikey says angrily.

I get chills at the thought. The guy could have a gun, and everywhere around us is already closed for the night.

"Mikey, come on. Just get me home. It's probably just some kid." I don't want to risk getting in any more trouble.

I don't believe my own words. The figure looked too tall to be a kid, but I'm tired and nowadays I hate confrontation.

"You're right."

Mikey breaks our few minutes of silence when he turns up the volume of his radio.

"Today marks a year since local woman Eva Willems went missing. The Mendex Police are still urging anyone with information to contact them," a monotone voice through the radio says. Once I hear that name, I block out the rest of the news report.

Eva Willems. The mere sound of her name gives me goosebumps.

Eva and I went to high school together — she'd moved to the States from the Netherlands during her junior year. She was athletic, with long blonde hair, blue eyes, and pale, clear skin. I used to get jealous of all the attention she got from boys. There was one boy in particular that she and I feuded over — Dennis Formont. Typical jock, great at sports, with a smile to kill for. He ended up choosing her over me and they briefly dated, but after one big blowout senior party, they broke up. That party, like the night I killed George Dawson, stays buried in my mind.

After that party, Eva just sort of fell off the map. She didn't go to college out of state like she'd planned; she stayed in Mendex with her parents. The only time I saw her after that was one night at a bar a month before my incident. By that time, she had a bad reputation and had gotten into an altercation with one of the other jocks from school. He asked her something inappropriate, which set her off. A part of me wanted to step in and come to her aid, but being the person I am, I just stood by and watched.

Mikey looks over at me. "Did you not hear about Eva?"

I shake my head, still in shock.

"She went on some trip out of town and never came home. She packed a bag but left everything else behind. She hasn't been heard from since."

"Wait, haven't I heard something like that before? Two sisters — they had similar names. Um . . . Mary and Mariah. Didn't they go out of town and never come back too?"

Mikey frowns and shakes his head.

"It was a huge deal at the time — not long after I graduated high school. All that stuff on the news about how women should carry pepper spray and not walk alone at night."

"Troublemakers," Mikey says, recognizing the story now. "Didn't they run off with a biker gang?"

"Nobody knows."

When I just sit there in silence, Mikey says, "I didn't forget about the pepper spray. But I thought that was statewide, to do with the Monroe Murderer? I can't believe no one told you about Eva. Especially your father. It's not safe out there. You shouldn't even be walking home this late at night. You look a lot like the women the Monroe Murderer went after, Max."

The Monroe Murderer. I haven't thought of that name in a long time. Whispers of a potential serial killer in Wyoming started back in 1997, after a third body was recovered in the span of three years. They say he goes after young women who bear a resemblance to Marilyn Monroe — blonde and beautiful.

Everyone thinks this guy killed Eva? I prefer to think she set off to make a new start. But she does look a bit like the women who were killed all those years ago. Kind of like the Smith sisters.

As far as I know, only five bodies have been recovered, but a few reporters have tried to link other missing women to the case. All the women found were missing for some time before their discovery. The first body was found in 1993 in an abandoned farmhouse right outside the town of Kelly. I remember seeing it on the news as a little girl. She had been missing for three years and had been shot to death. Another was found the following year, buried in a shallow grave a mile or so from a highway on the outskirts of Jackson, a resort town in Wyoming. By the time they found her, her body had decomposed, but they'd been able to identify her through DNA. It was one of the earliest cases to use the method. Both women were from the same town, both were blonde and attractive, and both styled their hair a little like Marylin Monroe. Then three more bodies were found, all years after their deaths but with similar looks to the other women, and all within a fifty-mile radius.

The police threw a lot of resources at attempting to iden-tify the killer, but they had no leads. Eventually the case went cold. Journalists always revive it whenever a blonde woman goes missing.

All in all, over fifteen missing women have been linked to the same killer, across twenty-three years. All of them young, beautiful, and with blonde hair. I think it's wishful thinking on the journalists' part. Even if there is a killer still out there, he must be old. Too old to continue kidnapping women.

"If you want to worry about me being ambushed, it shouldn't be by some serial killer. It would most likely be someone from town."

"That's incredibly insightful, Max, thanks," he says sarcastically, and I laugh, lightly punching his shoulder.

When Mikey parks his Jeep on the side of the street, I look over and see we're now next to my place. I was so deep in conversation, I forgot to give him directions.

"Wait, how'd you know where I live?"

"I worked for your dad for a year or so and remember all his rental homes. I assumed you would be living in this one as it's the only one I've seen not occupied."

"Creepy, but thanks for the ride." I open the Jeep's door.

Before I can step out of the Jeep, Mikey touches my arm.

"I hate to ask, but are you sure you're okay, like, mentally? With the accident."

I sigh. I know Mikey is only trying to help, but I hate being faced with this question. It feels as if I'm being asked if I'm going to commit suicide. They don't seem to realize that if I had wanted to do that, I would have done it in prison. I've had time to sit and think about the horrible thing I did.

"Shit, that sounded bad," Mikey says when I don't answer.

"It's fine. Yes, I'm okay. Don't worry about me. I'm really happy you're not mad at me," I explain.

I get out and close the door and as I begin walking to my front door, I hear Mikey's voice yell, "Hey, Max. When's your next shift?"

Turning around, I see the passenger side of the Jeep's window open and Mikey leaning across the seat, staring at me.

"The day after tomorrow. Why?"

"I think I should give you a ride home again."

I cross my arms. "That's really not necessary."

"I'm not trying to hit on you. I just don't want you walking home alone. What's your number? I can always text you, let you know I'm coming."

I'm overcome with embarrassment. I don't even have a cell phone anymore. I can't afford it, nor do I know when I will again. Not that I'd have many people to call anyways. My father pays for the house phone just so he or Almeida can get ahold of me.

"I don't have a cell. Can't really afford it on my budget," I explain.

"Okay, well, I'll just stop by around the same time I did tonight, okay?"

"Mikey, really, it's—"

"Don't make me beg, now," he says, cutting me off.

I roll my eyes, pretending to be annoyed. "Fine, since you are being so adamant."

"I am. Goodnight, Maximillian," he says, before rolling the window up and driving off.

I stand there a couple moments, unsure if allowing him to do this is a good thing. I had made a pact in prison to be a good person. Hanging out with an ex-boyfriend who's now married is skirting the line between good and bad. I need a friend, though. I've become so lonely. I thought getting out of prison would erase all the loneliness, but now I suffer from it more than before. Besides, it's just a ride home.

I begin my walk down the paved sidewalk to my house, and for the first time in a long time, I'm not miserable. That is until I realize that tomorrow, one of my only days off this week, I'm supposed to go to AA. I know my father and aunt made it a condition of my living here because they care. I just feel ill every time I have to speak about how alcohol ruined my life. It's like reliving that night over again.

CHAPTER FIVE

October 9th, 2009
11:46 p.m.

He watches as Maxine moves back and forth across her living room. He has never felt such deep hatred for anyone. He hates her, but he can't help admiring her beauty. It is an uncomfortable and irritating feeling. The desire to strangle her mixes with the wish for her to be naked while he watches the air leave her lungs. That isn't his plan for her, oh no. It's just a fantasy.

Maxine Masterson — even the sound of her name vexes his blood. It has been six months since she was released from prison. Five years for murdering another person.

Unknowingly, she has ruined his life. He needs her to know all the pain she's caused him. All the plans for his future she has ended.

He watches as she continues to pace around, looking distraught. She does this most nights. There's a bottle of vodka on the coffee table — she gets it out and puts it there some evenings. She never drinks the vodka. Sometimes she even goes to the kitchen and holds the bottle over the sink, as if willing herself to dump it down the drain. She never does. Instead, she puts it back in the cabinet and gets ready for bed.

After she's done pacing, like clockwork, she puts the vodka away and disappears. He moves from his spot behind a hibiscus shrub and crosses the street, looking both ways for any signs of neighbors or bystanders. Once he's on her lawn, he goes to the left side of Max's house, toward the double-hung window of the bathroom. The blinds aren't closed. He kneels, waiting for the bathroom light to come on.

When it does, Maxine is in there, her back to him, taking off her work top. Underneath she wears a beige bra. It's the same one she wears most nights she works. He wishes she would switch it up, wear a rose-pink push-up one with lace. He loves pink on blondes. It's always turned him on. He already has a set of lacy lingerie for when he captures Maxine.

While still wearing her bra and panties, Maxine walks to the mirror and examines herself. She presses her hands to her sides, as if checking for any difference from the previous day. At first, he suspected she was suffering from body-image issues, but he now knows it's the exact opposite. She fancies herself. She just wishes someone were there to see and touch her.

Each night it gets harder for him not to force himself in there, to be that someone. She has an ethereal beauty — she's slim, toned, and graceful. When she wears her long hair pulled back, he could lose himself just staring at her.

After examining herself, Maxine turns the faucet on and begins to wash her face. This is his favorite part. From his angle, he gets a look at her small, heart-shaped bottom as she leans forward. Every time he watches this, he considers breaking the front door down and taking Maxine then and there. Before he saw Maxine for the first time, it was easy for him to keep his hands off women. Now that he spends nearly every day watching someone he desires to have and hurt, it's become an onerous task.

Maxine soon goes to the curtains and shuts them. She usually does this before showering. He wishes just once she would forget so he could watch her undress completely. After she showers, she generally goes to her room and closes both blinds in there as well.

He waits by the bathroom with his ear pressed to the window. He hears the shower start. He waits until it turns off to sneak to the right side of the house where her bedroom is. He barely gets a moment's glance at her walking in, a towel draped around her body, before she closes both blinds. He longs for the day she forgets.

For the past four months, he has been planning to take her, but for someone who has so much on the line, it hasn't been easy finding the perfect time. He's spent the last six months keeping tabs on her. She spent the first two months of her probation in a halfway house, her every move monitored. Now she lives on her own, it's opened more doors, but she still has family who check on her frequently.

There might be a better, cleaner way of getting this woman into his home. He just needs a little time. If he wants to get away with the crime, he needs to be patient.

He presses his palm against the glass of the window. He tightly closes his eyes, once again imagining himself killing her. He wants her to bleed. He wants to lie with her as she bleeds out, desperately clutching to a life about to expire.

CHAPTER SIX

October 10th, 2009
5:25 p.m.

Thirty-five minutes until AA is going to start. I'm still home, but if I walk fast, it's generally only a twenty-minute walk. Once a week, Jay Semmers rents out Mendex's community center to hold the meeting. He's been running the meetings there for years now, even before I was arrested. My father reached out to him before I was released, asking if I could join. Jay likes keeping the meeting tight-knit. Mostly, he doesn't want any nosey townsfolk coming in to get gossip.

Jay is a nice-enough guy. A devoted Christian now, he was previously a severe alcoholic that lost his wife and two children due to his drinking. Every time we get a new member, he goes into detail about the repercussions he faced from his alcohol abuse. He's over eight years sober now but has yet to have contact with his family due to the sins he committed while under the influence.

Although I hate going, it's somewhat comforting knowing I'm not the only one who ruined their life over alcohol. There are around twelve of us that attend the weekly meetings. Some others occasionally miss a couple meetings but end up coming back to restart their sobriety. Today I'm two hundred and twenty-five days sober. Every day, I've craved a drink. Anything to take my mind off what I've done. Jay explains that that is a part of the process, and that I should continue coming to AA until that need is gone. Sometimes I feel that could be tens of years from now.

Before leaving my house, I pull a gray hoody over my head. Once winter is here, walking everywhere will become a real pain in the ass. The summer months were nice. I got exercise and a tan from all the walking I did.

Wyoming is known for its especially cold winters. Thankfully it hasn't snowed yet, but as soon as it does, I plan on begging my father to loan me one of the old jalopies collecting dust in his garage, although I'm sure the idea of me being behind the wheel of a vehicle again terrifies him.

* * *

I arrive at the community center with ten minutes to spare. Jay's red Ford Ranger is already in the parking lot. When I walk inside, he is setting up chairs in a circle. A part of me wants to offer to help, but another part hates the thought of another one-to-one conversation with him. Although it's supposed to be forbidden, I'm afraid Jay will relay everything I say to my father.

Instead, I go to the left, toward a narrow staircase leading to the restrooms. As I head up, another person coming down nearly crashes into me.

His hands latch onto my shoulders, stopping me from falling on my ass. I look up to see who has such quick reflexes. It's a man, very tall and lanky. He has dark brown hair with floppy bangs. His eyes are a vivid forest green, and although they are semi-covered by his bangs, they are big and bright. Like pine trees in springtime. While most people with green eyes have specks of blue or brown, his are intensely green and beautiful. He's wearing a dirty tan T-shirt over a black long-sleeved top.

I don't recognize him at all. Not from my days as a barfly, nor from school or AA meetings. He's the type I would have latched onto in the old days. He has handsome but delicate features and smells of mint aftershave.

Once I have steadied myself, the man lets go and clears his throat. "I am so sorry, I didn't see you."

I move a strand of hair out of my eyes. "No worries, this staircase isn't large."

"Yeah, I noticed that." He grins. Yellow teeth.

So, he doesn't have great oral hygiene. I don't mind. I mean, at least they aren't crooked. Crooked or missing teeth are usually where I draw the line. Or I did when I was sexually active. It was generally a sign that they were junkies of some sort. That, or they didn't take any care of their teeth. A smile is one of the first things you notice in a person, and because of that I try my best to keep up my oral health. In high school, I religiously used teeth-whitener strips that burned the enamel off but made my smile brighter. At the time, I was trying to get a better smile than Eva Willems, who seemed to have me beat in every other feature. If only Dennis Formont had noticed before he chose Eva. Not that it mattered in the end, considering what happened with them.

"Yeah, well, I don't think they really have the budget to fix it. I mean, the carpet in his whole building is from, like, the 1960s."

I'm blabbering like an idiot. Being stuck around mostly women while in prison has taken away all my charisma when it comes to men. The girl I was before was so confident that she didn't need to say more than five words to a man she was trying to get into bed.

The man chuckles. "Yeah, it kind of reminds me of an acid trip gone wrong."

Not wanting to say anything stupid, I simply chuckle.

We inch past each other. As our arms brush, I catch a whiff of his breath. It reeks of coffee and, I swear, a bit of rum. As I climb the stairs, I look back and find that his eyes are on me. We both share an awkward smile before I look away and book it up the stairs.

Once in the women's restroom, I immediately go to the bathroom mirror to examine myself. I curse myself for not paying more attention to my appearance. Lately I've lacked any desire to put on makeup, and mostly stick to putting my hair in a ponytail. It's been so long since I've been on a date or even got laid. Now with Mikey showing back up in my life and this attractive stranger, I wish I looked pretty. I think of all the money I made in tips last night and decide a portion will go toward purchasing makeup.

I pull my hair from its ponytail and run my fingers through the strands until they perfectly curl over my shoulders. There's a wave in the middle from my ponytail, but the rest looks decent.

Before I leave the restroom, I take my hoody off. There's a bit of mud on it where the stranger grabbed my shoulders. At least now I don't look like some crackhead outside a gas station begging for change. I'm in an old white V-neck blouse. My everyday beige bra doesn't do my breasts much justice, but the V-neck somewhat makes my bust look larger.

I arrive back just as everyone else is taking their seats. There's one open spot left for me and sadly it's across from the new stranger, not beside him. I notice his eyes on me as I enter, but I keep mine straight ahead as I make my way to the plastic seat.

Once I'm seated, Jay starts the meeting the same way he always does, and I can't help but zone out as I attempt to sneak glances at the man. He has stopped looking at me but is instead staring at Jay with interest.

As if noticing my eyes on him, he looks over in my direction. Embarrassed, I look away and cross my legs. A part of me wishes I had worn a short skirt or dress so I could pull a Sharon Stone in *Basic Instinct* moment. In my early twenties I saw that movie and admired her character, Catherine Tramell. I took mental notes and attempted to come off as sexy and mysterious as she was.

Maybe with some money, I can buy a black dress. Lord knows, I need a new wardrobe. Most of the clothes I own now are old and selected by my father. He gave away all the slutty ones I owned. Now I'm left with worn T-shirts, jeans, and dress pants. Aunt Almeida gives a portion of my paycheck to my father to hold on to in case I waste it on trivial items, but thanks to tips, I had a little left to pretty myself up.

I zone back into Jay's introduction to hear him say, "We have a new member here today. Everyone, welcome Clark. Clark got ahold of me a couple days ago, wanting a chance to give up his addiction to alcohol. Clark, why don't you stand up and introduce yourself, son."

Finally, I can look at him without appearing creepy. I don't recall ever meeting a Clark in my whole life.

Clark pushes himself up to stand. He slouches shyly. I was the same way when Jay made me introduce myself. My hands would get clammy and I would stutter as I explained my predicament.

He clears his throat. "Hello, I'm Clark and I'm an alcoholic."

In unison, everyone says, "Hi, Clark."

Clark looks ill at ease. "Can . . . can I be honest?"

"Of course, Clark," Jay says. "Everything you say stays here with us."

Clark nods. "I'm not even a day sober. I had some rum with my coffee before coming here. It's a daily thing I do. I'm nearing six or so cups a day. As the day goes on, the amount of coffee becomes less and less. It's the only thing that relaxes me. Sometimes I feel, uh, life's stresses are too much to bear. I just can't control myself when I'm drinking; it's like a light goes off and I'm a completely different person."

There is pain in Clark's emerald eyes as he speaks. His words are slurred and shaky. When I went cold turkey, I sounded the exact same. I am empathetic to what he's going through. I want to speak to him more than ever. Learn about his past and what he did to seek help from here of all places.

"Life stresses, now that is a big one," Jay says. "Things get too hard, so you turn to liquor. You think it will help, but in all reality, it clouds your mind from solving these issues. Clark, would you mind sharing what in your life is causing you to turn to alcohol for relief?"

Clark stands frigid for a moment as if contemplating what to say. I don't blame him. Jay can get personal during these meetings. I can tell new people just lie, ashamed of their past. The longer they come, the more down and dirty they get with their truths. I, on the other hand, had to be honest since the entire town knew about my accident. In a weird way, it allowed me to be vocal about what happened, and unleashed a lot I had built up. Thankfully I didn't have to speak of my prior sins, just the new one.

"My brother, he recently got a terminal disease. He's only a couple years older than me, and I've been entrusted with taking care of him along with his home and all the bills. I know it doesn't seem like much, but he sometimes gets angry if I don't do everything in a specific way. I also work full-time as a construction worker, so it just makes everything unbearable. I drink on the job constantly and don't sleep much."

That explains the mud on my hoody. And now I notice his clothes are dirty, as if he just got off work. My father wears the same three pairs of work pants on repeat during the week. So, the part about being a construction worker I'm positive is true; the rest is difficult to gauge. His story seems too elaborate to be made up, but you never know at a meeting like this. People can surprise you.

Jay shares some of his own battles with life and how he once thought turning to liquor would solve his problems. He thanks Clark for taking the first step to recovery, which is coming here today. He asks some others in the group to stand up to introduce themselves, to give Clark a perspective on how others have started drinking. I tremble as the guy seated next to me gets up. I don't want Clark to know what I've done. To know my actions caused a man to die.

I zone out, engaged in my anxiety before hearing Jay in a loud but monotone voice say, "Max! Earth to Max."

I look at him and force a smile.

"Why don't you stand up, dear? Introduce yourself." His lips curve into a soft smile.

I reluctantly stand up and take a deep breath. "Hi, I'm Max, and I'm . . . an alcoholic."

Everyone says, "Hi, Max."

I feel Clark's eyes on me, and I know soon enough he'll know I'm a horrible person who killed someone, and will want nothing to do with me. Unlike mine, his drinking problem sounds as though it is still a seed in the dirt, not a whole goddamn ancient pine tree.

"I'm two hundred and twenty-five days sober today. I used to drink quite often. One night, a little over five years ago, my drunk driving resulted in a man's death. I spent five years of an eight-year sentence in prison. I traded anything I had to obtain fermented contraband, whatever I could to get my hands on real liquor. It was stupid, but it was the way I handled my guilt. When I was released, I made a promise to stop drinking. I realized that if I continued to drink, I'd just cause more damage. I wanted to reenter civilization sober."

I don't go into extensive detail out loud, but in reality, expunging the guilt from my mind was the most difficult part of prison.

I'll never get rid of it all — how could I? But I had to if I really wanted to leave prison sober and mentally capable.

Jay begins to elaborate on my crime and the damage it had done to my life and the family of the deceased. He does this with every member. I feel mine is the worst, and I know he does it to keep me on the wagon. As Jay goes on with his consolations, I peer at Clark. I expect him to be put off by my statement, but he's still eyeing me. I can't tell if it's in disgust or interest.

CHAPTER SEVEN

October 10th, 2009
6:02 p.m.

Thirty minutes later, I have made it through another AA meeting. I'm safe for another week. Jay closed the meeting with his weekly ritual, congratulating those of us holding strong with our sobriety and attempting to boost those who'd stumbled. Clark didn't speak up again. That's not unusual for newcomers. They like to keep their distance, like a new kid at school who knows no one. I feel an uncanny attraction toward him. It must be his demeanor, eyes, and the sound of his voice. Or maybe it's because he's new. Someone I haven't met before. Someone who doesn't know all my wrongdoings.

I pull my hoody back on as I leave through the front doors of the community center. The sun is halfway down, illuminating the sky with tinges of orange and pink. This is one of the few good things about AA. The walk home is always peaceful and beautiful. This time of year, the light doesn't last long, and I have to hightail it home to avoid the night chill.

Before I set off on my walk home, I hear a voice yell from behind me, "Hey, Max!"

Clark is coming out of the community center.

"Hi. Clark, is it?" I know damn well what his name is, but considering the number of times he caught me staring at him, I can't come off too keen.

"You walking home?" he asks, putting his hands in his jean pockets after feeling the brisk air.

"Uh, yeah."

"God, that must suck. It's fucking freezing out here."

Small talk, about the weather, gas prices, or politics, bores me. For Clark, I muster up a smile and shake my head.

"It's not too bad. I get to witness Wyoming's gorgeous sunsets."

"I would offer you a ride, but I guess since we're strangers, that might come off a little creepy."

"I mean, we're not exactly strangers anymore, right? Thanks to Jay, you know what a degenerate I am."

Clark chuckles. "I wouldn't say that. You made a terrible mistake, but I can tell you're trying to make amends with what you did."

"Thanks. Hey, um, speaking frankly, it doesn't seem like you belong there with us. You're not hurting anyone with your actions. Just trying to stay afloat with stressful shit."

After saying that, I realize I'm enabling Clark. Jay would hate that. It's the truth, in my opinion, and if Clark's story is true, I'd do the same. I know my father drinks much more than he would if he hadn't been straddled with me — or my mom.

"I like that perspective, Max. I guess I just wanted to give this whole AA thing a chance. At least it gets me out of my house."

"I like that perspective too. I spend far too much at home — or work. It's a never-ending cycle."

"Being an adult is great, isn't it?" Clark jokes.

"Yeah, I tend to complain a lot. My father thinks I have persistent depressive disorder. He's the one that makes me go to these. Thinks it'll help rehabilitate me."

"And has it?"

It should be an easy question to answer. That, yes, in a way it does help to hear I'm not so alone, but no, because telling everyone what I did is like reliving it all over again — which makes me desperate for a drink.

Thankfully, before I have to answer, the rest of the group begin flooding from the building. Nearly all of them stare at us.

"Y-yes, it's a very rewarding group," I finally say.

Clark grins slightly. "You don't have to lie to me, Max."

"Sorry, that's another habit of mine. Not lying. I'm horrendous at that. I want people to think I'm trying to change. I am, but AA makes me relive that day all over again."

"You don't need to lie to me. I like honest people."

"People say that, but the minute you are, they accuse you of being an asshole."

"I spent my life around assholes. I think I can handle your assholeness, Max."

Every time Clark says my name, he says it with an edge. Like we know each other already and he likes the feel of my name on his tongue.

"It's your funeral." I cross my arms over my midsection and press my hands into my sides. They're starting to go numb in the cold.

"So, if you walk everywhere, why the hell aren't you wearing an actual winter coat?" Clark asks, noticing my stance.

"I've never been good at dressing for the weather. My mother used to scold me for it all the time," I explain, trying to appear less chilly than I am.

"Well, give me a sec. I can get you a jacket." Clark jogs off before I can protest.

He gets into a 1992 Toyota Cressida. The same model I used to drive. The one I ran George over with. The color is different. His is a bright firetruck shade of red, while mine was white.

I gulp, remembering the blood on the headlights and shattered windshield. What are the odds Clark would drive the same shit box I used to?

He retrieves a thick dark brown-and-black flannel jacket. As he runs back toward me, I can't help but stare at his sedan, memories of that night engulfing me. All the blood. The man staring deep into my eyes with hatred as he bled out. Those last words he uttered: *They're going to make you pay for this.*

Clark sees my discomfort. "It's just an old jacket of mine. Really, I'm not a creep."

I shake my head and muster up a fake smile. "No, it's not that. Your . . . sedan — I used to own the same model. Just brought back memories."

"It's my uncle's. He gave it to me to get to work and back. Piece of shit, really."

I laugh. I like how Clark can cuss around me so easily. Most men apologize like it's a tragedy to say such words around a woman.

I take the jacket from Clark and put it on over my hoody. I press my hands into the wool pockets, my numb fingers instantly warming up. The jacket is insulated with down. It also smells of a mix of Clark's cologne and plywood. I hope he doesn't ask for it back. I'd love having a nice warm jacket to walk with, all the while getting a whiff of his manly scent.

"Thank you. You really didn't have to do that."

"I really don't wear it anymore. Besides, it looks better on you."

I probably look like a snowman with all these layers but appreciate Clark's kindness anyhow. That drive home he's offered doesn't seem so bad anymore. A big part of me wants to get in his car, take him to my house, and ride him all night. Five years without sex or a man's touch has brought out a horniness in me I haven't felt since Mikey. I've been home for four months, and with my current reputation, I've been too scared to try sleeping with anyone. I feel the only men who could ever want me are ones like Red. But in ways I can't understand, Clark is different.

"Anyways, once again, not a creep, but—"

"You don't need to keep saying that. It almost makes me suspect you are one," I joke, laughing that Clark feels he has to keep reassuring me.

"Sorry, I'm not good at talking to girls — pretty ones, especially."

I blush again, wishing it weren't so damn cold and that I could shed these layers. Show Clark my body, make him yearn for me. I know for a fact it wouldn't disappoint. I've been staring at myself in my bathroom mirror for months, wondering when I'll get another opportunity to wow a man.

"You don't have a girlfriend, do you?" I don't need another married man being nice to me.

Clark shakes his head. "Haven't really had time for one."

"Hey, me either. Boyfriend, anyways."

"Now that's surprising. You're the prettiest girl I've seen in this town in a while. Surprised no one's snatched you up."

Clark's compliment brings butterflies to my stomach. In the past, it wouldn't have meant as much. I was used to receiving compliments on my appearance when I was younger. Five years surrounded by women gave me a newfound appreciation for it.

"Men around here tend to avoid me. I mean, no one in this town wants to be known as the man who's dating a convicted felon."

"Well, lucky for you, I don't scare so easy. I also don't care what people think."

"Where have you been all my life?" I say with a tinge of sarcasm, but Clark's eyes still light up.

"I mean, if we had met sooner, would it have been the right time?"

43

I shake my head, knowing it wouldn't have been. I had already trashed my relationship with a nice guy back then. My old selfish self would have done the same with this guy.

Instead of answering that question, as I'm certain Clark already knows the answer, I say, "So . . ., that ride."

Looking pleased I have agreed to the ride home, Clark beams and begins to walk me to his sedan. Before we make it halfway there, Mikey's black Jeep drives into the parking lot. *What the hell is he doing here?*

I like Mikey, but right now I don't need him around. I want Clark to give me a ride home. He's a charming, attractive man I want to take home and fuck.

"Know him?" Clark says, noticing I've stopped walking.

"Y-yeah, sort of."

I consider running to Clark's sedan and hiding behind it, but before I can, Mikey's eyes find mine. He smiles, but that soon fades once he spots Clark at my side. He gets out of the Jeep and begins striding our way.

"Mikey." I force a smile that I know he'll recognize as fake.

"Max, your dad said he wanted me to give you a ride home. It's getting cold," Mikey says, continuing to stare at Clark like he had just been caught trying to abduct me.

There's no way that's true. My father likes the fact I must walk everywhere I go. Thinks it's punishment for what I did. Mikey must've found out my whereabouts some other way.

"That's awfully nice of you, but Clark's offered me a ride home."

Mikey walks closer to Clark, looking him over. He offers his hand, and Clark takes it with an awkward smile.

"I'm Mikey, a good friend of Max's. Her dad wants me to drive her home. But thanks anyways."

Clark looks just as dismayed as me. I wonder if the two men will start arguing.

"Sure." Clark presses his lips together.

"Max, come on." Mikey casts a glare at me before walking away.

I don't want Mikey to make things more uncomfortable, so I decide to go with it.

"I'm sorry," I say to Clark.

"Don't worry about it. Next time?" Clark's shoulders slump in defeat.

"Sure. It was nice meeting you, Clark. Thanks again for the jacket."

Clark nods, and I follow Mikey. Before getting in his Jeep, I take one last look at Clark. He's still standing in the same spot, in the same position. I offer a wave that he returns before turning and walking to his sedan.

I am so agitated. I am ready to let Mikey have it, but he beats me to the punch.

"What the hell was that about, Max?"

"I was just about to ask the same. What are you even doing here? My dad doesn't give a fuck if I walk around in this weather. He'd let me walk through a snowstorm before offering fifteen minutes of his time to drive his shithead of a daughter home."

"Well, I'm not your dad, Max. I'm not letting you just walk home, or letting some stranger take you home. Do you even know that guy? Jesus, Max, you're smarter than that."

"Are you calling me dumb?" I ask, incredulous.

"No, I was just trying to help," he says calmly. "I was dropping off some weed for Tayen, and he mentioned you have AA today. I called and asked Almeida when you'd get out."

"So, you're stalking me now?"

Mikey laughs, like that question itself is silly. He starts his Jeep and backs out of the parking lot. I spot Clark's sedan on its way out, heading in the opposite direction of my place. I cross my arms, despising Mikey for cockblocking me. He's not the one who has to go home to a cold bed. I don't understand why he cares so much about a girl who cheated on him five years ago. Remembering Clark taking a liking to my honesty, I decide to do the same with Mikey.

"Why do you care what happens to me?"

"What?" he asks, keeping his eyes on the road.

"I mean, you owe me nothing. I cheated on you, and now you are married with a toddler. Why do you care who I'm riding with?"

"That's a damn good question. As you seem completely oblivious to the dangers around here."

"This Monroe Murderer thing again?" I ask, sighing. "Not every blonde woman who skips this one-horse town has been murdered, Mikey. Answer my question: Why do you care?"

"Five years later and you're still a royal pain in the ass, Max."

"Me, the pain in the ass? You're the one who——"

I stop, realizing I'm about to tell Mikey he just cockblocked me. A part of me is afraid to tell him I wanted to take Clark home today. As if he's still my boyfriend. Or as if telling him would make him think less of me or — worse — no longer want to be around me.

"I'm the one who what?"

I stare out the passenger-side window, watching the neighborhood houses going by. We should be back at my house soon.

"Forget it. Just take me home."

CHAPTER EIGHT

October 10th, 2009
6:28 p.m.

The rest of the ride is in silence. As soon as we reach the rental, before Mikey can put his Jeep in park, I'm out of the car. I plan to get inside, get in bed, and touch myself. The same thing I do nearly every other day to quiet my horny thoughts. I'm pissed at Mikey for causing my horniness to be wasted on my own fingers.

As I walk to the front door, I hear Mikey's door close. I look around and see he's following me.

"What are you doing?" I ask.

"You have coffee?" he asks.

"Yeah, but—"

"Didn't you invite me to coffee the other day? Or is that off the table now?"

"You're the one that said no."

"Well, in Maximillian fashion, I've changed my mind."

I huff, hating that he just called me that. Such a stupid nickname. I don't despise it nearly as much as my first name, Maxine. At the age of nine, I announced to everyone my name was Max. I told my mother the day she died, thinking she'd reject the change. When she didn't, I decided to fully commit to it.

"Don't call me that." I walk to the front door to unlock it.

I go to the kitchen and as I prepare a pot of coffee, Mikey takes a seat on the vintage western-style love seat in my living room. I stare at him from the corner of my eye as I put the grounds of coffee in the paper filter. I shouldn't have let him in. If anyone in town sees his Jeep on the street right across from my house, we'll both be in trouble. Even though Mikey has only lived in Mendex since he was twenty, he's made a lot of friends.

Once the coffee is done, I pour us each a cup. Still somewhat angry with him, I sit on the old recliner.

"This place looks nice," Mikey comments.

Fucking small talk. It's insulting for him to even bother. This place is a shithole my dad uses to make a little extra income. If it weren't for me living here, he'd make a measly five hundred from it. It's a one-bed, one-bath; the kitchen is small, as is the laundry room, barely fitting the out-of-date washer and dryer. All the furniture is used and refurbished; my dad vacuumed all the dirt and grime from between the crevices to make it look newer.

When I don't answer, Mikey exhales, saying, "Look, I'm sorry. I know I'm being overbearing, but I really do mean well. It's dangerous out there."

"I can take care of myself."

"I know you can. I really am just trying to help. It's not a bad thing to accept help, you know?"

"I appreciate it. I guess I just didn't expect to be getting help from you."

"Yeah, funny how that works. We had good times together. Maybe I'm just stuck in the past. This marriage to Adrienne, and parenthood . . . it's just stressful."

A part of me wants to sit next to Mikey. To console him like I used to. We spent a lot of time together during those three months we dated. Talking about our problems, the good things, and even random topics. After a long day at work, we would shower together, and I would wash him while offering comforting words.

I can't do that now. He's married. I already despise myself enough for killing someone; sleeping with a married man would incinerate my self-worth completely. Every moment spent in this man's company deepens the urge.

I decide to be cold and point out the reality of the situation. "Mikey, you're thirty years old. This is how life works. You married her, she had your child."

He frowns at my unsympathetic words. As if feeling the chill, he grabs his coffee cup and takes a drink from it. Then he reaches into the pocket of his brown jacket and takes out a bag of joints and a lighter.

"Mikey, no," I say, standing up.

"I'm due home in like twenty minutes. This is me dealing with life."

"If my dad smells it, I'm going to kill you."

He laughs me off, lights one of the joints, and takes a deep drag, all the while staring at me. We used to smoke together quite frequently back when we dated. I preferred liquor, while Mikey preferred weed.

"Just tell Pops it's mine."

"Yeah, I'm sure telling him that my now-married ex-boyfriend was at my house smoking weed would make him real proud," I say.

"We sometimes smoke together. He might buy it. He knows I'm unhappy."

I sigh. I bet my dad knows the feeling of hating your wife and life. It probably brings back horrid memories for him.

"He knows I still think about you too. I asked how you were doing a lot when you were gone."

"Stop talking about me to my dad," I order, embarrassed.

"I can't help it. You did some voodoo on me, woman."

49

I laugh. "Voodoo," he calls it. Must've been all the sex we had when we were together. It was always fantastic. Afterward, we'd pass out in each other's arms. That must be what this is. Mikey is sex deprived and trying to rekindle an old relationship.

"You never visited, you know? Must not have missed me that much."

"I was angry with you. Then, when I got over it, I was already dating Adrienne. She hates you, so . . . I just wanted to keep the peace between us."

"Is this what you call keeping the peace?"

"I don't care anymore, if you couldn't tell." He shrugs.

Sweat is beading on my chest. I remember I turned the heat up and just drank half a cup of coffee. I stand up, taking my hoody off, take it to the coat rack, and hang it next to Clark's flannel.

When I turn around, Mikey is looking me up and down as he takes a hit from his joint.

"You look good, Max," he tells me.

"Shut up," I say, hiding my blushing face.

I could undress more for Mikey. Really get a reaction from him. But I remind myself I'm angry with him for taking that chance I had away. I will not be the other woman.

"We had coffee. Now you should leave. You have a family to get home to."

Mikey finishes his joint, drops the butt into his coffee cup, and stands. He moves closer to me.

"Mikey, stop," I hiss.

"You can't keep your feelings bottled up forever, Maximillian."

"Don't ca——"

"Thanks for the coffee. I'll see you tomorrow." He smiles briefly, then he's gone.

As soon as the door is shut, I lock it and run to the kitchen where I keep my pint of Nikolai vodka. I purchased it a few days after moving in here. I did so as discreetly as possible, going to the liquor store across town. The one my father doesn't visit, as he hates the owner. For extra insurance, I wore a ball cap and sunglasses when purchasing it. It's been nearly four months, and I've left it untouched. I don't know why. Every night, I find myself taking it out and wishing I could drink just one small sip.

Drinking used to calm my anxiety. Why do I have to be such a coward and not just drink the damn vodka? It would warm me up, expel all these erotic thoughts I have for Mikey. He said it himself, even he's calling my bluff.

If I drink it, there will be no going back. I couldn't lie about it. I'd have to stand in front of Jay and the rest of the AA members and tell them I'm back to day zero of sobriety. I have to do this for myself and my family. They believed in me when I didn't even believe in myself.

I pace around until my anxiety gets the best of me, and I put the liquor away. Then I go to the living room and begin to cry. If I could have anything in the world it would be just a drink of that vodka. Or Clark and Mikey in my bed.

CHAPTER NINE

October 10th, 2009
8:15 p.m.

It isn't like him to be at Maxine's house this early in the evening. A half-moon hangs low in the clear sky, adding a yellow light to the darkness. Neighbors will still be up and about, possibly looking out their windows. They could spot him, hiding in the hibiscus shrub in front of the empty house. It's the spot he always goes to first, so he can watch Maxine from afar while he scopes out the neighborhood: lights on at other homes, cars driving by, bystanders. He's always been cautious. Tonight is different.

He can't stay up late to see her, not again. He has work tomorrow at six. After that, he must get the van ready with everything that he'll need to grab Max once she's off work. That's when he plans to take her.

He lingers at the other end of the street for nearly half an hour before making his way to Maxine's lawn. He makes sure no neighbors have their curtains open and that no vehicles have driven by in a decent amount of time. When he arrives near the house's front window, he peeks through. She isn't in the living room, nor the kitchen.

Keeping low to the ground, he makes his way to the back of her house. She has two bedroom windows. One has the shades completely drawn, but the other has a shade only two-thirds of the way closed. He presses his back to the wall and checks his surroundings again. Being here is risky, and he knows that. The neighbor has a dog. If they were to let it out now, the dog could bark, alert the neighbors to his presence. That's why he prefers to wait until after 11 p.m., when mostly everyone in the neighborhood is asleep.

He keeps an eye on the neighbor's back porch light. It's automatic, so it should alert him if the neighbors do decide to come out. He's dressed in all black, along with a dark ball cap, so he should blend into the night if any vehicles drive by. He'll only stay a moment.

When he's sure the coast is clear, he peeks through the window. What he sees nearly brings him back down to his knees. Maxine is lying on her bed in a white tank top and nothing else. Her legs are spread open, and she has her right hand between them, her other arm resting just above her head. She's pleasuring herself. Her eyes are closed. She's concentrating hard as she works her fingers. She opens her mouth, and he imagines her moaning.

It doesn't take long for him to get a hard-on. He stuffs his hand into his pants, imagining he's there with her. He forgets all the hatred he has for this creature and begins pleasuring himself. He envisions all the fun he'll have once Maxine is in his control. He's never had sex when it's against someone's will, but if that's the only shot he has at having her, he'll bend his own morals. He won't cause harm to her if he doesn't have to.

It doesn't take long for him to finish. It's a better, longer-lasting climax than usual. A tight moan escapes his mouth.

His attraction to this creature is different from the rest. Ever since he saw Maxine, he hasn't been able to control his desires.

The satisfaction from his orgasm is cut short when an older man's voice yells, "What the hell are you doing?"

Startled, he drops to his ass. It's the neighbor with the dog. He's been too engrossed in watching Maxine to notice the porch light go on. He zips his fly and sprints as fast as he can in the direction of his van.

He dodges into an alleyway, thinking he's in the clear, but then he hears the dog barking behind him. He glances back and sees it round the corner into the alley. When the dog is only a couple yards away from him, he jumps onto a nearby dumpster and hops the fence. His foot catches on the fence, and he falls face down on the freshly mowed grass. Thankfully the yard to the house he had fallen onto doesn't have automatic lights. He gets back up and runs across the lawn and onto the next street, hearing the dog barking and scrabbling at the fence.

His vehicle is only another street down, parked in the next alleyway. Once inside, he wipes a few beads of sweat from his forehead, relieved he escaped scot-free. He hopes the ball cap was enough to shield his identity.

He can't be brainless like that again. No more early-evening trips. If he gets caught, Maxine will never be his.

As he drives, he can't help but think back to what he saw in the bedroom. He has to control his lust for Maxine.

After what Maxine did, he deserves to do what he wants with her. He just has to rid himself of all empathy.

CHAPTER TEN

October 11th, 2009
7:58 p.m.

Someone is watching me. Following me. They saw me in my most vulnerable state. I don't want to believe it; in fact, I'm still trying to convince myself it must all be a coincidence. But I can no longer ignore it. First, there was the man standing outside the restaurant. Now a man has been caught watching me through my window. I'm in danger, and I have no idea who to fear.

Today has been one long nightmare. I hardly got any sleep last night after discovering someone had been spying on me while I was masturbating. I was convinced I'd shut both of my blinds, but I had been so horny, I didn't make sure to check. After Mikey left, I cried for an hour or so before going to the kitchen to make a quick dinner. After that, my fantasies about both Mikey and Clark took over, and I went straight to my room. I just wanted to feel good for a couple moments.

Just as I was reaching orgasm, imagining past sexual experiences with Mikey, the possibility of having Clark touch me, there was a loud knocking on my door. A wild part of me thought it would be Mikey attempting to seduce me. Thankfully it wasn't, because at that moment I would've thrown any morals I had away.

The knocking was my next-door neighbor, Robert. He was already in his pajamas and looked a complete mess. It was the first time he had ever been at my front door. He and his wife were quiet neighbors, usually in bed early.

Robert informed me he caught a man masturbating outside my window. When he yelled at him, the man had taken off.

"Bella chased him off," Robert told me, patting his golden retriever. "I'm sorry I didn't get a good look at him. He had a ball cap on, so I couldn't see his face. Not sure I'd have made him out even if he hadn't been wearing it. I didn't have my glasses on."

Robert called the cops and helped me file a police report. I wanted to die when they asked what I had been doing. I lied and said I was getting changed. In the end, without a description of the man's face or his vehicle, they couldn't do anything.

After that, I checked all the curtains and blinds in my house, making sure they were all fully closed. But the darkness only made me more worried. Unable to sleep due to the lurking thoughts of the man breaking into my home, I kept my bedroom light on and locked the door.

Who is he? Why has he chosen my house to watch? Is it someone I know? Could it be Mikey? I haven't seen him at all in the four months I've lived here, and now he's suddenly maneuvered himself into my life again. But Mikey wouldn't do something so horrible to me. There's also Red. He was angry after I rejected him the other day.

When I showed up for work today, I couldn't concentrate. All I could do was imagine that man watching me. How did he know to look through my blinds at that very moment?

"You should have called me right away," Aunt Almeida tells me when I ring her up. "You didn't need to come in after a shock like that."

"I'd much rather be here than home worrying myself to death about some creep lingering around the house. Only now that I'm here does the whole ordeal keep running through my head. I'm messing up my orders."

"Well, I'll be there soon. I'll close for you."

I don't want to walk home alone today, that's for sure. I could tell my dad about the peeping Tom — that might stir him up enough to help me out — but I fill up with shame just thinking about that. So, I pick up the phone and call the only friend I have.

* * *

As I cash out my last ticket for the night, Mikey enters the restaurant on cue. I tell my customers thank you and watch as they leave. I make sure to clean the table, watching Mikey wait by the host stand with his hands in his pockets. Today he's wearing a blue-and-white button-up flannel with nice dark blue Wrangler jeans.

I go to the back and take my apron off. Aunt Almeida looks as exhausted as me. I feel guilty. She already pulled an opening shift before coming to save me, but she insisted on staying till closing rather than calling in one of the other waitresses. The evening regulars love it. They generally don't get to see her on the night shift, and although weary, she still manages to handle multiple tables with a smile and small talk. I, on the other hand, feel like a ghost haunting the restaurant.

"Mikey Connolly called me yesterday asking when you got out of AA. Is he the one giving you a ride home?" she asks, hands on hips.

"You know Dad won't," I protest, seeing dismay in her eyes.

"He's a married man, Max."

"It's just a ride." I put Clark's flannel jacket on.

"Are you actually wearing a winter jacket? I don't believe it. New?" she asks.

"A man from AA gave it to me," I explain.

Almeida chuckles. "Look at all the male attention you're getting."

"I'm not getting any attention, just a jacket and a ride."

"You forget I'm twenty years older than you. I know where both of those things lead."

"You're being silly. Thanks for covering for me."

"Don't mention it. Just do me a favor. Be careful around these men. There's a serial killer out there."

I look at Almeida in surprise, but she's serious. It's highly unlikely the serial killer is out roaming the streets of Mendex. Only three women from this town have gone missing in the past twenty-three years since the killer has been active, and none of them have been linked to the Monroe murders. Eva, Mary, and Mariah were all troubled women — they probably just wanted a fresh start somewhere people wouldn't judge them all the time. But I'm not going to say all that to my aunt. She might think I want to skip town too, and I don't want to worry her.

"I will." I give Aunt Almeida an air-kiss. "Love you."

Mikey's sitting on one of the ruby-red leather couches by the front door. He stands up as I approach and gives me a hug. Once he lets go, I scan the restaurant for anyone who could've seen that display. Someone here is bound to jump to the wrong conclusion and tell Adrienne.

"Sorry, it looks like you needed that."

"Thanks for picking me up."

As we leave the restaurant, I ponder telling Mikey about what occurred last night. I don't want him worrying about me more than he already is. Not that I don't like it.

During my early twenties I was too fearful of getting into serious relationships. A part of me could only think of my parents' relationship and how that ended. My mother hadn't taken to being a stay-at-home mom, and once she'd started self-medicating with pills and alcohol, my father started an affair with another woman. When my mother found out, her already-crumbling mental stability shattered completely.

Then there was Dennis, the boy I spent my high school years fawning over. The way that ended made me fearful of the harmful things I'm capable of doing when I'm in love.

When we get inside Mikey's Jeep, he turns to look at me. Not like he looked at me last night. It's a sympathetic expression.

"Did something happen today at work or last night? I mean, don't take offense at this, but you look beat to shit."

"I didn't get a lot of sleep. That happens. You have a kid. You should know the feeling."

"I was just asking." He sounds hurt by my outburst.

I realize I am displacing my frustration onto him, and it's not fair. He's been nothing but kind to me. Even if he wants to get in my pants.

"I'm sorry. I just don't know how to act around someone like you."

"Like me?"

"Someone that gives a damn. In prison, it was just me. Before then, I just sort of . . . freaked out when someone cared. I don't know why I'm like this. I think when my mom—"

"Max, Max, you don't need to talk about her." Mikey touches my shoulder, pulling me back from the deep end.

I was only nine when my mother ended her life, but I remember everything that happened. I remember the way she looked at me before she died. The pain in her eyes. How everyone told me her actions were not in any way my fault. No one realized I wasn't hurting because I thought it was my fault; I was hurting because I hadn't been enough to stop her from doing what she did. Of course, now that I'm an adult I know she badly needed psychiatric help that she didn't receive.

I haven't spoken about my mother in years. Everyone in town knows what unfolded before she took her own life. It made national news. Now after my crime, the Masterson name has been even more soiled. I really need to get out of this sinking ship of a town.

During our whole relationship, Mikey never once asked me about her. It's one of the things I liked most about him. Not like the others, who apologized and asked how I dealt with it. Asked if I remembered how my mother acted before she went crazy. People can be nosy. Mikey was different. He did what I wish everyone in the world would do: act like it never fucking happened.

"Just know I do appreciate our friendship, and I like having you in my life. Even if I'm shit at expressing it," I say.

"I know, Max. I know."

When we get to my place, Mikey doesn't offer to come in, and I don't tell him what happened last night. Before getting out of his car, I reach over and give him a hug. He takes a deep inhalation of my hair before I leave the embrace. I thank him for the ride and go into my home, locking the door behind me.

CHAPTER ELEVEN

October 15th, 2009
7:40 p.m.

The next four days passed in a blur. By the time it's my last night shift before one of my days off, I am less than ecstatic. I've enjoyed spending time with Mikey. Most nights he takes me home and we sit in his Jeep in the restaurant's parking lot, talking about the past and all the fun times we had. Even the times before we dated.

He talks about his family. Although he seems to truly love his son, he's not said one good thing about Adrienne. Unless asked, he won't even bring her name up. I expect at some point he'll stop showing up to take me home, because sooner or later, word of our relationship will spread around town. The rest of the staff have seen him coming in and waiting till I'm off. He's even come in earlier to have some coffee, and requests a table in my section. Adrienne is bound to put a stop to it when she finds out.

The unselfish version of me hopes he will stop showing. My emotional interest in him has been rekindled, and that scares me. And talking about the past while knowing I'll never be able to relive those days is stressful. I'll never be able to change all the things I've done.

Yesterday I even took a walk to the drugstore nearby and bought some makeup.

Today, since I know it'll be the last night I see Mikey until my next night shift, I took nearly an hour on my appearance. I curled my long blonde hair, a tedious task I normally am too lazy to take the half hour to do. I've even brought a bottle of hairspray to keep the curls intact as my night shift is nearing its end. I blended a mix of pink and warm brown eyeshadow on my eyelids, then applied two coats of mascara.

I'm eating a complimentary order of fries thanks to Tayen when Casey, the other waitress on shift tonight, tells me I have a table. Tonight has been slow, and I assume it will be my last customer. I hope it's Mikey, but he's not due in for another hour or so. When he does come in, Casey usually gives me more attitude about it.

I grab a stick of gum so my breath won't reek of fried potatoes and head to the booth near the front of the restaurant. The customer is facing away from me, wearing a ball cap, looking over the menu.

Notepad in hand, I put a fake smile on my face and approach him.

"Good afternoon, sir. Can I grab a drink for you while you look over the menu?"

The man peers up and I am taken aback to see that it's Clark. With all the time I've been spending with Mikey, I nearly forgot about the cute stranger from AA I had been flirting with. He looks somewhat exhausted, but at the sight of me, he lights up. He's wearing a tight-fitting, short-sleeved Henley shirt. He isn't heavily built, but his arms are toned.

"Max, hey." He sets the menu down.

I try to hide my surprise. "Clark, how are you?"

"Living the dream. I didn't know you worked here."

"I've never seen you around. You come in much?"

"No, I did as a kid. I just figured after this week I deserved a treat. Little did I know the treat would be seeing you." He winks.

I blush and, remembering I'm on the clock, lift my notepad up. "Can I get you something to drink? Homemade iced tea? Lemonade?"

"Just a coffee for now, please."

Clark did mention he drank a lot of coffee at AA. I wonder if he's waiting to pour some rum in it from a flask hidden in his back pocket. From here I can't smell alcohol on his breath, and he doesn't appear intoxicated.

"Cream with that?"

"No, black's fine."

I jot that down on my notepad and excuse myself. I make a fresh pot of coffee and hurry back to Clark's table. Casey notices my happy flushed face and glares at me as I make my way back to him. Most of the other waitresses don't like working with an ex-con like me. But I suspect Casey also doesn't like me because before I started, she was the cutest waitress here. Most of the customers we get are older folks, families, or stoners — slim pickings, but I guess she doesn't like the competition anyway. Clark is certainly the cutest customer I've had since working here, apart from Mikey, that is.

I bring Clark his coffee. He gives me a wide smile, showcasing his yellow teeth. "Thank you, Max."

"Ready to order?" I ask.

"Sure, I'll just take a cheeseburger, no onions or mustard. Oh, and can I also get a side of mozzarella sticks?"

"You not a fan of onions and mustard, huh?"

"Don't really like them on my burger. Is that bad?"

"No, I like mine the same."

"Good taste," Clark says with a wink. I smile as I take his menu.

After I tell Tayen Clark's order, Casey comes up behind me, her arms crossed. Casey has never attempted to be nice to me. She'll barely speak to me unless she's barking out cleaning orders.

"Another suitor for Max Masterson?" she says sarcastically.

"Didn't realize I even had one to begin with," I say, playing coy.

She smirks. "He's kind of cute. Never seen him around. You two know each other? You should introduce me. I mean, you already have Mikey Connolly. Don't be greedy."

"You want to know him so bad, go introduce yourself," I say, sick of her sarcasm.

"Don't mind if I do."

I start wiping down tables. As I do, I see Casey approaching Clark. I can't hear what she's saying, but she's making a lot of hand gestures and has an overly large smile on her face. A part of me hopes that Clark will reject her, and I see my wish is granted when she doesn't linger by him long. After she leaves, he looks to the side and makes eye contact with me, grinning.

So that I have a reason to talk to him, I grab a pitcher of fresh coffee and walk over to Clark.

"Refill?"

Raising his eyebrows, Clark takes a glance at his still-full cup and shakes his head.

"That other waitress, Casey. She seems nice."

The tone Clark uses implies he doesn't actually think that.

"She's a ray of sunshine," I say as seriously as I can in case Casey is listening nearby.

"Hey, what did we say about lying?" he jokes.

"You started it."

"She said I should be careful around you. Is that true? Should I be careful around you?"

I shrug. "I guess that's for you to decide."

"I think I like a little danger. Makes it interesting."

64

I want to flirt back, but I feel guilty. *Am I doing something wrong?*

"I should go check on your order, Clark."

I leave as quickly as I can. I enter the employee break room and take a deep breath. I stare at myself in a nearby tiny, smudged mirror hanging on the wall.

"What is wrong with you?" I ask myself.

Why am I blowing off this sweet man? It's Mikey's fault. All this time I've been spending with him is toxic. It's making me not see the available man sitting there, obviously flirting with me. Just a few days ago I wanted to sleep with Clark. Now here I am, feeling guilty for flirting.

I fix my hair, moving it over my shoulders so it flows perfectly down, landing a couple inches below my chest. I grab some pink lip gloss I brought and slide the wand over my lips. After taking a couple deep breaths, I walk back out and continue clearing tables. Clark's still sitting in the booth, reading today's newspaper while sipping on his coffee.

After the peeping Tom incident, Aunt Almeida made sure I was never the last waitress left to lock up the restaurant. If for some reason Mikey can't make it today, I'll be getting off work just in time to ask Clark to give me a ride. Once we're alone, I can be myself and not worry about others watching us. Thankfully Casey hasn't said too much about my past. I mean, Clark already knows about my prison time, but I'm sure if he knew about my mother, that would be the final straw.

When Tayen rings the bell to indicate Clark's order is ready, I hastily grab it and head to Clark's table. By now his coffee cup is empty, so I also offer him a refill.

"Anything else?"

"No, this looks good. Thank you, Max."

Butterflies flutter in my stomach just hearing him say my name. I was an idiot to rebuff him. I have been guarded long enough, and having only two friends in this town isn't healthy. Especially since one is family and the other is a married man.

"Sorry if I made you feel uncomfortable," he says, before I can walk away.

"It's not that, it's just . . . this town talks. After what I did, I think everyone wants me to just die alone. If I get too close to someone, people take notice. Not that I blame them."

"That's, like, super fucked up. It was a mistake. You've done your time," he consoles me.

"That's Mendex for you."

"That's why I don't go out much."

"I guess that's why I've never seen you around. You live here your whole life?"

Clark scratches his head and nods.

"Did you go to high school here?"

"Homeschooled."

"What do your parents do?"

Clark presses his lips together, and after some thought, he says, "My father farms."

No mention of his mother. Was she the one who homeschooled him?

"Does he like farming?"

He nods. I want to ask more questions, but Clark seems to have grown uncomfortable. I have enough experience with a dysfunctional family life to know not to pry.

"I always wanted to go to a normal school," he says. "How'd you like it?"

Such a big question. People normally have one of two answers. The ones who were bullied would say they hated it. The popular ones, like me, would say it *was* a blast. It was a blast, but one incident ruined all that. Now whenever I think about high school, I think of one night.

"It was okay. I did okay."

"That's two okays, so I'm guessing not so okay. You come off as the sociable type, so I thought you would've said great."

"I come off as sociable, really?"

He's not wrong, but for some unexplainable reason, I don't see how Clark could've caught on to that. I'm a shell of the girl I used to be back in high school. That one night took all that sociability out of me. After that, drinking numbed the pain. Now being painfully sober, I can't escape it.

"Yeah, pretty, and blonde. Those teen movies always say blonde girls are the popular ones."

"Well, those are movies. But yeah, I did okay in high school. I played tennis."

"Any good?"

"Not really. I mainly did it to get out of class. And to survive."

"Well, you're lucky. School is where they say you learn social skills."

"Yeah, I guess."

The phone starts ringing, and I excuse myself, somewhat happy to get out of the conversation. Not that I don't appreciate being in Clark's presence, but the topic of school makes my stomach ache. I think of that night. All the shots I took, the way Dennis put his arm around me, acting like nothing had happened.

"JJ's Family Restaurant. How can I help you?"

"Hey, it's me."

Mikey.

CHAPTER TWELVE

October 15th, 2009
7:58 p.m.

"Mikey, hey," I answer.

"Just letting you know, I'll be there in five. Can you be ready by then?"

I gulp, wanting to tell Mikey a lie. Tell him Casey offered to drive me home. But I've already told him about how all the waitresses dislike me. Perhaps he won't remember that. Thinking of all the little moments from our relationship he still somehow remembers from five years ago, I doubt that.

"Yeah, but if you're busy I can always catch a ride from Casey. She might need help closing," I explain.

I find it best when lying to tell half of the truth. Casey would love the extra help even if it is from me. She's lazy and wasn't too ecstatic to be the closer.

Not that I would stay to help her. I'd simply catch a ride with Clark. Try flirting with him when we're alone. Just the thought of grasping his toned arms, feeling his hands on my waist, brings goosebumps to my flesh. If I just have sex once, I feel I'll be cured of my constant need for someone's touch.

"Don't be silly. She hates you anyways, right?"

"Yeah, but it's really no big deal," I press on.

"Max, it's no big deal for me. I already told Adrienne I wouldn't be home till eight."

"How long are you going to keep lying to her about us?"

I catch Casey's eyes on me from afar. I must cut this conversation short before she hears us. Getting any dirty intel for the other waitresses would be the highlight of her day.

"Do you want an exact date or . . . ?" Mikey chuckles. *Why is he taking this matter so lightly?*

"You should just tell her the truth. If she's so against us being friends, then maybe that's a sign I need to find another ride home."

It pains me to have to say that, but I can't sit idly by and let Mikey continue to lie to his wife.

"Am I just a ride home to you, Max?"

I tightly close my eyes. "Of course not. You know what I mean."

"We can talk about this in person, okay?"

"No, Mikey—" But he has already hung up.

I catch Casey smirking at me, and I mimic her. Tonight, I must tell Mikey we can't keep this charade going. I can take care of myself and, with Clark's winter jacket, the walk home won't be all that terrible. I'll purchase some pepper spray for added protection.

I notice Clark has finished his meal. I grab his check. When I give it to him, he hands me two twenties, which is double the actual total of his bill.

"I only need one of those," I say, attempting to hand the second twenty back to him.

"That's for you."

"No, Clark, I can't," I say, my cheeks flushing.

"It's nothing. You're amazing. An . . . amazing waitress, I mean."

"Hardly, but thank you."

"So, are you almost off work?"

I nod, already knowing what he's getting at.

"If you'd like, I can give you a ride home."

That's the exactly what I want. I didn't even have to be the one to ask. But because of damn Mikey, I can't say yes. I mean, I could and tell Mikey to back off, but it wouldn't be right. He deserves a proper explanation of why what we're doing needs to stop.

Before I can answer, the front door chimes. As if on cue, Mikey strolls in. He goes to the hostess stand, looking around for me. It doesn't take long for him to spot me, and he smiles before seeing who I'm serving. His smile fades. Noticing my eyes on him, he purses his lips, walks over to the couch, and takes a seat.

"I can't tonight."

Clark casts a look over at Mikey and frowns. "He your boyfriend?"

I shake my head. "No, just an overly protective friend. He's been giving me a ride home because he thinks it's too dangerous for me to be out walking the streets."

"Must be a good friend. Well, I won't keep you long. Thanks for everything." Clark wipes his mouth with a napkin and stands up.

Feeling I've finally ruined my chances with this man, I ask, "Will I see you at AA?"

"Sure, sure." Clark's already walking away.

Clark and Mikey stare daggers at each other as Clark leaves. I close out Clark's ticket and clean off my last table before clocking out. I go to the back and tell Tayen goodbye before grabbing the flannel jacket and putting it on. I let Casey know I'm leaving and roll my eyes as she makes a sarcastic comment about Mikey.

"I'm ready," I say, making my way to Mikey, who still looks irritated.

"Casey looks like she would have definitely given you a ride home." Mikey scowls, standing up.

"Stop it," I say, turning and walking out the door, not waiting for Mikey.

A brisk wind is blowing. I button up the flannel and continue my walk to the parking lot at the back of the restaurant. It doesn't take long for Mikey to catch up.

"Max, hold on," Mikey says, and I begin to walk faster.

He puts a hand on my shoulder. I stop and scan the parking lot. Is Clark still here? I don't want him to hear us arguing. His sedan is already gone. Did he really hightail it out of here that quickly? Hopefully he wasn't angry with me.

"We should hurry. Your wife is expecting you at home." I brush Mikey's hand off my shoulder and speed up.

"Max!" Mikey exclaims.

Usually I take pleasure in the way Mikey says my name, but now it only invokes frustration. Why is he trying to chase off the one suitor I have?

"Just take me home."

"Wait. I got you something."

"What?" I ask, confused.

Mikey is holding something behind his back. Gifts are crossing the line of our relationship.

"Look, Mikey, I really think what we're doing—"

"Hold that thought for one second, please," he interrupts, showing me what he has in his hand.

It's a small velvet box. I gasp, a huff of cold air entering my mouth. Mikey opens the box, and inside is a diamond-studded necklace with the letter M. I stare at it in disbelief.

"I got this for you, back when we were dating. I was going to give it to you before . . . well. It doesn't matter. It's yours," he says, closing the box.

I just stand there, leaving my hands at my sides. He chuckles, taking my right hand and placing the box in it. Once I have it, my arm slumps back down to my side. My body is numb and it's not due to the cold.

"Why'd you . . . why . . . why would you keep this?" I ask, dumbfounded.

"I don't know. I almost pawned it several times, but I couldn't. It's yours."

"No, no, I can't," I say, attempting to give Mikey the box back.

Mikey grabs ahold of my hand and, moving his face toward me, whispers, "Please."

I blink back tears. It's the first time a man has given me jewelry. I have to keep my emotions under control. This is a married man with a child, giving me jewelry. I know tonight will be the hardest yet, keeping myself from chugging that liter of vodka at my house. I want to get drunk.

"Unlock the Jeep," I softly tell Mikey.

"I forgot to mention how beautiful you look, especially with the moonlight behind you."

"Mikey," I protest, looking him dead in the eyes, praying he'll stop.

"I wish I could've saved you from that night. I tried calling. I wanted to reconcile. If only I'd called earlier. Maybe things would be different."

"Don't be ridiculous. What about your little boy?"

"Yeah, he's my whole world. I just can't help but wonder sometimes."

"You need to lay off the dope. It's making you think crazy."

"I'm one hundred percent sober, Maximillian."

"Don't—" I protest, pressing my free hand on Mikey's chest, but before I can finish, he leans over and plants his cold lips on mine.

72

CHAPTER THIRTEEN

October 15th, 2009
8:09 p.m.

I don't pull back, not right away. The feel of his soft lips on mine makes it too difficult. He isn't lying about being sober. I don't get the faintest taste of weed on his breath. He tastes like peppermint toothpaste. Before another second can pass, I use all my inner strength to gently push him away.

"I had to do that, if only once," he whispers.

I bite my bottom lip and say, "Take me home."

He just nods, unlocking the doors to his Jeep. I quickly climb in, placing the box with the heart necklace in the pocket of my jacket. Mikey gets into the driver's side and starts the Jeep. An old song begins to play, "We'll Meet Again" by Vera Lynn. Mikey and I glance at each other before looking away. We drive in silence.

As I get out of the Jeep, the wind is cool against my face. I hope it cools my flushed cheeks. Once inside, Mikey throws his keys onto the coffee table, and I take my jacket off and go to put it on the rack. Mikey grabs me by the waist and pulls me closer. I feel his breath on my neck as he gently kisses me. Heat rushes to my cheeks again. I turn around and, before I can let my better judgment stop me, kiss Mikey on the lips. Our kiss deepens, and we slowly migrate to the love seat. As we kiss, he fumbles with his work boots, trying to pull them off. We giggle, and I kick my sneakers off with ease.

He slowly moves my shirt up and over my shoulders and tosses it on the ground nearby. The room is dark, but he stops kissing me to stare at my nearly undressed body. As he does, I remove his bomber jacket, then his lime-green polo shirt.

"Fuck, it's dark in here," Mikey whispers, looking around at the drawn blinds.

I haven't told him about the peeping Tom. So many times, as he drove me home and I sat in his Jeep, I wanted to, but I couldn't. I worried he would want to stay over, sleep on the couch. I couldn't do that to him. Not that it matters anymore. What we're doing right now is deeper than that.

Mikey gently sets me down on the love seat and climbs on top of me. Soon his hands are over my bra.

Just as I feel his hand begin to inch underneath the wire of my bra, he asks, "Is this okay?"

I should say no, but I don't. My brain is no longer calling the shots; my body is. I nod. I want his hands on me. My body is on fire, burning for the pleasure I've been deprived of.

Mikey moves his hand under my bra, taking a firm grasp of my breast. I bite my bottom lip to suppress the moans. I don't want him to know how good this alone feels.

As we continue making out on the couch, Mikey's erection presses into my leg. I wish he'd speed things up. He always did like foreplay, taking things slow as we made love. I'm the opposite; I often fantasize about quick sex. Sex that couldn't wait a second longer, clothes that needed to be ripped apart to get to it.

Mikey moves his hand lower. But suddenly somebody hammers loudly on the window next to the front door. Mikey and I both freeze. Only moments later, there's another frenzy of knocks.

Mikey jumps up and rushes to the window, then opens the dark green curtains I had closed completely. The night sky illuminates the living room. Is someone outside, watching?

I think of the man watching me, following me. Could it be him? I wrap my arms around my body, wary of how exposed I currently am.

Mikey must see something I don't because as he looks outside, he exclaims, "What the fuck?"

CHAPTER FOURTEEN

October 15th, 2009
8:27 p.m.

"What?" I ask, pulling on my shirt and going over to Mickey. Now I see where his anger has come from. His Jeep's windshield has a crack running the length of it. Finally, the realization of what just occurred seeps into my mind. How could I have been so foolish?

As I stand there, frozen on the spot, Mikey puts his shirt and boots back on and runs outside. If this wasn't the man watching me, who could have done this? Adrienne? I check my watch and see it's nearly eight thirty. Mikey is late. Perhaps someone saw his car outside my house and told her. Or, even worse, it could be that peeping Tom, outraged by the sight of Mikey and me going into the house together.

Mikey comes back inside, slamming the door.

"Was anyone out there?" I ask. It's a stupid question, as I doubt Mikey would've returned so quickly if there was someone.

"No. I know who did it, though." He's running his fingers through his hair like he wants to pull it out.

"Who?"

"Adrienne's brothers. Casey knows Adrienne. She must've seen us outside the restaurant and called her. Knowing Adrienne, she probably called one of her brothers to check and see if I was here. Shit!" Mikey's pacing around.

"Maybe it was just some kids playing a prank," I suggest.

Mikey shakes his head. "No. This . . . this was personal. I know it."

"Then you need to go home, sort things out."

Mikey puts his bomber jacket on and comes closer. Just being near him again, I feel guilty. I could have pushed him away when he kissed me. I could have told him how wrong it was that we were doing this.

"I'll go home, make sure at the very least that they leave you alone," he says, placing his hand on my cheek.

I don't want to, but I move his hand from my face. "What we did was wrong, Mikey. You need to go home."

"I'm sorry, Max. I knew better and still went for it. I just can't help it. Being around you has made me feel—"

"Please go," I say, unable to take the sorrow in his eyes.

Mikey sighs, nodding. He leans in and kisses my cheek slowly.

Once he's gone, I close the blinds again. Then I go to the cabinet, find the vodka, and without hesitation take a long swig.

Just like that, I am back to day zero.

CHAPTER FIFTEEN

October 16th, 2009
8:12 a.m.

The next morning, my pounding head isn't the only thing that wakes me with a sudden jolt. Somebody is banging on the door. My first instinct is that it's Mikey. That he's come to tell me all the details of what happened to his Jeep last night. I pray Adrienne doesn't know. That the knocking on my window and the rock thrown at his windshield had been some kids playing an over-the-top prank.

Mikey is supposed to be working today. So, unless he called out, it is someone else.

Getting out of bed, I take a glance at the bedside table, seeing the nearly empty vodka bottle. Now that I'm awake and the liquor has worn off, everything is hitting me like a Taser to the back. I grab the liquor and take a sip, hoping it'll reduce my headache.

Thankfully I don't have work, but I do have an AA meeting later this evening — which I hope will be easy and not require any speaking on my part. I don't want to admit what I've done to the group. I'd rather talk to Jay in private, explain what happened, hopefully get some words of wisdom. I think about calling him, but really all I want to do right now is stay in bed, leave the lights off, and wait for the pounding to stop. I can't do that, though.

I go to my front door and peek through the peephole. My full bladder nearly erupts at the sight of the person on the other side of the door. It's Adrienne. Last time I saw her, she had long, perfectly curled coffee-colored hair, which is now greasy and tied back in a messy bun. She's wearing an oversized purple hoody with gray sweatpants. Her arms are crossed, and she's tapping her foot impatiently.

I consider my options. I could be a coward — not answer and hope she goes away. I've avoided responsibility in the past. That night at the party. I'd even considered doing it the night I killed George Dawson. Then I think of all the pain I caused when I played the role of the coward. I can't become that person again. That version of myself died the night I killed George. I need to find my courage and face this woman whose husband I was making out with just last night.

"I know you're there, Max. Answer the fucking door!" Adrienne yells, glaring directly into the peephole. It's obvious she knows what happened.

I take a couple deep breaths and unlock and open my door. I decide that as a reward for not being a coward, I can lie and deny anything happened between Mikey and me. Maybe all she knows is that he was in my house last night. It's not like he was here long. I can say we were just catching up, which would still piss any wife off but somewhat lessen the blow. I tell myself if Adrienne's brothers really are as crazy as Mikey says, I need to lie to keep him safe.

"Sorry. I was sleeping." I can't meet Adrienne's angry gaze.

"I bet you were. Messing around with someone's husband must really take it out of you."

"I-I don't know what—"

"What I'm talking about? I'm talking about you kissing my husband at that shitty-ass restaurant last night," Adrienne says, cutting me off.

So much for denying it.

"How . . . how did you—"

"Casey told me everything. About how Mikey's been giving you rides home and about how you two kissed in the parking lot. I know everything, Max."

So, she doesn't know his Jeep was parked outside my house after the kiss at the restaurant. But if she didn't send her brothers over, then who damaged Mikey's Jeep?

"Adrienne—"

"Cut the shit, Max. I don't have the patience or time to listen to your sorry-ass excuses. I came here to tell you to stay away from my husband. You already destroyed one family's life, and now you're going after a second?"

Adrienne's words burn because she's right. I kissed Mikey in that parking lot. I want to blame my actions on my constant yearning for sex, but that would be a lie. I like Mikey, and after all these years, I still have feelings for him. He's one of the only good people I have in my life, and a part of me will always despise myself for ruining things with him. If I hadn't cheated five years ago, things could have been drastically different. I might never have gotten in my car that night. Drove that road home. Hit George.

"You're right, Adrienne. Mikey and I just have a past, and with everything going on, it's been hard to bottle up my feelings."

"You're a piece of shit, Max. You're exactly like your parents."

I unclench my jaw, ready to speak up for myself, but . . . don't. She's right. I can't tell which of those insults sting worse: being called a piece of shit, or being told I'm like my parents.

Adrienne scoffs at my silence. "Typical. I really wanted to come here and beat your skinny ass, but I don't feel like going to jail. I'm here to warn you. Stay away from Mikey. Be the better person, for once in your life."

I continue to just stand there and stare. As Adrienne waits for a reply, I simply nod. It's all I can do to hold back the tears. I will not allow her to see me cry. If prison has taught me anything, it is not to cry in front of anyone.

"Don't make me come back here," she warns.

I don't wait for her to get to her vehicle before I slam the front door. I press my back against the door and slide down it, tears flowing down my face. Nearly everything Adrienne said was right. I am a piece of shit, but I am not like my parents.

After prison, I've really tried being a better person. I want to distance myself from my family's reputation for doing horrible things. I don't want to be like my dad, who had an affair and broke my mom's already-crumbling mental state. I don't want to be like my mother, who, after finding out about the affair, took revenge in the best way she saw fit.

All she needed was the help of her nine-year-old daughter.

A part I played perfectly.

CHAPTER SIXTEEN

October 16th, 2009
1:45 p.m.

After this morning's visit from Adrienne, I've once again decided to be a better person. While in prison, I promised to do so more than once, but after the events of last night, I need to stick to it this time. I have to get Mikey out of my mind. Maybe one day in the future, if they can't make it work, we can try again. For now, I'm letting him go.

In order to do that, I need to do one thing. I need to have sex. If I get it out of my system, I might finally be able to get Mikey off my mind.

AA is tonight, which means I have a chance to seal the deal with Clark, if I didn't blow my chances with him last night. Guys like women that play hard to get. Perhaps seeing me leave with Mikey has intensified Clark's attraction to me.

I finish the remainder of the vodka. It thankfully heals my headache. I need just one last bottle. I waste no time getting dressed and walking down to the farthest liquor store from home to purchase a larger bottle of cheap vodka. It takes an hour to walk there and back, but the anonymity is worth it. I stop at a nearby Goodwill store to look for something cute but casual to wear to AA. I find a front-buttoning blue chambray skirt that rests perfectly on my hips. For the top, I choose a long-sleeved white crew-neck blouse. It's one size too big, and when I undo the three buttons on the top, you can see the top of my beige bra.

I pray this isn't all in vain. That Clark will be at AA tonight, and he'll offer to take me home. If he doesn't, I'll have enough liquor in my system to ask him myself. If the world truly wants me to be better, it needs to give me this one thing. If I get this, I'll ignore Mikey. I'll tell him to leave me alone. I'll get help from Jay to once again start over on my sobriety.

Once home, I doll myself up for Clark. I barely recognize myself in the mirror. I had been precise while doing my makeup. I know Clark already likes me but if he's angry with me over last night, my appearance could sway him back into no longer being upset with me.

Before leaving for AA, I grab an empty water bottle and fill it with vodka and a splash of old cranberry juice I have in the fridge. My heart's beating fast. I'm unsure if it's due to the fact I could be rejected by Clark, or that I am about to go into AA half drunk with an alcohol-infused drink in hand.

After going through all the options on the table, I leave my house. I know what I want.

* * *

5:45 p.m.

Fifteen minutes until AA starts and Clark is nowhere to be seen. My head begins to taunt me, telling me to go inside the building before it's too late.

As some fellow members begin to show up, I hide behind the building, scoping out all the vehicles while taking chugs of my drink. I can no longer fake sobriety. Jay is trained in sensing this. I could wait for the others to show up and for the meeting to begin to make a run for it.

There are only a few minutes until Jay will shut the front doors of the community center. After that, I can make a break for it. Just as I am prepared to make my escape, the familiar sight of that old sedan comes into view. My heart skips a beat, and the water bottle nearly falls from my hand. I run from my spot behind the building and book it toward Clark's sedan.

As I run in front of his car, he watches me. I force a smile and give a small wave, which is returned by a puzzled look. I must look like a nutcase. I had so much confidence built up, but now, as I am nearing the end goal, I have no idea what I'm about to say. Or how I'm going to say it. I don't have much time.

Once Clark has rolled his window down, I put on a fake smile and say, "Clark, hey."

Clark gives me a small grin and waves awkwardly. "Max, what . . . what are you up to? Thought you'd be inside by now."

I move a strand of hair behind my ear and say, "I'm having a bad day. Was trying to avoid the inevitable."

After I blurt that out, the look on Clark's face is pure confusion. He must smell the alcohol on my breath.

"Have you been drinking?"

I shut my eyes, my cheeks going hot from the mix of alcohol and embarrassment.

"No! I mean, yeah, a little. I've been having a rough day — days."

When Clark's expression continues to remain blank, I turn around and say, "Forget it — I'm sorry."

I begin to walk off, prepared to run home. The sound of a car door opening behind me stops me in my tracks.

"Wait, Max. Sorry. I guess you just kind of surprised me. Would you like to go inside?"

I purse my lips, trying to figure out how to put what I'm about to say.

"Or would you like to take a ride around town? Tell me about this rough day — days — of yours?"

I just nod. Clark takes my hand in his. As our hands touch, my stomach flutters. I look down as he walks me back to his car.

"I don't want to be the reason you don't go to AA," I say once we reach his car, our hands still intertwined.

"I'll let you in on a secret." He leans in, whispering, "I only came to see you."

"Me too." I bite my lip while I look up at him.

Clark winks at me and gently lets go of my hand. His eyes never leave mine as he gracefully walks back to the driver's side of the sedan. We both get in at the same time, and I realize his sedan is still running.

"So, this bad day . . . want to talk about it?"

"Trust me, you don't want to know. You'd think less of me."

"Try me."

"I just keep fucking up. That guy, Mikey, we dated before I went to prison. I thought we could just be friends, but he's married now and . . . his wife didn't like that."

"This Mikey guy, you have feelings for him still?"

I can't be completely honest with Clark. I hate lying, but if I tell him that I do, he may push me away. Tell me to get out and drive off.

"No, he was just someone I felt I could talk to. I don't have very many friends in this shithole town."

"I think sometimes we miss the things that are right in front of us." He lays his hand on top of mine.

85

CHAPTER SEVENTEEN

October 16th, 2009
6:37 p.m.

It doesn't take long to drive around Mendex. Twenty minutes later and Clark and I have driven around most of the town's streets. It may be more, but I'm unsure; time seems to soar by.

As we've been driving, he's caught me several times staring at him with admiring eyes. I can't help staring at his grimy clothes and the dirty patches on his arms. I want to rip his dirty clothes off, get him in the shower, and wash him clean.

"You know, I don't even know how old you are," I say, after a minute of silence.

"Twenty-eight," he says with a chuckle.

He looks older, but construction work can take it out of you. My father also looks older than his years, though that's not all thanks to his job.

"Aren't you going to ask me how old I am?"

"A gentleman never asks how old a woman is. But since you insist, how old are you, Max?"

"Twenty-seven."

Clark nods. "Do you normally go after older guys?"

"Older guys meaning . . . you?"

"Well, yeah, a year can do a lot to you. I'm definitely wiser."

"How do you figure that?"

"I don't rebuff someone who's clearly interested in me, not once but twice."

"I'm not good at picking up on that stuff."

"Guess I'll have to teach you, then." Clark takes my hand and, bringing it up to his lips, gives it a soft kiss.

I get goosebumps. I stare at his lips after he's put my hand down. They felt soft and inviting.

"Pull over," I command, unable to take the feeling of not having those delicious lips on mine any longer.

"What? Wait, I'm sorry, Max. I didn't mean to—"

"Just pull over."

Looking as if all the air has left his body, Clark puts the blinker on and pulls over on a side street. As soon as he has put the sedan in park, to ease his worry, I remove my seatbelt and move to the middle seat. I stare deep into his eyes. I move his bangs completely out of his face to get a closer look.

"You have beautiful eyes," I whisper, keeping my hand on his cheek.

He looks down, ashamed. Like he's unworthy of my compliment. I bring his head up to look back up at me. We stare at each other, and I get a whiff of spearmint and coffee on his breath.

"You're beautiful, Max," he says, moving his hand up to rest on my waist.

I lean in, closing my eyes, and press my lips to his. We kiss only for a short moment before I move away. When I open my eyes, he still has his eyes closed and looks like he is in another world.

"Would you like to go to my house?" he asks.

"Is your brother home? We can always go to mine."

"He's at the doctor's right now. We'd be all alone."

"Where do you live?"

Clark takes a deep breath. "It's an old farmhouse, about twenty, twenty-five miles out of town."

CHAPTER EIGHTEEN

October 16th, 2009
7:14 p.m.

By the time we arrive at the farmhouse, the sun is a blazing half disc sinking down below the distant mountain, reds and oranges setting the horizon on fire. The day whispers its goodbye. It's the perfect romantic scene for Clark and me. Before we even come to a complete stop, I have the urge to move closer to him, to press my body to his and cuddle him tenderly as we watch the sun go down.

I've lived in Mendex my entire life, but I've never been out here before. It's beautiful, the perfect escape from town. The last house we saw was over ten minutes back, and that was abandoned, from the look of it. The farmhouse looks on the verge of being abandoned too.

We drive past an aged white picket fence that surrounds the house. There's a barn nearby, its red paint thin and flaking. A lone cow stands a couple yards from the barn, chewing on a loose stack of hay. It looks thin and lethargic.

The farmhouse casts a gloomy shadow before the setting sun. It's not how I pictured it. The faded gray paint is chipped, and the curtains drawn across the large windows are full of holes. Outside, the porch is sagging.

I glance warily at Clark as he parks his sedan to the left of the house. Something in the pit of my stomach casts doubt. That doubt turns to fear when I see the front door. It's the same shade of red as the red door at the party Eva and I were at, sparring over Dennis.

Clark touches my thigh. "I know it looks like a complete shithole," he says. "After my brother got sick, I couldn't afford the upkeep."

"I see." I gulp. "So, this is where you live?"

"Grew up here. It's been in the family a long time."

I nod, wondering how long his brother has been sick. This house looks as though it has been decaying for a while now. The house I grew up in wasn't pristine either; my father was too busy working on richer people's homes to take much care of ours. This sort of negligence on a home doesn't just happen in the span of a couple years.

"It's beautiful out here," I offer, taking another look at the sunset to push away that ache.

"It's nothing compared to you, Max," Clark says, a small grin on his face as he casts his eyes on me.

I smile, moving closer to Clark. I debate kissing him on the lips but instead rest my head on his shoulder. I can hear his heartbeat, and it calms me even though it's rapid. He must be nervous. He puts his arm around my shoulder.

"I never saw myself with a girl like you."

"You don't give yourself enough credit, Clark. You could find someone better than me."

I gulp, hating myself for saying that. The words just flew straight out of my mouth before my brain could stop them. I keep bringing my past up like I'm yearning for Clark's approval. Or anyone's approval as to who I am as a person. With Mikey, and now Clark, it's been nice to hear their words of compassion and reassurance.

Clark takes a deep breath. "You made a mistake. You were young."

"Thanks, but I have to pay for what I did."

"Haven't you already?"

I pull away, staring at Clark. His big green eyes show so much compassion. He doesn't stare at me like the killer I am. He would if he knew the other unforgivable things I've done.

"I'm not a good person, Clark. That man — George — he was the only one who I didn't run from when he needed saving. I've sat by and watched bad things happen and done nothing. They say there are two types of bad people. People who do bad things and people who see bad things being done and don't do anything to stop them."

"You did the right thing with him, though?"

"Yeah, but I still took a man's life. I just wish I could've saved him. It could have washed me free of my prior sins. Made my life mean something for once."

Clark is silent for a moment as if considering what to say. He looks away from me and off in the distance as if pondering a college-level math equation.

"One day," he says eventually, "you may get that chance again."

I shrug, knowing God will never offer that.

"Let's go inside." Clark leans over and plants a soft kiss on my forehead.

We begin to walk up the porch. The steps creak under my weight. On the porch is a gray plywood rocking chair and a couple plastic lawn chairs. Sitting on the arm of one lawn chair is an ashtray full of cigarette butts. On the ground by the rocking chair are a couple bottles of rum. The rum makes sense, but does Clark smoke?

Clark uses a single key to unlock two different deadbolts located on the red door, and as we both walk through the door, my heart does another leap. When he closes the front door, he relocks both deadbolts from the inside. I stare at it wondering how long it would take for me to undo those locks myself. Why have two deadbolts? Is there a danger of intruders this far out of town? Perhaps being out here, so far from town, gets a little scary.

"My brother's kind of paranoid," he says, seeing my eyes on the two locks.

I nod. We're in a large open-plan kitchen with a dark walnut floor. The mustard-yellow fridge looks like a vintage model. On the wall next to the fridge is an old landline phone that is a rustic red color. I follow Clark into the dining room area where there's a circular drop-leaf table with five chairs tucked under it. The table I can tell must not be used often, as I can see a small film of dust collecting on it. By a tall record player, a dozen or so records sit on top of an end table.

The staircase leading to the floor above is only two yards from the front door. My eyes are drawn to a door with a large padlock on it, to the right of the stairs. A basement, maybe? I wonder what they keep in there for it to be locked.

"Bathroom's at the end of the dining room," Clark tells me, nodding to another door.

"What's the room by the stairs?" I ask.

Clark gulps. "Leads to the basement. Has family heirlooms. And the laundry room."

This house and all its old furniture make the hairs at the back of my neck stand on end. That, or it's the temperature in the house. It feels chillier in here than outside. I doubt this place has a working heater. I still want to take off the jacket that I'm wearing, let him stare at my new outfit with wandering eyes. It's been so long since I've been able to tease a man with my body.

"Would you like anything to drink or eat?" he asks.

I take a deep breath and, setting my attention on Clark, shake my head.

"Can you take my jacket off?" I ask, turning toward Clark and slowly unzipping it.

Clark steps closer to me so we're only a few inches apart. He puts his hands on the shoulders of the jacket and pulls it off, letting it run over my arms and fall to the ground.

He takes ahold of my hand and lightly pulls me to the stairway. "Would you like to see my room?" he asks.

I nod and run my free hand along the handrail of the stairs as we walk up. The wood feels rough and, as expected, the stairs are creaky. It's been a while since I've been in a house with two stories. It takes me back to that party in high school, walking up the stairs to a room I should've never gone into. I take a deep breath, inhaling the stale air as I try to push those thoughts away.

On the top floor, there is a narrow hallway that goes both left and right. At each end there is a small window. The left side has only one door, while the right side has two. Clark takes me to the left.

His bedroom furnishings are sparse: desk, laundry basket, double bed, dresser. The bed is perfectly made and has a navy comforter. The floor is the same walnut as downstairs. One door of the closet is still open; I spot a couple jackets and long-sleeved shirts on hangers. The only light in the room comes from a window. The sun has nearly gone down, diffusing all the pretty colors into a faint glow.

Clark reaches for a light switch, and soon a flickering bulb illuminates the room. He reaches into his pocket, takes out a black wallet, and tosses it onto the desk.

I wrap my arms around his waist, going up on tiptoes to give him a tender kiss on the back of his neck. Clark shivers, but then he turns around to face me.

"I'm going to run downstairs, get some water. Would you like anything?" he asks.

I want to grab him and keep him in the room, but when an idea pops into my head, I decide not to.

"Water's fine. Come back quickly." I run a single finger down his chest and stop just below his shirt, where I feel the hair on his stomach.

"Oh, I will." Clark walks out and closes the door behind him.

Once I hear the creaking of the staircase, I quickly take my shirt and skirt off. I leave my bra and panties on and sit on his bed. It smells just like Clark's jacket. When Clark doesn't appear after a minute, I stand back up, collecting my scattered clothes. I leave them neatly folded on the desk.

Keeping my ears alert for the creak of the staircase, I open one of the desk drawers and find a large sketchbook. I grab it and flip it open. The first drawing is of this very farmhouse but in much better condition. A few cows and horses graze by the barn. The artwork is impressive. Clark never mentioned he could draw.

I flip to the next picture: a portrait of a woman. Folded in the corner is another picture. I grab it and see it's a Polaroid and the exact same picture as the one drawn on this page. The woman is beautiful. She has a soft, gentle smile with laugh lines on each side of her lips. Her hair is short, blonde, and curled perfectly. She is wearing a short-sleeved button-down dress and a silver heart locket around her neck, landing just above her chest.

I wonder if this woman could be Clark's mother, or maybe an old girlfriend. If she's a girlfriend, why would he keep it? Clark said he hasn't had a girlfriend in a long time. I want to ask, but that would be admitting I snooped in his belongings.

As I gaze at the photograph, the creak of the stairs causes me to drop the sketchbook. I grab it quickly and stuff it back into the drawer as I close it. Just as the door begins to open, I lie down on the bed, keeping my head up and my arms outstretched.

When Clark walks in and sees me, he freezes. His eyes begin looking at my body slowly. Like he's taking a mental picture. I beckon him over.

Clark sets a glass of water on the floor and removes his shirt. He's slim for a construction worker, slenderer than I thought, almost undernourished. He has a six-pack, though, probably from laboring on sites all day rather than working out. Once he's near, I sit up and run my hand along his body, feeling the bumps of his ribs under my fingers.

Unable to help myself, I lean in and begin kissing his upper abdomen, moving down slowly. Soon I am right above his belt. I undo it, unzip his pants, and quickly shove them down to his ankles. His boxers are light gray, and he already has a hard-on. I look up at him and mischievously smile, biting my bottom lip.

"I want to see you," he whispers, bringing me up.

He reaches around me and unclips my bra. Once it's off, he lays me down and slowly removes my panties. He stands there, his hand moving down his boxers to grab himself as he looks at my body.

"I hope I do okay. It's just, I've never been with someone like you," he whispers, getting on the bed to lie on top of me.

"Don't say that," I whisper into his ear, feeling his heart beating fast.

We kiss passionately until finally I cannot take it anymore. I burn to be touched, to be ravished.

For the first time in a long time, I'm excited. Excited to have a man enter me, to ravage me, to touch every inch of my body. It's been so long since I've been touched, this feels like some lucid dream. Any moment I'll wake up and Clark will be gone. Like his existence was pure imagination. Something I dreamt up, to escape my depressing existence.

Clark is kissing me all over now. My skin feels hot, and I tighten my thighs in anticipation. He chuckles and continues kissing down, grasping my hips. His fingernails dig into my skin causing an eruption of pleasurable pain. Once he's down to my belly button, he opens my closed legs. Then, just like that, his mouth is on me. I see fireworks. I grip the top of his head, pulling at his hair.

I look up at the ceiling. If I keep watching him, I'll orgasm any second. I want this moment to last. I shiver at the motion of his tongue. To stop myself from orgasming, I tighten my legs around his head and think of something else.

"Does that feel okay?" Clark asks.

I look down to see his big green eyes fixed on me. I nod and push his head back down, too close to orgasm to speak.

At this exact moment, things go from good to revolutionarily spectacular. All my worries and doubts about this old house have vanished. I'm no longer worrying about missing AA. I no longer hear Adrienne calling me a piece of shit. And, most importantly, I'm no longer thinking of George Dawson.

CHAPTER NINETEEN

October 17th, 2009
Time unknown

I wake up in the middle of the night. I'm wearing a pink cotton bathrobe. A chill wind is blowing. I open my eyes and see I am lying on the porch of Clark's house, right in front of the red door. The paint is freshly done, some of it running down the bottom onto the wooden porch. The rocking chair and lawn chairs are gone. The windows are completely dark.

I attempt to stand up, numb and disoriented. As I get up, my limbs are heavy, almost like I've been drugged. The waxing crescent of the moon lights up the farmhouse with an unnatural glow. One much too light to be coming from the moon. Beyond that, everything is dim.

Clark's sedan is no longer parked out front, and the white picket fence has vanished. All I can see in the darkness are weeds and a couple pine trees nestled in the background like a painting, frozen in place.

Nothing about last night would explain why I've woke up on the porch. Perhaps I sleepwalked here. But wouldn't Clark notice me go?

I walk toward the red door, remembering I still haven't figured out why it's been freshly painted. It's too similar to that damn red door from the party.

Max, there's nothing you could've done.

But I could've done plenty. Now because I didn't, the red door haunts me. A lifeless door intimidates me. Pressing that horrible night into my brain.

Just as I put my hand over the doorknob, ready to turn it, somebody starts pounding on it from inside. I am so aghast at the noise, I nearly fall to the ground. I slip a couple feet back, grabbing ahold of the wooden barriers to the porch.

"Hello?" I say, my voice is low but echoing in the distance.

"Max, Max, help me!" a young boy calls in a frail voice.

I step back to the door and press my hands against it. Warm liquid oozes onto my hands and I pull them away. A distinctive metallic smell. It doesn't smell like paint.

"Max, Max," a female voice now rings from the inside, sounding stagnant.

I have heard these voices before. I know them, but I can't recall how.

"Who's there?" I yell, my voice hoarse.

"Why didn't you help us, Max?" both voices ask together, changing from frightened to toneless.

I no longer want to know what's behind the door. I want to turn around and run off into the nothingness. Take my chances out there. Somebody hammers on the door again, more aggressively. Soon the pounding turns to kicking. I jump back, forgetting the steps behind me, and tumble down the stairs. I sit up, my back burning from the blow of hitting the ground. The door locks break, swinging it open, hinges creaking.

There's nobody there. Instead, the red liquid on the d begins to pool out. At first, it's light, like rain down a storm d

Then the liquid increases like a flash flood, dripping down the stairs and onto me. The liquid drenches my lower body, and as I attempt to move, the liquid comes thicker and faster.

I can't stand up. I crawl away from the incoming spurts of liquid. Some enters my mouth — bitter, metallic. *Not paint. Blood.*

Now the blood is rushing out from the bottom to the top of the door. I attempt to regain my footing, falling face first into the ground. Soon it envelops my entire body. I close my eyes. Blood stings beneath my eyelids.

I begin to swim up, eyes closed. I'm running out of air. I am going to drown. Just when I feel my body going numb, I feel cold air on my outstretched hand. I use the last of my strength to push my head above the sea of blood.

I breathe in the fresh air and open my eyes. I'm no longer in a pool of blood, but instead water: a green, scummy pond, calm, unlike the waves of blood I saw coming from the door. I'm no longer on the farm. I'm twenty yards from land. I can see a forest of Rocky Mountain juniper trees and tall weeds on the land. It's bright out, but the sky isn't blue. It's a black abyss.

I know this pond. It's like a punch in the gut, as I had never dared return here. This is one of the last places my mother took me the day she killed herself. After picking me up from school that day, she took me to get ice cream. Afterward, she took me to the park. She was so kind and full of life.

I begin swimming toward dry land, my body on the brink of exhaustion. The liquid I ingested is filling my lungs and suffocating me. I've never been a good swimmer, wouldn't even get in the water until I was thirteen. Any time I dared to go in, all I could think about was this cursed pond and what I witnessed my mother do.

Just as I am nearing the land, a voice behind me calls out, "Help me, Max!"

It's the same voice I heard from behind the red door. And now I do remember who that voice belongs to.

A small blond boy is thrashing in the water. Bowl-cut hair and large eyes. I swim back to him as fast as my body will allow. When I make it to the drowning boy, I put my hands under the water, under his arms. It's too deep to put my feet on the ground, so I tread water.

"Help me, Max!" the boy screams again.

The boy is spindly, but I can't lift him. It's as though cement blocks are tied to his ankles. I let out an exhausted breath as I tighten my grip, forcing him to stay above water. I'm growing weaker with every moment that passes. The water becomes thicker as I kick, trying to keep us both afloat.

My strength is gone, and we both go under. I keep my eyes open, searching for what could possibly be bringing us down with such force. The boy's tiny legs do not have a rope tied to them.

"Why did you let me die, Max?" he asks.

His words came out crystal clear, like we aren't beneath the surface. I crane my head up to look at the boy. His face is pale blue. His thin lips, purple. His once-sweet-looking eyes are half closed as he stares daggers into my soul.

"I didn't mean to," I say, shocked at the words smoothly escaping my mouth.

I no longer feel my lungs being filled with water. The drowning sensation is gone. The boy is no longer immensely heavy. We're just wading now.

"You let me die. It's your fault, Max," he says brutally.

"I'm sorry, Billy."

The boy stares at me, his face turning more pale and dead. He closes his eyes for a couple seconds, then opens them. Their green has faded to milky white. I scream at the sight of him, but he merely smiles. I never could have saved him; he's been dead all along. He died waiting on the help of the girl who lured him to his death.

I let go of the boy, his body remaining in place. I swim back to the surface of the pond. I begin choking out all the water built up in my body. Once I regain my breathing, I start my swim back to land.

The boy never returns to the surface, and I am able to swim to the shore. As I crawl out, I look down and see I'm no longer in the bathrobe. I'm wearing a cranberry-red minidress. As I look down at my now-changed outfit, I notice both my palms are still covered in the blood from the door. I wipe my hands on my exposed thighs, but nothing comes off.

I go back to the pond and put my hands into the murky water, rubbing them together. When I bring them out, they are still red. I angrily shove them back in, scrubbing them harder. Still nothing.

"Max, is that you?" a voice says.

I look toward the sound. Eva Willems is standing by a quaking aspen tree, its leaves crimson-red colored. Her long blonde hair, straightened, lands just above her waist. She's wearing the same body-hugging, backless, satin blue dress she wore to the party — in fact, she looks exactly the same as she did that night. I remember fuming with anger at how beautiful she looked. Dennis couldn't keep his eyes off her. To think of it, the cranberry-red minidress I'm wearing now is also the one I wore that night. I spent nearly two hours deciding on what to wear, praying Dennis would prefer me over her.

"E-Eva?" I ask, gulping.

"Max, why did you abandon me?" she asks with a look of disappointment.

"I-I was drunk, I wasn't thinking."

"You ruined my life. All for a fucking boy."

"No, no, no! This can't be happening!" I scream, putting my hands over my face. The red of my palms fills my vision.

"You thought you could just run away, act like nothing happened. You wanted to do that the night you killed George Dawson. But you couldn't. You couldn't run away like you did with that little boy and me. Their blood is on your hands."

"Please, stop," I beg, removing my hands from my eyes to be face to face with Eva.

Her dress is now ripped, the satin torn at the end. The straps hang down. Her perfect complexion is smeared with makeup.

I step back, but Eva grabs a tight hold of my wrists, bringing my face to hers.

"You're a fucking coward, Max!" she screams. Her spittle lands on my face.

I pull away from her. She laughs and digs her nails deeper into my wrists. I scream in pain, and she laughs more. Finally, she loosens her grasp, letting me fall to the ground. Now standing a few feet across from Eva and looking down at me is a man with a bloodied face. George Dawson, on the night I killed him.

"You killed me, Max," George says, his voice deep.

"I'm sorry. It was an accident." My heart is beating so loud that I can't hear myself speak.

"You let me die," another voice says, and I look over to see the drowned boy coming from the pond.

"Oh God, please . . . stop!" I shut my eyes, wanting this nightmare to end.

"Welcome to hell, Maxine Masterson," Eva says, and I open my eyes to see all three of the individuals I'd crossed coming closer, their hands outstretched.

CHAPTER TWENTY

October 17th, 2009
3:51 a.m.

I jolt awake, screaming. After the scream leaves my body, I feel breathless and start coughing from the cold gust of air filling the room. Opening my eyes, I expect to still be on the shore of the pond with Eva, George, and Billy still coming for me, wanting their vengeance. Instead, I am in a darkened room, wearing Clark's oversized shirt. It takes me a couple moments of heavy breathing to control my shaking body.

Soon Clark is sitting up, startling me. I shrink back. The room is too dark; it brings me a feeling of claustrophobia. I jump out of bed and find the light switch. The light blinds me momentarily. The first thing I do once my eyesight adjusts is look at my hands. They're clean, no blood.

Clark is at my side a moment later, his hands on my shoulders. I look up and see his hair is tousled, his bangs waved in different directions. His eyes are half closed.

"Are you okay?" he asks, sounding groggy.

"Sorry, sorry. I had a bad dream." I place my hand on my heart, wishing it would stop beating so erratically.

"It's okay, you're safe. I'm here." He enfolds me in his arms.

I rest my head on his chest, listening to his heartbeat. We stand there for a couple moments, holding each other.

Staring at Clark calms my racing heart. I remember last night and all the wonderful things that happened. Clark and I showered together after our foreplay in the bedroom. In the shower, Clark pushed me against the tiled wall and took me from behind, before turning me around and picking me up. I wrapped my legs around him and we climaxed together, lost in each other's gaze.

After, we sat in his bed and talked for a while. I learned his favorite color is a warm sunset orange. I told him mine is white, which he informed me isn't an actual color. We then discussed things we liked to do as kids. His being drawing, which had brought me back to the sketchbook in his desk drawer. I wanted to comment that, apparently, he still enjoyed that too, but I didn't. He would tell me of his own free will when he was ready. He told me how he thought I would look really good in pink. I didn't agree, but I humored him, saying next time we saw each other, I would try wearing something pink. He replied that he would buy me something. That made me warm inside, as a man had never bought me clothing before.

After talking for nearly an hour, we had sex for a second time. This time I could tell Clark was feeling depleted. I wasn't. I could have gone all night long until morning. I wanted to just ravage his body, memorize every inch of it.

My thoughts of last night and Clark's emerald eyes staring deep into mine with compassion pull me fully from that awful dream.

"I'm . . . I'm sorry," I say again.

"Shh, it's okay. I get them sometimes too." He moves his hand to the light switch. "Let's go back to bed."

I stop him. "Can we keep the light on? Just for a minute, please?"

Clark grins and gives me a soft kiss on the forehead.

"Would you like to lie down? Talk about it?" he asks.

Talk about what? The fact I am completely losing my mind. My demons are coming out in full force. If I tell him the full story, Clark will boot me out of his house; he'll never want to see me again.

"You . . . you don't want to know," I say, walking away from him and sitting on the side of the bed.

Clark sits down next to me. He presses his thumb to my cheek and wipes away a few tears.

"It might help if you talk about it."

"You'd think I'm a piece of shit." I wince at the echo of Adrienne's words.

"Try me."

I look away from my knees and up at Clark. Those green eyes are alert, inviting. He makes me feel safe. I've never told a stranger about my mom's last terrible acts. People know, but after I became an adult, no one really asked how I felt about it. How it continues to follow me.

"I've wronged some people in my life, Clark. Like, really wronged. They were in my dream, all of them."

"Them?"

"George Dawson, Billy—"

"Billy?" Clark asks, tilting his head quizzically.

I take a deep breath, knowing it's time to speak. Clark may be the only person left in the world who will ask.

"When I was nine years old, my mom did a very bad thing. She wasn't a horrible mom, just deeply depressed and suffering from psychosis. My father became very distant and began having an affair at some point. The result of my dad's affair was a little boy, Billy. My mother discovered my father's affair when Billy was five. She wanted to get revenge on my dad for hurting her.

"It started out like any ordinary day; my mom was getting me ready for school. Before she dropped me off, she asked me to talk to Billy. To befriend him. I did, and after I got off school, I told her all about it. She took me to get ice cream and fries. She was being so nice. I thought she was finally getting better. I was excited to have my real mommy back."

I pause, wishing the story just ended there: *Mom got better, and we lived a happy life together.* In reality, my mother just wanted to share one last precious moment with me. Speaking of what she did always brings a sour feeling to my stomach. I point at the glass of water on Clark's nightstand. He hands it to me, and I drink the entirety of it, hoping to get the staleness out of my mouth.

"Afterward, she took me to a park. The same park where I had told her Billy would be. She instructed me to play with him and take him to this wooded area where there was this nasty stagnant pond. Kids weren't supposed to go to this area. I did as she said and took Billy there. She said she had a surprise for us. What was I supposed to think? Then she came . . . came out of the wooded area. She was smiling the whole time. She . . . she—"

I stop speaking, the words sticking in my throat. Clark keeps his eyes on me, gently caressing my back. Everyone in town knows this story, but I feel like I'm sharing a deep dark secret held only between my mother and me.

"You can stop if you want." I know he genuinely means it, but I'm too far in to not go on. I have to let it out.

"She grabbed him like he was just a stuffed animal. She took him into the water and . . . and he was begging for her to stop, but she just kept going. I asked her what she was doing. I couldn't understand what was happening. Oh God, I was so scared. Billy screamed my name, asking me to help him. I barely even tried. Then she . . . she drowned him. I just stood there and watched."

Tears are running down my face. I can still hear Billy's screams, how he called to me for help. My mom's stern voice stopping me.

Clark has the same sympathetic look on his face. He doesn't look shocked or despairing, like I've been expecting.

"She told me it was all my father's fault. At the time I believed her — hated my father for breaking our family apart. She called him, told him what she'd done. She drove the two of us out to this mountain, took me up it—"

Breathe, Max. Breathe.

"She told me to be brave, then she told me to turn around, and she jumped."

The ending feels so anticlimactic. My mom killed herself after doing a horrible thing. She took the easy way out. The townsfolk were happy to be rid of her. My father was left reeling from the consequences. He lost a son. Was left with the daughter of the woman who killed him. He went deep into debt, paying for my therapist.

"And Billy's mother?" Clark asks. "What happened to her?"

"She moved away. Never spoke to my father again."

I clench my dry lips together.

"I'm sorry, Max." Clark's hand never strays from my back. "You've probably heard this a million times, but you have to know it wasn't your fault that boy died. We . . . we can't control what our parents do. They are the ones who mold us into who we are. They are the ones we listen to; it's instinct to do what your mom told you to do that day."

Clark speaks so firmly on the subject. Like he knows about having toxic, mentally unstable parents. It makes me feel better that I have chosen him to tell this story to for the first time.

"You're not a bad person. Please don't say you are."

I crack a brief smile through my tears. Clark once again clears some from my cheeks, leaning in and pressing his nose to mine.

"You deserve to let all this guilt go. Learn from your mistakes but don't dwell on them. If you do, you'll never move on. You deserve to heal." He moves his face away from mine and takes my hand.

"Why are you so nice to me?" I ask.

"Bad things happen to good people. From what I've seen, you're a good person, Max. You had a rough childhood. I mean, you could've done worse. Some have."

Little does he know I *have* done a horrible thing. A thing I've blamed on my upbringing.

Clark's last remark makes me wonder if he's talking about himself. "I still don't really know much about you."

"What would you like to know?" he asks.

"How come I've never seen you around?"

Clark exhales. "My mom left when I was only five. After that, my father homeschooled us. I guess I've spent most of my adult life on construction sites, till my brother got sick, and I began taking care of him."

"And your father?"

Clark looks a bit uncomfortable at that question. I'm beginning to think his father is the reason he can relate so much to my story.

"He, uh, left a couple years ago. Comes around every so often."

I frown, feeling there's more to the story than Clark is letting on. He didn't look away from me when I was talking; now his eyes are on the wooden floor. I've just told him my story; what is keeping him from telling me his? What if it's worse than my own?

"Hey, what's your favorite candy?" he asks, looking up at me with a smile.

"Candy?" I ask, chuckling.

"Yeah, your favorite candy. Hershey, Twix, Almond Joy, Snickers . . ."

I haven't really had candy in quite some time. I try to remember the last one I had. Aunt Almeida poked fun at my weight the other day, saying I'm too thin, and gave me a bag of M&M's.

"M&M's, I guess." I shrug.

"What type?"

"Type?" I ask. Clark nods.

"Uh, regular? What's this for?"

"Tomorrow I am going to take you to work and bring you some lunch with a treat. Because that's what you are, a sweet treat." Clark leans over and kisses my neck.

The touch of his lips brings goosebumps to my body. I hope he's not starting something he can't finish.

"How'd you know I have work tomorrow?" I ask.

He stops kissing my neck for a second. "Wild guess. If you're not, I can take you out to lunch." He starts again, deeper kisses, making his way down to my shoulder.

"Like a date?" I ask. I haven't been on one of those in a long, long time.

"Yeah, silly. Up, please?" he asks, tugging on the bottom of the T-shirt.

I laugh and lift my arms in the air so he can remove my shirt. His hands are all over my body. I look down at him, a big smile plastered on my face as he takes in the sight of my body like it's the first time again.

"Shit, I do have work. You were right. I'll have to take a rain check. I don't know if you know this but I, Max Masterson, haven't been on a date in a long while."

"Lies," he says, pushing me down on the bed and getting on top of me. "Well, I guess I'm the luckiest guy in the world." He leans down to kiss me passionately on the lips.

As he does, I can't help but think about how easily he changed the subject. What is Clark hiding about his father?

CHAPTER TWENTY-ONE

October 17th, 2009
9:56 a.m.

I wake up alone in bed the following day. The shades are closed, but through the cracks they let in a little morning light. I sit up in Clark's bed, rubbing my eyes.

Last night's events begin running through my mind. All the sex Clark and I had, the moments we shared, and, most importantly, what I told him. At first, upon getting to this eerie farmhouse, I had wanted to get laid and get out. Now, after last night's events, I feel I will forever remember this place. I will remember the way Clark held me, how he kissed my neck as I cried. Maybe it's far-fetched, but I feel like we were destined to cross paths.

I'm still naked. I pull on Clark's oversized shirt again, then I find my skirt and other belongings. Instead of wearing the skirt, I go through Clark's dresser and find a red flannel printed pair of boxers. I put those on and open the door, walking out into the hallway.

After using the restroom, I go downstairs to the kitchen and dining area. Clark is nowhere to be seen. In the kitchen, I find a glass in one of the rustic wood cabinets above the sink. I pour myself some water and begin wandering around the home. It's bare of photographs and knickknacks, aside from a couple old-timey western-style paintings in the dining room. Everything is covered in a layer of dust; it's surprising anyone at all lives here. The only thing that looks heavily used is the coat rack, which holds some heavy jackets, gloves, and, beneath, work boots.

My interest is piqued by the door by the stairs. I walk over and jiggle the large padlock attached to it, but it's locked firmly. What was it Clark said was in there? Heirlooms? Does Clark's family have so many precious heirlooms that they have to take precautions and keep them all hidden away? Why not use some of them to decorate the house a little? I know it's all men that live here, but even my father has photographs of his family.

Just as I am about to walk away from the door, I hear a light banging sound downstairs. Or I think I do. Maybe it's just my early-morning senses imagining things. I press my ear to the door, waiting to hear anything else. This time when I hear a noise, I know it's coming from downstairs. I knock on the door softly, my heart hammering in my chest. More banging sounds.

"H-hello?" I say, wondering if Clark is downstairs.

A muffled sound comes through the door and my heart leaps. "Clark, is that you?" I ask.

More banging sounds come from below. I step away from the door, unsure what to do. Just as I am walking backward from the door, a hand touches my shoulder, causing me the shriek. I turn around to see Clark standing directly behind me.

"Good morning," he says, offering me a cup of coffee.

I force a smile and, taking the cup of coffee, say, "Th-thank you." *Something is downstairs, and it isn't Clark.*

I can't help but side-eye the phone sitting next to the fridge. My whole body feels tense.

I'm overreacting. It could just be a faulty pipe or the washer. I'm sure their washer and dryer are as old as everything else in this house. Whether or not it's something — or someone — I have to keep my cool. I can't just ask Clark why there is some unknown sound coming up from the locked basement.

"I was just feeding the animals," Clark explains, although I didn't ask where he's been.

"It's cool."

It's cool? When have you ever said that?

Clark frowns at my now-tense body. He looks past me at the basement door. The worry on his face makes me tense up even more.

"Did you want to see in the basement?"

Why would he ask me that if there really is nothing down there? I'm just being paranoid. Maybe all the worries deep down in my stomach from being at a stranger's farmhouse out of town are just now surfacing again.

Clark is a sweet guy. He's been a listening ear, heard all my troubles, and still held me tight. We have an undeniable chemistry. I have to stop this absurd worrying.

He also is still a man you only just met.

"No . . . no, I was just being nosy." I crack a smile, trying to look relaxed.

"No need to be. You can see anything you like. I could even show you around outside. It's not much, but I think you'll like it."

"I'd like that." I take a sip of the coffee.

I just need to go outside and get some fresh air. My mind is just playing tricks on me. I'm sure drinking the coffee Clark gave me and getting some sunlight will ease my mind. After he shows me around, I can ask him to take me home. I glance once more behind me at the basement door, and then I put the flannel jacket on.

Once outside, we walk toward the old barn. Once my feet land on the dirt trail leading to the barn, I realize I've forgotten to put my sneakers on. The barn, like the farmhouse, looks rustic and practically abandoned. The door is large, taking up nearly half the front of the building. Once Clark slides the door open, I'm met with the smell of stale straw and animal manure. The light from outside shows dusty air, wooden stalls with a couple pitchforks, shovels and milk pails leaning against them. All the stalls are empty of any animals; so is the rest of the barn.

"We used to have a bunch of animals, but after my father left and my brother got sick, we had to get rid of them. We have a cow, but she's grazing right now. The chicken coop is at the back end of the barn," Clark explains.

Despite the fresh air, I can't stop thinking about the basement. So much so, I can't form a reply to what Clark said. A part of me wants to ask him to take me downstairs. To see with my own eyes that nothing is down there. What if something is, though? I would be walking down to my own demise.

I force a smile, taking a sip of my coffee while avoiding eye contact with Clark. I pretend to look around the barn, avoiding eye contact with him.

"Want to see the chickens?" he asks.

I need to go home to my safe place. I can no longer ignore this bad gut feeling I'm getting. If I'm by myself, I can properly sort through my thoughts.

"I should probably—"

Before I can finish my sentence, the sound of a vehicle pulling up outside stops me. I look toward the open barn door, momentarily seeing a dark gray van drive past, toward the house. I'm relieved, thinking it may be a friend or coworker of Clark's, someone who can pull me out of being alone with him any longer. That way, he can take me home quicker.

"Shit," Clark mutters. His face has gone pale. It's definitely not the expression of someone whose friend just pulled up.

"Who's that?" I ask.

"My dad."

CHAPTER TWENTY-TWO

October 17th, 2009
10:32 a.m.

Clark's dad? By the look on Clark's face, they're not on good terms. Hopefully now he'll definitely want to take me home. He won't want a girl he barely knows around to meet his estranged father.

"Were you not expecting him?"

Clark gulps and takes a tight hold of my hand. "No."

Clark is frozen. *It's as if he's trespassing on someone else's land, and the owner just showed up,* I think uneasily. Outside, the van's engine dies, and two car doors open and shut. His dad isn't alone. Maybe he picked Clark's brother up from the hospital.

"Fuck, you didn't bring shit for bait," a deep voice says jovially. *Bait?*

"Fuck you, you're the one who brought the shitty poles," a different man jokes back.

It doesn't sound like his dad is here for a visit. It sounds more like he lives here, and he just got home, back from some fishing trip. Did Clark lie to me?

"Where's your shithead son?" the first man says.

Clark's grasp on my hand tightens more. I yelp, pulling my hand away. He doesn't seem to notice; his eyes are still on the barn door. This situation is not right. I look around for an exit. There's a back door, which appears locked, and a couple windows between the stalls. One is open. My exit, if I need it.

"He not at work?" the other man says, the one I know now is Clark's father.

"No, Samuel called me. Said the little prick didn't show up this morning."

The things these men are saying about Clark are not pleasant. I somewhat understand his frozen state. He wasn't lying when he said he hadn't been expecting them. He had a reason for lying to me. Which I now can conclude he did in fact do. His father never left; he lives here. This other man who mentioned work must be his boss.

"Clark, what's going on?" I ask.

"Shh!" Clark puts a finger to his mouth.

"I'm going to beat that little shit's ass. Not that it'll do any good," Clark's father says.

"Maybe he's watching Maxine again," the other says, and now it's my turn to freeze.

He said my name, my full name. *Watching? Again?* How do they know my name?

It can't be.

Someone has been watching me. The peeping Tom from the other night. I imagine Clark outside my window. I want to scream.

Did I really go home with the man who has been stalking me? I take a step back. The window is two stalls down, approximately four yards away. Clark is within a couple feet of me. His eyes have shifted from the door to me once again. They're different. I'm no longer staring at a man I know, but a stranger. I look at the half-full cup of coffee I still have in my hand. It's my only weapon. I grasp it harder.

I don't want to believe it. This can't be.

"Clark, what's going on?" I ask.

Clark bites down on his lower lip, hard. Blood drips from his lips. He doesn't say a word, but takes a step toward me. For five excruciating heartbeats we just stare at each other.

"Max, don't freak out. It'll be worse if you do." He raises his hands like he's trying to calm an animal.

"Moe, I found your son," a voice says.

I turn around. There's a man standing in the doorway. He has a dark green fishing tackle box in his hand. He looks to be in his fifties and has a large beer belly that his ragged T-shirt doesn't completely cover. He's grimy from his fishing trip. He's looking directly at me, a lecherous grin on his face. The type of man you wouldn't want to meet in a dark alley.

"Graham, get your ass out here right now!" a voice jeers in the distance.

Who is Graham?

"No, Moe, you might want to come here. We have company." The big man's creepy dark eyes never leave mine.

The other sighs deeply, then I hear his footsteps coming closer. I take another step back, toward the window.

"You're in so much trouble, boy," the man says.

I edge toward the stall with the window. Clark shakes his head, urging me to stop, moving closer. I'm shaking so much, I feel I might drop my only weapon. I could throw it at Clark and make a run for it. I don't have the best aim, but the drink is still hot so it could buy me some time. This other man won't be able to fit through the window or chase me. Clark could, so he's the one I'll have to hurt.

Just as I am considering my options, Clark takes a giant leap toward me. I raise the coffee cup and, before Clark can come any closer, bash the cup against his face. The cup breaks into shards and the liquid goes all over Clark's face. I spin around and book it toward the window.

CHAPTER TWENTY-THREE

October 17th, 2009
10:34 a.m.

"Moe, Moe, get the van!" the other man yells as I run toward the window.

I unlatch the stall door and push it open. I squeeze myself through the window. Just as I do, someone grabs my arm — Clark. His nose is gushing blood; the right side of his face has cuts from the hit. He doesn't look nearly as angry as I thought he would. He presses his hands against the windowsill.

"Maxine, please, don't do this."

Just hearing him call me "Maxine" sickens me. I wriggle to the ground and begin running as fast as my legs will let me. I jump the white picket fence. A glance back shows that Clark has climbed through the window and is running after me. I continue to run, but the fields stretch away into the distance with no sign of other houses.

I can hear a vehicle's engine starting up behind me. My bare feet sting from hitting rocks and sticks but I don't dare stop.

Soon I make it to another picket fence, which I hastily climb over. The weeds here come up to my knees. They hinder my running, and my lungs feel like they're going to explode if I don't stop. I look behind me to see Clark a little farther back now, approaching the second fence. In the distance, the van is hauling ass our way.

"Maxine!" Clark screams, seeing I've slowed down slightly.

"Help me!" I scream, regretting it as the extra air leaving my body causes my lungs to burn more.

I can't outrun a vehicle. I want to slow down, pause for a second to breathe, but I push on. I catch sight of a house in the distance, sitting on a hilltop. It looks abandoned but maybe I can find a weapon there, or at the very least lock myself inside.

I switch directions toward the house. It has to be a quarter of a mile away. I can do it. I just have to outrun them. Naked desperation courses through my tired feet and legs, making them move faster.

I chance another look behind me. Clark has gotten closer; the van has just busted through the second fence. As I stare back, my foot collides with a rock, throwing me into the air. I try to regain my footing but fail and tumble to the ground. I throw out my hands to break my fall but only cause a sharp wrench of pain in my wrists.

I attempt to stand back up, my feet aching from the pain, but before I get to my knees, Clark collides with me. He pushes me onto my back. His face is beet red, dripping with sweat, and the blood from his nose has leaked all the way down to his T-shirt.

"Help me!" I scream, wiggling my body.

"You need to calm down." Clark presses his weight down on me, taking hold of my wrists and moving them under his knees.

"Get off me!" I shriek, kicking my legs out.

Clark leans down and speaks into my ear. "I'm going to fix this, I swear." His sweat drips onto my face.

The overweight man has jumped out of the van and is sprinting toward us. I can only see half of his body through the tall weeds. He has a white rag in his hand.

"No!" I scream, guessing what the rag is. Chloroform.

He chuckles at my screams and pushes the rag toward my face. I twist my head away.

"Hold her the fuck down, boy!" the man screams at Clark.

Clark forces my head the other way. When he successfully does so, the man is quick to press it against my face.

"Hold it!" he orders Clark, who takes the rag and continues pressing it roughly against my face.

The rag has a chemical smell mixed with a hint of old red wine. Soon I feel faint and dizzy. As my movements slow, Clark removes the rag from my mouth.

I'm facing the vehicle now. I hear a door open. A few moments later, a man comes into view. His body blurs like a sun dipping below the horizon. He's wearing old blue overalls and, like Clark, has dark brown hair, but his is cut short and graying.

"I'd recognize that face anywhere," he says, looking down at me, and hocks a spit of tobacco out of his mouth.

The tobacco lands directly in front of my face. My eyes begin slowly closing. I will them to stay open, but they fight back harder to shut.

"Graham, I asked you to do one fucking thing," the man says directly to Clark.

I open my mouth to speak but no words come out. Soon my eyes force themselves closed, and not long after, I pass out completely.

CHAPTER TWENTY-FOUR

October 17th, 2009
10:41 a.m.
Graham

"Get those ropes around its ankles, you fucking idiot," Graham's father orders, giving him a hard shove off of Maxine's unconscious body.

Graham, still out of breath from the intense chase after Maxine, slowly gets to his knees. Uncle Joey tosses another pair of paracord ropes to him. He catches them and starts tying them around Maxine's ankles. Once he's tied them tight, he stares at her closed eyes.

Graham has been watching and planning to kidnap Maxine for the past four months. Finally, he has achieved just that, but instead of feeling victorious, he feels defeated. He had always been strongly attracted to Maxine, but getting to know her has changed so much. After one night with her, he was willing to throw away five years of careful preparation and planning.

Since the night Maxine killed Graham's brother George, he and Moe have been planning to make sure Maxine suffers for taking his life. They stayed away from the court proceedings to ensure she would serve less time.

Since her release, Graham has spent nearly every night watching Maxine. He knew his lust for her was dangerous but never planned to fall for her. He had merely decided to create the persona of Clark and meet her, to help with the kidnapping. He felt it was the only option left when her ex-boyfriend got in the picture and gave her a ride home from work. He knew that one ride would turn into many.

They knew taking Maxine would be difficult. Not like the other girls they have taken. She has a family who is constantly watching her to make sure she obeys the rules. Moe and Graham rarely took girls from Mendex. Too close to home.

The newspaper has been calling them the Monroe Murderer for years. Catchy, but a misnomer. Moe and George (before he died) weren't killing women due to some obsession with Marilyn Monroe. It was Graham and George's mother, Hannah, who bore a striking resemblance to the actress. Her hair curled, golden blonde, a bright white smile, and an hourglass shape. Graham doesn't know why Mother decided to abandon them. He just knew what Father told him. *She's a whore who abandoned you because she couldn't take the pressure anymore.*

He suspects his father treated her poorly. As far back as Graham can remember, Moe has always been an ill-tempered, psychopathic individual. Moe takes these girls to assuage all the rage he has built up from Hannah's abandonment. He likes to imagine the girls he takes are Hannah and he's killing her again and again. Playing sick, psychotic games with her like God.

George, Graham's older brother, was a willing participant in all the games. He was exactly like Father, uncaring and brutal. He lured the girls in with his good looks and charming personality. Once he persuaded them to come home with him from some bar, Father would be waiting in the back seat to either bash their head against the dashboard or press a rag of chloroform to their mouth.

It's been nearly seven years since Graham felt tender toward any woman. He had learned that love only ended in pain. Mary and Mariah, the two sisters from Mendex his father kidnapped — they really loved each other. He's dreamed of having that kind of love his whole life. He remembers them always holding hands tightly as his brother, father, or he descended the steps to the basement. Before Father had finished them off, they'd even kept eye contact, telling each other how much they loved each other. Graham can barely remember the last time he had been told he was loved.

To this day, he blames himself for the sisters' deaths. Father knew he had been getting close to them. Graham had attempted to stop it, to tell his father he didn't care whether they lived or died. But he knew they were only being kind to him so he would let them go. The moment that happened, they would run away and never return. Just like his mother.

* * *

He wishes he would die; this isn't how he had wanted this day to go. If Maxine had just listened and kept calm, he could've avoided this. Hid her in the barn until his father and Uncle Joey went inside. Snuck her out to safety. After last night, he no longer feels the hatred he once had for her. Or maybe he hasn't felt hatred for her since the moment his eyes landed on her. It's just now, he is no longer in denial about it.

"You barely caught it. Jesus, I mean, it's a girl," Uncle Joey taunts him.

"Put it in the back," his father orders, spitting out tobacco as he saunters back to the van.

Maxine is not an "it." But Father will strike him if he calls her something other than "creature" or "it." One of Father's many rules for the women they take: never call them by their name;

never call them "her." The creatures are not human beings; they are objects.

"Yes, sir." Graham grits his teeth, devastated.

Graham picks Maxine up, letting out a breath of drained energy. He carries her to the back of the van, drops her in, and jumps up after her. He shuts the back doors, and the van immediately begins driving forward.

He takes a seat next to Maxine's head. He runs his fingers through her tangled blonde hair, a few tears escaping his eyes. He never intended things to go this way. At first, when Maxine agreed to go home with him, they were. He knew his father would be angry about bringing her here sooner than they'd planned, but he thought at the very least Moe would be proud of him for catching her. Now things have changed. One night with her has done that.

When Graham and Maxine first arrived at the house, his feelings for her were already getting a little muddled. The way she stared deep into his eyes like no other woman ever has and called them beautiful. How they drove around town, jamming to music. It was the most fun he's had in years. For the first time in his life, he felt like a real human being. Like he wasn't just a deprived slave to his father. Like he and Maxine were teenagers, driving around without their parents' permission, talking and getting to know each other.

When they arrived at the farm yesterday, he still intended to follow through with his plan. He pushed aside all his newfound feelings for Maxine just before walking through the front door. Forced himself to see only the woman who killed his brother. He planned to wait until her back was turned and strike her. Then she asked him to take her jacket off. The moment he saw her in that white T-shirt that ever so perfectly clung to her, he knew he had to have her.

Graham's first encounter with sex was at the age of twenty-one. He had snuck out to a bar twenty miles out of town while his father and brother were out of town scouting for a new girl. It had felt great — but meaningless. So had the other times after that. With Maxine, though, it was different. He had never had sex with a girl in the shower, but the way the water from the shower head hit her body as he held her in his arms felt like magic. Her moans were music to his ears. Like it was his first time ever.

After they fell asleep, wrapped in each other's arms, Graham felt ashamed of what he was planning to do to her. Feeling her heartbeat flutter against his chest, he wanted to keep her safe. To keep his father from hurting her — and even himself. All those years of sitting at home and waiting for the moment to exact his revenge had completely vanished.

Graham's feelings grew heavier when Maxine woke up from a nightmare in a fit. After she confessed what her mother had done in front of her very eyes, he wanted to confess everything. What happened to his mother and all the killings his father had done since then. All the times he had Graham clean up the bodies and all their blood from the basement's concrete floor. Confess so she would know he understands her trauma. That he has lived a life full of his own personal trauma and the demons that came with it. She would feel connected to him. However, that might have broken the illusion of him being the perfect guy for her. She might have screamed, called him a monster, and tried to run away.

When they arrive back at the house, Graham opens the back doors and gets out of the van. He grabs Maxine by her ankles and pulls her out, throwing her body over his shoulder.

Once inside the house, Graham walks to the basement door. He watches as his father takes out a set of keys and unlocks it. Less than an hour ago, the two of them had been standing here and Maxine had been acting strange, as though she already knew something was going on downstairs. If only Father had showed up twenty minutes later. Graham would have taken Maxine home, would have had time to figure things out.

Now time is his biggest enemy. He has to use it wisely. Father's games will begin soon. He has to protect her without letting Father know. Graham has to convince Father he wants her dead just as much as he does.

CHAPTER TWENTY-FIVE

October 17th, 2009
10:56 a.m.
Graham

There are two cages in the basement, used for keeping the girls locked up. Each cage is eight feet wide and four feet long. All they have is a cot and a bucket. Nothing else, as Father doesn't like taking a chance on giving them anything they can use as a weapon. So, he gives each girl a large bucket to relieve herself when needed and an old army cot of Uncle Joey's. Father is careful every day when checking on the girls to make sure the cot isn't missing any parts.

When Graham was only fourteen years old, one girl took one of the metal rods and tried attacking Father with it when he came in to give her food. She only got in one blow to his legs before he grabbed her and strangled her to death. Since then, he tells each girl that story, making sure they know they'll pay the ultimate price if they attack him.

Another item kept in each cage is a chain welded to the ground. Depending on their behavior, they either have the chain connected to their foot or their neck. Generally, the new girls get one on their neck, as Father doesn't trust them.

Each cage is made of steel, the bars tightly spaced. Each has a locked door that only Father has the key to, same with the chains that add extra security. Father only gives Graham the key if he's out of town and needs him to watch the girls, which is rare.

The empty cage's door is already open; it has been cleaned out for months in preparation for Maxine. Graham takes Maxine into the cage and sets her down on the cot. She doesn't move at all. Graham wonders when she will awaken. The chloroform generally keeps girls out for around half an hour or so. He will need a minute alone with her, when she's awake, to explain things. Tell her he will do whatever he can to keep her safe. Reassure her he isn't the monster she now believes he is.

"Get the chain on it," Father orders, hitting him behind the head.

Graham begins to secure the shackles around her ankles. Before he can finish, Father hits him on the back of the head again.

"Not around its ankles, you idiot. Around the neck," he orders.

Graham sighs. He knew that would happen, but he wanted to test it anyways. He grabs a nearby neck shackle and secures it around Maxine's neck. He throws the ankle shackle out of the cage. Both Father and his uncle are staring daggers at him. He has to act as though he does not care for this woman. Her life depends on it.

Graham knows the next step in the process. Grab the garden hose used to bathe the women and blast cold water, waking Maxine up. He heads over to the faucet, but as he passes his father, Moe grabs ahold of his shoulder, stopping him.

"We need to talk." Moe walks back upstairs, and Uncle Joey follows him.

Another beating, Graham assumes. As if the coffee cup smashing into his face wasn't enough. That side of his face is still throbbing from the hot coffee. Maxine is the first woman to hurt him this way, and although it should've angered him, it didn't. It made him happy: Maxine is a fighter.

When he gets upstairs, he finds Father at the kitchen sink, wetting a washcloth. He tosses it to Graham. Graham barely catches it, shocked his father cares. He and George had beaten him up plenty of times and never offered any remedy. It must be because a woman was the one who hurt him.

"Clean yourself up," he says coldly.

Graham does as he's told, washing away the blood that has run all over his weather-beaten face.

As he does so, Father begins pacing the room. He often does this when deciding what he's going to say or do. It could mean he's exceedingly angry, or it could mean he's pondering his next move. He might not beat Graham after all. Is he going to question Graham about the previous day's events? That would be worse than a beating. Graham has never been a great liar, but with Maxine's life at stake, he will have to muster something believable.

"How'd you get it here?" Father asks, stopping in his tracks to stare at Graham.

"Definitely wasn't by force," Uncle Joey points out.

"I-I-I've been going to its AA meetings."

Father frowns. One of his rules is never to engage with the girls they've chosen before a kidnapping. He doesn't want people to see any of them with a girl.

"And?"

"And I got it to trust me. Told it my name was Clark."

His uncle lets out a loud, obnoxious laugh.

"Like Superman?" he asks.

That's exactly it. Graham thought by giving Maxine the name of a superhero, she would perceive him as such. As a child, Graham owned many Superman comics, dreaming he could be as powerful and charming as Clark Kent.

"It had an old boyfriend giving it rides everywhere. I thought there was no other choice but to get it that way."

His father purses his lips. "Okay, but that still doesn't explain why the creature is here so early."

Graham thinks hard and fast. He has to say each word carefully. He has to act like George. Uncaring and only interested in one thing.

"I wanted to fuck its brains out. I knew you wouldn't let me."

Uncle Joey laughs again, while his father only grins.

"And you convinced it to do that?"

"It wanted to go home with me, so . . . yeah."

"And?"

"And I took it back here and fucked it. I was about to knock it out in the barn before you guys showed up. I know you said not to touch it while you were gone, but . . . I just . . . just wanted—"

"He wanted to get his rocks off, Moe. Can you blame him?" Uncle Joey pulls a dirty handkerchief from his pocket to cover his laughs.

"You shouldn't have disobeyed me."

"You're right. I'm sorry, sir."

Father turns away from him, walking around again.

"How was she?" Uncle Joey asks. "She's too thin for my tastes, personally. Would be like fucking a skeleton."

His father casts a glare at Uncle Joey. Uncle Joey used the word "she." Father has a rule to never call the women by "she" or "her". Just "it" or "creature". The only somewhat feminine title he would call them was "bitch". Towering a couple inches above Father and over eighty pounds heavier, Uncle Joey doesn't abide by Father's rule.

Graham shrugs. "It was fine."

His plan will work if Father takes the bait. He has gotten Uncle Joey on his side. It isn't hard getting approval from Uncle Joey, a colossal perv, by mentioning sex. All the big man thinks about is women and using them. As long as he keeps his hands off Maxine, having him on Graham's side will cause no problems.

"Your son is finally becoming a man," Uncle Joey says.

"Right . . . Well, I'm not thrilled you went behind my back, but George used to do the same thing. What do you want to do with it?"

"Uh . . . what, sir?"

"Are you deaf? What do you want to do with it? Since you're a man now, got the bitch here, I guess I'll allow you some fun. Then it's my turn to turn it inside out."

"We should play Russian roulette again," Uncle Joey says. "That's always a blast."

Graham gulps, shaking his head. It's been six months since they played Russian roulette. They all went downstairs, loading two revolvers with one bullet apiece. Then pointed them at each girl.

Graham's grandfather had fought in the Vietnam War, so both his father and uncle know quite a bit of the history of the war. They started off asking the girls trivia questions. If they got one right, the trigger wouldn't be pulled. If they were wrong, it was.

Graham doesn't know how smart Maxine is. She could easily lose a game like that. He has to choose something that will buy him some time with her.

"I want it again. I want to see fear in its eyes this time. Cut it up if it doesn't listen to me."

Father turns back around to stare at his son. He remains silent, as if mulling over the idea. Thinking of the risks and if he really wants Graham down there alone to do that.

"You've never asked me for something like this before. Why now?"

"That thing killed my brother. I've had a lot of time to think about this. I have to make it suffer. Shooting it won't be enough."

Graham makes sure to keep his face placid, hiding the remorse he feels at his words. Maxine has brought a version of himself out that he has never known before. This version is willing to do what it takes to save her. To say these things he's never said before. To stop whimpering at his father. He begins to wonder if it is love causing this shift away from cowardice.

"Fair enough. Joey, come help me unpack our shit. Then we'll wake the bitch up. Graham, go take a damn shower, you reek of it."

CHAPTER TWENTY-SIX

October 17th, 2009
11:13 a.m.

"Hey, hey. Are you alive?"

The sound of a voice wakes me from a horrible nightmare where Clark has just chased me over half a mile through a field. I mean, it had to be a dream, right? Clark's soft voice in my ear as he forced my body into the dirt replays through my head. My head is aching worse than any hangover I've ever had.

Something metal and heavy is around my throat. When I breathe in, the air smells musty, like old, damp clothes. I want to keep my eyes shut, imagining any moment Clark is going to wake me up. I'm in his bed, and he's cooking me breakfast downstairs.

My legs are aching. That dream of running so fast and so far felt so real. So did the fall — my ankle is still throbbing with pain.

"Wake up!" a voice yells, with the clashing of metal upon metal.

When I open my sleepy eyes, I'm met with a blinding dose of fluorescent light. I raise my hands to block the rays, but when I do, I find my wrists are bound with gray paracord rope. The walls that surround me are concrete, and so is the ceiling, which is covered in cracks. Something cold is around my throat; it hardly allows me to take a full breath of air in before constricting it. I reach my bound hands to my throat, feeling a thick metal bracket and a padlock in the middle connected to . . . chains.

I slowly sit up. My head throbs in time with my heart. I look down at my feet and see they are tied together too. My vision blurs in the flickering light. I'm lying on top of a green army cot, inside a cage with vertical bars on three sides and a stone wall on the fourth. I must be in the basement. It explains the stone walls, the concrete floors, the stale air.

But I'm not here alone. That voice I heard . . . was female.

"Hello?" I say.

"I'm over here," she says. I know her voice, that distinctive accent.

Even so, when I look at her, a faint shriek escapes my dry mouth. Standing only a few inches from me, her hands squeezing the bars, is Eva Willems.

CHAPTER TWENTY-SEVEN

October 17th, 2009
11:15 a.m.

She looks so different, almost like someone else: rawboned, sunken cheeks. Her hair is greasy and unkempt. Her blue eyes are bloodshot, and her skin is bleached. This has to be a dream; I saw Eva in my dream just last night. Except, in my dream she didn't look so . . . dead looking. She'd appeared the same as she had in high school.

"Maxine Masterson. Of all the people they could have stuck me with," she says in a dead tone.

We stare at each other for a painful amount of time. I tightly shut my eyes, begging for this nightmare to end. Eva's been missing for over a year; how could she be here with me? I thought Mikey was being stupid, linking her disappearance to the Monroe Murderer, but now I realize I was wrong. My body shakes as I come to a sickening realization. The Monroe Murderer has been committing crimes for two decades. For so long that I thought they were too old to continue. What if there's more than one of them? A father and his son. The son who so happens to have brought me here.

My head is pounding. I try pinching my legs, wondering if the self-affliction will awaken me to the real world.

"That won't work. I tried it," Eva says.

"What won't work?" The pressure of the lock on my throat cuts my voice low.

"Pinching yourself. I thought I was dreaming too. You're not."

I turn on the cot to face Eva. A part of me hoped I'd meet her again. Not like this, though. In a normal setting. I'd apologize for all the pain I caused her. Hope she forgives me. Now I realize this nightmare is real, and she's the last person I want to see. Which must be a reciprocated feeling.

The basement is quite large. It looks like it's used as a dumping ground for old furniture: there are a couple wooden chairs and an empty bookshelf, a large black hot-water tank, and a single cupboard sitting above a rusty white sink, plus a row of shelves full of tools. A single grimy window has bars attached to it from the inside — it looks too small to squeeze out of. There are four lights, two outside the cages and two inside. There is a rusty floor drain directly in front of each cage. They are stained dark red. I slowly look directly up from the drains. Hanging between the two drains is a meat hook.

I feel as though I'm either going to vomit or pass out again.

"What's happening?" I ask, my whole body trembling.

"They got you."

"They?"

"The Monroe Murderer."

I gulp. So, it's true. Clark, if that's his name, is the famous Monroe Murderer. The big, kind, green eyes I'd been staring into this whole time are those of a monster. That must be how they work. His father sends the good-looking son to lure us in. Makes sense for me, but Eva? After high school, she barely spoke to anyone at all. Maybe she sought shelter in the same beautiful eyes I did.

"Clark is the Monroe Murderer?" I ask.

"Clark?" Eva asks, confused.

I recall another name I heard the man in the overalls call him earlier.

"Graham?" I correct myself.

"No, he's just the lackey. His father — Moe — he's the sick son of a bitch running things."

The man in overalls, the one who approached just as I lost consciousness. His voice was gruff and terrifyingly baleful. *I'd recognize that face anywhere.* What could he have meant by that? My face? Why would I be recognized by a murderer? Had the two been after me for some time? Clark — Graham — has showed up in my life an unusual number of times this week. First, a new face at my AA meeting, asking if I needed a ride home. Next, at my work, once again kindly asking if I needed a ride home. I practically begged for a lift yesterday.

The peeping Tom, the sicko caught watching me — it must have been Graham. Who knows how long he's been watching me. But why me? I've seen pictures of the women in the Monroe case, and like I told Mikey, I don't fit the type. Not enough for the killer to plan to kidnap me — to know my work and AA schedule.

I fell for it all. Graham's understanding nature, his telling me everything I wanted to hear. I trusted him too quickly, had feelings for him right away that I hadn't felt in a long time. Maybe that's why I was their target. A lonely girl with no real friends who had committed a horrible act. Graham saw all the pain I felt for my misdeed and was a sympathetic ear. All the while he only wanted me to end up in this cage as Daddy's new pet.

"You've been missing a whole year," I say. I find hope in the fact that Eva's still alive after all this time.

Eva's eyebrows arch, her eyes wide, like this is the first she's hearing of it.

"A year, huh?"

"We've got to get out of here." I stand up, but my feet are still tied together, and I nearly fall to the cold ground.

I grab on to the thick chain and find the end. It's welded to the floor. I pull on it with all my strength. Nothing.

"Don't you think I've tried that already?"

I let out a sigh, dropping the chain to the ground. I go to the door of the cage and begin shaking it. The padlock rattles. The bars are spaced widely enough that I could stick one of my arms through, but not both. Not when they are tied together. I look at Eva. She has a chain too, but it's only locked to her right ankle. Her hands are free.

"Have you tried—"

"I've tried everything. Anything I haven't tried, another girl has. I know what you're thinking. Don't. The fat guy — Joey — he bit a girl's hand when she tried grabbing him. Took a chunk clean off and spat it back at her."

My stomach churns at the thought of someone biting into me like some savage zombie. No one's down here now, though. Eva could try grabbing the lock. Breaking it — or using something to unlock it. If only I'd worn my hair up, used a bobby pin.

"No one's had a bobby pin?"

Eva chuckles at my question. "They take everything from you."

No longer able to control my panic, I fall to my knees, feeling all the dirt on the floor digging into them. The ground is cold; it's almost like kneeling on ice. Unable to stand the feel of it, I sit on my bottom instead, bringing my knees to my chest.

"You're wearing his clothes," Eva comments.

I look down at myself. I'm relieved to still have Graham's clothes on from when I was drugged. I hope it means no one's touched me.

"Why are you in that freak's clothes?" Eva asks, irritation in her voice.

"I don't know what you're asking."

She's still in the same spot, her face pressed against the bars.

"He never lets any of the girls wear his clothes."

What can she possibly mean by that? I threw them on this morning, unaware of the horror that was awaiting me. I wore his shirt to bed; he happily gave it to me. Were other girls treated differently than I have been? It would make more sense, seeing as these guys are serial killers. Why has Graham been so kind to me? Why didn't he knock me out as soon as I set foot in this house?

Then there's the way his eyes bulged when he heard that van make its way up the driveway. The way he told me to be quiet. Was he not planning to bring me down here? He certainly didn't expect his father to return home when he did. I grimace. He might have been the only one looking out for me, and I slammed a coffee cup into his face.

"How did they get you here?" Eva asks.

I sigh, pressing my lips together. I don't want to tell her how easy I made it for them. How I was seduced by the man she's calling a freak. There's no way he did the same to her. Every girl must be different.

"How'd they get you here, Eva? Everyone thought you just ran off."

Eva snorts and lets out a heavy breath. "I tried. I got fifty miles and broke down on the highway. They offered me help, and I knew they were up to no good. I mean, you out of all people know what happens when you trust a man, right?"

I look away, unable to keep eye contact with her. Nine years later, a year of being trapped in a cage, and she still hasn't forgotten.

"Look, Eva—"

"Tell me how you got here. Now."

Before I can even begin to spit out the story, the door upstairs opens.

CHAPTER TWENTY-EIGHT

October 17th, 2009
11:20 a.m.

As soon as the basement door opens, Eva moves to the far corner of her cot and hugs her knees. She looks down at her lap and is no longer the strong person demanding to know how I got here. Seeing her sudden fear, I move quickly to sit on my own cot. We both glance at each other for a moment before staring at the three men walking down the stairs.

First comes Graham's father, Moe. He's still wearing the same dirty overalls but now is holding a lit cigarette, which he takes a huge draw of before grinning at the sight of me. Behind him is the heavyset man, Joey, then Graham. I stare at Graham, trying to search his eyes for any sign of remorse. He's different now, like back in the barn. A scared animal with its abuser, keeping its eyes glued to the ground.

The three men stop at the meat hook. The fluorescent light brings out Moe's dark eyes. It's spectral, like staring at the devil. It's almost like looking into eyes that have been gutted from their sockets. No wonder he has Graham lure the women in.

"Damn, she's already up. We don't get a wet T-shirt contest," the heavy man says.

I barely even hear the other man's words. I'm so engrossed in the sight of Moe's dark eyes, as if staring at a TV with a screen full of static, that it takes me a moment to realize he's holding a sharp knife, the sort a hunter uses to eviscerate an animal. The blade is stained a deep red. Now I can see why Eva retreated so quickly to the corner.

"I've thought of this moment for a long time. Now that I'm here with you, I don't know what to say. Don't want to say much of anything. Just stick this blade straight in your throat." Moe ducks past the meat hook to come closer to my cage.

I inch back in my cot, until my back hits the wall. Moe chuckles, bringing his cigarette up to his mouth for one last drag before dropping it to the ground and stomping on it. He opens his mouth to let the smoke out and brings the knife up, licks the blade. Blood comes from his mouth, and he spits in my direction. He smiles, his yellow teeth stained red. I want to scream for help, but there is none. Eva is keeping her body in a small ball, and Graham has yet to take his eyes off the ground.

"Who are you?" I ask.

"I'm the closest thing to the devil you'll ever meet. Here to take what you owe, Maxine Masterson."

What I owe? How do I owe these people anything?

"Speak English, Moe," the other man says, laughing at my confused, terrified look.

"How rude of me, speaking riddles to brainless creatures. I'm Moe Dawson. You don't know me, personally, but you met my son, and not the one standing in this room. My other son, George."

I feel the air leave my lungs. This all makes sense now. Graham coming into my life, watching me. They want revenge for killing one of their own.

"It . . . it was an accident," I say, my voice wobbling.

"Oh, it was an accident. Shit, my bad. Let me just get the keys, let you out." Moe reaches into his right pocket and takes a copper key out.

He drops the key to the ground. It lands a few inches from my cage. I want to leap to the ground and grab it. My wrists tied together can't fit through the bars, but they could fit through the gap underneath the door. But then there's the way Moe is staring at me. It's almost like he wants me to go for it. I look up at Graham. His eyes are wide, and he shakes his head slightly.

"Be a doll and grab me that key," Moe says.

I shake my head, knowing this is a trick.

"Pick it up, or I'll have to come in there myself," he commands.

His eyes force me up. I can't walk, so I kneel and pull myself toward the bars. The key isn't far from the cage, and if this man is planning to do what I think he is, I can avoid it. Just take the key as fast as I can. This is clearly a lose-lose game, but I feel bound to play. If I don't, things will get worse.

I stop when my head is near the cage door. Moe is watching me with a sly grin on his face. It would take no time at all for him to bring his foot down on my hand. I breathe in the dank air that now smells like cigarette smoke, then, without a beat, move my fingers under the cage door and over the key. Feeling like any moment Moe's boot will come down on them, I move as quickly as I can. Moe's feet don't move an inch during the whole endeavor.

Once my hands are back inside the cage, I shrink back. I have the key. Now what? I could always keep it; after all, they can no longer get to me. Stupid idea — why would they not keep a spare key?

"Unlock the door."

"Why?"

"Because I'm telling you to, creature."

Creature. Why does he keep saying that word?

"Look, sir, please. I am so sorry for what happened to your son. Please, don't do—"

"Oh fuck, another beggar," the other man says, once again letting out a disgusting laugh.

"Unlock the fucking door," Moe orders, his words slow and cold.

I look over at Graham, using my eyes to beg him to stop this. He hasn't said a single thing this entire time.

"Get your eyes off my son, or I'll cut them out." Moe bangs his knife against the metal cage.

I look away from Graham, nodding my head. Tears fall from my eyes as I stand up. I shuffle slowly toward the cage's door. I locate the padlock once again, trying to determine how long it will take me to maneuver the key into the lock. Even if I do get the door unlocked, I still have this bracket locked around my throat.

"Give me the key to this." I point to the padlock on my throat.

Moe raises his eyebrows. "Of course."

I gulp, not anticipating that. He reaches into his pocket and takes out a set of two silver keys. He takes one off and tosses it to me. I narrowly grab it and press the key into the lock constricting my throat. It unlatches. I drop it, feeling that any minute this charade will end. I breathe in and out a couple times, getting as much air in as I can. Moe continues to stand there, staring at me.

"Cut the ropes . . . please," I ask, shakily moving my wrists up.

This must be the moment they put an end to this sick game. Then again, these are seasoned killers who have a taste for torturing women. At least, I assume so. With Eva still here and alive a year after being kidnapped, they must enjoy these women being tortured. They don't just outright kill them like most serial killers. Moe glares at my request, giving me hope this will all be over soon.

He lifts his knife up and stares at my bound wrists. I gulp, sick at the thought of letting this man near me with a knife. He could grab them and slit them with ease. Add another layer of bloodstain to the knife.

Don't be a coward, Max. I don't have it in me to be brave, so not being a coward will have to do.

I take a deep breath and lift my wrists toward the bars.

CHAPTER TWENTY-NINE

October 17th, 2009
11:26 a.m.

I imagine Moe taking that knife and cutting me up like a hunter would a freshly killed doe. His eyes stare deep into mine. I know it won't be the first time he's butchered someone.

In the next three seconds my heart feels as if it's no longer beating. Just anticipating having that knife dig deep into my frail wrists. Instead, he pokes the knife through the bars and in one movement cuts through the paracord. I watch as it falls to the ground, and just as my heart starts to beat again, I have moved my hands down to my sides. A breath of trapped air escapes my mouth.

"Thank you," I whisper.

Would it be testing my luck to ask him to cut my ankles free? Even if he is willing to, I don't think I can put my mind through it. Even the anticipation of being cut into bits by that sharp knife is aging me.

Maybe if I do this, they'll just take the key from me, lock the gate, and laugh. Or I could be quick; I could push the cage door against Moe, knock him out of the way. If he drops his knife, I can grab it. Threaten Graham and the other man with it while cutting my ankles free.

I look at the row of shelves on the wall, at the tools on them: a hammer, utility knife, drill, and screwdrivers. If Moe doesn't drop the knife, I could grab any of those and strike the other man, then Graham. It's a brainless plan but it's all I can think of.

Holding the silver key, I reach out and ease my hand through the bars. My hand fits through more easily than I originally thought. Thanks to my slim wrists, I can just about grab ahold of the padlock.

I glance over at Moe, who is only a foot from the door, his body at ease as he watches me. I want to look back at Graham, see if he's shaking his head or nodding. Trying to tell me anything. Then I remember what Moe said about cutting my eyes out.

My hand is shaking. I attempt to put the key into the padlock. I miss and try again. It won't fit.

"Oh, didn't I mention that isn't your lock's key?" Moe asks.

I drop the key. Before I can pull my hand back into the cage, Moe grips my hand tightly, trapping it. I scream as he moves the knife to my hand. I use all the strength I have in me to try to pull my hand from his grasp, but before I can, he takes the knife and cuts my pinkie clean off.

CHAPTER THIRTY

October 17th, 2009
11:28 a.m.

I'm so shocked — he's so quick — that the pain doesn't start until I see blood shooting from the stump. Then a jolt of electricity shoots through my mutilated hand and into my entire body. I scream and Moe finally lets my hand go.

I pull my hand into Graham's shirt, stuffing the end of my pinkie into the fabric. Blood soaks through, warming my stomach. Joey is mocking my shrieks of pain.

"What the fuck is wrong with you?" I scream.

"A lot," Moe replies, "and you, creature, are about to discover all of it. I've been waiting for this moment for five years."

I want to cuss him out, but I can't. I suddenly feel dizzy, as though I am going to pass out. I backtrack to the cot, nearly falling over as I do so. I sit down, cradling my hand in the wet T-shirt.

No one here will save me. I am being tortured by serial killers. Graham clearly is under his father's thumb, too much to help me. If I could get him alone, I could attempt to talk to him. Remind him he doesn't have to do this.

"Dad, you said you'd let me—" Graham begins to say, but Moe angrily raises his hand to stop him.

"It's a pinkie. You'll still get some," Moe says.

Still get some? Some what? A piece of torture for himself? Graham has finally spoken up, and that's what he's questioning. He sounded so sincere when he told me I did the right thing as I wept over killing his brother. He could just be an incredible actor, like I've read other serial killers can be when fooling a victim into trusting them.

Moe leans down to grab the key I dropped; he puts it back in his pocket. He begins looking around the floor for something. I watch as his eyes wander the floor before stopping on an object. My pinkie. He leans down and picks it up.

"Don't worry, this . . . this is just the beginning." He looks at me with a grin. "Clean this mess up," he orders Graham.

Graham nods his head reluctantly. As he passes his father, Moe grabs ahold of his arm.

"Fuck this up and you won't get anything," he whispers.

Graham nods again, and the two older men walk back up the stairs. Once they're gone, it's silent. The only sound is coming from my heavy breathing and the old water tank rumbling. Graham goes to the back of the basement and disappears through a door I didn't notice before. He comes out a couple moments later with a plastic bottle and some washcloths. He approaches my cage.

"Get . . . get away . . . from me," I mumble, my vision starting to blur.

Am I bleeding out? I've never felt this weak before. I can hear my heart hammer in my chest.

"I'm not here to hurt you, Maxine."

Hearing him call me by my full name makes me feel more nauseated.

"You . . . tricked me."

"I'm going to help you."

It's a game, that's it. I can't trust him. He just sat by and watched his father cut my pinkie off. If he wanted to, he could have stopped him.

"I don't even have a key to your cage. I'm not here to hurt you. Just let me help you. I think you're going into shock from the blood loss," he pleads.

That explains the nausea. I look at the washcloths and plastic bottle he has in his hands. It's a bottle of rubbing alcohol. I need it. The shirt I've wrapped my hand in is soaked in blood. But this could be another trick to get my hand out of the cage. Cut off another finger.

Be brave, Maxine.

Can you bleed to death from a severed pinkie? I can't take any chances. I'm already weak from the loss of blood. That, or the mere sight of it is making me woozy. Either way, this could help me regain my strength. I need that cloth to tie around my hand and stop the bleeding.

"Keep your other hand away from your pocket," I order him.

"Sure," he says calmly, lifting his left hand up to grasp the bars.

I slowly stand up. I forget about my ankles being tied together and when I go to take a step, I fall to the ground. I roll onto my back in agony.

"Maxine, are you okay?" I hear Graham say.

I don't even answer. I can't muster up any words. Instead, I begin to slowly push my body toward the cage. Once my hand makes contact with one of the bars, I grab on to it and pull myself into a sitting position.

I take my hand from inside the shirt and lift it up through the bars. Fresh blood completely covers my hand, with more still oozing out of the stump. The sight makes me want to hurl.

"I'm going to open this, okay?" He picks up the bottle of alcohol.

I nod, watching as he unscrews the cap. He pours some onto one of the washcloths. I flinch as he takes my hand gently. My head is urging me to pull away, not risk anything. My heart, on the other hand, knows I need this and wants to believe he only yearns to help me. That me being caught was all a mistake.

"You can trust him. He won't do shit."

I'm startled at Eva's words after the long silence. I look up to see she's standing now, glaring at Graham.

"Shut up, Eva," Graham tells her. I recall that earlier, she called him a freak.

He takes the washcloth with alcohol on it and presses it against my pinkie. My hand throbs from the sharp pain of the alcohol coming in contact with my wound. I attempt to keep my trembling hand still as Graham cleans it.

"I'll get you more clothes soon." He looks down at my bloodied shirt.

Once he's done, I quickly pull my hand back and bandage it with the washcloth. The bleeding finally seems to be subsiding.

I want to sit back on my cot, get as far away from Graham as possible. But I stay still. Although I'm no longer bleeding, I still feel disoriented. If I try to stand up, I could fall again.

Instead, I look over at Graham, whose eyes are on me. If I killed his brother and they really have been planning this for five years, then why is he being nice to me now? Perhaps he saw how badly I was bleeding, and thought I could die before he was able to torture me. Me dying would put a damper on all the torture.

"Why are you helping me? Don't want me to die before you can have all your fun?" I ask.

"No, Maxine. I'm going to save you, okay?"

"Why?"

"Because . . . I think I love you," he says, forcing a smile.

CHAPTER THIRTY-ONE

October 17th, 2009
11:37 a.m.

I want to shrink away from those words. Nobody has said they love me in a very long time. Not a man, anyways. My own father hasn't even said that since I was a young girl.

Eva chuckles, covering her laughs with her hand.

"Why . . . why . . . what?" I stammer.

"I thought I hated you. I did, for a long time. But, Maxine, me and you, we're the same. I see that now. I've been put through so much shit by my father. I never wanted this life. He's been pulling the strings. I was telling the truth, about my mom leaving when I was young. My father blamed my brother and me; he's always used it against us. After last night, I promised myself I would keep you safe. My father coming home, that wasn't planned."

"Then get me—" I glance at Eva and correct myself. "Get us out of here."

"I don't have the keys. I'll get them soon, though, I promise. I just need you to trust me."

"Trust you? You lied to me, told me your name was Clark and that your brother had cancer. You've been stalking me. You . . . watched me through my window."

I need to stop. To be nice to Graham. I can't help it, though. The sense of betrayal is overpowering me. Making me despise this man for landing me in this cage.

"I did. I've always had this overwhelming attraction to you. I can't help it. I will save you."

Graham grew up in the house of the Monroe Murderer, co-opted by his father into aiding and abetting his crimes. He must be suffering from complex childhood trauma — something I was tested for many times after my mother went crazy. He is right to see a similarity between us from what we've both suffered because of our parents.

But it means something else too: he doesn't really love me. He loves the *idea* of me. He loves the idea that he can bond with me more than anyone else in his life. It means I can't trust him, no matter how sincere he thinks he is, but I have to pretend I do.

If I survive this, I will try to get Graham the help he needs.

I look at my bandaged hand. My vision is starting to return to normal, on the plus side. Does that mean I'm in the clear now? I still feel the unruly pain.

"I need a hospital, Graham," I say.

Graham bites his bottom lip. "I know. I will figure something out."

I sigh. He doesn't have a key to my cage, but there must be something he can do. My mind flashes back to the phone by the fridge.

"You could call the police. That phone in the kitchen."

I hear Eva chuckle, as if my begging is funny somehow. I'm sure she's tried asking for all the same things.

"My father is up there right now."

"After he goes to sleep, then?"

Graham nods his head. How many more fingers will I have to lose before Graham does something? His father isn't a young man; Graham could overpower him easily. I want to scream this at Graham, but I know it's better I don't. After my mother died, my dad told me she was a bad person. That only made me hate my dad. "What did your dad mean, you'll still get some?"

"It's all I could think of to keep him at bay from killing you. I told him I wanted to . . . to have sex with you one last time."

"No," I say, disgusted.

"I'm not going to touch you. It was just all I could think of. I've tried helping girls here before. Father found out and made their deaths much more excruciating. For now, I have to act like all I want is . . . to have you. Act like you mean nothing to me. It'll keep you alive longer. So, I need you to do something for me, Maxine."

"What?"

"Put your neck bracket back on."

"Are you crazy?"

"I must follow my father's orders. If I don't, you'll be fair game. Just trust me for now."

Fuck. He wants me to willingly put this death trap back around my throat. Be more locked up than I am now. Do I really have a choice? He's all I have.

"Okay." I manage to move my body and find the key.

"You won't regret this. Here, I'll get you painkillers and some water." Graham jogs to the room in the back.

"You fucked him, didn't you?" Eva asks me, a look of disdain on her face.

Graham returns from the room. He runs back to my cage and hands me two blue pills and a plastic cup filled with water. I grab them and hesitate.

Seeing my hesitation, Graham says, "It's oxycodone. My brother used to take them all the time. I never knew where he got them, but they're powerful."

He's right. Oxycodone is a highly potent pain pill. It could make me tired. What if I fall asleep again, granting them easy access into my cage to do whatever they please? Then again, I'll do anything to make this goddamn pain subside. I put the pills in my mouth and take a large gulp of water. I am so parched I finish the whole cup.

"Th-thank you." I offer Graham a smile.

I put the bracket around my neck again. I already feel my air constricted and consider throwing it on the ground. This is just another trap I am getting myself into. Another step away from freedom. But what choice do I have? Graham said he could save us.

I lock the padlock and toss the key to Graham.

"I'm going to get you out of here, even if I have to kill him."

I wish he would just go kill him now. His father is a lunatic. But I know what's stopping him. After my mother died, I still took her side for years. I blamed my father for tearing our family apart. But I was a child then; Graham is an adult.

"I tried to hold on to the idea that my mother was innocent for years. It's hard to let go of someone, especially when they are your own blood, but I believe you can." I crawl over to the cage, put my uninjured hand on the bars.

Graham moves down to his knees, grabs my hand, and holds it tightly. He nods and kisses it.

"We can run away, start over."

I have to agree, play up to the idea that once I've escaped, I'll blindly go anywhere with him. He's sick and needs help.

When he's gone, Eva gives me a look.

"You're going to have to fuck him again. You know that, right?"

CHAPTER THIRTY-TWO

October 17th, 2009
11:40 a.m.

I turn to look at Eva to see if she's joking, but her expression is somber, like any feeling she had has died. If she's been here for a year, I'm sure she's gone a little mad.

"What are you talking about?"

"He won't kill his father. He'll say he's going to help, but he won't. He tells every girl here the same thing. You have to get him into your cage. Fuck him and kill him."

"And how the hell do you expect me to do that?"

"I don't know. I think he keeps a pocketknife in his pocket. If he comes into your cage, that means he has a key. You think of the rest."

What she doesn't understand is, I don't have it in me to kill another person, not deliberately. Much less someone who desperately needs help. Someone who trusts me. If Eva is telling the truth, that Graham has said he would try to save every girl that's come in, it could be a problem. He could be telling me the same thing he's told the others. But if he truly loves me, maybe it'll be different this time. Maybe he'll finally be able to turn on his father.

"I don't think I can kill someone."

Eva lets out an exasperated sigh. "We're going to die if you don't. I get it, you two fucked and now you have some pathetic feelings for him but—"

"I don't have any feelings for him. I just don't want to kill him. He's clearly being brainwashed by his father."

"And has been for many years. You think that means anything? When push comes to shove, he'll let Moe slice you up. He's watched and cleaned up the mess when it's happened to other girls. I promise you; it will not be pretty. They've been planning this a long time."

"Well, you've stayed alive a long time. You must be doing something right."

Eva scoffs. "Yeah, I stayed away from that freak. Didn't listen to his bullshit. I'm not like you. I don't fall for psychopathic assholes. I don't let them get in my head and fuck over anyone they want."

I freeze. I know exactly who she's talking about.

"Eva, it's been nine years. I'm not the same person I used to be."

"Did you change before or after you killed that guy? Or maybe it was before, when you let me—"

"Eva! Look, this isn't going to work if we're against each other. I know you hate me, and I don't blame you, but if we don't work together, we're both going to die."

Eva is silent for a couple moments as if pondering that idea. She looks so frail and exhausted. I can't let her get too caught up in our past. It'll muddy her thinking. I want to save her more than I want to save myself. It's a dangerous idea, but she might be right about Graham. I could lure him into my cage, get the key. Knock him out somehow and lock him in here. I could call the police with the phone upstairs.

"I thought you were in jail. They already released you?"

I sigh. This isn't exactly what we need to be talking about right now.

"I got out six months ago."

"So, you're probably on some sort of probation, right?"

I shrug. "Not anymore. I got released from parole for . . . good behavior."

"Bullshit," Eva scoffs. "How about your dad, your family? Will they know you're gone?"

Till now, I've been so caught up in trying to figure out how to get out of here on my own, I haven't even thought of the possibility that someone might come to find me. I'm supposed to be at work this afternoon. In the six months I've worked for Aunt Almeida, I haven't called out once. She'll be notified immediately about my no-show. She'll call my father, and he'll go to my house to check on me. If not today, then the next day when I don't show up again. If they don't suspect I'm on some bender. Knowing my father, that's exactly what he'll conclude.

No one saw me leave the AA meeting with Graham. No one even knows about him besides Casey . . . and Mikey. Casey just thought he was another customer; she won't bat an eye. Mikey, however, might have a suspicion. But he won't be aware of my disappearance right away, not the way we ended things. After some time, though, he'll be questioned. He's smart. He'll piece together what happened to me. It's a long shot, but right now Mikey might be the only one who can identify Graham. He saw his vehicle. Not too many people drive that car model in Mendex.

"I was supposed to be at AA yesterday. But I bumped into Graham outside and left before it started. Nobody saw us."

Eva lets out a sigh. "You work, right? Please tell me you at least have a job."

"I work for my aunt. It's not like me to not show up. My dad will probably think I relapsed. He'll go to my house and see all my stuff is still there."

"How long do you think that will take?"

"A day or so. Only one person really saw me with Graham, though."

"Who?"

I take a deep breath, wishing I didn't have to tell her. With any luck Eva doesn't know who Mikey is.

"Mikey Connolly, he's an ex-boyfr—"

"I know Mikey. He's married, you know?"

"Yeah, I know. He was . . . giving me rides home from work. Was worried something would happen to me if I walked instead."

Eva chuckles. "And still you were stupid enough to end up here."

"I was lonely. Graham was pretending to be someone else, and we got close. I wasn't thinking clearly. It doesn't matter. Mikey saw his car — he might be able to lead the police to us."

"The Toyota? Hopefully he hurries, then."

"What do you mean?"

"Moe only got that for his plan for you. Thought it would be fitting, since that's what you killed his son with."

That car should have been a red flag the moment I saw it in the community center parking lot. I wonder if it's actually my old sedan. After the accident, it was hauled to the dump. But it only needed a new hood, headlights, windshield, and radiator.

"You realize you don't have that much time? Moe wants you dead, and Graham can only stall him for so long. You need to get that freak in your cage."

It pains me to admit it, but Eva's right. We don't have the time it would take for the small possibility of Mikey getting involved and making that connection.

"I'll try to get Graham in my cage, okay? But I'm not going to kill him. I have a better idea where we all come out of this alive."

CHAPTER THIRTY-THREE

October 17th, 2009
12:48 p.m.

Graham returns nearly an hour later. In his hands are two plates with sandwiches, and hanging over his shoulders are my clothes from yesterday. I would have preferred more comfortable clothing. But I'll take anything that isn't currently covered in my own blood.

In the hour he's been gone, the oxycodone has kicked in majorly. I feel immensely better. It's no wonder these are so addictive. Now I just fear when their effects will wear off.

He approaches my cage. "I got you some food and clothes."

"Can I wear something of yours? It's just so cold in here."

His smile fades. "Father says he wants you out of my clothes."

I frown and begin to slowly hobble to the front of the cage where Graham is.

"How are you feeling?"

"I'm okay. The pills are working."

"Good. I have more I can give you later."

I nod. I don't want to wait down here long enough to need more. I need a hospital. Before I can voice this, however, I hear Eva growl.

"I haven't eaten in over a day," Eva whines, her attention on the food.

Graham casts a glare at her. He goes to her cage and shoves a plate roughly under the door; the sandwich on it falls to the ground. Eva doesn't seem bothered; she crouches by the food and snaps it down like a wild animal. He walks back over to me, carefully taking the sandwich from the plate and tilting it inside my cage.

"Thank you." I take it from him and bite into it.

It's turkey, lettuce, and tomato. I've been so full of pain and fear, I haven't realized till now how hungry I am. I savor every bite. By the looks of Eva, being fed isn't a daily occurrence here. I'll need every calorie I can get to keep my mind and body sharp.

Once I'm done eating, Clark hands me my clothes. I consider putting them on the cot and waiting till he's gone to change. But I have to attract Graham. Let him see my body. Get him to want to be inside my cage as soon as possible.

I set my clothes down and start by taking Graham's boxer briefs off. The shirt he gave me is three sizes too big; it hangs just below my fingertips. Graham sees this and goes silent. I see Eva in the background, a small smile on her face. I slowly turn around and bend down to pull on my panties. I slowly move them up and over my hips.

When I turn back, Graham is red-faced. He looks as enraptured as he did the first time he saw me undressed. Next, I put my hands over the end of the shirt and gradually pull it up and over my head. I stand there, topless, staring at Graham. My lower body is covered in dried blood from the shirt, but still his mouth is ajar.

"Were those drugs stronger than I thought?" he asks, chuckling.

I can't let Graham know that I'm trying to turn him on, so I simply nod. There's no bra in the pile of clothes, so I slip the white T-shirt on. The idea of Moe or Joey seeing me this vulnerable terrifies me, but for now, I have to keep my eyes on the prize and pray they don't come downstairs anytime soon.

Before putting my skirt back on, I walk over to the door of the cage, only a couple inches from Graham. I can hear his heart pounding from here. That, or it's mine.

"I'm scared, Graham." I keep my voice low and as weak as possible.

"I am too. I'm going to figure this out. I just need time."

Graham glances over at Eva, who's still sitting by the empty plate, as if lost in thought. I hope Graham doesn't guess we already have our own plan. Even if I could bring myself to trust him, he didn't really answer me when I asked him to try calling the police.

"I don't have time, Graham. Look." I lift my bandaged hand in the air.

He frowns. "I know, I know. Don't worry, I've seen girls survive much worse."

Is that supposed to make me feel better or worse? Graham beckons me closer to him. I press my head against the cold bars.

"She's not your friend. Don't believe anything she says."

I look back at Eva. I can tell she's attempting to listen in. It's not like we're being subtle about discussing her.

"Why?" I whisper.

"Why do you think my father has kept her alive this long? Think about it."

Does he mean Eva is helping Moe? I shake my head, not wanting to believe it. What he's insinuating is that Eva is just as evil as Moe. Maybe there is a reason beyond just staying away from Graham that she's been kept alive this long.

"Put your clothes on. Father and Uncle Joey have been drinking. Uncle Joey is a sick fuck. I don't want him seeing you like this."

I nod and grab my skirt, pulling it on without hesitation.

"Good, I'll be back soon. I'm hoping they get tired. Decide to wait a night before doing anything else."

"Graham, please. Wait for your father and uncle to leave the room and call the police."

"When he's asleep."

"What about sleeping pills?"

"Uncle Joey might have some, back at his house. I would have to leave and—"

"No, no, please don't leave me alone with those men," I beg.

"I won't. I'll look around. Father might have something else."

"Please just don't leave me here alone." I reach out to him.

Graham grabs my hand and gives it a soft kiss. "I promise I won't. I love you."

CHAPTER THIRTY-FOUR

October 17th, 2009
2:21 p.m.
Mikey

"What do you mean she didn't show up to work?" Mikey asks Almeida Masterson.

Mikey has been worried about Max since last night when he went to collect her from her AA meeting, arriving just as everyone was leaving. Max wasn't among them. He even waited for the man running the group, who was the last to leave and who locked the door. He felt guilty — more guilty. Had all the stress of the previous night's events caused Max to miss a meeting?

Next, he stopped at her house to see if she was home. He knocked at her front door and stood there for ten minutes. The curtains were shut. Either she wasn't home or she was ignoring him. Or worse, she was in trouble. He finds it frustrating that people don't seem to grasp the fact girls around the state of Wyoming with blonde hair keep going missing; some are even found dead. The Monroe Murderer has been around for decades and, like the Zodiac Killer, has never been caught. People in Mendex like to gossip about serial killers, but they never take them seriously. Because, according to them, bad things don't happen here.

His suspicions about Max avoiding him grew when he got home and Adrienne told him that she'd visited Max that morning. She said she told Max to stay away from him. "And that goes for you too, Mikey," Adrienne said. "If you see Max again, I'll tell my brothers, so help me." Like he's her own personal possession.

Mikey no longer cares about the consequences. Let Adrienne do her worst. He just needs to see Max, at least once, so she knows how sorry he is for causing all this havoc in her life. He also wants to see her in the flesh, to make sure she's safe.

When Mikey got home from Max's after his vehicle was vandalized, he was surprised to find that Adrienne's brothers weren't there waiting for him. Just Adrienne, seething. Turns out one of the snooty waitresses saw him kissing Max outside the restaurant while on a smoke break. What Mikey still can't figure out is who busted his windshield. If it had been Adrienne's brothers, they would have been at his home that night ready to rip him a new hole. Adrienne only seems to know about the incident at the parking lot, not Max's house. So, who broke his windshield?

That night things escalated further than he had planned. He wanted to spend more time gaining Max's trust, becoming her friend again. He never intended to go inside her house, but the way she kissed him made it impossible to resist. And there's the man he's seen twice around Max. The guy's been staring at her with a sparkle of complete and utter attraction in his eyes. So, Mikey's jealousy played a part too.

He planned to give her the necklace much later, but Max was slipping from his fingers. She was lying to get out of him giving her a ride. He had to get her back. He couldn't let some creep come into the picture and take her away.

Now he's at the restaurant, being told Max hasn't shown up to work. Her overworked and tired-looking aunt has come in to

complete Max's shift. Almeida doesn't care for Mikey; he can tell
by the way she is staring at him.

"She didn't go to AA last night, either," Almeida says. "The
group leader called her father and said she was a no-show."

"Is it like Max to do that?" he asks.

He already knows the answer is no. Max has too much on the
line to be missing work.

"No, that girl hasn't called out of work once in four months,"
Almeida says.

"And that doesn't strike you as odd?"

Almeida crosses her arms. Her tired eyes are alert, as if she's
ready to spit out harsh, honest feelings about the matter.

"You know what strikes me as odd?" she asks.

"What?"

"That a married man is standing here grilling me about one
of my workers. Don't think I haven't heard the gossip going on
around here."

"I'm just worried about her."

"Go worry about your own family." Almeida turns to walk off.

Mikey grabs ahold of her arm. She stops and stares at his hand
as if he's struck her. He quickly lets go.

"I'm sorry, ma'am. I'm just really worried about Max. She must
be somewhere. I feel partly to blame. I don't want her off ruining
everything she's worked for."

Mikey is partly telling the truth. He is worried that Max has
fallen off the wagon, but mostly he's worried she's with that man.
That man who doesn't share his concern for her. Who can't care
for her the way he does. This last week Mikey's been trying not
only to get closer to Max but also to keep her out of trouble. She
is prone to trouble like a clumsy person is prone to tripping.

"If Max hasn't showed up to AA or work, she's already destroy-
ing everything she's worked for."

"What did Jerry say?"

"Her father's at work, said he'll go over to her house after to check on her. For Christ's sake, Mikey, I don't know what else you want to hear."

"Has anything odd happened to Max these last few days?"

Mikey feels as though he's a police officer with his questions. He won't give up until he has a lead. If her family refuses to offer any help, he'll have to go to the police. Ask them to do a wellness check or something.

Mikey suspects Almeida is about to tell him off but then she takes a deep breath.

"There was one thing. I thought she would've told you, though."

"Told me what?"

"Thursday, she came into work an utter mess. Called me and said a neighbor had caught a man watching her through her window."

Mikey feels as if he's about to pop a blood vessel. Why didn't Max tell him this? She must not have wanted to worry him. If she had, he would have stayed with her. The first night he was at the restaurant, there had been that figure watching them. Mikey had nearly forgotten it happened, until now. Then Thursday, someone had been watching Max. It couldn't all be a coincidence.

There's one obvious suspect for the stalking: Clark. They met in AA, and then he's eating dinner at the restaurant. Max said she had just met him, but what are the chances he had just shown up to her work exactly when she was about to get off? That was the same night she had tried lying to Mikey about a coworker giving her a ride home. It had been Clark who offered her a ride. Just like he'd tried giving her a ride home from AA.

As he was leaving the restaurant that night, Clark had given Mikey a vexing glare, as if Mikey'd ruined some plan of his. Then that same night, when he went into Max's house, Mikey's wind-shield had been broken. And then someone banged on the window. Now that he thought about it, that was pretty weird. Like they'd wanted to interrupt whatever was happening inside.

"Did they catch him? The peeping Tom?"

Almeida shakes her head.

Mikey knows what his next step is. He has to call Max's AA group leader. If Clark was at the meeting, the group leader must have his number. He didn't see Clark leaving AA last night. It can't all be a coincidence.

"Do you have her AA sponsor's number?"

"Jay? No, try Jerry. I'm done with this conversation, Mikey. I have work to do. If you find Max, tell her to give me a call."

CHAPTER THIRTY-FIVE

October 17th, 2009
2:41 p.m.
Mikey

After calling Max's father four times, Mikey finally reached him. Jerry reluctantly gave him Jay's number. Jerry, like Almeida, didn't seem too worried about Max. He said she'd most likely gone back to drinking. Mikey likes Jerry and knows he's gone through a lot of hardships in his life, and knows his ability to deal with his daughter is faltering.

Jerry and Mikey have been acquaintances for the last five years. Jerry occasionally asks for help from Mikey with construction work on weekends when he can't get workers. Mikey mostly only comes to ask questions about Max. Mikey can sense Jerry knows he still cares about his daughter, but Jerry's warned him that she has issues when it comes to relationships and friendships.

Mikey dials the number Jerry gave him, and it rings three times before a man answers.

"Hey, sir, my name is Mikey Connolly. I'm a friend of Max's," he says.

"Hey, how is she?" Jay asks.

"I'm trying to figure that out right now, sir. You see, Max didn't show up to work today, and I'm getting a little worried about her."

There's silence over the phone. Mikey begins to think of how to nonchalantly ask about Clark. He's already come off as a weirdo to Almeida and Jerry. He just needs someone who will not automatically assume Max is on some bender.

"Well, Mikey. I'm not supposed to discuss our members' business."

"Please, I wouldn't ask if it weren't important."

Jay sighs deeply. "I'm not sure what your relationship to Max is, but I think she may be off with a man from AA. One of our members had arrived at last night's meeting late and saw her in another member's car."

Mikey catches his breath. A lead, finally. Clark drives the same model Max drove when they were dating.

"Do you have his number, by any chance?"

"I mean, I do, but I can't just give it to you."

"I think we both know she needs help. I'm worried she may have gone back to the bottle. If she does that, she'll lose everything. She'll be jobless and homeless. Please, Jay."

More silence.

"Okay, I do care about her. The girl's had a hard life. The guy's name is Clark. He only came to one meeting, in fact. Seems like a good kid from what I saw. Works for a construction company."

Mikey knows nearly all the owners of construction companies around town. There aren't many. He also knows most of the workers from his own time in construction. He's never heard of this Clark guy, so either he's new, or he's lying.

After getting the number Clark used to call Jay, Mikey says thanks and that he would let Jay know as soon as he got ahold of her. Jay has been a lot more helpful than her family, but he agreed too easily that Max might have gone back to the bottle.

Mikey knows it can't just be that. All these weird situations with Clark are too coincidental. Now he only has an hour until he's due home from work. He'll make one last call before heading home. He doesn't want to, but he knows he needs to stay on Adrienne's good side. He can't fend off her brothers while he's trying to find Max.

He dials the number Jay gave him. He feels his left leg shake as he does so.

If Clark does answer, what is he even supposed to say? He's been able to get information from Almeida, Jerry, and Jay, but he knows them. He didn't know this man.

The phone rings four times before someone picks up.

"Joey's Lumberyard, how can I help you?" It's a man's voice.

Lumberyard? Has Jay given him the wrong number, or is Mikey right to think that Clark lied about working in construction? Mikey considers hanging up right now, but he doesn't want to give up his only lead.

"Yes, hello, I'm looking for Clark."

There are a couple moments of silence on the other end before the man says, "Clark? There's no employee here by the name of Clark."

Think, Mikey, think. Clark used this phone to get a hold of Jay. Mikey thinks of anything else he can ask. What identifiers does he know about Clark? His raggedy haircut is one. Or his sedan. He curses himself for not remembering the license plate number, but he does remember it was a tacky red.

"Oh — maybe I misheard his name. A friend of mine and I were hanging with a fella at the bar the other night and he forgot his . . . wallet. There isn't any ID in it. He was driving a red sedan. I think it was a Toyota."

Mikey's leg is shaking more now. He puts his hand on his knee to steady the shakes, as if the man over the phone might hear.

"Oh, Graham? That's the owner's nephew. He's not in today. If you'd like, you could drop the wallet off here. We don't close until six."

Graham? Is Clark a made-up name? Perhaps he made up the name for AA — some people might be ashamed enough to do that. Then again, in a town like Mendex, it's hard to keep secrets.

Mikey has heard of the lumberyard — it's the only one in Mendex and is on the edge of town.

"I'm at work right now. Does he have a phone number I could reach him at?"

"I can't give out employees' numbers, sir. If you'd like, I can get ahold of him myself."

Shit, that will only end in disaster. For the time being, Mikey has hit a dead end. He can't ask for an address and can't have the employee calling Graham. If Clark really is Graham, he'll know someone's made the connection.

"You know what, I could drop it off tomorrow. When do you guys open?"

"Our office opens at 8 a.m. Graham should be in then."

"Great, thanks." Mikey hangs up.

He wants to keep looking, do anything but wait. But doubt begins to creep into his mind. Is he overreacting? Perhaps Max really is with Graham of her own free will. It's not like she hadn't been trying to do the same exact thing the other night at the restaurant.

Is he acting like a stalker himself, now? Looking for a girl that doesn't want to be found? If Graham really was the man following her, why would he have been seen in public with her all those times? No kidnapper is that brainless.

Mikey exhales. Maybe he just needs to come to terms with reality. He lost her, but he will still wait. Wait to see her in the flesh to know she's safe.

CHAPTER THIRTY-SIX

October 17th, 2009
3:26 p.m.

A couple hours or longer must have passed since Graham came downstairs to feed us and give me my clothing. I'm on edge, listening for any sounds of someone possibly coming down the rickety staircase. About thirty minutes ago, some old country music started blaring from above.

Eva said it's Moe's music. That he plays records whenever he's drinking, which happens to be nearly every night. If it plays for too long, she says, that is a bad sign. That he's drinking extra heavy and will get bored. Bored means he'll come downstairs to play games. The two girls that were here before each ended up being killed on a night like that.

I contemplate asking Eva what these games are, but I don't want to further traumatize her. I need her mind sharp.

Is there a possibility Moe and Joey could drink so much that they pass out? That'll give Graham the chance to call the police or, better yet, take Moe's keys and let Eva and me out. I've just got to make it until they fall asleep. That's it.

I'm depending on too many people. Neither Eva nor Graham seems reliable; each one has warned me against the other. What if, when the time comes, Eva tells Graham of my plan to seduce him so I can grab his keys? Would that mean she'd get better treatment? It's not like she is my biggest fan.

"Why does Graham have such a hard-on for you anyways?" Eva asks.

I bite my lip, wondering if I should tell her. I remember Graham's words. *Don't trust her.* Then again, he could just not want me to get close to her.

"I don't know. He's sick. Just looking for someone who can relate to him."

"You told him about what happened to your mom?"

I nod.

"You're perfect for each other."

I frown. Eva's smirking at me.

"And how is it you've been alive in this basement a whole year? You said two girls have come and gone since then. It can't just be because you treat Moe's son like dirt."

"Because I was smarter than them, that's why." Eva crosses her arms.

"What does that mean?"

"It's really none of your business, Masterson."

"I'm just trying to figure out if I can trust you to help me get us out of here."

"There is no way out of here. Not unless you nut up and kill that freak."

"Humor me."

"Don't you get it? These psychopaths have been doing this shit for years. They know what they're doing and are true to their words."

"And those words are?"

"All the blonde girls die here."

Eva says that in a singsong voice, like she's a robot repeating what's been said to her a dozen times.

All the blonde girls die here.

Why is it that Moe is going after just blonde girls? I think of everything I saw in the farmhouse yesterday. The house seemed off, in the sense it didn't have any family photos or much of any decoration. Wait — that drawing and photograph I found in Graham's room. The woman in it. I feel so shortsighted for not realizing it before. That woman in the photograph has to be Graham's mother, who disappeared. She was beautiful and had an uncanny resemblance to Marilyn Monroe.

So, Moe got his heart broken by the mother of his children and decided murdering innocent girls was the best way to cope. There must be something else to the story. You don't kidnap and torture women because of a broken heart. Moe must have been like this before his wife left.

And if Graham truly is the only son he has left, why treat him so harshly? Does Graham remind Moe of his wife? Or is it to mold him into a sociopath? Continue the family tradition?

"Do you understand now?" Eva asks, breaking my train of thought.

"Understand what?"

"We're going to die down here."

"Don't say that. I just have to think," I reassure her.

"There isn't anything to think about."

"We have a plan. Just trust the plan."

"We don't have shit. You can sit there and talk all you want, but all you care about is saving your own skin. Doing what's best for Max Masterson."

It's not true. I wish I could scream at her that I'm not the same person I used to be. What good would it do? She clearly has never stopped hating me.

What if she's right, though? If I have the chance to escape this house without her, would I leave her behind? My heart says

I would save her. My head, however, thinks of what the safest bet would be. Like it did the night of the party. My head told me what to do, and no matter how much my heart screamed at me to help her, I didn't listen.

"I came to the realization a long time ago that I'm going to die down here. I just don't understand how God would be evil enough to make it be with you."

"Eva, listen—"

"No, you listen. You ruined my life, Max. I know you had a horrible childhood; hell, I even tried to forgive you, thinking of how traumatic it must have been seeing what you saw. But all you did was sit by and watch what happened to me. All for what? A fucking high school boy."

"Now isn't the time for—"

"No, you are going to listen to what I have to say!"

Eva's words startle me. This is the most emotion I've seen her convey since I've been down here. Suddenly she looks awake rather than gloomy and fatigued. I'm sure she's had plenty of time to rehearse this to herself in the year she's been held hostage. I'm just not ready to hear it.

"I felt sick because of how happy it made me that you were going to prison. Justice had finally been done, even if it wasn't for me. But as time went on, I didn't feel better. I still was the same scared girl I'd always been. Afraid to get close to anyone. Then Dennis moved back to Mendex, only a couple blocks from my apartment — you didn't know he was back? Him, his wife, and a couple kids, all happy as can be. I had to pack up and leave. I didn't have a plan or the money to do it, but I couldn't take it any longer. I didn't tell anyone — not even my family. Then my car broke down, and guess who decided to help me out?"

A girl stranded on the road, her car packed with bags. No one to miss her.

"You're saying this is all my fault?"

"I don't like to point fingers, but yes. If you had just done the right thing that night, those boys would be in jail. I would have gone to college. Moved away from this shitty fucking town years ago. Graduated and became what I always wanted to be."

"Fine, this is my fault. I'm the bad guy. How is that going to help us?"

"It's not. I'm just relieved that at least you'll be dying too."

"That's a great boost of confidence."

We both sit in silence for a while. My goal has been to get Eva out of here safely, but I can't do that if she is unwilling to cooperate. She's been down here for too long. She's been around only psychopaths for a year. I can't blame her for no longer believing in a chance for survival.

"I just want us to work together. I want to get us both out of this shithole. What do you want from me?"

"You can tell me the truth."

"The truth?"

"About everything you saw that night."

"It was years ago; it doesn't matter any—"

"It matters to me!" Eva screams, so loudly I'm worried they'll hear us upstairs.

If they do, they'll come down. Drunk and ready to play a game. Eva has tears streaming down her face, which is bright red with anger. It will be more than apparent we have been arguing. I need to mitigate this problem, but she's asking me to talk about the one thing I've kept bottled up for years.

"I'm sorry. Of course it matters. It's just—"

"It's just what?" Eva interrupts me.

"This will create a barrier between us. We need each other."

"It will create a bigger barrier if you don't own up to the past."

This is going to be a big mistake. Telling her my account of that night will crush her. She already has a faint idea of what happened. But she doesn't know the entire truth of it. The things I witnessed and turned away from. I still remember how she stood on my porch the following morning, looking an utter mess. She asked me to tell her the truth then too. I turned my back on her, thinking she deserved her pain for stealing Dennis away when she knew I liked him. I'd finally won a losing game. I became like my mother, hell-bent on getting my way no matter who it hurt.

I take a deep breath and say, "I remember everything. I was drunk but . . . coherent. I got to the party around ten—"

Before I can finish, the basement door opens. I'm almost relieved, but then I see the three shadows making their way downstairs.

CHAPTER THIRTY-SEVEN

May 26th, 2000
11:32 p.m.

I've been at this party for over an hour, and Dennis Formont has said a total of four words to me. I've done everything to outdo Eva Willems this year, and she's bested me yet again. I swore for our last senior end-of-year party I would finally make Dennis notice me.

So here I am, hair lightly curled and braided in a Britney Spears homage, squeezed into this cranberry minidress that lands just below my ass and squashes my boobs so I can hardly breathe. And yet the moment I walked into the party and saw Dennis's arm draped around Eva, I knew she had won again. Without making nearly as much effort as me. All she's done is straighten her hair like she always does and put on a shimmering blue satin dress. She isn't even wearing jewelry, or heavy makeup. It's as if she's just finished a volleyball game and is glistening with sweat.

I hate her, and I hate my father for never getting me the nice things she has. Her teeth are whiter than mine, she's in better shape, and always wears the cutest clothes, her style effortless. I had to beg Dad for months to get me this dress and the black wedge slides to go with it. Eva's wearing ankle straps, which I had considered going with instead. Not that it would have mattered. Everyone would have seen me copying the perfect Eva Willems.

It's my past; it has to be. I've spent years trying to leave my family's dysfunctional past behind. By sophomore year, I solidified my place in the standings at school. Boys started noticing me; other girls beamed at my beauty. Then it all came crashing down when Eva enrolled in our school, fresh from the Netherlands. She was perfect at volleyball and became a starter her junior year. What took me two years to do, she did in under six months. Became the most popular girl at school. The one all the boys talked about and all the girls followed, dying to be a part of her clique.

I even tried being her friend. She was getting invited to all the big parties, and that meant I would have the chance to be there. I just wanted a chance with Dennis Formont. We had English class together, and I'd managed to talk to him a couple times. Every girl in school wanted him, and perhaps that's why I wanted him too. Then Eva showed up with her ridiculous Dutch accent and shiny long blonde hair. All my months' work of getting Dennis to notice me was for nothing.

I made one last-ditch effort to steal Dennis away from Eva. I wasn't even rude or malicious about it. Eva and I had been hanging out by that time. I told her I'd had a crush on Dennis for months. She plastered a big fake smile on her face and said we'd be the cutest couple. Not two days later, I found out the two were going out.

This party is supposed to be my time to show Dennis what he's missing. Show him I can outshine any stupid pretty Dutch girl. Maybe there's still time. I just need a drink. Something to loosen me up.

The party is at the house of David Spiker, one of the linebackers. His parents are always out of town, so this isn't my first time at a party here. I head for the drinks table and find an assortment of liquor. WKD Blue, hooch, a few bottles of wine, and a couple six-packs of beer stuffed in buckets of ice. They really are going all out for this party. If it weren't for my plan and taking over two hours to get ready, I would've been here earlier, already blacked out. Or in their pool, swimming with my friends.

I settle on a bottle of Cîroc vodka and pop the bottle open. I take a gulp, watching as Dennis and Eva smile at each other while they talk to a group of football players. That should be me.

I'm only eighteen, but my tolerance for liquor is already higher than my friends'. A couple shots will do them for the night. I need nearly half a bottle. It must be a genetic effect from my mother. That, or it's thanks to the nips I'm always sneaking from my father's drinks cabinet.

As the two continue to chat, I take some more gulps of the vodka. I'm unable to keep my eyes off them. Watching Dennis stare at Eva the way he does makes me clench my fists.

"What are you doing, Maxy pants?" a man behind me says, and a moment later I feel a hand graze my lower back.

David Spiker. He's a large guy, towering six foot five and over two hundred and twenty pounds. He's a cocky drunk, but I figured out a long time ago to stay on his good side. He's slept with nearly the entirety of the cheerleading squad and volleyball team. I know this because a list he made got spread around the whole school, ranking the girls' bodies. I find him appalling, but since his parents are loaded, he gets away with it.

"Don't call me Maxy pants."

"I wouldn't worry too much about her," he says.

"Who?"

"Come on, Maxy. I know it, Dennis knows it. Hell, the whole school knows you love Dennis and hate that Dutch chick."

Have I been that obvious? I've always tried to keep it low profile. I've even gone out on dates with other guys in school. Of course, none of them meant anything. I just wanted to make Dennis jealous.

"I-I don't hate Eva. She's just not right for him."

"Well, after tonight, you won't have to worry about that."

I take another gulp, wondering what David could possibly mean by that. Eva and Dennis have been inseparable since they started dating six months ago. Did she do something that everyone knows about, except Dennis? Was David going to tell Dennis about it tonight?

"What do you mean, after tonight?"

David pats my back and winks at me. Without answering, he walks toward Dennis and Eva. Oh shit, is he going to tell him I've been over here fawning over him for the last twenty minutes?

"David," I call out, wanting to reach out and grab his arm, but he's already too far away.

I watch as he leans over and whispers something to Dennis. I can't take this. I turn around to hide, hopefully making David look like the stupid drunk he is. Actually, he isn't wasted yet, which is unusual. Normally he gets drunk before I do. Maybe tonight he's trying to remain sober to remember whichever girl he sleeps with.

I go to the bathroom and lock myself in. I pee and continue taking swigs from the bottle. The bathroom is large and in disarray thanks to the party. I mull over whether to make myself throw up, so I won't feel so sick in the morning, but that risks giving me vomit breath.

I go to the large round mirror above the porcelain sink and look at myself. My vision is blurry. I blink hard several times to clear it. My skin is red, despite my foundation. I splash some water on my face and take a swig straight from the faucet.

When there's a knock on the bathroom door, I take one last drink from my bottle before unlocking the door. I stumble past two of my classmates, who laugh at my clumsiness. Or are they laughing because they know I'm hopelessly in love with Dennis? It induces a feeling of anger in me I've never felt. How is Eva better than me? Word around school is, she won't even have sex with Dennis. I would've. Doesn't he understand my commitment to him?

Maybe that's what she's planning to do tonight — give herself to Dennis. Is that what David was talking about?

I go back to my spot by the drinks table. Now all the people walking by me have begun to blur together. I don't care how drunk I am. If this is what will give me the confidence to talk to Dennis, then so be it. There's so much I've wanted to say to him. Now may be my last chance.

David is no longer standing near Dennis. Eva is, though. Her arm is around his waist and she's pressing her body into his.

As soon as the two of them see me approaching, Eva rolls her eyes. Almost like she's been expecting this.

"Dennis, I need to talk to you." I try to maintain my balance and keep my words from slurring.

"Max, what's up?" Dennis asks, looking at me with big amber eyes, a half-smile exposing those perfect white teeth.

I open my mouth to speak, but now that I'm here, the alcohol in my system has flooded my brain. The monologue I had prepared turns to mush as I stare into those dreamy eyes.

"I just wanted to talk in private. It'll only take a couple minutes. I promise," I finally say.

I can say what I need to if I can get Dennis alone. Get away from Eva and the constantly moving bodies around us, chanting and yelling. If I can get him away from all this, I might be able to think properly.

"Dennis is busy." Eva leans down to my level like I'm a child.

She looks as drunk as I am. She has a red Solo cup in her hand, and as she staggers, the drink spills out. Her eyes are glazed over like mine. She might even be more intoxicated. It's strange seeing her this drunk.

"I just want to talk for a—"

"She's already wasted. She's always fucking wasted," Eva murmurs to Dennis, cutting me off.

I want to clock her in the face. If I don't get the chance to talk to Dennis, I'll just punch her instead.

"I'm not wast—"

"When are you not wasted, Masterson?"

She's not wrong. I drink as heavily and as often as the football players. Mostly, I drink to escape my family's past. Is that why Dennis doesn't like me?

"I got it, hon." Dennis lays a kiss on Eva's cheek and takes a step toward me.

He puts his arm around my shoulder and turns us around to walk a few feet away.

"Now's not really a good time, Max," he whispers to me.

"It'll just take a second. I just . . . want . . . wanted to tell . . . you—"

"Go drink some water. I'll find you in a bit, okay?"

He doesn't give me time to respond. Instead, he flashes one of his signature smiles and goes back to Eva, who's eyeing me like a hawk. I want to hit her, to push her to the ground. Wipe that smug look off her face. But Dennis said we'd talk soon. Maybe he's going to break up with her tonight. He must have seen how drunk I am and wants to wait until I'm sober to express his feelings for me. Tell me he's sorry for choosing Eva over me. David said I wouldn't have to worry about her anymore. Those two are good friends; that must mean something.

I trust that Dennis will be back. In the meantime, I'll do as he says. I'll drink some water.

CHAPTER THIRTY-EIGHT

May 27th, 2000
1:04 a.m.

It's over. Eva has won. I haven't seen the two of them in over twenty minutes. I went to the bathroom and failed in my attempt to throw up. When I returned, the two of them had disappeared. Now I am sitting at the kitchen counter nursing a plastic water bottle, on the brink of tears.

Everyone at the party is three sheets to the wind. I would be too if it weren't for Dennis telling me we'd talk later. I put the bottle down an hour ago so I could be better prepared to talk to him.

Now he's gone and I hate him. And I hate David for giving me false hope. I want to find David and give him a piece of my mind, but he, too, has disappeared. It could have all been one big joke: giving me hope that I had a chance and then watching as I cry in the kitchen all by myself.

This is all my mother's fault. When I was growing up, she never trained me properly, and now I'm falling for someone I can't have. Everyone around me knows what she did, and they can only see her in me. Even my father sees her in me. I can tell by the way he avoids me with his work and liquor. He doesn't even notice I'm out every weekend doing whatever I want. He probably enjoys my absence.

As I sit in the kitchen feeling sorry for myself, one of my friends, Brooklyn, walks in. She's in a swimsuit and dripping wet. I should've just gone swimming in David's massive pool and had fun. Brooklyn, seeing me at the counter, frowns. She already knows about my feelings for Dennis and has repeatedly told me that falling for a jock is an easy way to get your heart broken.

"What are you doing?" she asks.

"Drinking away my sorrows." I put the water down and raise the bottle of vodka to take a swig. I haven't had a drink in over an hour, and now that my stomach feels better from the water, I might as well get back at it.

"What happened now?" she asks.

"Dennis told me earlier we would talk, but then he disappeared with Eva."

Brooklyn sighs. She leans closer to me and whispers, "Denise told me that Roger saw those two head upstairs, like, twenty minutes ago. I'm only telling you this because I think Eva's finally going to let him go all the way."

"And this is helping me how?"

"Walk in there. Tell Dennis your feelings."

"I don't really want to see that. Besides, he'll think I'm some crazy stalker."

"So what? He's been stringing you along way too long."

I'm silent as I realize she's right. I don't deserve this. These whole two years I've been pining for Dennis, he's been casually flirting with me. He even flirted with me after Eva and he started dating. If I want a chance of finding any shred of courage, I need to come out with what I'm feeling. That what he's been doing to me is unfair. In the end, he may call me a lunatic and never want to speak to me again, but at least I'd finally be at peace. Knowing once and for all it was never meant to be.

"Fuck, you're right." I hoist myself off the counter.

"Fucking A, I am," Brooklyn cheers, grabbing a nearby can of beer and cracking it open. "You got this."

I lift my bottle and we clink our drinks together. We both take a drink, and then I head for the stairs.

I ascend to the second floor. By this point, the newly imbibed alcohol in my system has taken over, and I have to tightly grasp the handrails to go up every step.

I try the first door I see, but it's locked. I knock on the door for a full minute until a boy on the basketball team, who is undressed and blocking his crotch with a throw pillow, answers. Sitting on the bed is a girl covered in blankets.

"Trying to join the fun, Max?" the boy asks, winking at me.

"Get out!" the girl on the bed screams at me.

"Sorry," I stammer, walking off and hearing the door slam behind me.

I stumble into a lamp, knocking it over. I take a few steady breaths as I begin to realize how crazy this idea is. What if the door's locked and they don't answer? What if they do, and the sight of Eva and Dennis together is too much for me?

Be brave, Max.

I lean against the wall, stepping over the tipped-over lamp. I narrowly miss running into a console table sitting between the bathroom door and the room I'm guessing is David's. As I stand outside the door, I take more deep breaths. The door is a bright firetruck red. It's giving me a headache.

It's now or never. Time to let go of these emotions. If he rejects me, at least in the end I'll know I tried.

I debate knocking but decide against it. Eva will just force Dennis not to answer. I put my hand on the doorknob and swing the door open.

Am I hallucinating? Is my mind playing tricks on me? Because this . . . this is far worse than anything I ever expected to see.

CHAPTER THIRTY-NINE

May 27th, 2000
1:16 a.m.

Eva is lying face down on the bed, her dress hiked up over her waist and panties down to her ankles. Another football boy — Red, I think his name is — is standing directly behind her, his pants undone. There are three other boys in the room as well. Another senior I cannot recall the name of, David, and Dennis. They're just standing by watching, a beer in each of their hands.

"Dennis?" I say with a gasp.

The boys all stare at me. The only person who doesn't is Eva. Her eyes are half closed and she's staring at the wall like a psychiatric patient getting a lobotomy. Red quickly pulls Eva's dress down to hide her exposed body and buckles his pants back up.

"David, what the fuck? You were supposed to lock the door," he yells.

"Shit," David says. He steps toward me.

I move back, my mouth ajar, unsure what to say or do. I'm frozen in my drunken state. I can't run; I can barely breathe.

"I got this," Dennis says, stepping in front of David.

Dennis's eyes are calm, as if I didn't just walk in on Red about to . . . well. What have I walked in on? Were they about to take

185

turns on Eva? She's too drunk to consent. What do I do? Run? Dennis is looking at me with fiendish eyes.

Dennis puts his arm around my shoulder. He's more sober than I originally thought.

"Max, come with me," he says, turning me around and leading me out the door.

He is practically carrying me. All the alcohol I've consumed finally feels like it's about to come out again. Dennis shuts the door behind us. He rests my body against the wall next to the door.

"What . . . what's going on?" I ask, pushing my weight against the wall and clutching my stomach to stop myself from vomiting.

"Nothing, Eva's just sick. She drank too much and needed to lie down," Dennis calmly tells me, resting his hand on my shoulder and looking directly into my eyes.

What does her being sick have to do with her dress being hiked up and her panties being down to her ankles? My thoughts are running wild. I look away from Dennis and at the freshly vacuumed ivory carpet.

"Why are you up here? I told you we'd talk." Dennis leans closer to me and tilts my face back toward him.

I want to scream, to run away. What's going on in that room isn't right. What can I say, though? I'm drunk, and if I go downstairs and even attempt to explain what I saw, everyone will look at me like I'm crazy.

"You disappeared. I just wanted to find you," I finally say.

He smiles lightly. "I'm sorry, Max. I haven't been fair. You know I like you, right?"

Like me? That aching need to throw up is gone momentarily.

"No, I didn't know that."

"Silly girl. Of course I do. I was going to put Eva to bed and come talk to you. I just wanted to give you time to sober up. Talk to the real Max."

"It just seemed like what I saw in there wasn't—"

"Hey, you're my girl." Dennis caresses my jaw with his thumb.

I can't let him distract me like this. I just can't imagine Dennis, my Dennis, being a part of something so horrific.

"Dennis—"

"Shh." He leans over and faintly kisses my cheek.

I can't explain it, but suddenly the feel of Dennis's lips on my cheek erases my racing thoughts. I've dreamed of him kissing me for years.

"I'll meet you in the kitchen in fifteen minutes, okay?"

I slowly nod. "For real this time, right?"

"Absolutely. I've been wanting to talk to you all night."

I blush, looking away.

"I'll see you in fifteen?"

"Okay."

I watch him disappear back into the room. This time, when the door closes, I hear it being locked.

Shit, just a kiss on the cheek and I've allowed Dennis to twist my mind up.

Help her. You have to help her.

I stare at the door, wondering how I can help her. I could get a group of boys downstairs. Get them to bust the door down. I'm sure one of them would have the moral capacity to stop what is happening. Or at least find a girl that would. Would they even believe me?

You know I like you, right?

Dennis's words ring in my ears. I imagine us holding hands, kissing tenderly on the lips. Him looking at me the same way he looks at Eva. After this, he'll be done with Eva. What did she ever do to help me anyhow? I remember her poking fun at me being drunk all the time. Now who's the one that's too wasted? She probably won't even remember anything that's happened to her. That might be for the best.

Something shifts in my head. The earlier thoughts urging me to help my archnemesis disappear. Now I'm only thinking of that talk I'll have with Dennis. Now's my time to have the boy I want.

I'm going to hell, I think as I walk downstairs.

CHAPTER FORTY

October 17th, 2009
3:57 p.m.

Eva and I go to our cots and press our backs to the wall. Staying as far from the door as possible. I don't know if I'm relieved or terrified by Moe reentering the basement. On one hand, I was able to avoid telling Eva the truth. The truth of what I decided to ignore. Saying it will break me, will rattle my brain back to that night. I can't do that, not here. I need to stay sharp and plan our escape. Digging up the past won't aid in that.

I attempt to calm myself. I know my face is still flushed rosy red. I look over at Eva and see she's red hot with anger and tears are streaming from her eyes. Moe will just assume we're angry and miserable. It's not like he cares how his captives are feeling.

Once again, Moe is leading the group and Graham is in the back. He instantly makes eye contact with me; his shoulders are slumped, and his face appears filled with stress. Moe stops in front of the cages and crosses his arms, looking at both Eva and me.

"You two having a party down here?"

We don't respond. I pray the redness in my cheeks will go away and Eva will stop crying. The way Moe is staring at us frightens me. Like he can sniff the uneasiness in the room. All the women he's taken, he must be able to read our pain with ease.

"They look like two little girlies who lost their teddy bears," the uncle says, before taking a drink from a mason jar filled with a clear substance.

"What's wrong?" Moe asks.

Eva casts a quick look my way. She shakes her head.

Say something! Say anything except the truth.

"I don't blame her. I wouldn't like that bitch, either," the uncle says.

"No, no, no. It's never been like this. What was it saying to you? Was it trying to convince you into trying anything?"

Eva remains silent. I wish she'd say something, anything.

"Because if it was, you know the consequences, right? You've seen the consequences."

He's smart, too smart. He stares at us for a long while, as if attempting to read our thoughts. I do my best to appear normal.

"Hey, aren't they both from here? Maybe they know each other," Joey points out.

Moe raises his eyebrows as if a lightbulb has just turned on above his head. *Oh no.*

"You two . . . you two know each other?"

My heart drops. I hold my breath to stop myself from shaking. Even Graham is looking at me suspiciously. What would he think of me if he knew the truth?

"No," I say as casually as I can.

"I wasn't talking to you," Moe says.

He takes out the same knife that he cut my pinkie off with and approaches Eva's cage. She keeps her eyes down and wipes her tears away.

"I asked you a question. Tell me, do you know each other?"

Eva sighs. "We went to high school together."

That's all, just say we went to high school together and leave it at that. I know a psychopath like Moe won't care what happened that night, but it might give him ideas for torturing me. Get in Eva's head. End our chance of working together.

"It certainly is a small world, huh?"

"Why'd the bitch lie, though?" the uncle says, pointing at me.

"Yeah, if it's that simple, why did it lie?" Moe asks Eva.

I wish I could speak. Come up with a clever excuse. *Just say we were fighting over a boy. Don't share the rest.*

"We didn't get along." Eva wraps her arms around her body.

"Probably over a boy," Uncle Joey comments.

"You're both the same age, right?" Moe asks.

Eva nods.

"Well, don't keep me in suspense. What happened?"

Why does Moe care? What is he getting at? Just like when he dropped the key, I don't know. Sure, I had a feeling it would end badly for me, my hand smashed up or something, but never did I expect him to cut my pinkie off. I'm in the dark when it comes to the way Moe thinks.

"She wanted the guy I was dating."

Oh God, Eva, just stop! He's playing with us. He doesn't care. Just drunk and, as she put it, bored.

"Don't tell me it stole him from you? You're much prettier than that thing. Should've seen the missing pictures around town. You were a looker."

Until you took her and turned her into a malnourished crazy person. Doesn't Eva see he's just playing mind games with her? Trying to get her to crack?

"You can say that." Eva's crying again.

"Eva—"

"Shut the fuck up!" Moe yells at me, causing me to shrink back like a dog being yelled at by its abusive owner. "Tell me what happened."

"Father, why does it matter?" Graham asks.

"Why does everyone keep interrupting me?" Moe asks, casting a look back at his son.

Graham bows his head.

Eva speaks up. "She was in love with my boyfriend."

"Did he cheat on you with it?"

Please, no. I think of that night. All the liquor I drank. The way Dennis kissed my cheek so softly and looked at me with his beautiful sparkling eyes. How his gaze made my mind numb to contrition.

The next morning, when I woke up with a hangover, the night's events really cemented in my head: that I had left Eva in a den of wolves. And just as I was processing that, there was a knock at the front door and Eva was there, looking a mess. She wept on my doorstep. Even in her drugged state that night, she'd heard my voice and remembered that. But she didn't remember anything else. She begged me to tell her what had happened to her — had Dennis raped her? I told her to stop making things up, that Dennis was mine now and nothing she could say would change that. And then I slammed the door in her face.

"No, it wasn't that. Max, why don't you tell him?"

Everyone's eyes shift to me. I freeze. I've been preparing myself to tell Eva the truth, but not like this. Not as a part of Moe's twisted game. Why is she doing this? Has her anger over the years really boiled up so high that she's ready to feed me to the wolves? I am not her enemy here. I am her enemy from high school. These men will kill her once they're bored.

"This isn't their business." I put on the bravest face I possibly can.

"Maxine, just tell us," Graham says.

I don't have time to react or reply. I look over at Graham just in time to see Moe swiftly slap him across the face. It's a hard enough slap that Graham shrinks away.

"Don't ever call it that! Do you understand that, boy?" Moe yells, moving as if to strike him a second time.

"Yes, sir," Graham says, shielding his face.

I don't understand why Graham doesn't beat this old man down. He's small, but he could easily overpower him. Moe is old and just as thin as Graham. He really does have Graham convinced he's still the alpha male. I need to remind Graham that's not the case. That his father is manipulating him.

"Either you can tell us, or I can assume you deserve to die right here, right now." Moe lowers his hand and turns to face me again.

When I don't speak, he says, "Graham, hand me the pliers."

CHAPTER FORTY-ONE

October 17th, 2009
4:06 p.m.

Pliers?

"Wait, wait. Okay, okay," I yell, my throat aching from the pressure of the bracket.

I look over at Eva. I try to imagine we're alone. I remember her face from that night. How she lay on David's bed like a rag doll. I knew she had been drugged. I knew if I left that room, she wasn't going to be put to bed. That those boys would have their way with her. I ignored the thought of all her pain and suffering. Only thought of how she took Dennis from me. That if I ignored all I'd seen, he'd be mine. I thought of myself and only myself. She deserves to know, and I deserve all the consequences.

Tears are forming in my eyes. I wipe them away, hating myself for crying again in front of these men. Eva looks at me hopefully. Like she is going to hear something she doesn't already know but desperately wants to. But she knows what those boys did. She has to. I didn't hide my expression well the day after, when she came over. She needs closure.

"What's the last thing you remember from that night?"

"I remember you coming up to us in the living room, and realizing I was drunk. I only had three or four drinks. Dennis made them all for me. I remember your voice later, but I don't remember where I was. After that, things get dark."

Three or four drinks? I had triple that. There's no argument; she was drugged.

"That night at the party, I went upstairs to David's room. I went up there to demand answers from Dennis. He said he'd talk to me later, but he hadn't come to find me, so I went looking for him. I thought I'd walk in on just you two. You were . . . you were in there. I walked in on you half passed out on the bed. Your . . . dress was hiked up over your body, and your underwear was down. One of the football—"

I choke as I speak. As I'm explaining what happened, it's like I'm back in that bedroom. Watching the worst and ready to just walk away. I feel more tears fall from my eyes.

"Are you seriously the one crying right now?" Eva asks.

"I was a stupid teenager. I know that's no excuse—"

"There were other boys in that room?"

Eva is pressing her hands against the bars that separate us. If those bars weren't there, she would be on me. Choking me, forcing the rest of the story from my mouth.

"Red Adkins, he was standing over you. He got angry at David for not locking the door. Reece Jefferson was in there too. And David and Dennis. Dennis told me you were sick."

"Are you kidding me?"

"I didn't think Dennis would lie to me."

Another lie. I knew he would lie, I just didn't want to care. Didn't want to annoy Dennis.

"Bullshit!" Eva yells, pounding her fists on the bars.

"And . . . I left. Dennis came down twenty minutes later. Told me to never speak of what happened, and I . . . did what he told me."

Eva scoffs, pressing her forehead against the bars. At this point I'd rather take Moe's beating than be stuck in this room with her.

"There were four of them in there?" Eva asks, after a minute.

I nod.

"And you stood there at your door while I begged you to tell me the truth. You saw what it did to me. For years I thought I was crazy. I thought it was just Dennis who raped me. Thought maybe he paid you to keep his secret."

"No, he just broke it off with you and started dating me. I'm sorry. I was just a stupid teenager. I didn't—"

"Shut up, Max! You give that stupid excuse again, I swear to God."

Eva's body is shaking with anger. I've felt guilty about this secret my whole life, but now as I'm telling her, I feel as if I've submerged my entire body in the reality of what I did. It brings me back to my dream last night. How real it felt. How I felt like I was drowning in that water. How Eva, George, and Billy were there. The ones I hurt. It meant something. I cannot go back and save George or Billy, but I can save Eva. I must save her.

"I really am sorry, Eva."

Eva doesn't speak; she just continues to stare at me. I wish it were only us in the room. That I could tell her that if it's the last thing I do, I will save her.

"And I thought we were the bad ones." Uncle Joey begins laughing.

Moe has a tiny smirk on his face. It's as if he's gaining pleasure from watching this. Graham looks dumbfounded. He must despise me.

"I think it's time for some retribution," Moe says.

"Retribution?" Joey asks, still laughing.

"For the creature," he responds, taking a set of keys out.

He unlocks the door to Eva's cage. She cowers away from him, still shaking. Moe, knife in hand, enters her cage and unlocks the chain that secures her ankle to the ground. He pulls the chain out of the cage, and Eva, like a dog, follows him on her hands and knees.

"Get your girlfriend out." Moe throws his keys at Graham, who's clearly still in shock.

Graham misses the catch and fumbles to pick them up. I stare at the ground as he approaches my cage, making sure I don't make eye contact with him. Graham cuts my ankles free first, then the bracket around my throat. He grabs me by the arm and takes me from the cage. I look at my surroundings, wondering if there is any chance of escape. If I could grab Eva and bolt with her upstairs. Graham's hold on my arm is soft, almost like he's caring for a wounded animal. His hand is shaking as if he's unprepared for what's about to unfold.

Joey stands guard at the bottom of the stairs, his arms folded like a bodyguard at a club. There's no way I'll be able to overpower him and get past, but if I could, I could certainly outrun him. The only one here I know I can't outrun is Graham. *He's the one who caught me. Why didn't he let me get away? Perhaps he thought Moe and Joey would've caught me eventually anyways.*

Graham said something about going to his uncle's place to look for sleeping pills, so that means Joey doesn't live here. If Joey leaves, perhaps I can talk Graham into overpowering his father.

"Put it there," Moe instructs Graham, pointing to a spot a couple yards across from where Eva is standing.

Is Moe going to grab me like some sadistic killer in the movies and put me on the meat hook? Let everyone watch and take turns stabbing me as I shriek? Make me the laughingstock I deserve to be? Would it bring Eva some happiness, watching me suffer at the hands of these men? Would she think it's a fitting punishment? But doesn't she want me alive, to get Graham into the cage? Perhaps her mind is so far gone and the desire to see me suffer so ingrained she no longer cares about surviving.

"I've only ever done this once, and, well, that . . . that was for fun. Eva, this is for you."

Everyone in the room looks at Moe in amazement. He just said her name. Although he had struck Graham in anger for saying mine, he just used Eva's.

"What's for me?" she asks.

"Hit it," he orders, pointing at me.

Eva looks at me and back at Moe. *What game is this?* He can't care about what happened to Eva. He just wants to see me in pain.

"Go on," he says casually.

Eva and I stare at each other for a moment longer. She moves toward me, and I instinctively take a step back.

"Hold it down," Moe orders Graham.

"But Father—"

"Hold it down!" he screams.

Graham takes a tight hold, securing my hands behind my back.

"Eva, you don't have to do this." But a part of me knows that isn't true.

Eva stares at me with the same pure hatred she had when I told her about what happened at the party. Her big blue eyes seem to flash red — am I hallucinating?

This is what I deserve. I know the pain I've caused her. I can't imagine what's going through her head. She thought she had been raped by her boyfriend, which was bad enough; now she's discovered it was a gang rape. And the one girl who could've stopped it but didn't is standing right in front of her.

Eva moves closer to me, till we're only a couple inches apart. I can hear her heavy breathing. She lifts her right arm in the air and in one swift movement, slaps me across the face. I hardly wince. The pain isn't significant. It's like being slapped by a child.

"Come on, that's it? This is the thing that let you be railed by four different guys," Moe says. Joey chuckles.

Eva angrily stares at them. She looks back at me and instead of lifting an open hand she balls it into a fist and, with a loud grunt, punches me in the face. That has more kick. Then another punch lands on my left cheek with more force. I taste blood on my gums. I refuse to give these men the satisfaction of seeing me in pain again. I take the hit, hardly wincing.

"That was a little better. You got to put more force into it. Try to think of that night. It didn't care you were brutalized, so why should you care if you hurt it?" Moe says, his eyes never leaving mine.

I'm irritating him by not begging for mercy. That brings me some relief. I swear I will not allow him to win this. I got punched a couple times in prison by other women. Those women were bigger and stronger than Eva. I took it then; I can take it now.

Eva once again raises her fist. She steadies herself this time and pulls her hand back more before punching me again. I spit blood onto the ground. I bite my lip to save my face from showing any pain. This time I look down to keep my composure.

"Bitch can take a hit," Joey comments.

I feel Graham's heavy breathing in my ear. I get a whiff of rum. I wish I could have had a drink earlier. That would've made this more bearable.

"Again, Eva," Moe orders.

"Fuck you, Max Masterson," she breathes, striking me.

My knees buckle this time. Graham's hold on me loosens and he lets me fall. I stare at my blood and tears mingling on the cold ground.

That last hit felt the most personal. Eva is enjoying this. I hope this breaks her hatred toward me. I hope this will give her closure.

"That's enough, Father," Graham says.

Eva snarls at Graham's request and grabs ahold of my hair to pull me back up. Before I can flinch, she punches me again. Her knuckles are bleeding.

Eva lets go of my hair and I fall to the ground.

"I said that's enough!" Graham screams, coming between us.

He pushes Eva away. She's already out of breath and falls to her ass like a rag doll.

CHAPTER FORTY-TWO

October 17th, 2009
4:12 p.m.

I appreciate Graham coming to my aid, but I know he'll pay for sticking up for me.

"All right, calm down." Moe takes ahold of Graham's shoulders. "Why do you care? That thing killed your brother. Now you're stopping someone else from getting their vengeance?"

"You took it too far. Look at it." Graham points at me just as I am spitting more blood out.

"Don't be such a pussy," Joey says.

"Fuck you," Graham mutters under his breath.

"Fuck you!" Joey screams, leaving his spot by the stairs and stomping toward Graham.

I expect Graham to cower back, but he does the opposite. He squares up to the bigger man. I crawl away to avoid the oncoming fight. The stairway's unguarded now. Is the door at the top unlocked? If I make a run for it, how far will I get? Could I reach Graham's car or that creepy van? Would the keys be in the ignition, or somewhere in the house? My head aches so much from the beating and the loss of blood, I can barely think straight.

"What? Now you decide to grow some balls?" Joey's face is a mere inch from Graham's.

"Yeah. I caught it. I decide what I want to do with it."

I inch my way toward the stairs. Eva's still on her ass, cradling her knees with her bloodied hands. I should be angry with her for punching me, but I'm not. I deserved it. And I have a goal: to save her.

Graham and Joey continue to argue while I take slow steps backward toward the stairs. Moe's attention is on both of them. If the door is open, I could make it. Lock the door and use the phone to call the police.

I may never have this chance again. I can't keep waiting around for Graham to save me.

Be brave, Maxine.

Taking a deep breath, I bolt up the stairs.

CHAPTER FORTY-THREE

October 17th, 2009
4:14 p.m.

I'm halfway up the staircase. I can do this.

"Moe, Moe," I hear Joey say behind me, obviously noticing I have made a run for it.

I make it to the top. The door is shut. I grab the doorknob. It doesn't turn.

Shit.

I beat my fists against the door. Someone grabs ahold of my hair and pulls me back.

"No!" I scream, hands outstretched to the locked door as I'm forced back down the stairs.

At the bottom, I feel whoever grabbed me press my body into theirs. I peer behind me to see Joey, a wild look on his face. I attempt to escape from his grasp. He tightly secures an arm around my waist and takes a knife out of his pocket, holding it close to my throat.

"Why you leaving? The party's down here," Joey says, taking a long lick along my cheek. His stubble presses into my cheek.

The smell of his breath is revolting. The smell of his body odor is worse. It's as if he hasn't showered in days and has spent said days under the sun. The saliva he leaves on my cheek is thick and reeks of tobacco. The smell is so bad it momentarily distracts me from the blade scraping against my throat.

"Let me go!" I scream, moving my head from his.

"Joey, take her upstairs and outside," Moe says.

The two smile at each other as if that's code for something. What could be so awful about going outside? Is that the final area where they slaughter the girls? Joey picks me up like I weigh nothing and carries me up the stairs, through the door, and into the kitchen. I see through the holey curtains that it's still daylight out. It felt like I was down in the basement for an eternity, but in reality, it can't have been more than a few hours.

At the front door, Joey sets me down to unlock the two deadbolts.

"Move and I'll slit your throat," he whispers.

I can't hear anyone else following us. They must be locking Eva back up. Where is Graham? I need him here now before this repulsive man can spend another minute alone with me. Moe may be the most daunting of the group, but feeling Joey's hands on my body gives me the creeps.

I remember early on he mentioned Graham hadn't showed up to work, so that must mean they work together. If anyone out there can remember me being with Graham and figure out his real name, his job might come up. I know the time I was supposed to be at work has been and gone. Aunt Almeida must have called my father. Maybe they'll band together and call Jay. Find out about the new guy at AA.

Once the door is unlocked, Joey shoves it open and pushes me outside. He takes a sharp right and herds me toward the barn. But we're not going in there — we walk past it.

"Uncle Joey, what are you doing?" Graham yells from behind us.

Joey hoists me up again, as if anticipating trouble. "Your little girlfriend's staying the night in the graveyard."

Graveyard. What is that? I begin squirming, frantically kicking my legs in the air.

"Stay still!" Joey yells hoarsely.

He sets me down but still keeps a tight hold of me. As I try to wiggle free he presses the knife against my throat. The blade nicks my skin, and I feel warm blood trickling down my chest.

"Wait, no. She doesn't need to go down there."

Graham attempts to put his hand on Joey's shoulder, but the older man turns the knife on Graham, pointing it at him. He raises his hands in the hair.

Joey once again is lifting me up and moving forward. Around the back of the barn, I see a metal box with a door on top surrounded by long weeds and grass. It's the width of a small dumpster. One that would be used as a slurry pit. Something a farmer would dump dead animals' bones or things they can no longer find a use for.

"Open the hatch, boy," Joey orders Graham, who has once again caught back up to us.

"She'll die down there," Graham pleads.

"She'll be fine. Still fuckable, I promise."

"Just put her down. Let's talk about this."

"You'll do no such thing," Moe says from behind us.

Moe has a pistol and a pair of handcuffs. He walks to face me with the handcuffs open. I scream, kicking my legs out and hitting him on the knees. Uncle Joey sighs and throws me to the ground, hard. I scream again as he gets on top of me. His weight is unbearable, and I feel the air leave my lungs.

Moe handcuffs me.

"Dad, no!" Graham yells.

Moe, clearly losing patience with his son's disobedience, points the pistol at Graham.

"Get back in the house, boy!" he yells.

Graham looks at me, to which Moe responds by angrily clubbing the pistol across his face. He falls to the ground, touching the side of his face where the gun made contact. The side I already hit with the coffee cup. It's bruised and has scratch marks on it from the cup.

"Yes, sir." He slowly gets to his feet and, with one last look at me, turns around and runs off.

I want to curse at him. Curse at him for leaving so easily. He's the one that's supposed to be my savior. How can he be defeated just like that? I've lost my finger and taken a beating, and I've still stood up more to Moe in the past five minutes than Graham has this whole time. At the very least he could go inside and use the phone to call the police. I watch him disappear out of eyesight. I can barely breathe under Joey's weight, let alone talk. So much for the plan. I'm about to be dumped into this pit and left for dead.

I hate Graham. Hate myself for believing he could have been my savior. Hell, I wanted to save him from this. The man is twenty-eight years old and still acting like a scared child when it comes to his old man. Eva was right all along.

Moe is shaking his head. "Fucking kid."

He walks to the pit and opens the metal hatch. The lid rests against the barn wall. Inside the hatch is complete darkness.

"Ready to put the bitch in?" Uncle Joey asks.

Moe nods, looking down at me. "It's timeout time."

Moe takes me by the arms, and Joey finally gets off me and grabs my legs. They lift me up and start walking toward the hatch. I use all the strength left in me to wiggle my body every which way I can. It does nothing and soon my feet are resting against the opening of the hatch.

"When was the last time you threw a bitch down there?" Joey asks.

"Dead or alive?"

Joey chuckles. "Will the fall kill her?"

"I doubt it. Make sure to lock the hatch so it can't crawl out."

The pit stinks worse than Joey. I scrunch my nose in disgust. I press my feet to the sides of the metal box as Moe pushes me inside.

"Do you want to go headfirst? I promise it'll hurt a lot more." Joey grabs my feet and forces them away from the sides of the crate.

Once my feet are off the sides, Moe pushes me down into the dark hole.

CHAPTER FORTY-FOUR

October 17th, 2009
4:19 p.m.

It's not as deep as I thought it would be. I land on my ass in a cloud of dust, and something crunches underneath me. I cover my mouth as I begin coughing. Moe and Joey are laughing somewhere above me. I look up. The hatch is about eight feet above me. Moe and Joey are staring down at me.

Moe reaches into the front pocket of his overalls and pulls out a cigarette and a lighter. That explains the ashtray outside of the house. I watch as he lights the cigarette and looks down at me. He's enjoying my pain.

I want to scream at them. Plead with them to take me out of wherever it is I am. Some burial ground for animal carcasses. Although I hate both men with a fiery passion, a desperate part of me would do anything to get out of here. Before I can speak, the hatch slams shut. Everything goes pitch black.

"Let me the fuck out of here!" I scream, coughing up more of the dust entering my mouth.

Their laughter fades as they walk away. I am alone in this hole. This hole that most definitely holds animal waste — and perhaps human. I quiver at the thought, and panic rises in me.

The dust is settling. I take a couple deep breaths and pinch my arm. Anything to snap me out of this panic. It could be worse — I could still be trapped in that basement with Eva. The girl who hates my guts and most definitely is no longer on my side. I could be alone with either one of those creeps, Moe and Joey. Down here they can't hurt or rape me. That word sets me shivering again. Would that be karma? I let it happen to Eva by twice as many men.

Is that what Moe does to the girls here? He hates women for existing, that much is clear. I try to remember any news articles I've read about the Monroe Murderer. Were the women they found raped? I'm not sure. It's never been said in the papers that they were.

Moe promised Graham he could have sex with me one last time before they kill me. So that means he's okay with it happening. Has he let Graham do that to other girls? Is Graham capable of rape? Eva did say he watches his father kill women — and two women have been murdered since she has been here. I know Graham isn't as twisted as his father, but after growing up watching that, it being normalized in his head, how could he still have any good in him?

I reach out and try to get a sense of my prison. When I stretch my arms above my head, my fingertips graze what feels like cracked cement. I kneel down and touch the floor with my uninjured hand. The dirt floor is ridged with something hard and smooth . . . bones? I crawl about to see how far this box goes. I only make it a couple feet before I feel cracked cement walls.

I shift my body to sit on my bottom. I need a few minutes. I need time to stop myself from hyperventilating. Everything in here feels like bones, rocks, and trash. What if I'm sitting right next to the dead body of another of Moe's victims? What if they leave me to rot in here?

"God, if you're up there, please help me," I whisper, lacing my fingers together.

Nothing . . . makes sense. Even if there is a God, why would he help me? I never even went to church to pray for forgiveness. Not after I let my mother kill my little brother, nor in prison after I ran over George.

Then again, I shouldn't feel guilty about George, now that I know the truth about his family. George was a murderer.

They're going to make you pay for this.

I had nearly forgotten his last words to me. They finally make sense. George knew his family would have their vengeance.

You saved lives, Max. You killed a man who tortured innocent women. I wonder if God will forgive me for all I've done. And I might have to kill someone else if I want to get out of this alive. I've never read the Bible, but I'm positive murder is still murder regardless of who it is.

CHAPTER FORTY-FIVE

October 17th, 2009
4:19 p.m.
Graham

Graham runs back into the farmhouse, heading straight to the kitchen sink. His face is once again gushing blood, today's beatings written all over it in bruises and cuts. He wets a washcloth and cleans the blood from his nose. Once he's done, a burst of anger goes through his body and he screams, throwing the washcloth at the wall as hard as he can.

One threat and a pistol-whipping from his father and Graham had bowed down to him. Just like that. Just like every time he's tried to help a girl out. After all these years his father still has a hold over him. Is still silently using what he did against him. Except it was supposed to be different this time. It's Maxine's life on the line. Maxine, who was begging him to help her. He loves Maxine, and the thought of her alone in the animals' boneyard makes his blood boil. He wishes he could grab his dad's shotgun, blow both his father and uncle away.

Killing his father and uncle isn't a part of his plan, though. All he wants to do is get his father's keys while he sleeps and let

Maxine out of the cage. Sneak her to the car and drive off. They would have the night to get as far away as possible.

The plan sounds perfect but would only end with Maxine calling the police or making a run for it as soon as they made it to town. Especially now that he's allowed his father and Joey to throw her in the pit. She must be angry with him. He just needs some time alone with her to apologize and promise this will all be over soon. He needs to regain her trust. Make her realize he's the one she belongs with. For the time being, he decides to keep her locked up.

Graham hasn't had time to process the story Maxine told them all about Eva at that party. He knows Maxine is a disturbed individual, but never did he think she could be capable of allowing such harm. Twice. It was understandable that she couldn't prevent her mother's actions when she was nine, but as a teenager, sitting back and doing nothing?

He's sat by as both a child and an adult and let his father do evil things. He's watched him torture and butcher girls for the better part of his life and done nothing. He tries to make himself feel better by helping the girls as much as he can. He even assures them he'll get them out, to safety. There's no harm in giving them a little hope. In the end, he's never actually taken the initiative to rescue or release them.

Instead of anger or disgust at what Maxine has done, he feels learning this truth strengthens their bond. They both share the trait of being a watcher. Someone who stands by and watches as someone suffers. Unable to act, unable to help.

He fetches the bloodied washcloth from the ground by the wall and finishes cleaning his face. As he does so, he stares at the front door, waiting for his father and uncle to return. Uncle Joey and Graham both have work tomorrow at seven, so with any luck his father is going to take Joey home soon. Then Graham will be faced with only one opponent instead of two. He'll also have time to talk to Maxine as his father drives Uncle Joey home. The hatch will be locked, but he remembers the last time Father locked a girl down there, he was able to open the door a couple inches to drop things down.

Graham grabs a Ziplock bag from one of the kitchen cupboards. He wants to take her water, but he doesn't have any water bottles small enough to fit. Instead, he goes to his stash of mini plastic bottles of the rum he puts in his coffee. He fits four in the Ziplock bag. The liquor will numb the pain.

He searches another cupboard filled with random items and finds a miniature flashlight. One that will fit through the crack of the hatch. Light may put Maxine at ease. He can't imagine being stuck down in that graveyard in complete darkness. Thankfully it's not a form of punishment Father uses frequently, as he hates the smell of rotting corpses.

His father returns a couple minutes later. He grabs a nearby jacket of his and puts it on. He looks over at Graham, who has hidden the Ziplock bag and flashlight in the back pocket of his jeans.

"I'm driving Joey home. I need you to do something for me," he says.

"What, sir?"

"You remember where that creature lives?"

Graham furrows his brows in confusion and nods his head.

"Go to its house and pack a bag."

They've never done that before. Then again, besides Eva and the twins, they hadn't taken a girl from Mendex in over a decade. He hates to admit it, but his father is right. People will soon notice Maxine's absence if they haven't already. She has a job and has already missed a day. Then there's that ex-boyfriend of hers.

He has the ability to free Maxine from the hole and take her to town. It's what he should do, but that would mean the end for him. He would never see Maxine again. Hell, he would never see the light of day again. He has to let Maxine see he isn't the bad guy, that they belong together. He needs just a little more time with her.

"Yes, sir."

"Good. If you don't fuck this up, I'll still consider letting you fuck the pig."

Graham clenches his fists in order not to jump his father at that remark. He's heard his father call the women that they take many vile things, but never has he felt this heated over it. He's even sort of got used to it. Maxine is different, though. She's his last chance at love and a normal life.

Maxine belongs to him; there is no other alternative than the two of them being together. Graham would rather kill her than let her run away. He imagines how painful it would be to wrap his hands around her throat and watch the life leave her body. Only a week ago the mere thought gave Graham a rush of adrenaline. Now he knows there's no going back. If Maxine is to die, so will he.

CHAPTER FORTY-SIX

October 17th, 2009
4:27 p.m.

As time drags on, I begin to rethink my opinion that being in the pit is better than being in the basement. It's true nobody's cutting off my fingers down here, but being in complete darkness with the foul smell has my stomach filled with dread. My head feels on fire after the beating from Eva, and my wounded hand's hurting again — the pain pills Graham gave me are wearing off.

More tears stream down my face. Are they planning to leave me to rot? Is that the "proper punishment" for killing George? Without water, I won't last more than two days. The smell alone is torture enough. Even if I do manage to live longer than that, my hand will surely get infected in such unsanitary conditions; I'll die screaming. Add in the rancid smell, darkness, with numerous dead bodies down here with me — this could be the ultimate punishment in their eyes.

Prior to the events that just unfolded, I had stupidly hoped that, with Graham's help, I could get Eva and me out of here safely. That as long as I played along with his idea of running away, I could figure out a way to get him help. But then he let his family throw me down here.

He's twenty-eight years old and has sat by and let his father do these horrible things. I did that twice, and it has haunted and ruled my life since. How much morality can Graham really have?

For a couple minutes all I can hear is the wind blowing above me, but then a vehicle starts up. Who's leaving? Perhaps Joey — Graham said he didn't live here. He arrived with Moe, so someone else must be giving him a ride home. After the vehicle starts, I hear its engine roar as it drives off, and it's silent again. A couple minutes pass and I hear the sound of footsteps in the grass. I clench my uninjured fist, terrified of who could possibly be headed my way.

I hear Graham's soft voice above me. "Max, hey, it's me."

Graham? He's still here? That means his father gave Joey a ride home. I can convince him to call the police with the phone inside the house. My hopes begin to rise again.

"Graham, thank God you're here. I heard a vehicle outside. Is . . . is your father gone?"

Graham hesitates, then speaks in a rush. "N-no, Joey just took the van home."

He's lying. I want to call him out on it but don't want to risk him getting angry with me.

"I see. Are you okay?"

"Am I okay?"

"Yeah, your dad, it seemed like he hit you pretty hard."

"Oh, right. I'm fine. Forget about me. Are you okay? I'm so sorry I let them throw you down there. I don't know what happened. I lost control again."

I am not okay. You let your father throw me in this godforsaken hole!

I take a deep breath. I can't say that. I have to remain calm.

"It's okay, Graham. I . . . I actually feel safer down here than up there."

I grit my teeth to keep my voice as even as possible. I must treat Graham like he's glass, or he'll shatter and so will our relationship. I can tell by his voice he's on the brink of a mental breakdown.

"How . . . how many girls has your father thrown down here?"

"Not many. I brought you some stuff."

Stuff? Stuff because he knows I'm going to be down here for a while. I bite my lip hard so I don't say what I'm thinking. He's avoiding my unspoken question: *How many bodies am I down here with?* That doesn't take the chills away.

The hatch opens a couple inches, letting in some light. A couple seconds later an item is dropped through the space and down to me: a plastic bag with four plastic bottles. I hold them in front of what little light I have and see they're bottles of rum.

"Sorry, it's all I could find that would fit."

Water would've been a hundred times better, but this will do. Better than being dehydrated for however long they plan on keeping me here. I quickly open one of the caps and take a swig of the rum. It cools my empty stomach and sends a glimmer of warmth to my nose.

"I also brought you this." A few moments later another item falls from the hatchway.

I grab it. I hold it up in the light and realize it's a mini flashlight. I switch it on, adding a little more light in front of me. I look up and nearly scream at what it illuminates: skeletal remains. A body? No, it has — had — four legs. Its body is short, and the head appears to have fallen off. Must have been a pig. A cow's carcass wouldn't fit down here.

I tremble at the thought of moving the flashlight beam around anymore. Just the sight of a pig's decaying carcass almost sent me into a panic. What if I find an actual human's body next? I mean, they must be disposing of the bodies somewhere. Why not here? It's easy and doesn't require digging a hole.

"Graham, thank you for this, but I need to know how many bodies are down here. Please."

Graham sighs, and I can hear as he fidgets his feet in the dirt above me.

"Father has had me bury a lot of women along the property. He doesn't like to dispose of his bodies somewhere they can be easily discovered."

Just that answer alone keeps me from moving the flashlight anywhere else. I take a deep breath, trying to calm my shaking body. It does little to none as I'm shivering from the cold air coming into the hole.

"You have to get me out of here, Graham. I'll freeze. You know that."

"Don't worry about that, I brought you this." I hear him trying to force another object through the gap in the hatch.

A couple moments pass before I see a large item fit through the hatch and slide down toward me. I pick it up, smiling when I realize it's the flannel jacket Graham had given me. I pull it on and press my arms against my body. My shivering subsides. Once I have gained some warmth, I push my hands into the pockets. I had my house keys in them. I could use them as a weapon if need be. But they're empty now. Which means someone has taken them.

"You take my keys?" I ask.

"Yeah, Father wants me to go to your house. Pack a bag for you."

I bite my lip again. I want to urge him to either call or go to the police. Tell him I'll do my best to make sure he doesn't take any blame for what's happened. I wouldn't be lying, either. Although I'm angry with Graham for letting all this happen, I still do care about him. He's not well in the head. He needs help.

"Graham, you should go to the police. You can end this and save Eva, me, and even you. I can tell them none of this is your . . . fault. I can—"

"This is my fault, Maxine. I'm not an idiot. Is that what you want? You want me to be put away in a loony bin or, worse, prison? While you go home and are exonerated for the wrong thing you did?" For the first time I can hear the bitterness in his words.

I want to tell him he's being selfish, but I need to keep the peace.

"That's not what I want, Graham. I want to save us, all of us. Eva, you, and me."

Graham scoffs. "Eva, really? The minute she got to the police, she'd rat me out. Rat you out too. She's not on your side."

I don't care whose side she is on. She may have beaten me up, but I deserved it.

"She's a human being, Graham. All the girls who died at the hands of your father, uncle, and brother were. You know this is wrong. You have to."

"I know. I'm going to fix this. I just need time. I'm going to save you and get us out of this place."

I keep hearing Graham make these promises, but at this point, it's hard to believe he's going to grow some and stand up to his father. Eva said he's told all the other girls he would save them. Then, every time he's had the chance, he's been a coward. I have to ask him if what she said is true.

"Did you tell the other girls you were going to save them too?"

There's a moment of silence before Graham asks, "Did Eva say that?"

I don't answer. I don't want to get her in ány trouble.

Graham sighs. "Yes, I told others that. I just wanted to make them feel better."

Is that somewhat kind or utterly evil? Giving these women false hope, knowing he wouldn't be doing anything?

"Is that the same thing you're doing with me?"

"No, Maxine. You're different. I'm ending this."

He could end this right now: call the police, turn himself and his family in, get me to a hospital. But he clearly isn't going to. He's playing for time. I try reasoning with him.

"I know what it's like being afraid to speak up."

"With Eva?"

I gulp and grab for another of those plastic bottles of rum. I take the cap off and swallow the entirety of it. It warms my stomach. I wish I had ten more. Anything to take away the pain.

"Yes, I was afraid. Not for her — but for what others would do if I spoke up. I cared so deeply for the boy who did it. I didn't want him to get in any trouble. I wasn't a good person."

"How long did you date this guy for, exactly? I mean, it obviously didn't work out, so why didn't you speak up afterward?"

"We broke up after he was in college for a semester. While he was gone, I finally realized what a godawful person he was. It was too late by then. I had already told Eva I didn't see anything. At that point, I thought speaking up would just be foolish. I've kept it burning inside my body for nine years now."

"Try twenty-three years."

"Have . . . have you ever killed any of them?"

Graham is silent for a couple moments before saying, "The girls? No."

That's a bit of a relief. But Graham had said "girls" as if making it clear he hadn't killed one of the women they've had here specifically.

"Have you killed . . . anyone?"

"Maxine—"

"Graham, please. It'll help, you know? Letting it out."

"I did kill once. It was for my brother. Or, at least, that's what I like to tell myself."

"Your brother, George. What was he like?"

"He was cruel and evil. Like my father. I thought I knew him better than anyone else. Before he died, it turned out I barely knew him at all."

"How so?"

Graham takes a deep breath. "I was in his room, around a week before he died . . ."

CHAPTER FORTY-SEVEN

June 7th, 2004
9:21 p.m.
Graham

Father is out fishing with Uncle Joey, and George has disappeared for the third time this week. Now may be the only chance Graham has to look inside his brother's room. He's been off lately. He's agitated more than usual, taking it out on Graham or the creatures they have — the creatures they *had*.

His agitation got the best of him yesterday when he took a knife to a creature's throat for spitting in his face. Girls have done that many times before; most of the time he just laughs and beats them. This time, without hesitation, he slit her throat. Graham witnessed the whole thing. George told Father that Graham had nearly let it escape and he had had to kill it himself. It's not like George to lie like that. In exchange for his lie, Graham got a belt whipping from Father.

Now Graham is the agitated one. He needs to find some dirt on his brother. Anything that can get Father on his side. He's been their whipping boy for too long now. There must be something George is hiding, something that is causing him to act out.

George has always been the mirror image of Father. He's always shown little to no emotion. Especially toward women. He grew up copying the evil things his father did. By the age of thirteen he'd killed his first victim. But his normal antics are nothing like this. He didn't just slit the thing's throat out of pure anger. He would play a dehumanizing and torturous game with it. He didn't do things he knew would anger Father and prevent them from having their fun with the creatures.

When Graham does mess up, George lectures him, maybe even hits him, but he has never got Father involved. Never lied about it to save his own skin. He's been going out a lot more often by himself. He isn't bringing back creatures or coming home drunk, so he has to be doing something off-limits.

His appearance has also changed. George usually wears his chestnut hair cut short. A month ago, he shaved it all off and has kept shaving it since. He's also been shaving his facial hair often, instead of just once a month or so like he normally does. George, although a psychopath, is a creature of habit. He likes his appearance the way it is and has treated Graham the same for years. It all means something.

Graham makes his way up their staircase and goes straight to George's room. It's locked, but Graham has found out where he keeps a spare key. George always has a spare key to everything, as he often drinks heavily and loses his. Father and George are different in that way. Father keeps one set of keys and always keeps track of them.

When he gets to George's room, Graham puts the key in the lock and opens the door. It's been a while since he's been in his brother's room. He remembers when George used to show him kindness. He would take his brother into his room and show off his knife collection. When Graham got older and hit puberty, his brother even taught him sex education and showed him a collection of nudie magazines he kept hidden under his mattress.

George's room is as bare as Graham's. It has a small closet filled with oversized black clothing. He also has a laundry basket filled with dirty clothes. Graham starts there when he sees a dark brown Carhartt jacket George often wears even though it's summer and nearly every day is over eighty degrees out.

Graham never understood his brother's need to wear such baggy, unflattering clothes. Perhaps so he could blend in better. His brother is a lot more muscular than Graham. He works out and goes for runs daily. His body is the selling point he uses when going after creatures. They are often swayed by his rugged good looks and muscular body. Graham wishes he could have a body like his brother's.

Graham grabs the jacket on the top of the dirty clothes and searches through the pockets. In them he finds some crumpled receipts. As he reads through them, he sees they are all for local bars in Mendex. One, however, is from one of Mendex's grocery stores. For a six-pack of beer and . . . flowers. Why would he ever buy flowers? Does his brother have a secret girl he's seeing? Dating or getting close to anyone outside the family is strictly prohibited by their father.

Graham likes to imagine a normal world where he has a girlfriend. A girlfriend he could buy flowers for and regularly have sex with. Nothing like the grungy girls he occasionally hooks up with to ease his sexual urges. A girl he finds perfect in his eyes. One who understands him and doesn't treat him like he's an embarrassment.

He remembers one of the first girls he saw naked. She had been in one of the magazines George showed him. *Playboy*'s April 1996 cover. Samantha something. Her smile was bright and white. Graham had later cut the picture of her out of the magazine and kept it stashed under his bed. He had only been fourteen at the time and had hopes that one day a woman like that would be his.

Graham puts the grocery store receipt in his pocket and goes to the bed. His brother used to like keeping all his secret items there. They were children when he did that, but Graham knows George isn't the most intelligent man and will most likely keep to his old ways.

He kneels down and lifts the old, stained mattress. He sees the nudie magazines, some knives, and cash. Not much else. Before dropping the mattress, he catches sight of another magazine hidden in the end corner of the bed's frame. Maybe an old one George stuffed in the back, forgot about?

Graham eases the magazine out of its hiding place. He looks at the cover. Then he drops it to the ground and takes a step away.

CHAPTER FORTY-EIGHT

June 7th, 2004
9:29 p.m.
Graham

The magazine is white, and in blocky red words at the top reads *Playgirl*. On the front page is a buff, shirtless man in tight black pants.

It must be under his brother's bed by mistake.

Father has always taught the two brothers to hate homosexuals. That it was a sin to be into the same sex as your own. Graham never fully understood the hate. George, on the other hand, would always say slurs toward gays.

After taking a deep breath, Graham picks up the magazine. The pages are scuffed, as if it's been looked through many times. What does this mean? Is this dirt Graham has on his brother? Is George questioning his sexuality? Or has he always found men attractive?

As for having dirt on his brother, this is the ultimate thing to hold over George's head. If his father knew about George keeping a men's nudie magazine, he would probably beat him — possibly kill him. He remembers his father and him meeting a homosexual couple at a gas station in Mendex. After they had left, his father proudly exclaimed he would rather his son be dead than gay.

If Graham says anything to George, he knows he'll lie. Make up some convoluted story as to why the magazine is there. Or he'll explode and beat him up. Graham will have to hide the magazine. Threaten him with it.

Graham hides the magazine under the sink drawer. He doesn't plan to keep it hidden there long.

Graham goes to the kitchen cupboards and finds a bottle of rum. He just bought the bottle last week, and already it is nearly gone. He's been drinking heavily since his brother and father both started ganging up on him. There was a time when Graham and George would sit together at the table and share a couple shots after watching their father with the creatures. The drinks, at least for Graham, would numb all the hurt he felt in his body witnessing such crimes. George on the other hand, Graham didn't know for sure why he drank.

An hour passes before Graham hears the noise of a vehicle in the distance. He prays it's not his father getting dropped off by Uncle Joey. He needs time alone with George. He gets up and jogs to the front window. Once he sees the van with George sitting in the front seat, he goes back to the table. He takes deep breaths to remain calm and relaxed. If he shows any fear, his brother will pounce on that. His brother has a good eye for other's weaknesses.

Graham takes one last chug of the rum, finishing the bottle. The front door opens. Graham gulps, staring at his brother's huge frame. The brothers are both tall, but George outweighs Graham by over fifty pounds.

George glances only momentarily at his brother as he removes his boots and puts his coat on the rack. He heads to the fridge and rummages through it.

Good luck finding anything in there besides beer and expired salad dressing.

This household has never found much need to keep food around. Especially now that there are no creatures in the basement. Father mostly eats at Uncle Joey's. If Graham buys any food, he barely gets the chance to eat one meal before it's all taken by his brother.

"Why didn't you go grocery shopping yesterday?" George asks, slamming the fridge shut.

"Why didn't you go today?" Graham asks.

"Because I'm not the bitch in the house, you are."

Graham tenses and, before he can stop himself, says, "You would know."

"What the fuck did you just say to me?" George pushes a chair aside so he's standing right in front of Graham.

Graham takes a deep breath. Is it too late to change tactics? He can apologize and sneak the magazine back into George's room before he notices it's gone.

Don't be a coward.

"I said you would know, George." Graham stands up so they are eye to eye.

"You better watch it. If Father knows you're talking to—"

"If Father knows you have a male nudie mag under your mattress, I don't think he'll give a fuck how I'm talking to you."

George's eyes widen and his body stiffens. The next moment, face red, he grabs Graham by his shirt collar and pushes him against the wall.

"What the fuck are you talking about?"

"I think you already know."

George's eyes flash to the stairwell. He shoves his brother hard against the wall and runs up the stairs.

"You won't find it up there."

George stops in his tracks.

"Where'd you put it? You motherfucker, I'll kill you." George rushes back down the stairs.

Graham is expecting this. He grabs a pocketknife from his jean pocket and points it at George. He has a feeling his brother will call his bluff, as he's never physically threatened someone, let alone harm anyone in front of him.

"Stay away from me."

"Or what?"

"Or I'll kill you. Father will understand if I show him that magazine."

George forces a tight grin and, lifting his hands in the air, says, "Okay, fine. Why were you in my room, little bro?"

"You've been treating me like shit these last couple weeks. I was tired of it. I knew something was up with you."

"You can't tell him."

"That all depends on you."

"What do you want?"

"I saw a receipt in your coat pocket. It was for flowers."

"Why the fuck did you—" George begins to scream, but after closing his eyes tightly and taking a deep breath, he asks, "What about it?"

"Who are you buying flowers for?"

"It's none of your business."

"You made it my business with how you've been treating me," Graham says.

"I'll stop, okay?"

Okay. That should be it. George gave his word. But Graham still has no answers for his brother's behavior. He wants him to trust him. To tell him what's been going on. Graham won't judge his brother.

"Are you . . . gay?" he asks, with a gulp.

It's a simple question, but George's eyes flash with anger. The same anger when he heard about the magazine. The same anger when the creature spit in his face. He runs toward Graham, and before he can react, he takes the knife from his hand and punches him in the jaw. Graham falls to the ground, his brother on top of him. George presses the knife against Graham's throat. The blade nicks his skin.

"You ever call me that again, I'll slit your fucking throat. And no one will miss you."

"Then why, George?"

Graham knows he is pressing his luck but no longer cares. He hasn't cared for his own life in a while. As he sat by and watched so many creatures die, a part of his own self-preservation must have died.

"I'm just confused, okay. It's nothing. You ever mention this to Father, I'll make damn sure I cut you to pieces before he can get to me. Things are fine the way they are. Leave it be and mind your own business!"

George takes the pocketknife from Graham's throat and throws it aside. Just when Graham thinks his brother is going to get off him, George punches him in the face again. He feels blood gushing from his nose.

George gets off him. "Where did you put it?"

Graham points toward the sink cupboards. He's in too much pain to speak. George walks to the sink and grabs the magazine.

"Don't bring this up ever again."

After that, he walks upstairs and goes into his room, slamming the door.

It takes Graham a few minutes to recover from the beating he just got. He slowly sits up, putting his hand to his nose. His blood is boiling with anger at how he cowered before his brother, how he gave up the magazine so quickly. He should've known his brother would have overpowered him. He just didn't realize how the mere question of his sexuality would set him off like that.

Graham needs to think of another plan. Telling his father is no longer a viable option. But if Graham can find out who George bought those flowers for, he may be able to use it against him in another way. A way to get free of this hell house forever.

CHAPTER FORTY-NINE

October 17th, 2009
4:39 p.m.

Graham falls silent.

George sounds like the spitting image of his horrible father. Cruel and psychotic. Why is it they both ganged up on Graham? Was making him play along with their games a game in itself? I want to hear more. I want to know if Graham ever did attempt to escape. Clearly not, if he's still living in the farmhouse five years later. His father must've never found out about George's sexuality if he is so strung up on getting revenge for him.

"I have to go, Max."

"What? Why?"

"I have to go to your house. Father will want to know why I haven't set off yet."

I open my mouth to argue but stop. If I argue too much, he'll realize I've guessed he's lying about his father still being here.

"Please hurry, Graham. I can't stay down here all night."

"You won't. I'll be back soon. I . . . I love you."

Graham says it so sincerely. He really seems to believe that. But if he truly loved me, he wouldn't stand by and let this all happen to me. He would call the police and save me.

"I don't believe that, Graham," I blurt out.

"Why?" he croaks.

"You have the power to stop this and won't. True love doesn't look like that."

There's silence for a couple moments between us. I begin to think he's left before I hear a deep exhale.

"I do love you, Max. I love you so much, I don't want to lose you. If I go to the police, I will never see you again. I'm being selfish, I know that. I can't help it."

Is he afraid to lose me or go to prison for the rest of his life? At this point, I really don't know.

"It is selfish, Graham. I'm going to die if you don't make the right choice. Then I'll be gone forever."

"I'm not going to let that happen."

I don't reply. I don't have the energy to. I feel pain form in my hand. I flash the light over and see the fall has stained dirt on the cloth. It'll need to be changed again soon. I have to be more understanding toward Graham to get out of this. Or at least out of this hole.

"I love you too, Graham. I trust you'll do the right thing."

Graham lets out a sigh of relief, and then I hear him stand up and walk away, and the sound of a vehicle starting soon after. I sit alone with the flashlight now shining in front of me, on the empty bottles of rum. I want to leave the flashlight on the ground but I'm curious to look around. See what I'm alone with.

I turn the beam to my left. The walls are made up of cracked cement with dirt smudged inside the large cracks. How long ago was this hole dug? Perhaps before Graham or George was even born. It looks on the cusp of coming down.

I take a deep breath and continue moving the beam clock-wise. The pit is around the size of a large walk-in closet. I find another pig carcass. After seeing the first one, I don't feel nearly as nauseated at the sight of its decayed body. Maybe I have an over-active imagination; there might not be any human dead bodies down here.

The rapidity of my heartbeat subsides, and my shaky hands grow steady. My flashlight beam, now at three o'clock, shines upon another object. It's not another animal's body. I close my eyes and take a deep breath before I open them again. My skin grows chills from fear, and goosebumps form over my arms. The object is leaning against the cement wall. It is covered in a light blue film. Plastic?

I inch closer, keeping the beam on the object as if that's the only thing keeping it from pouncing on me. It is a body. I can tell by how it's leaning against the cement, with its legs stretched out on the ground. The plastic it's wrapped in makes it appear like a butterfly in a cocoon.

Just get away from the fucking thing, Max. Get as far away from it as possible. Turn the goddamn flashlight off if you have to.

As the more logical part of my brain urges me to move away, I find my body overpowering it and continuing to move closer. It's been down here for a while. I see white bones beneath the plastic film. I am close enough to see the glint of a skull.

Whoever killed this woman — I'm sure it's a woman — wrapped her in plastic and brought her down here themselves. They rested her against the wall to decompose. But why only this one? Was the smell too offensive to keep dumping bodies down here? Did Moe decide burying the bodies elsewhere would be safer? If so, why did he never rebury this one?

I inch to the left of the plastic-wrapped body. I flash the beam down at its feet, then move it up. I see she's still dressed. She's wearing a lemon-yellow dress that is covered in holes. I move my free hand toward the skeleton. I poke the thigh. It's a hard yet soft feeling. I move the flashlight toward the skull. No flesh, no hair.

My fearlessness begins to vanish. Bile rises up in my throat. I'm going to be sick. This body has been left here to rot, to frighten other girls who dare catch an attitude with Moe.

As I back away, the light shines on the collarbone, and I see a bump in the middle. It's a necklace. A flash of recognition: the drawing and photograph in Graham's sketchbook. That woman was wearing a silver heart-shaped necklace that fell in the same place.

Is this the woman from the photograph?

The plastic is too thick to see if this necklace is the same one the woman in the photograph was wearing. I take a deep breath and pray if there is a God, he will forgive me for doing this. For messing with the dead.

I dig my nails into the thick plastic, attempting to rip it away. My severed hand pulsates with pain from doing so. I bite my lip to numb the pain and continue. I set the flashlight on the ground and use all my strength to rip a hole in the plastic. Once I have, I feel a moist sensation on my fingertips. I take my hands away, feeling sick. Must be the flesh. The plastic turned it into a sludge from years of being so tightly wrapped up. The body shifts slightly, and I shriek.

"I'm sorry," I mumble to the corpse.

I grab the flashlight again and shine the beam over the now-ripped plastic. Time stops when I see the silver heart locket. It glimmers in the light. There's no more room for doubt. This is the skeleton of the woman in the photograph.

My burning question is, who was she?

CHAPTER FIFTY

October 17th, 2009
6:22 p.m.

By the time I hear a vehicle approaching, I am close to falling asleep. After taking the necklace off the skeleton, I thought I would never sleep again in my life. But I'm exhausted. I closed my eyes to try to shut out my racing thoughts, and not much time passed before I began to doze.

It's wrong to steal from the dead, especially from someone who suffered at the hands of a sadistic killer, but I need to show Graham the necklace. If he has a photograph of her, she must have meant something to him, whoever she was. It could be a dead end, but there's a tingling feeling in my stomach that tells me there's a deeper meaning to it.

I hope it's Graham and not Moe arriving. But Moe left before Graham. He also was just dropping someone off, not packing a bag in a house he doesn't know.

Then again, if Graham is taking a long time, it could mean someone caught him going into my house. My neighbors or my father. I try not to cling to that hope. Graham has been watching me for a long time. He must be competent at watching someone from afar without being detected.

I hear the vehicle shut off and, soon after, the sound of shoes moving through the gravel and grass.

I hold my breath as the sound gets closer. Who is this? Who do I even want it to be?

Graham's voice floats down from the hatch. "Max, are you okay?"

I let out a heavy sigh. So, he wasn't caught.

Now that he's back, I need to convince him to get me out of here. My hand is hurting more and more as time passes. I can feel the dirt going through the bandage.

"I'm . . . hurting, Graham," I say a couple moments later.

"I'll get you more of those pain pills," he offers.

Not exactly what I wanted to hear.

"I got some of your belongings."

"No one saw you?" I blurt out accidentally.

Graham senses the regret in my tone and sighs heavily. "No, I've snuck around your house plenty of times."

I tightly close my eyes, remembering when my neighbors had caught him watching me.

"You were caught once."

"Yeah, about that—"

"It's okay."

"I normally didn't come that early. I just needed to see you."

I need Graham if I am to escape, and I do want to get him psychological help, but I'm repulsed by all the things he's done. Not just watching me. Allowing his father to harm all these women. His brother and father brainwashed him, but he could've done something. What is keeping him from going to the police? I can't let myself forget all the lives that have been lost while he sat by and watched.

I consider telling him about the necklace in my jacket pocket. What will he do? Will he be angry at me for snooping? Will I be able to tell who the necklace belongs to from how he reacts?

"Hey, Graham."

"Yeah?"

I catch my breath. This should wait till I'm out of here. That way I can see the look on his face when I tell him. See if he'll lie to me or freeze up.

"D-did you enjoy watching me?" I ask, changing my tone from solemn to flirtatious.

"Y-yes, I touched myself."

My skin crawls at the thought.

"What if I told you I was thinking of you when I did that?"

It's partly the truth. I was also — mostly — imagining Mikey.

"Really? Me, not your ex?"

We don't have time for this.

"Like I said, he's just a friend."

"I saw you two that night he kissed you. I saw you take him into your house."

"It had been a long time since I'd had sex. I wanted to take you home that night, you know? He stopped that."

I hear Graham chuckle. "Maybe I shouldn't have thrown that rock at his Jeep, then."

So, Adrienne's brothers hadn't caught us after all.

"Well, you stopped us, so mission accomplished."

"Do you like him?"

I catch my breath. Now I do have to tell a lie.

"No, I mean, not in that sense. Not anymore."

"Okay, I believe you."

I hear disbelief in his voice. I need to work on my charm and convince Graham of my undying love for him.

"I want out of here, Graham. I'm really hurting."

When Graham doesn't reply I add, "I'm dirty too. You could clean me up."

"But my father is still—"

"I know your father isn't here, Graham."

"Am I really that bad of a liar?" he asks with a chuckle.

"I won't run, if that's why you lied. I promise. I just want out."

"Okay, but if my father comes back — we'll have to figure something out."

"When will he be back, you think?"

"The fact that he's still gone means he's probably drinking with Joey. We should be okay — for a while."

Once Graham leaves, I let out the breath I've been holding. I need to keep my cool. With Moe gone I may be able to reach that phone in the kitchen. I could do that if I were to knock Graham out but . . . the thought of harming him doesn't sit right with me. Even if it's for the greater good.

I can't explain the queasy feeling I get in the pit of my stomach every time my brain tells me to hurt Graham to save Eva. I do still like Graham. I look into his emerald eyes and see something I never really have in a man. I see . . . myself. Graham and I have both played an evil part in others' lives. We didn't intend to but still did. Graham may be the only person who I will ever see my sick self in. I push these feelings away for now. Act as though my heart doesn't exist in this game.

Graham returns a couple minutes later, and I hear him hammering, shaking the hatch door. He does this for a while, breathing hard.

"What are you doing?"

"I couldn't find any bolt cutters, so a hammer is going to have to do."

It takes a dozen more blows to the lock before the hatch door swings open. The sight of light shining through the square opening brings chills to my cold skin. A part of me thought I'd never see the light of day again.

It's insane to imagine less than twenty-four hours ago I was free; I felt safe. A drunk girl, all happy-go-lucky, going to a stranger's home. Does any of that matter anymore? If I hadn't come willingly, it sounds like Graham was planning on kidnapping me regardless. In a sick way it's good I came of my own free will. If Graham and I hadn't had that time together before he kidnapped me, he would never have found out the truth about me. Now he thinks he loves me, he thinks I trust him, and I can use that to escape.

I hear the hollow clunk of something metal hit against the side of the hatch. I look up and see a silver ladder sliding down.

Once the ladder reaches the dirt, I approach it. I put my hands on the cold metal and prepare to take my first step up.

"The ladder is a little short, so be careful. I'll help you the rest of the way up," Graham calls down to me.

I look up to see he is holding both sides of the ladder steady. It is a couple feet short of the hatchway. I shiver, wondering if Graham may accidentally lose control of the ladder and drop me. The fall wouldn't hurt any less than the first time.

The ladder shakes as I climb. I keep my eyes on my hands as I slowly bring them up each side one by one. The pressure from each grasp of the ladder brings more jolts of pain to my injured hand. When I look up, I'm only a couple feet from his face. He smiles faintly and begins to get to his feet. He reaches his hand out and, against my better judgment, I take it.

"Just a couple more steps, Maxine," he assures me.

I gulp, looking down. If I go any farther up, my hands will no longer have anywhere to hold on to, except Graham's hand. The top of the ladder is rusted and sharp. If he drops me and I fall, I will hit it. I imagine it hitting me straight through the chest. Blood spurting everywhere. Falling back down into the hole to bleed out.

As if seeing straight into my gory thoughts, Graham says, "You can trust me."

I nod, my throat too dry to respond.

I take my other hand from the ladder and get a tight hold of Graham's arm. I take the last couple steps up the ladder. It begins shaking tremendously, and eventually my weight brings it down. I yelp as my full weight is transferred from the safety of the ladder to Graham's hold on me. I expect any moment to fall back down, but Graham takes a deep breath and pulls me over the threshold. Right into his arms, into safety.

CHAPTER FIFTY-ONE

October 17th, 2009
6:38 p.m.

As Graham brings me up and out of the dark hole, the first thing I feel is the cold air as it creeps under the sleeves of my jacket and onto my skin. The second thing I feel is Graham's hands still holding on tight to me even after he's pulled me completely out. A small part of me says to push him away and run. I might have outrun him the first time if I hadn't tripped. He also no longer has his maniac father behind the wheel of their van chasing me. But I'm also more heavily wounded than before. My legs still hurt from my fall earlier, along with my feet from running barefoot. The phone is my smartest option right now.

"Are you okay?" he asks, taking his eyes off mine to look down at the rest of my body.

I look down. My bare knees are gashed and cut from landing in the dirt and crawling around in it. The body — the necklace. I have to tell Graham. I remove my hand from Graham's to put it into the pocket of the jacket where I've placed the necklace.

"Graham, down there I—"

"You don't have to talk about it. Let's get you cleaned up."

"But—"

241

"We don't have much time, come on."

He's right. I can tell him later.

"I'd rather go to the police now, Graham. The car's right there."

"Maxine, I already told you. I need time," he says sternly.

"Graham, I promise you I will not abandon you. I will do everything in my power to make sure it's your father who goes away."

Ignoring me, he puts a hand on my arm, his grip firm, and walks me toward the house. I can't break away, not in my state.

"If you don't get those cuts cleaned up right away, they'll get infected."

So, he wants to help me, but he doesn't want to let me go. He isn't prepared to own up to what's happened here. He isn't prepared to save Eva, and he probably isn't going to save me.

Inside the farmhouse, there's still no chance to break away. I look at the phone as we pass through the kitchen. Graham takes me upstairs to the bathroom. He follows me inside. I don't think I can undress in front of him. The flirting was mostly a means to get out of the hole. It worked, but now . . . I'm not ready to just shower with him and act like nothing horrible hasn't happened.

I turn to the dirty mirror. I let his jacket slip from my body and onto the floor. My once-white shirt is stained with dirt and ripped, exposing cuts on my waist. My face is grimy with dirt from the pit. My knees are grazed, dry blood caking my shins. My feet are in a similar condition, cuts covering them.

I tear my eyes away from the mirror, unable to look at myself any longer. I stare at my hand with the missing pinkie. The bandage is brown and torn.

"Shit. You need clothes," Graham says and turns away, leaving the bathroom.

The phone. I could get downstairs to the phone.

I stare at the bathroom door. It's closed. I imagine myself flinging it open and sprinting downstairs. Calling the police, then running outside to get as far away from the house as possible. Is it locked? I can't remember. Graham brought me inside so quickly it's hard to recall if he locked it behind us. It will only take a couple seconds to get out of the house, if he forgot.

I go to the door and wrap my hand around the knob, turning it. It's locked. Damn. What kind of bathroom locks from the outside? I need yet another way of getting to the phone. How much time will Moe be at Joey's? A couple hours? All night?

I am over by the bathtub, running the hot-water faucet full blast when Graham returns. I peer behind me to see he has a gray towel in one hand and in the other, hanging from a metal hanger, is an absurdly bright pink satin nightgown with a slit on the thigh.

He can't expect me to wear that. It could pass for lingerie. I remember him telling me he would fancy seeing me in pink. How long has he thought that? Since before, when he was watching me? When he wanted to torture and kill me? It sickens me to know he had most likely bought that with bad intent.

Noticing my bulging eyes affixed on the nightgown, Graham says, "It's the only women's clothing I could find."

I want to argue. Tell him to bring me his clothes. An oversized tee and boxers would be much more comfortable than that. Didn't he just go to my house and pack a bag full of my clothes? If he wanted, he could grab me those. I take a deep breath, remembering I have to play the girl he loves. As long as Moe and Joey won't see me in it. I don't trust them, and that nightgown gives them a clear view of my body.

"Thanks," I manage to say.

Graham smiles and sets the towel and nightgown on the sink.

"Take these. It'll help with the pain in your hand," he says, taking out more of those pills from his back pocket.

I smile and take the pills from his hand. Hopefully these will take away not only the pain in my hand but the rest of my body.

If I do get to that phone and need to run, it'll help lessen the pain I feel all over.

I watch the bathtub fill with water. Once it is full, I turn the faucet off. Graham lightly smiles at me before turning his back. I spot the toilet's tank lid. Could I grab it and bash him on the head with it? Would that kill him or just knock him out? What if I got caught grabbing it?

No, I'm not going to hurt him. I can't. Hitting him with that thing could seriously injure him, maybe even kill him. I can't do that.

I bite my bottom lip until it trembles from the pain and slowly begin to take my dirty clothing off. I drop my things in the corner of the room and, one step at a time, get in the tub. I leave my bandaged hand out, not wanting to soil the bandage further.

Once I'm submerged, I scrub the dirt off my arms and legs. I work on my face. The residue has already turned the once-clear water brown.

Realizing my naked body can no longer be seen through the water, I say, "You can turn around."

Graham turns around, peering at my bandaged hand.

"I brought some fresh bandages for you. I can change it out if you don't mind."

I nod. He smiles and walks toward the bath, kneeling down. He takes a roll of white bandage from his back pocket and sets it on the side of the bathtub. He gently begins to unwrap the old bandage from my hand. I look away, not able to bear the sight of it. *I can smell it.*

"Hey, Graham. Can I ask you something?" He begins to wrap a new layer of bandage over my hand.

Graham nods.

"Um . . . did you ever sleep with any of the other girls?"

What I really mean to ask is, did you rape them, Graham?

I still can't remember what the news articles said about the Monroe Murderer's victims. I suppose I might as well try to find out from the horse's mouth.

"Of course not," Graham answers, and I believe him.

"Did you have feelings for them?"

Graham finally looks at me. That question seems to have stunned him.

"Not sexual feelings, if that's what you're asking."

"Love feelings?"

"Not really. I cared for some. Two, in particular. They were sisters. Mary and Ma—"

"Mariah," I finish, gulping.

The two sisters from Mendex who went missing when I was nineteen. I can't bear to ask a question I already know the answer to. *Are they dead?*

"Yeah. I cared about them. They had a hard life. So did the other girls we took, I guess. But those sisters, they shared a bond. A bond I'd never seen."

"What happened to them?"

"My father noticed how close I was getting to them, and he . . . well, you know."

No, I don't, Graham. That's why I'm asking. But I'm beginning to wish I hadn't asked. *Am I going to die in the same way?*

How many other girls have died here? More than the police know about — they haven't even linked Eva, Mary, and Mariah's disappearances to the Monroe Murderer. It's just journalists and wannabe-investigators like Mikey making that leap of logic. I grimace. It stops here.

Graham finishes wrapping the bandage over my hand. I remove my hand from his.

"It was my fault. I got them killed and did nothing. That's why we're the same, you and me, Max. I understand what you went through with Billy and your mother. I've been dealing with it my whole life. I've let so many girls die."

"You can stop. I'll help you stop," I say.

We both smile at each other for what feels like an eternity. I can't tear my eyes away from those green eyes of his. Just like the first time we met, his bangs are partially covering them. I find myself lifting my hand and grazing his hair from his face for a better look.

"You know, after my mother died, I was never able to connect with anyone. I thought if I got too close to anyone, they would hurt me, and I'd be capable of doing what my mother did. So, I hurt them before they could hurt me."

Graham just stares at me with compassion. I realize I've never said that to anyone before. It was always too horrible of a thing to admit. Deep down, it's the terrible truth.

"I'll never hurt you, Maxine."

This time when he says my full name, I don't feel sick. It flows from his mouth so lovingly. For a moment, I shut my eyes and imagine that Graham and I are in a real love story. That our meeting happened by complete coincidence. That he hasn't chloroformed me and chained me up in a basement. It disappears fast as I remember the chilling reality of our relationship.

Graham helps me wash my hair. I feel rejuvenated but wracked with guilt. I'm being washed and somewhat cared for while Eva sits in the basement all alone. Has Graham brought her up for baths too? I need to stay focused. Stop allowing Graham to hypnotize me.

Graham turns toward the door as I dry myself off and put on the nightgown. It fits perfectly. I stare at myself in the mirror. It ends midway down my thigh, just above my fingernails. If I bent down, you would surely get a peek at the matching pink underwear I'm now wearing. It terrifies me to think of what Graham had in mind when purchasing this. Does he buy all the girls stuff like this?

Unable to process that set of grueling thoughts any longer, I touch Graham's shoulder, and he turns around. He stares at me in silence. By the look of that sparkle in his eyes, I know he bought this dress for me, and only me.

Once he's done staring, he reaches down, grabs his jacket from the floor, and hands it to me. I put it on and shove my hands in the pockets, feeling for the necklace.

"Graham, I have to tell you something."

"Oh, wait, I have to tell — no, *show* you something," he says, grabbing my hand.

He leads me out of the bathroom and down the stairs, never letting go. Once downstairs he takes me to the table in the dining room and sits me on one of the chairs. It creaks under my weight. He goes to the kitchen. My eyes go to the phone. It's a couple yards away, same distance as him.

"I forgot it outside. Give me a second." Before I can respond, he goes outside.

I stare at the front door. Then I look over at the phone. What if he catches me? There is a block full of kitchen knives on the counter.

Grab one.

And do what with it? Stab him? I must be out of my mind.

You're out of your mind if you don't consider it.

My body begins to twitch. A result of my brain fuming at the thought I am not moving toward the knives. A weapon to have on me would be nice.

Just as I am gearing to stand up, Graham appears again. He has something in his hand and a big yellow-toothed grin on his face.

CHAPTER FIFTY-TWO

October 17th, 2009
7:18 p.m.

It's M&M's. Graham has a packet of regular M&M's. That's the reason he has this big cheesy grin on his face. I remember him asking me what my favorite candy was, and that's what I told him. It had been a hasty answer. I don't eat much candy, but the last time I had, it had been M&M's. Just staring at the brown packet in Graham's hand churns my stomach. I'm starving.

"I remember you telling me these were your favorite." He hands me the packet.

I smile and tear it open. I pour a handful into my hand and toss the little candies into my mouth. Before I used to let the chocolate melt in my mouth, savoring the taste; now I chew a couple times and swallow. As I devour the packet, Graham goes to the kitchen and grabs me a glass of water. By the time he hands it to me, the M&Ms are gone. A minute later so is the water. I probably look like a wild animal.

"Thank you," I say.

Graham kneels down to be at eye level with me. He is still smiling and reaches a hand up to wipe water from the corners of my mouth.

"I wish things could have been different."

I'm unsure how to answer that. I'm his captive, ready to be executed by his crazy family.

"I will get you out of this, Maxine," he says when I don't reply.

"Is there any way we can break Eva from her chains? Get out of here before your father comes home?"

His smile disappears. He looks away from me, as if grief-stricken at my tasteless request.

"I doubt it. I barely got you out as is."

He's making excuses. Why is he making excuses?

"It can't hurt to try."

"Why do we have to save Eva? She's not a good person."

"Because of me. She's not a good person because of me."

"This is different."

"Why don't you want to save her?" I ask. "She's just like the other girls." I can't stand another minute of not knowing why Graham is so uncaring toward her.

"Eva has survived longer than any of the others in this house. You want to know why that is? Because she's deceived the others. There was one girl we had seven or so months ago. Father wanted to play Russian roulette with her and Eva. It's a game he's played before. He loads a bullet into a revolver and spins the chamber. He points the gun at a girl and asks a question. Usually a historical one. If she gets it right, he goes to the next girl. If she gets it wrong, he fires and . . . yeah. Either it goes off or doesn't."

I'm guessing Eva won the match. That's not her fault. My stomach knots up imagining the fear both girls must have felt.

"Well, Eva was answering all her questions correctly, and the other girl was not. They both knew the gun would fire sooner rather than later. It was the other girl's turn. My father asked her a question, and she wasn't sure what the answer was. She looked at Eva and Eva whispered something."

Graham takes a deep breath, looking away.

"What happened?" I ask, my hand on his shoulder.

"Eva purposely gave her the wrong answer, and when she was wrong, the gun went off."

"Eva could've not known—"

"She knew. My father never would have allowed her to get away with it had it been right. He enjoyed seeing Eva give the girl the wrong answer to save her own skin."

I feel frozen, unable to process what I just heard. Eva must've been frightened, wanting to live and believing the only option to do so was to let that poor girl take the fall.

"That's not all. There was another. She was only nineteen years old and so sweet and fragile. I saw her sad eyes and promised her I would do what I could to help her. Uncle Joey wouldn't stop staring at her, the sick fuck. So, I told her I'd give her a nail, something easy to hide. I told her if he was alone with Eva, she should use it. Joey doesn't even have keys to their cage. She was just so manic. I had to ease her stress. Eva heard the whole conversation, and after I gave the girl the nail, Eva told my father. He was so angry, he kill—"

"Stop." I close my eyes tightly.

"You cannot trust her, Maxine."

This changes everything. Eva has let two girls die to save her own skin. So what if it's kill or be killed here? It's still wrong. What if she does the same thing to me? Tells Moe our plan for me to lure Graham into my cage and attack him? But if she were going to do that, wouldn't she have already? I realize now the plan was never going to work. If I can't attack him here, when I am free, then I couldn't attack him in the cage.

Graham stands up and turns away from me. He walks over to the record table. He begins skimming through the vinyls, squinting as he does so.

"Um, what are you doing?" I ask, when in reality I want to ask him why he's trying to stray away from the important conversation we were just having.

He doesn't answer but instead continues skimming through the vinyls. He finally finds what he's looking for and takes one out. It's a rustic orange with five members of a band on the front. The Platters. Taking the black disc out, he carefully sets it onto the record player.

A beautiful melody begins to play. A man sings in a soft voice. Graham walks back over to me, holding out his hand.

CHAPTER FIFTY-THREE

October 17th, 2009
7:25 p.m.

He wants to dance. *Why?* I stare at him in confusion.

He's still offering me his hand. "Please, Maxine."

I close my eyes tightly, trying to clear out all the stress I'm feeling. Leaving my eyes closed, I outstretch my hand in Graham's direction. He takes it and pulls me close. He leaves one hand entangled with mine and puts the other on my waist. I let my free arm drape over his shoulder. I tightly grab on to the material on his jacket, unable to open my eyes, although I feel Graham's gaze burning through me.

"Why are your eyes closed?" he asks.

"Because I'm trying to imagine we're anywhere else. A crowded room or an open field. Just anywhere else where I'm not in danger. Where I'm not worried about a girl who hates me."

"I'm going to get you out of danger. Just trust me."

How can he expect me to trust him when he's the one who landed me here? And now that he has the chance to get us out, he's refusing because of what? Because he'll go to prison and lose me forever?

I wrack my mind, trying to understand his point of view in all of this. He's scared of not just losing me but being put away forever. How well would he fare in prison? Not well, I'm sure. Men's prisons are worse than women's. Could I have the power to get him put in a mental hospital? He isn't crazy, just brainwashed.

"I trust you," I finally admit.

"I guess it would be nice to imagine us anywhere besides this shitty house. Sharing our first dance. If I had to pick anywhere else, I would say our wedding."

I feel tears soak my eyes. I never pictured having a wedding. Before prison, I didn't want to get married. Married means there's a chance I could end up brokenhearted and crazed like my mother. Not only that, but I didn't think anyone would marry a felon. I imagine what wedding setting would be perfect. I love springtime and the rain. Not too cold but not too hot.

"This is crazy, you know? We just met," I say.

"I think, all circumstances aside, this is the most uncrazy thing to talk about."

I crack a brief laugh. How disturbingly right he is.

If Eva escapes, you will not get to be with Graham. He will be in prison for the rest of his life.

A shot of shame injects itself straight into my heart. I'm conflicted between the two outcomes. If I don't help Eva out of this, I'll be abandoning her again.

After all illusions of where we could be have passed, I open my eyes. Graham is staring at me; his eyes filling with tears. I stare at his features, seeing the scrapes on his cheek from when I hit him with the coffee cup. They are almost nothing compared to his red nose and bruised eye. He really has taken a beating today. I reach up and caress his damaged cheek.

"You're the first girl to hurt me like that," he says with a sigh.

"I was scared."

"No, I deserved it. Your survival instincts kicked in. You're a fighter."

The song begins to fade out and as it does, so does my calm and peaceful state of mind. Now I feel overwhelming pressure to save Eva again. A crazy thought comes to me. I'll have to act fast before I change my mind.

"Did I ever thank you for rescuing me from that hole in the ground?" I ask.

We're silent for a couple moments before Graham asks, "Did I ever thank you?"

"For what?"

"For giving me a reason to escape this hell."

I caress Graham's cheek again and lean over to him. He closes his eyes, but I keep mine wide open as I brush my lips against his. Our lips are dry and cracked. We begin to kiss, his eyes never opening.

He lifts me into his embrace, pressing his body to mine, and brings me to the dining room table, setting me on top of it. Our hearts beat in sync.

I think he keeps a knife in his pocket. Eva's words.

Was she right? If he has a pocketknife, I can take it and hide it in one of my jacket pockets. I move my hands around his waist. I slowly lower them to his butt before slipping my fingers into the pockets.

As I am searching the pockets, I feel his hands attempt to tug my jacket off. I can't let that happen. I take a tight hold of his hands, leading them to my chest. He takes my breasts in his hands, squeezing them gently. As he does so, I once again move my hands to the back pockets of his jeans. My hand grazes over something cold and smooth. I feel the button trigger that will release the blade of the knife.

He removes his hands from my chest and inches them to my waist. My heart rate increases dramatically the lower his hands go. My cheeks flush, and for a stupid split second, I hesitate. He opens his eyes just as I have the knife clasped in my hand. It's so heavy.

"Are you okay? Is this too much?" he asks.

I shake my head.

"I can stop." He starts to pull away.

I use my free hand to pull his body back into mine.

"I don't want you to stop," I whisper in his ear.

"I missed the touch of you, Max," he whispers, leaning down to nibble at my neck.

His lips on my neck cause a wave of shivers down my body. Shit, now is not the time to feel horny. I must remain on task.

As he continues to nibble my neck, going lower to my collarbone I hold my breath trying to ignore the tingles in my groin. Slowly, I slip the knife out of Graham's pocket. Once it is out, I look down at him. He hasn't noticed.

"I never thought I'd have the chance to touch you again," he whispers.

A droplet of sweat drips down my face. Now what? My original plan was to just take the knife and hide it in my pocket. Now I'm getting other ideas. My inner instincts know the right thing for Eva would be to stab it into his neck. I could save Eva and me right now. But in the process, I will kill Graham.

I feel another part of me lift the knife up so I can see it. Right by Graham's neck. Next, I press the trigger. The blade flicks out; it's smaller than the one Moe used to cut my pinkie off. Still, it would do some damage if pushed into someone's neck.

What am I thinking? Killing someone? Not just someone. The someone who has gone through a whole life of pain and hurt. The one who's forced to watch unthinkable things and tasked with the cleanup. The one who's been getting beat up trying to protect me.

I can't do this. I will find another way to save Eva and I. Anything but this.

I tighten my grip on the knife and, with my other hand, push Graham away from me.

I have to do this.

CHAPTER FIFTY-FOUR

October 17th, 2009
7:32 p.m.

For a moment, time stops. We both just stare at each other. I've decided to use the knife to get me to that phone. I'll call the police, and all of this will be over. Graham looks at me as if I'm a ghost. That look of love and longing to touch me is gone. He's never going to trust me again, but I don't have a choice. Moe could be home soon; we don't have time. I can't sit around and wait for Graham to do the right thing.

"What are you doing, Maxine?" he asks, taking a step toward me.

Be brave, be brave, be brave.

I point the pocketknife toward him. My hand is already shaking.

"I'm going to call the police, Graham."

Graham sighs and looks behind me, at the phone.

"Don't do this," he says, looking back at me.

"I don't have a choice."

"Maxine." He takes another step toward me.

"Get back!"

I take slow steps toward the kitchen. I can do this. I keep the knife pointed at Graham. He lifts his hands in the air and watches me as I walk. My heart is hammering in my chest.

I make it to the phone. Keeping my eyes and the knife on Graham, I grab the handset and bring it to my ear. I rest it against my shoulder and use my hand to dial nine. I don't hear anything. I quickly press the one twice. *Nothing*. It's dead.

"Hello," I say into the clearly dead phone.

"I'm sorry, Maxine. I wanted to tell you."

I turn my head to look over at Graham, but as I do so, I feel his hand tightly grasp my wrist. He pulls on it, and my hand, which I hadn't noticed is sweating, drops the knife. I go to catch it before it can land on the floor, but Graham beats me to the punch. Now the tables have turned. The knife is pointed at me. I drop the phone and hear it clash onto the floor.

I should have never grabbed that knife. I knew it could be a decision with dire consequences. I just didn't have enough faith in Graham to save Eva. There were so many better options. I could have gotten out of here on my own and gotten her help. But instead, I was rash.

I can explain to Graham I wasn't going to hurt him. That when he pulled me out from that hole, I knew I needed him more than he did me. He must believe in the end I never would have hurt him. Then again, it'll still be a devastating blow when he hears it was even a thought in the first place.

"Graham, I . . ." I stutter.

His eyes are filled with a fiery rage I've never seen before. For the first time, I see the same hate in his eyes that I've seen in Moe's.

"Why couldn't you just have trusted me? I *loved* you." A tear rolls down his cheek.

I try to caress his cheek. He shrinks away from me like I am a disgusting insect getting in his space.

"I'm sorry, Graham. I was just so scared. I didn't know what else to do."

Graham doesn't budge at my groveling.

"There wasn't a line I wouldn't have crossed for you. I was willing to risk it all if it meant saving you."

His words sting and fill my mind with a cloud of even more guilt.

"Just give me a minute to expla—"

"Get downstairs, Maxine."

"Graham, ple—"

"Go!" he shouts, bringing the knife closer to me.

I want to believe he wouldn't be so angry as to kill me, but I think of my mother. She was heartbroken enough to kill a child. When people feel like they've been wronged, they will do unthinkable things to hurt those who betrayed them.

Graham follows behind me back down the stairs to the basement. I had prayed that the next time I went down these stairs, it would be to save Eva. Not to be once again locked up with her. I imagine her face when she sees me again. Sees Graham taking me down to be a prisoner. Some savior I've turned out to be.

When we make it down the stairs, Eva is sitting on her bunk. She looks confused at the sight of us. Probably confused as to how I'm still alive. She probably thinks I convinced Graham to set us both free. Thinks she'll finally get out of that cage. Then I see her hope shift to anger when Graham leads me into my cage. I can practically feel her hate burn into my skin with each step I take back into the cage.

Graham closes the cage door.

I could try to barge out again, knock him off balance. I want to try, hoping that Graham wouldn't have it in him to hurt me. My heart, however, stops me, not wanting to try anymore.

Graham puts the new lock on the cage door and shuts it. He turns to leave, but before making it a step forward, he stops and turns back toward me. He reaches into his jean pocket and pulls out the pocketknife.

"If my father comes back before I do, use this." He passes the knife to me through the bars.

"Don't say a word, or I will kill you," he says, staring daggers at Eva.

This should make me happy, but it makes me feel ten times worse. This feels like Graham is saying goodbye.

"It was a mistake, Graham."

"Good luck, Maxine," he says hoarsely, making for the stairs.

"Graham, you promised you wouldn't leave me," I plead.

He stops for a moment but doesn't turn around. For a second, I think I might've changed his mind.

"You promised you'd trust me. I guess we both lied," he says and continues to walk away.

It's silent for a couple minutes. I feel Eva's eyes on me. I know she wants to know what all just happened. I don't think I can tell her. It'll just make all of it more real.

"I thought you were dead," Eva says, now standing by the bars that separate us.

I shake my head, turning my face from hers to wipe away some tears. I lean down to grab the knife. It feels cold in my hand. I may be on my own, but I have my last play right here. Whether I'll be able to use it when the time comes is another question.

"What happened?" Eva sounds sympathetic.

"I did what you said — or tried to, at least. Had the knife but couldn't kill him. So, I tried calling the police with that stupid phone."

"But he left you the knife?"

I nod again.

"You know what you have to do, then?"

I remember Graham's story about Eva.

"Are you going to tell Moe?" I ask. "Graham says you have a thing for ratting out girls with weapons."

Eva looks momentarily confused before rolling her eyes.

"I had to do that. That girl — she would've got us both killed. Her for having it and me for not telling Moe. Don't judge me; judge Graham for giving it to her in the first place."

I put my hands into my jacket pockets and find the necklace. The one that belonged to that mysterious woman. I take it out and stare at it. I forgot to show it to Graham.

"Do you know much about Graham's mother?"

"Not much. She's the reason Moe kills, I'm guessing."

I hold up the heart pendant. "They threw me in a pit, out behind the barn. I found this on a dead body."

"You stole it from a dead body?"

"No . . . well, yeah. I saw this necklace in a picture of a woman that Graham keeps in his bedroom drawer. I thought she had possibly been an old girlfriend of his. Now I'm not sure."

"You think it might've been his mother?"

Another nod.

"And what did you say when you showed it to him?"

I can't answer that.

"Jesus, Max. You didn't tell him? Why not? Maybe if he knew Moe killed his mother, he'd have a reason to kill that cocksucker."

"I tried — it just didn't happen."

"*It just didn't happen.* What are you thinking?"

Now Eva is irate, her words biting. Just like when she had showed up at my house the morning after that party. When I refused to tell her what really happened. When I left her to drown in uncertainty.

"Fuck you, Max Masterson," she had said in between her weeping, right before I slammed the door in her face.

"I'm sorry. I'll just have to kill him. We'll be okay, I promise."

Eva scoffs. She doesn't trust me, and I don't blame her.

"Just don't tell Moe."

"Give me the knife," she orders.

I scrunch my eyebrows, expecting that to be a joke.

"And why would I do that?"

"Because when the time comes, you won't use it. I will."

She's not wrong, but it doesn't matter. Graham gave me this knife to protect myself. I'm keeping it.

"No, Eva. When he comes down here, it will be for me."

When Eva doesn't respond, I say, "I know I've let you down, a lot. But I'm going to kill him, once and for all. For you, me, and all the girls before us."

CHAPTER FIFTY-FIVE

October 18th, 2009
8:14 a.m.
Mikey

Mikey has wanted to give up his search for Max. He tried convincing himself last night as he laid in bed. But something in the pit of his stomach warned him not to. That he had to at least know for sure she is safe. She would do it for him. He thinks.

Joey's lumberyard opened fourteen minutes ago, but Mikey's been sitting in the parking lot for over half an hour. He has sat and watched as all the employees slowly trickled into the building: laborers dressed in oversized flannel shirts and shrugging on fluorescent yellow vests, and a middle-aged woman dressed in drab office apparel, who showed up at 7 a.m. on the dot. Mikey assumes she must be the front desk clerk. Not long after that, an overweight man arrives, who Mikey recognizes as Joey, the owner.

Mikey has heard a lot about Joey. That he's a mean son of a bitch to work for. That he is a complete creep to women. All in all, none of the things he's heard about this man are glowing references.

Joey is apparently Graham's uncle. Mikey knows he could enter and talk to him, but as he watches the mean-looking man enter the building with a bottle of booze wrapped in a brown paper bag in one hand, a cigarette in the other, he now thinks better of it. Joey is a creep. A creep who would protect his scumbag family. No, Mikey knows he has to leave all his pent-up anger inside until the one who deserves it shows up.

Mikey sits for another twenty minutes until he sees a van pull into the lot. Graham is driving. If he was supposed to show up to work at eight, that means he's late. Is that usual for him? Does his uncle let him stroll in whenever he wants? Or is he never late, and this is an off day?

Graham parks near the front of the lot and takes a few minutes to exit his vehicle. Mikey watches as he just sits there and looks straight ahead at nothing. Before going into work at the butt crack of dawn, it's normal to get yourself together for a couple moments. But the way Graham just sits there is suspicious. His face looks blank.

When he finally does get out, his walk is slow, and his feet drag against the gravel parking lot. He's walking like a zombie.

Mikey puts his hand on the door handle, ready to get out and brave this ghastly-looking man. Before he can open the door, his phone rings. Max's father. It's rare he calls. Mikey takes a preemptive sign of relief, believing this could all be over. That Jerry has finally located her.

"Hi, Jerry," he says into his phone as he watches Graham. "What's going on?"

"I went over to Max's house last night," Jerry says, taking a deep breath.

"And—?" Mikey is beginning to feel Jerry is about to tell him something terrible.

What if he's too late? What if Jerry found Max's dead body, and Mikey did nothing to help her?

Flashes of her body lying dead on the cold ground of a field appear in his mind. Her skin covered in dirt and blood. Her warm brown eyes with orange tones still open in a look of pure agony.

"She wasn't there, but her suitcase and some clothes were missing."

She packed a bag. Was all this worrying about her well-being for nothing? Was Max really just going off the deep end? Did he not know Max like he thought he did? Would she be capable of throwing out everything she'd worked so hard for just for some guy? It couldn't be.

"The night Max missed AA, I saw her. She was with a guy who said his name was Clark, but he lied. His name is Graham, and he works at Joey's Lumberyard."

Jerry takes a deep breath. "Some people use a cover at those meetings, I'm sure. She probably just ran off with this guy. Wait . . . how did you find this shit out?"

"I . . . it doesn't matter. I'm at the lumberyard. I'm going to talk to him."

"Mikey, come on. You're going to get yourself in trouble. Max will come back."

Mikey doesn't want to just let this go. If he does and Max turns up dead, he will never forgive himself.

There are already so many horror stories of troubled women going missing and never coming back. Everyone thought they had just run off, but some of their bodies were found. Mikey couldn't just write Max's disappearance off like those other girls' loved ones had.

"I love my daughter," Jerry says, "but she's a troubled girl. I thought AA could help, but clearly her problem is beyond just that. She needs to go back to therapy."

Don't we all?

Mikey ends the call after assuring Jerry he won't do anything stupid. That he just wants to talk to Graham. Make sure she's at a safe place if she has begun drinking again. Which, after hearing about Max packing a bag, is Mikey's new plan. At first, he wanted to demand Graham tell him where she is and show him she's safe. Now he's not sure she is in trouble but has rather made the stupid decision to hit the bottle. Hopefully Graham will be helpful, tell Mikey what he knows.

Mikey drops the phone on the passenger seat and looks back up. Graham is still standing outside but has been joined by his uncle. Joey's angry. Mikey can see he's giving Graham an earful. Graham's hands are dug into his jean pockets. What's Joey telling him off about? Being late?

Mikey is parked over ten yards away but rolls down his Jeep's window, hoping he can overhear their conversation.

"You overslept? Are you fucking kidding me?" he hears Joey yell.

Graham's reply is short, but Mikey can't hear what he says.

"You know how weird that looks?" Joey shouts. "Right now, especially?"

What does he mean by that?

Graham's mouth remains shut, his eyes on the ground.

"Get the fuck inside. You're lucky I don't fire your ass right now."

Joey turns and stomps inside the building. Mikey needs to move now. Before that conversation, he had been doubtful about approaching Graham. Now, more than ever, he wants to speak to him. He jumps out of the Jeep and jogs over to Graham before Graham can follow his uncle inside.

Mikey sees Graham's eyes widen — like he's been caught doing something wrong. Just looking at him makes Mikey want to grab him by his shirt collar and demand he tell him where Max is. He restrains himself, knowing anger won't get him any closer to the truth.

"Hey, I'm Mikey. Remember me? I'm a friend of Max Masterson," Mikey says.

Now that Mikey is close to Graham, he sees the bruises on his face. One looks fresh, and he has a bandage over a swelling cut. Like he's been beaten up and hit with an object. His eyes look bloodshot and have dark circles underneath them. Mikey recalls noticing some minor bruising on his face when he first encountered him but nothing like the fresh bruises he has now.

Graham presses his dry lips together and clenches his fists. "Max? From AA, right?"

"Yeah, I was just wondering if I could talk to you for a moment."

Graham looks up toward the building as if he wishes he were anywhere but here.

"I'm running late for work. Would another time be okay?"

"I'll be quick. Max hasn't been home for a couple days, and she's missed work. I saw you two together and was just wondering if maybe you've seen her?"

Graham hesitates before letting out a breath, laughing.

"Something funny?" Mikey asks.

"Aren't you married, man?"

"And?"

"And you're wondering where this girl is?"

Mikey clenches his fists to keep his anger under control.

"And what was your name? Clark? Or is it Graham?"

"I don't share my real name at AA for privacy reasons. Why are you here?"

"Look, I'm not here to argue. I just want to know if you've seen Max. She's been MIA for two days, and no one knows where she is."

"I don't know what to tell you."

"Really? You don't know or you won't tell me? Because I think you know where she is."

"Why is that?"

"Because Jay, her AA sponsor, told me someone saw you two leaving the building together."

Graham looks as though he just got punched in the gut. He looks away as if he's trying to think up an answer.

Mikey has already caught him in one lie. He should just bring what he knows to the police. Would they be able to do anything? Could she even be considered a missing person? Her father and aunt don't seem to think so. It would take a couple days before they come around to that idea. Max may not have a couple days.

"Yeah, that does ring a bell. She seemed stressed out. Would you have had anything to do with that?" Graham finally says.

"What are you insinuating?"

"What I'm insinuating is, maybe Maxine doesn't want to be found right now. That life has been hard for her, and she needs a break."

Did he just call her Maxine? No one, not even her own family, calls her by her full name. It shouldn't matter, but hearing the way Graham says her name gives him the shivers. Like she's his dog or property. How does he even know she's called Maxine? Max never uses the name. She's preferred being called Max since she was a child.

"You don't know anything about her. I've known Max for years, and I care about her. She needs help."

"You don't care about her the same way I do. You're married," Graham replies coldly.

"It doesn't matter. If you know where she is, you need to tell me."

"What I'm going to tell you, Mikey, is that Maxine doesn't want to see you. She needs a break from you parasites."

Mikey is taken aback by Graham's sudden resentment and jealousy. He's no longer standing like a coward; his shoulders are straight, like he's ready to fight.

"If you knew anything about her, you'd know she hates being called Maxine."

Graham chuckles lightly. "She didn't have a problem with it last night."

All of Mikey's past plans of being nice go up in smoke. Graham just crossed a line. He feels all the anger he's been storing away start to boil up and into his head. Just the notion of this creep's hands on Max's body, ravishing her, makes Mikey want to punch him square in the face.

"Tell me where the fuck she is, right now."

"Or what?"

"Or I'll call the police."

"And say what?"

Mikey is bluffing, and it looks like Graham knows it. He's a lot more intimidating and intelligent than Mikey initially perceived him to be.

"Just tell me where she is. If she's drinking or doing drugs."

"She's not some little project for you. Just because you're bored with your wife doesn't mean you can just use her as some hobby."

"This has nothing to do with me. I'm worried about my friend who was last seen with a guy whose face looks like someone beat him up."

"I would never hurt her," Graham replies bitterly.

"Just tell me where she is, you freak!" Mikey screams, not sure how much longer he'll be able to keep his fist from colliding with Graham's face.

"I'm not telling you shit. Find another bitch to cheat on your wife w—"

Before Graham can finish, Mikey sucker punches him.

CHAPTER FIFTY-SIX

October 18th, 2009
7:42 a.m.
Mikey

It happens so fast. One moment they're talking, the next Mikey's nursing his stinging knuckles, and Graham's on the ground clutching his bleeding nose.

Before anything else can happen, the office door chimes. He looks up to see Joey running down the front steps.

"What the hell is going on?" Joey asks, out of breath.

"He punched me in the fucking face!" Graham yells, getting back to his feet.

Joey is smirking as he steps between the two of them.

"He knows where my friend is," Mikey says, pointing at Graham.

"What's he talking about?" Joey asks, his smirk disappearing.

"Max — or as that freak calls her, Maxine Masterson. She's been missing for two days and was last seen with him."

"Go home to your wife, Mikey!" Graham shrieks.

Mikey goes to take a step toward him, but Joey lightly shoves him away with his hand.

"Calm down, calm down, ladies."

269

"Just tell me where she is."

"The girl's safe," Joey says.

Mikey is taken aback. Joey has seen her. Been around her. That brings him more discomfort. Max must have felt uneasy being around this large creepy man. He smells of freshly rolled cigarettes, booze, and stale oil. Graham is a stick figure of a man — Max could take him if she tried — but Joey's another thing entirely.

If they did abduct Max, the only question is, why? Why Max? Has she just been unlucky falling in with a shady guy like Graham? And if they did take her, why would Joey be putting his skin on the line, admitting to a complete stranger that he's seen her? He doesn't seem close to his nephew. Quite the opposite.

"How do you know?" Mikey asks.

"I saw her at his place last night," Joey says.

"Willingly?" Mikey dubiously asks.

Graham makes a move toward Mikey, irritated by his question. Joey pushes him back.

"She was wearing his clothes, so . . . you do the math."

If this man weren't such a heavyweight, Mikey would punch him too.

Logic says Max is safe and has just been sleeping over at Graham's. But Mikey's gut says that isn't it. It says Max is in danger, and these guys are trying to fool him. His father always told him to trust his gut instinct. It's clear they are not going to be dishing out any truth, so he will have to think of a different plan. One that will allow him to get to Graham's house.

"If you're covering for him, the police will know."

"You aren't the one to be threatening me with the cops, boy. As I see it, you have two choices right now. You can leave, and I won't call the cops on you. Or you can stay and wait for the cops to arrive and go to jail on an assault charge."

Would the police being here do any good? If Mikey explained to them about Max, would they believe she's in danger? It's not likely. The police in this town are lazy, and right now there's more chance of Mikey being arrested.

He shouldn't have punched Graham. He just couldn't take that smug look on his face. At least he was able to discover his uncle is in on it. If they are here, that means they aren't hurting Max.

Mikey decides to leave — for now.

* * *

He doesn't make it far before pulling over. He plans to call Max's dad to tell him everything that just occurred and hopefully convince him to call the police. They'll listen to a relative.

Before he can dial Jerry's number, his phone begins to ring.

Shit, it's Adrienne.

He considers ignoring the call, but she might be calling about his son. He reluctantly answers it.

"Where the hell are you?" she snarls, before he can say anything.

"Work."

"You're lying. I called your work, and they said you called off. Where are you?"

Shit, shit. I don't have the energy for this right now.

Adrienne could get Mikey in trouble for calling his work, asking where he is. He's the only one who makes money in their house, and she's putting them in danger of losing that.

"You called my work? Why?"

"Because I knew something was up. I saw the look on your face this morning. Are you with her?" Adrienne asks, her voice breaking at the last question.

Mikey should feel guilty. He did at first. When he first saw Max at the restaurant and couldn't keep his eyes off her. She had changed so much, but just like the first time he laid his eyes on her, he was starstruck. Max really is the most beautiful girl he's ever been with.

It isn't just her appearance. It's that longing in her eyes. Especially before she went to prison. She had this extroverted party-girl persona, but deep within her eyes there was always a wanting. Wanting to be somewhere else with someone else. Like the people in this town knew too much about her.

She hates living in Mendex — has since before they met. She would never say it, but Mikey knows why. She feels they all judge her for what her mother did. It happened so many years ago, but people never forget when something so atrocious happens in a small town. Sometimes when they would be out, Mikey would notice people whispering, staring at Max like she was some sort of infamous celebrity. For that reason, Mikey never asked her about her mother or what happened. He still believes to this day that that is one of the only reasons she even dated him. He muted that awful event for her.

There was something else he felt she was hiding. Something more personal. No one avoided relationships like she did. Mikey wanted her to feel comfortable enough to tell him her other secrets. But getting Max to talk about her past was like trying to solve a Rubik's Cube.

"No, I'm not with her. She's missing, Adrienne."

"Missing? I just saw her, what, two days ago."

"Yeah, and that same day she went to AA and disappeared with some guy."

Mikey doesn't mention the fact that she packed a suitcase. It'll make Adrienne dubious, like the others.

"What guy? Wait — don't answer that. I cannot believe I am letting you get me wrapped up in that girl's life. None of this is our concern. Let her father figure it out. For Christ's sake, Mikey, *I'm* your wife."

"I know, I just don't want to do nothing and find out she's . . . she's—" Mikey cuts off that sentence when an image of Max's dead body flashes through his mind.

"Are you doing this because you feel responsible for her? For what we did while you two were dating?"

Mikey's hands start to shake. He wishes he had a cigarette or cold beer. Or both. Anything to not think about what he did.

Max still didn't know what he did while they were together. It was one of the biggest mistakes of his life. He had just reached a breaking point with her. With how distant she was.

The night before Max cheated on him, Mikey called her four times before she answered. All he wanted was to take her on a date or even hang out at home. Max was upset and drunk, wallowing in her sorrows. He begged her to let him stop by, so they could talk about whatever she was going through. She refused and told him to call her the next day.

He should've stayed home. But he felt so frustrated. He only stopped at Adrienne's because she said she had weed. He thought it would calm his nerves. Adrienne convinced him to stay and have a few beers with her. A few turned into a lot. Adrienne always had a big crush on him. One thing led to another.

He couldn't face Max, not at first, anyways. The next day he was the one ignoring her calls. He planned to tell her — just not that day. Then she betrayed him. Slept with one of his buddies. A sick part of Mikey felt relieved. He was no longer the cheating asshole. He shifted all his anger onto her.

"No, I'm not," he finally says through gritted teeth.

"Does she know?"

"It doesn't matter."

"Come home, Mikey," Adrienne says. She doesn't sound exasperated anymore.

Mikey doesn't reply. He can't form the words. He's been hiding from the anguish of hurting Adrienne for the last week at least. Now everything seems to have come to a head.

"I can't compare to her, I know that. It's killing me. Please, don't do this."

It's not often Adrienne shows her fear. She had gained some weight and let herself go since they had their son. Mikey never pressured her to take better care of herself. His whole life he's tried not to overvalue physical appearance. Max is beautiful and always has been. But it's not the reason he's been stuck on her for so long.

"I'll be home soon. I've got to go. I'm sorry," he replies, and before she can answer, he hangs up.

He must end this, whether he goes to jail or not. He doesn't bother calling Jerry. He won't listen. Instead, he pulls a U-turn and drives back to the lumberyard. He's going to sit there and wait for that fucker Graham to leave.

Once he reaches the road that passes the lumberyard, he sees that Graham and Joey are no longer in the parking lot. Neither is the van Graham arrived in. Mikey catches his breath, believing he has just made a horrific error.

Graham must have panicked at Mikey's presence. He knows someone is on his trail. Mikey could've inadvertently put Max in even more danger. And now he has no leads.

But no, Joey's truck is still in the lot. He will have to wait till the big guy leaves and follow him.

Mikey parks on the street across from the lumberyard. He opens his glove box. In it is his double-action revolver. He checks the chamber — only four bullets. He hopes he won't have to use any of them. He just needs the gun to force Joey to take him to Graham's house.

It's a crazy plan, but it's also the only one he has left. Max's life is on the line.

CHAPTER FIFTY-SEVEN

October 18th, 2009
8:09 a.m.

I awake to the light of the sun. I think I'm dreaming at first. The thought of ever seeing sunshine again seemed like a fantasy. Almost as though that day I ran across that field was years ago. I can't imagine how long the other girls went without seeing sunlight. How scared they must've been before being put out of their misery on a dirty cement floor.

All those girls' disappearances may never be solved if I don't escape. I remember some of the beautiful blonde girls' photos being shown on the news. Their families urging anyone who might have information to come forward. Their families deserve closure.

I barely slept last night. I kept waking up at every little sound. Most of it was the old house creaking or Eva's loud breathing as she slept. Every single sound awoke me in a jolt. I kept expecting Moe to come down. He'd be angry Graham moved me and start whatever torture he saw fit. No one would stop him. No one except me. I gripped the pocketknife in my jacket pocket all night.

I go to rub the crust from my eyelids, but I can't move my hands. I realize they are tied together behind my back. The rough feeling of the rope as I attempt to move my hands is all too familiar.

I open my eyes. I'm not in the basement. Through the window of the vehicle, I see a blur of trees. The vehicle hits a speed bump and I bounce out of the seat momentarily.

What's going on? Has Graham finally got me out of that cage? Is he taking me away? Of course, he can't trust me enough not to tie me up.

I look at the driver, prepared to see Graham again. I'll apologize for what happened. Then I'll beg him to take me to the police station.

I'm wrong. Horrifically wrong. It's not Graham in the driver's seat. It's Moe.

CHAPTER FIFTY-EIGHT

October 18th, 2009
8:09 a.m.

This is it. Eva said he wanted to use my old sedan to kill me, and now he's doing it.

Did Graham rat me out? Or did Moe just decide to go forward with killing me without Graham's knowledge? It must be the latter. I know Graham is angry with me, but I feel deep in my heart that he wouldn't allow this. Could I use this knowledge to my advantage? Tell Moe if he kills me that Graham will kill him? Would that even scare him? Can you scare a psychopath?

Moe glances back at me and makes a wicked grin when he sees I'm awake.

"Good morning." He looks back at the road.

"What are you doing?"

"I couldn't wait any longer. It's a beautiful morning, and my son is away. I see you tricked him into letting you out of the pit."

"Don't do this," I beg.

Moe chuckles, the wrinkles at the sides of his mouth creasing. "Why do you all beg? Maybe you're too stupid to know that begging just makes it all the more enjoyable for me."

He's talking about the other girls he killed. He's speaking of it with such a calm and collected state of mind. He's right, though. I can't beg for mercy when he's incapable of empathy.

"Graham will be angry with you."

"You're not the first one to use my son against me. You girls think you're so special."

"Girls." Not "creatures." That's a first. Perhaps the creature bit is just a façade. Something to control his son. Make him believe we're not human. Moe knows and sees us as women.

"Am I the first girl he's loved?"

Moe looks back at me as though we're two friends chatting over a nice drive in the country.

"He doesn't love you. He may think he does. He's confused. You two have an awful lot in common."

What does Moe know about me? The confusion must show on my face.

"I know all about you, Maxine Masterson. I know what your father did, and what your mother did in retaliation. You and your mother are very similar. I wasn't expecting that."

His words infuriate me. It took so long for people, including myself, to convince me I am nothing like her. She murdered a child for "love." She took her life in front of me to escape the consequences.

"I am nothing like her," I reply through clenched teeth.

"Oh, you don't think so? You're both alcoholics. You both fell in love with men who wanted a different woman. You both go after what you want even if it wreaks havoc on others. Then again, that sums up most women."

I am unsure how to respond, so I don't. He's getting some sick pleasure from this, I can tell. The same pleasure he got from hearing about Eva's rape.

I've wasted so much time trying to talk to this monster, and it's only made matters worse. I think back to Graham's last words to me.

If my father comes back before I do, use this.

I wish I had woken up when he came down to the basement to grab me. I must've been so sleep deprived I just slept through it. I still might have the pocketknife in my pocket. I thankfully kept it in my right pocket, which is facing away from Moe. I force my hands toward the pocketknife. I manage to grab ahold of the outside of the jacket's pocket and feel the weight of it. It is still in there. I scowl to mask my relief.

Can I get the knife and cut the rope from my hands? I hope so. But then I will have to stab Moe. It gives me a queasy feeling, but I have to. If anyone deserves to be stabbed, it's this man.

I remember the object that's in my left pocket. The necklace. I will use it to distract him.

"I found a dead body in that pit, you know," I say, as I work my hands into the pocket.

He just smiles, as if reveling in the thought of the fear that must've caused me.

I need to keep him talking. That way he may not take notice of my fidgeting.

"It — she had a necklace."

Moe seems uninterested in what I'm saying. As though I'm a child in the car whining about wanting to stop for McDonald's.

"It was the same necklace that a woman wore in a photo Graham had in his room."

Moe raises his eyebrows, finally showing some emotion. He doesn't speak, but his expression is enough confirmation.

"At first, I thought she might be some woman Graham loved and you took away. But I don't think Graham knows what love is. You made sure of that when you killed his mother and filled his mind with a hatred of women."

"Graham isn't as innocent as you think. He just hides it better. Did you ever wonder why he's been so loyal to me all these years?"

I'd have been an idiot not to. It's all I've been questioning. Why Graham won't stand up to his father when he is physically stronger.

"Graham killed someone before I ever did."

What? He's lying. He has to be.

"Graham and George's mother. She was going to leave me. Our marriage had been on the rocks for some time."

"So, you killed her before she could get away?" I ask, disgust in my voice.

Moe chuckles.

"I was at work the day she was planning to leave. I told her to take one of the boys but leave me one. I didn't care which. I just needed help keeping the farm up. So, who did she pick, you ask? Little George."

Moe is silent for a moment before continuing. "I came home from work, prepared to never see one of my sons again. Instead, I came home to find her dead body in the master bedroom and a pistol in guess whose hand?"

No, no. It can't be.

CHAPTER FIFTY-NINE

October 18th, 2009
8:12 a.m.

"Graham shot his mother. In the back of the head. He was so small, I don't know how the little shit aimed so perfectly."

I hold back a gasp. He's speaking with such conviction. Like he's been holding in this ugly truth for a long time and feels freed to finally let it go.

"You're lying," I say, my voice cracking.

Why or how could Graham do such a thing? He was just a little boy. How could he have the mental capacity to realize his mother was choosing his brother over him?

Why would he kill her? I stop forcing my hands into the pocket of the jacket while I question their family drama. It's as though this revelation is too strong to multitask.

"But he was just a child. He wouldn't have gotten in any trouble."

"Yeah, well, sadly it was a little too late when he figured that out. By that time, he had already participated in a few murders. Cleaned up the mess, hid the bodies."

"Is that why George was so cruel to Graham?"

"I told George she left because of them. Said she could no longer take the pressure."

"How did you not get—"

"Get caught? Hannah didn't have many friends. She hadn't spoken to her family in over fifteen years. I told Graham if he was honest with the men in blue, they would take him away to a very bad place. I gave him a choice that day. He could be honest, or he could lie. A lot of people never get that choice when they kill someone. So, he and George told the police the last time they saw her, she was leaving with a suitcase. My brother supplied me with an alibi. She simply became a missing person. Gone with the wind, like the others are now.

"After that, I tried my best to raise my boys to stay away from women — to ingrain into their brains that love is only temporary. That women are evil and loving them only ends in pain."

"You ruined their lives."

"I saved them from becoming boring and sad pieces of shit."

He could be lying. This could be some sick game. Make me hate Graham before dying. When — if — I see Graham again, I will ask him. I should be revolted if this is true, but Graham was just a little boy. A little boy who saw his mother choose his brother over him.

It would make sense as to why Graham has had the need to stand by his father for all this time. He covered up the murder of his mother for him.

"How many other girls were there?"

"I'm not sure. Fourteen? Maybe more. George had his own number as well. I liked it — more than I ever liked my wife. It felt good. I thank her every night for the hobby she gifted me."

I grit my teeth and curse myself; I'm an idiot for letting him entangle me in his disgusting lust for murder. I squirm my hands back into the jacket pocket. My left arm is too short to reach inside, but my right can graze it. Before long, I grasp the handle.

"You're the only person I've ever told this to, apart from my brother, of course."

"You're both sick, demented, rapist psychopaths," I curse at him, raising my voice, masking the sound of the blade opening.

"Rapists?" Moe asks, beginning to chuckle.

Once the blade is out, I maneuver it onto the rope and begin cutting. I make sure to turn my body toward him and although the sight of him disgusts me, it also blocks his view of my back completely.

"I never touched any of those whores. I could have, but my need for women vanished the day my wife left me. George and Joey, on the other hand, they took care of that form of torment. A little funny you're calling *me* the rapist, given your history with Eva."

I gulp. He's right. I let it happen.

"Oh — Eva. I should've let her kill you. I know she wanted to; I could tell by the look in her eyes. You did her wrong."

I want to tell him I was too drunk to understand the atrocious thing I didn't try to stop. That's the excuse I've been telling myself. But why should I? Moe knows the actual truth. I did it to get what I wanted. Just like he kills to get what he wants.

"I'm nowhere near the monster you are. I don't purposely kill others for some sick pleasure."

Moe laughs at that. But he doesn't know I am slowly using a knife to cut through the ropes that bind me. The same knife I'm going to stick into his foul body. I have to play along with the sick game he's playing in our conversation.

"I like Eva," he says. "She's not really like a woman at all — too strong, mentally speaking. Can't let her go, of course. She'd tell the police everything. She'd make sure the three of us never see the light of day again. We'd probably all get the death penalty. Graham hates her, of course. He wants to get rid of her, so no one knows what all he helped with. But I'm going to keep her around for now. Till he sneaks in there one day and takes her out."

I tightly close my eyes. If I am to get out of this, I will have to talk Eva into letting them think Graham is innocent in his family's escapades. That he was forced to participate in the murders. He said he only ever killed one person, which I'm assuming might be two now if Moe is telling the truth about his mother. But he was just a child then.

"Graham isn't capable of ending an innocent life." But I'm not sure I believe that.

"There are a lot of things that boy is capable of."

I gulp. He's messing with me. Trying to once again taint my view of his son.

"You're wrong."

"Before you killed George, there were two girls — sisters. Graham was very fond of them. Too fond — I had to get rid of them. I gave them a kitchen knife. Gave them the choice to kill one another. Told them it would be by my hand or their own. In the end, one stabbed the other and then slit her wrists. Quite beautiful."

I feel sick listening to that. I feel the gut-wrenching fear they must've felt. How Graham must've suffered witnessing it. Anyone he's ever cared for has been brutally murdered.

"Why are you telling me this?"

"Well, I tasked Graham with the cleanup. My own personal punishment for him getting too close to them. Told him to clean the blood from the basement and arrange their bodies for burial. He was down there for a long time. When I went downstairs to check on him, he was . . . lying with their bodies, between them, and snuggling them awfully close."

I want to grab a tight hold of my stomach to stop myself from vomiting. I instead hold my breath and tightly shut my eyes, forcing the images to go away.

"I think he was pretending they were both still alive and would lie with him like that."

284

I can't allow Moe to trick me. He's just trying to make me sick. Cause me to be weaker and easier to kill. If I survive, I will ask Graham if this is true. I'll believe him more than I ever would believe this psycho. Even if it is true, it just means Graham is a lot sicker than I originally thought. He's not dangerous. He's not like his father.

"I thought I wouldn't have to worry about him. That lying with those sisters would give him the contact and love he needed. Then he saw you for the first time. Out in the rain — standing over his dead brother."

Air escapes my mouth. I hadn't realized I'd been holding it in that long.

"He was . . . there?"

Moe nods.

No, he wasn't. Couldn't have been. If he was, what stopped him from killing me? Surely, he'd be angry enough to do so. That, or kidnap me and take me to his father.

"Why didn't he—"

"Kill you then and there? I asked that same question. He said that he wanted to do more to you. That killing you wouldn't be enough. I didn't really understand. George and he were never close. Then the police showed me a picture of you, and it all made sense. You are the epitome of that boy's fantasy. A broken, beautiful blonde, just like his mother. It was all his idea, you know. Staying out of the court and allowing you to be released sooner. I should've known it was to get closer to you sooner, but a part of me hoped he really did want to torture you."

This was all Graham's idea? The stalking and plot to kill me? I thought Moe had been pulling the strings. Did Graham just leave that part of the story out?

I am nearly done cutting through the rope. What is my plan after this? Stab Moe, hopefully somewhere vital. Somewhere that will hurt. He's driving at least fifty miles per hour, from the way the car is bumping about. If I stab him now, we'll crash. I'm not wearing a seatbelt, so if we get in a bad wreck, it could kill us both. I could jump out of the car door. The ground outside is all long grass. Then what, though? Flag down a passing car? The sun is barely in the sky, so it must still be early in the morning. I don't know how far we traveled let alone where we even are. I don't see any signs of life out here.

I stop worrying about my safety and just focus on killing Moe. He deserves to die. I stare at him as he adjusts the radio. "I Fall to Pieces" by Patsy Cline begins to play. Moe drums his hand on the wheel and moves his head to the slow country song.

"There it is." He points at a large oak tree in the distance. "I've buried several other girls there. It's a beautiful resting place. The least I can offer them."

I gasp. I'm running out of time. I continue cutting at the rope until it's cut through. I hold in a breath of relief. I'm going to kill this sick son of a bitch.

"The others, they weren't personal. Killing them was merely a game. But you — you are here for killing my son."

I bite my lip hard. There is no going back after I take the knife out. He could grab it before I get a chance to stab him. I could die. As we get near the oak tree, Moe finally lets up on the gas pedal. We slow down to twenty miles an hour. It's time to ask.

"Do you want your wife's necklace back?"

Moe raises his eyebrows. "You have it?"

I nod and look down at my left pocket. Moe reaches his hand toward me, and I grip the knife in my right hand. I'm gripping it so tightly it feels numb.

Be brave, Max.

CHAPTER SIXTY

October 18th, 2009
8:18 a.m.

Moe considers my offer. My hand is clammy around the pocket-knife. I worry I may drop it when I try to stab him. That, or he may catch me and wrestle the knife from me. He has so much more strength, and he's been murdering women for years.

If I do stab him, I know it will not kill him. I don't need him to die, just to be wounded. If I jump out of the sedan, he'll hopefully crash. Make it immobile. I'm counting on that happening because if it doesn't, he can just run me over. That must be a part of his sick plan. I don't see a weapon on him. He must have been planning to let me out and kill me the same way I killed his son. It must seem like retribution in his eyes.

He is nearly at the tree when he finally reaches for me.

Once his hand is inside my pocket I say, "I don't regret killing your son. I used to, until I found out he's a sick fuck like you."

He stares at me, his eyes burning with the fire of intense hatred.

Before he can speak, I move the knife from behind me and, with all the strength I have, I plunge it into his side. His eyes are on me the entire time. Blood spurts from his side and he lets out an angry groan.

"You fucking bitch!" he screams, sending spittle across my face.

I put my free hand over the door handle of the sedan. It's locked, of course. Since this is the exact model I used to own, I find the lock quickly, below the passenger-side window. I snap it up and open the door. Moe puts his foot down on the accelerator hard. The vehicle speeds up and just as I attempt to jump from the open door, Moe grabs my hair, stopping me from doing so. We're only ten yards from the oak tree. If we hit that tree, I will be thrown through the windshield to my death.

The knife is still jammed in his side. I put my hand over it and press it deeper into his side. He screams in pain and lets go of my hair. Once he does, I vault out of the car. I duck and roll, but the drop is still painful. Everything spins as I crash onto the ground. My body hurts all over. My arms are scratched to ribbons. But — I'm alive. I feel so much pain from the jump that I barely hear the sedan bashing into the tree.

As I lie on my stomach, reeling from the pain, I glance up toward the car. Smoke is coming from the hood. The music from the radio continues to play.

Did Moe survive the crash? He was wearing his seatbelt, so I know he didn't fly through the windshield. He hasn't stumbled out yet. I hope he's unconscious. I don't have time to lie here and wait.

I slowly get to my knees. My head spins and my vision is doubled. I lean on the grass feeling like I might either heave or pass out. I see splats of my blood on the ground, trailing behind me from where I landed and rolled. The grass is a couple inches high, which must've cushioned my landing. If it hadn't been there, I probably would have a concussion and broken limbs.

It takes me a minute to stand; my body fights me the whole way up. The air has been knocked from my lungs. I feel as though they might explode. My bare knees have gashes on them, and when I try to take a step forward, I feel them wobble. I look at the wreck, still seeing no movement. Is it possible Moe is dead? I could try getting in the car. Driving to safety, if it isn't too damaged.

I should run — well, walk — away from this. Get as much distance between us as quickly as possible. I don't know how far I'll make it on foot. Taking a couple steps causes unrelenting pain. *Fuck.*

I begin limping toward the vehicle. My feet drag as I walk. If Moe is passed out, I can pull that knife out of his side. I heard you're never supposed to take a knife out of where you've been stabbed. It would wound him even further. If he's still alive, I can stab him in his nonexistent heart. If I don't have the courage to do that, I can toss him out of the car. I may not make it very far before the engine fails but any distance from this man is good.

I approach the driver's side and peer inside. The broken windshield has steam covering it and is allowing the engine fumes in. I make out Moe's body. It's still. I put my hand on the door handle and slowly open it. I prepare myself to slam it shut in case of any sudden movement. I try to remember I am in control right now. Moe is more injured than I am.

Once the door is open, I look him over. He must've broken his nose, banging it on the steering wheel upon impact. It's oozing blood and looks bent. He's leaning back with his head kicked back, eyes closed. Slow, ragged breaths escape his now-open mouth, blood from his nose flowing into it.

I grab ahold of the collar of his shirt and attempt to pull him toward me. He's heavier than I expected. That, and I'm still weak. I gasp as my pain makes me beg for mercy.

Once I get him out of the sedan, this will all be over. I'll be safe. I chant these words to myself repeatedly. Soon Moe's face is eye to eye with my own. I stop for a moment, inhaling a deep breath. I tightly shut my eyes as I do so. When I open them, I'm looking directly into Moe's eyes. They are wide and angry.

CHAPTER SIXTY-ONE

October 18th, 2009
8:25 a.m.

I let out a half scream. Moe grabs my throat, so the scream is lost inside me. My breath had already felt low and shaky, but now it's worse. Even after getting in a crash and breaking his nose, Moe is still strong. His eyes bore into mine. Anger radiates out of them.

"This was a nice car, you bitch!" he screams at me, saliva hitting my face.

Those eyes. The eyes of the devil. He has watched and enjoyed the pain of so many women. I remember my father telling me that if I ever were attacked, I should go for his balls or eyes.

I grab him by the ears, pulling him closer. He lets out a scream of agony. I press my thumbs over his pupils and jam them straight into his eyes.

Moe lets go just as I feel on the verge of passing out from lack of oxygen. He throws me down. My head clashes against the ground and I begin to hear ringing. I attempt to stand up, but I'm coughing too hard.

I roll over onto my stomach and crawl away from him. I'm moving slow, too slow. Even if Moe is momentarily blinded, I can't get away from him fast enough. I am too scared to look back. I hear him making grunts and moans of agony.

A minute or so later, and I'm still crawling away. My lungs slowly filling with air. I attempt to get up on my knees. As I am doing so, there's a sudden stab of pain in my right ankle. I glance behind me to see Moe standing above me, pressing his big black boot on it. Thankfully it isn't soul-crushingly painful. Either he's too weak to properly stomp on me, or I'm filled with so much pain I'm almost too numb to notice.

I let out a yelp and pull my foot away. He's staring at me with that same crazy expression he had when he strangled me. I don't seem to have damaged his eyes at all — I guess I didn't press as hard as I thought.

The pocketknife is still sticking out of his lower abdomen. Blood has nearly covered his entire upper body. He and I are both in bad shape. If I could trip him up, it could hurt him more, buy me time.

"I underestimated you, kid," he says. He reaches into one of the pockets of his overalls.

This is the end. He has a gun in there, and he's going to shoot me.

But it's not a gun he takes from his pocket. It's a pack of cigarettes. He puts a cigarette in his mouth and drops the packet on the ground. He pulls out a lighter and lights it. He takes a slow drag. His eyes roll to the back of his head, and he blows the smoke down in my direction.

"I've never been stabbed before, you know? That shit hurts. No wonder you all scream so loud," he says.

"I hope you bleed to death," I grunt through the pain.

"Did my son give you this?" he asks, pointing at the knife protruding from him.

I nod.

"Goddamn it. I never wanted kids. Fuckers just break your heart."

"You don't have a heart."

"You got me there." Moe coughs loudly as he puffs out another cloud of smoke.

I say nothing, only pull my feet away from him. He grins and this time stomps properly on my ankle. He had been going easy on it earlier. This time I scream out in pain. I sit up and push at his legs. He leans down and, before I know it, punches me in the jaw. I fall back to the ground, guarding my face, ready for another hit.

Moe winces. He grabs ahold of the knife handle and, taking a deep breath, pulls it out. He spits his cigarette out and holds in a scream.

"Well, Maxine Masterson, this is the end of the road," he says, raising the knife.

CHAPTER SIXTY-TWO

October 18th, 2009
8:29 a.m.

I'm not going to let him kill me. He is weakened by blood loss and he must have a concussion. I need something to hit him with. I look around for a rock, but there's only grass under my searching hands. I feel Moe's eyes on me. I know he wants to laugh at my efforts. He's probably watched many girls struggle to find a weapon, any weapon, when he's this close to spilling their blood.

I can't let him win, but my chances are so slim. There are no rocks nearby, and all my strength is gone. I've never felt weaker. I think about Graham. A part of me is angry at him for abandoning me, but another part of me understands his hurt. He must've hoped I could defeat his father, or he wouldn't have given me the pocketknife. If I die, I pray he will kill Moe. End this cycle.

Even if he kills me, Moe will have to go to the hospital after the damage I did. They will ask questions. Questions I hope he cannot answer. He is very manipulative, though. I could see him getting out of it. No, this will all be down to Graham and whether his love for me is strong enough to end his father's reign of terror.

I just hate leaving Eva alone. My one goal, and I failed. I wanted to save her so badly. To right my wrongs. I'm not a good person, but she is. All she ever got in this world is pain and heart-break. It all started with me.

Moe plunges the bloody knife toward my chest. I hold up my hands to protect myself. I'm ready for the blade to go either through them or straight into my chest, piercing my skin and ripping through my heart.

"Father, stop!" somebody screams. Graham.

I turn toward his voice. He's only a few feet away, in a dirty brown T-shirt and blue jeans. In his hands is a shotgun; he's pointing it at his father. I must be hallucinating. How could he have found us?

Then I remember Moe saying he's buried other girls at this exact location, and Graham saying, back when I was in the pit, that he was the one who had done the burying.

Graham does care after all.

Moe freezes. He looks just as shocked at Graham's presence as I am.

"What are you doing here?" Moe angrily asks.

"You can't have her, Father," Graham says. His hands are shaking.

Even with everything going on, most importantly that knife close to slicing into me, I can't help but feel a glimmer of hope. *You can't have her.* He still cares.

"Oh, for fuck's sake, son. She's just a girl. There's millions of them just like her out there."

"None like her."

"You fucking idiot. She's using you, don't you see? We let her go, and she's going to go straight to the police."

"I don't care. I'll shoot you, I swear to God."

Just shoot him now! Moe's not just going to let me go. He'll manipulate Graham into changing his mind. Or he'll see Graham is hesitating to pull the trigger, and he'll finish me off anyways.

But there's something about Graham that makes me think things are different this time. Graham looks less intimidated. His back is straight, and his expression is cold. Moe must see this, or he would have stabbed me already.

"Really? Is that how it's going to be? You finally decided to grow some balls for this bimbo?"

"I guess I did."

"She killed your fucking brother."

"I know, and I wanted to hate her for it. I pretended to for a long time but, Father, George was a horrible person. He deserved it, and you know that."

"He was more of a man than you'll ever be."

"I said get off her!" Graham shouts.

"You won't shoot me. Don't you remember all I've done for you? What you did to your poor, sweet mother?"

Graham cocks the shotgun and steps a foot closer to him. Moe, finally realizing Graham is prepared to shoot him, releases my ankle. I scoot toward Graham. I'm slow and can't get away from Moe fast enough. It doesn't matter — Moe is afraid of his son. I'll be safe soon.

"You'll thank me for this someday," Moe whispers, his voice so low I barely hear him.

"Thank you for what?" Graham asks.

Moe gives his son a sly smile. And suddenly he lets out a shriek and throws himself toward me.

I knew this would be it. All Graham had to do was pull the trigger, but he still wasn't prepared to. Or has he been bluffing this entire time? After all, it's his father or me — a woman who he barely knows, a woman who killed his brother, or the man who raised him and hid his mother's murder.

"Father, no!" Graham screams.

CHAPTER SIXTY-THREE

October 18th, 2009
8:31 a.m.

It all happens so fast. There is an ear-shattering bang, and Moe never quite reaches me. Blood explodes everywhere, landing in my eyes and blinding me. My ears are ringing again, and this time I can't hear anything else.

I wipe the blood from my eyes. It burns. Everything is burning. My mind feels as though it's being rocked back and forth. I know what just happened, but I feel too dizzy and dazed to really grasp it. I'm not dead, but someone else is. His blood is all over me, and he's lying near me. It's all too much. My breaths come in short, sharp bursts. I'm beginning to hyperventilate.

As the ringing in my ears starts to clear, I realize Graham is saying something.

"Maxine," he says again. He is kneeling beside me.

He goes to touch my shoulder, but I shrink away.

"It's okay, it's okay." Graham soothes, and I look up to see his eyes are on something behind me.

Behind me is Moe's lifeless body. Just an inch from his hand is the bloody pocketknife. His eyes are wide open with a permanent look of shock and betrayal. He really didn't think Graham would do it. Hell, those last couple seconds I wasn't sure, either. But he did. He saved me.

Graham is still staring at his father. I sit up and put my hand on his cheek. They feel wet with tears and blood.

"Graham," I breathe, turning his face to my own. "Don't look."

Graham shuts his eyes tight. He opens them to look at me and then hugs me. I shake from the pain.

"Are you okay?" he asks, caressing my hair as he continues to hold me close.

I'm not, but I nod anyways. I'm better than I was a minute ago. That part is true.

"You saved me." I press my face into his shoulder.

He doesn't say anything, but releases me from the hug and leaves my side. He walks toward his father's body.

"Graham, no," I plead, not wanting him to have to stare at his father any longer. It could traumatize him further.

He ignores me and begins to search through his dad's pockets. Soon he finds a set of keys. The keys to the cages. I sigh with relief.

"Come on, let's get you out of here," he says.

Before I can tell him I need a minute before I attempt to move, he puts one hand under my knees and the other under my armpits. With a grunt, he lifts me in the air. I see his van is parked fifty feet away. That's why I didn't hear him coming.

He carries me to the van in silence. I can feel the fast beat of his heart the entire time.

He sets me down by the passenger door. I open it and get in. Shortly after, he takes a seat behind the wheel. The engine is still running.

"How did you know where to find us?" I ask.

"He forced me to bury the bodies of the sisters out here. I figured since he knew about us, he would kill and bury you in the same place."

The sisters. The women Moe said he caught Graham lying with. I think about his mother, remembering that revelation as well. I gulp. Moe must have been lying. Trying to get in my head.

"Were you close to them?"

Graham peers over at me as he puts his hand on the shifter. I don't even need an answer. I can see the yes plastered all over his face. I'm not as disgusted as I should be. Graham had a messed-up childhood; his family abused him. No one ever told him they loved him. Those girls must have shown him a glimpse of what love looks like.

"Let's go." He reverses the van and turns it around.

"Wait, Graham." If I don't ask him about his mother now, I never will.

"Your father, he told me—"

I stop, growing dizzy again.

As if sensing my pain, Graham reaches over to the glovebox and opens it. Inside is a plastic baggie of white pills. He takes a couple out and places them in my palm. I stare at them quizzically.

"For the pain," he says.

Right. I take the pills and force them down.

After I swallow them, I clear my throat and ask, "Your father told me that your mother was planning to leave. That she was going to take George and leave you. He said you . . . you killed her."

Graham tightly closes his eyes. I see more tears fall down his face. Oh my God, it's true. It must be.

"I was so scared, so hurt. Mom was the only one who made living here worth it. She was kind and caring and he . . . he was so hateful. I don't remember much — I just remember feeling so dejected."

"Shh, shh. It's okay." I reach over and take his hand.

"I'm sorry I lied to you."

"Lied to me about what?"

"I've killed two people in my life, not one. I hope you can understand the second one. I remember it clearly. It was the night you killed George."

CHAPTER SIXTY-FOUR

October 18th, 2009
8:43 a.m.

Who did you kill, Graham? But before I can ask, Graham glances back at the car.

"We have to go," he says.

Go where? We should go into town and to the police station. I think of Eva all alone in the basement. Where is Joey? What if he goes to the farmhouse and harms her?

"What about your uncle?" I ask.

"He won't be off work until five. I'll kill him then."

Graham says that with so much ease and certainty. Nothing like the way he had spoken about killing his father. Perhaps he no longer cares that Joey is family. Then again, I wouldn't treat my worst enemies the way Graham's family treats him.

If we have until five, there is time to go into town. Graham could take me to the hospital, and I can tell them to send the police to the farmhouse. He doesn't have to kill his uncle if the police are there to arrest him.

"I need to go to—"

"The hospital, I know. Just let me kill Joey. He needs to die."

"The police can—"

"Take him to prison? So he can continue to live? No."

"But Graham—"

Graham takes my hand and looks me deep in the eyes.

"Please, Maxine. After he's dead, we'll do whatever you want. It's not just killing him I want."

I gulp.

"What else is there?"

"I just want to spend a little more time with you. If we go to the police, I may never see you again. I know I'm being selfish, I know I've let you down, and I'm sorry for everything. Just give me a little more time. Please."

I open my mouth to deny it but stop. I can see the pain in his eyes. He needs this. In a sense . . . I need this too. Graham has let me down many times. He's made horrible decisions and let his father commit heinous crimes. But I still care about him. I want to be with him. I don't know why — maybe I've gone mad.

I nod.

Graham smiles for the first time since he arrived. His eyes are bloodshot and still wet with tears. I'm not sure but it looks like he has a brand-new bruise on his eye, like he's been hit again. If I had to guess, it was probably his father after finding out Graham got me out of that hole in the ground.

I've never felt this much . . . love for a person. It's insane, loving someone who is so sick. He understands and accepts me for who I am. Me, the girl who has sat by and watched others suffer. We are the same. He may be the only man I'll ever meet who will love me just as I am. How can I go to the police now? The plan was to get him help, but what if I can't do that? What if they lock him up? Eva is the only other person that could help, but I can see her laughing in my face if I ask that.

Graham takes my hand and brings it to his lips. He closes his eyes and gives it a wet kiss.

"What — what made you come back?"

"I made you a promise and, even though you hurt me, I couldn't break it."

"I wasn't going to kill you. I just wanted to save Eva."

"She's safe now."

I pray he's telling the truth. I just need to talk to her, one on one. I want to convince her not to tell the police about Graham. Or at least say he was a puppet in it all. That he had no choice but to go through with all the murders his father committed.

I decide to let it go for now. I will give Graham time to grieve and pull himself together. I can tell by the red veins popping out of his eyes and the dark bags underneath he's not in the right headspace.

I reach into the jacket's pockets. I feel the necklace. Graham's mother's necklace.

"Graham . . . I need to show you something."

He nods.

"I found this necklace in that hole," I say, taking it out and putting it on the middle seat.

Graham looks down at it, at first with tired eyes, but upon seeing it they widen. Clearly, he recognizes it.

"When I first got to your place, you went to the bathroom, and I found a photograph of a woman. She was wearing this same necklace. I found a body . . . that had the same necklace."

Graham gulps. "It belonged to my mother."

"I know. Your father told me."

We turn onto a dirt road.

"You draw beautifully," I say.

Graham forces a smile. "I have one of you. It's my favorite."

Me? He drew a picture of someone he wanted dead for five years. I wonder why. I mean, before we got to know each other he didn't know anything about me. All the struggles and trauma we shared. Yet he still had some deep-rooted fascination for me. It seems too improbable to believe he had just been struck by my looks alone.

"I saw you on the night George died," he adds.

"Your dad said that. I didn't believe him. Graham, I need to know what happened that night. Please."

Graham takes a deep breath.

"You really want to know?"

I nod.

"I did something bad."

I put my hand on his knee. "So did I."

CHAPTER SIXTY-FIVE

June 14th, 2004
12:04 a.m.
Graham

Usually when George left the farmhouse, it was late at night, and after a six-pack or a couple swigs of a bottle of Everclear. Almost like he needed to be drunk to go where he was going. He would always wait until Father was either asleep or over at Uncle Joey's.

After the disaster of a conversation the two had a week ago, Graham knows he should just let the whole thing go. George is dangerous and never tells someone what to do more than once. But Graham can't let his behavior go on much longer. He's wreaking havoc with his actions.

His brother has always been the golden boy in the house. The one who doesn't disappoint Father and is just as unforgivingly vile. But it has all been some ruse. He has male pornographic magazines and keeps slipping away into the night. The two must be connected. Graham would let it go, if only his brother would trust him and let the two bond over this secret.

The thought of George possibly being gay — or at least curious — is something Graham hasn't even fully processed. He doesn't care, but his father would. It's risky and it's bizarre. George has

303

always been a ladies' man. The one with a muscular body and dark charming eyes. Graham has seen how easy it is for him to sway women. Like chewing gum. He's always admired his brother for that. But maybe it has been a façade this entire time.

Graham is hiding in the back of his father's van as his brother drives it somewhere unknown. They hit Mendex only a couple minutes ago — Graham can tell by the streetlights that appear as they drive. He is expecting George to go to some bar where he will attempt to pick up men. Mendex is a small town, so it doesn't have any exclusively gay bars, but there are some he has heard George describe as "too fruity to pick tail up."

The drive goes on for too long for them to be stopping at any bars. Graham has made secret visits to some the past few years and knows how long it takes to get to them and back. He had to. Father keeps a tight leash on him.

What will he do when he discovers what his brother is up to? Tell Father? Try to blackmail George into treating him better? Either could end up in bloodshed. George has already made it clear what the penalty is for blackmailing him.

Graham is jealous of George for being brave enough to make a life of his own. Being at the farmhouse around all the violence and murder would make anyone lonely. Graham dreams of meeting a nice, pretty girl. One who is pure and kind. Who he loves and who will love him in return. But in the end, he would be putting that girl in danger. It would be selfish. Graham is bound to this life. But if he is, then so is George.

A couple minutes later the van makes a sharp turn and stops. George puts the van into park and gets out. Once the door is closed and Graham can hear his footsteps retreating, he peeks through the window. His brother is walking toward a navy-blue house a couple houses down from where they are parked.

They appear to be in a middle-class neighborhood, the houses close together. George walks to the front door and knocks a couple times before a man answers. The light inside shows a tall man in his late twenties of average build. He wears a pale-yellow button-up shirt with brown slacks. His face brightens at the sight of George. Only a woman would dare smile like that at his brother. Then his brother smiles back.

Could it be some drug deal? George, when he has the cash, will occasionally buy cheap drugs like meth to keep him awake and, as he calls it, "proactive." But drug dealers don't smile at customers like that, and they don't usually invite customers over to their homes.

The man goes in for a hug and George, after peering around his surroundings, hugs him back. Graham hasn't hugged his brother since they were children. George hates being touched. Only tolerates it when it involves getting women to sleep with him. Or enticing them away from crowds and into the dark, to bind and gag them to take to Father.

After the two men have gone inside and closed the door behind them, Graham exits the van. The house has a large ground-floor window that is only partly closed off by curtains. Making sure there are no bystanders, Graham slowly creeps up to the window and peeks in.

He is looking at a living room — worn-looking couch, small TV on a wooden stand, brown rug, shabby beige walls. It's modest, but it's too tidy to be a drug dealer's house, he thinks.

George and the man are sitting together on the couch, inches from each other, as if they are close friends. But George doesn't have any friends. The brothers aren't allowed. Friends might stumble upon the family's dark secret.

If only the window were open, then Graham could hear what the two are talking about. George seems different than normal — he isn't rigid and menacing.

They both are deep in whatever they are talking about. The other man looks worried as he speaks, using a lot of hand gestures. Graham can't get over how nicely dressed he is. He's the polar opposite of George, who's wearing a dirty black hoody and his torn work jeans.

Graham looks around for any other windows in the house. He desperately wants to hear what the two are talking about. He spots one beyond the living room. In the open-plan kitchen, above the sink. He ducks his head below the window and tiptoes around the house. The window is latched but not locked.

He pushes the window open a couple inches and pushes his ear in as far as he can. The house is silent except for the voices of the man and George.

"I told you that I don't like you coming here this late," the man says.

"I didn't have a choice, Dean," George says, and for the first time in a long time he sounds melancholy.

"How long do we have to live like this?"

"Not long."

"You've been saying that for weeks. What is it you are so ashamed of?"

This sounds like a conversation a couple would have.

"Nothing, you just don't know my family."

"Fuck them, George. You can't let them control you."

Control him? He's the one that's been in control, enjoying every second of it. Or at least he's a good actor, pretending to enjoy it. So, George wants out. Why doesn't he just say that? Graham would do anything to get out of this family. He just never thought that was an option. His father knows his deep, dark secret. He knows all of George's dirty secrets too. He owns them.

"I'm trying."

"Not hard enough, damn it, George," the man says.

306

"Dean—"

"No, don't."

George puts his arm around Dean's shoulder, pulling him close. They stare at each other for a couple moments before moving in for a kiss.

Graham nearly falls to his ass in surprise. It all makes stupid sense. The dirty magazines. George's odd behavior. He's been in the closet all these years, and unable to hold it in anymore, he's gone out and met someone. Someone he possibly loves. Someone who has no idea what a monster he is. No idea about all the women he has tortured and killed.

Graham is filled with rage. He wants to love someone, but he has never had the chance. George has spent years tormenting him over not being man enough to go through with the things they do. He calls Graham a pussy anytime he shows remorse for the lives they've taken. Turns out, his brother is just as soft as he is. He's just better at hiding it.

Graham should go back to the van and hide. Wait till he gets back home, then rat George out to Father. But would Father even believe him? It would be his word against his brother's. Then George would beat him, possibly kill him for discovering his secret.

He has to do something. George doesn't just get to live this double life. To be happy. It isn't fair, and Graham wants to make him pay.

He goes back to the van and begins searching for a weapon. After rifling through the tarps, duct tape, and handcuffs, he finds a pocketknife. It has a small blade, but Graham is in too much of a hurry to care. Before he can change his mind, he walks to Dean's front door. Holding the blade in one hand, he uses the other to knock on the door.

He hears hushed voices before footsteps approach.

Dean opens the door, a bewildered expression on his face. He has kind eyes. It is a punch in the gut for Graham, who knows he's about to end this innocent man's life. Father has always told them to never get close to anyone or they could end up dead. Getting close means getting hurt. Better to avoid it to escape the pain you will face in the end.

"Hello, can I help you?" Dean asks.

Graham expects his brother to be at the door any moment. Then he remembers George will do anything to hide his presence in this house. Dean is out in the open, with a coward as his only possible savior.

"I'm . . . I'm sorry," Graham says softly.

Before Dean can answer, Graham thrusts the pocketknife straight into Dean's gut. Then, just as Dean is about to fall to his knees, he pulls it out and slashes his throat. He has to. A stab to the gut with a blade this small won't kill him. George and Father have always said that a slit throat will kill anyone within minutes. It's an easy kill. Bloody — but easy.

Blood sprays across Graham's jacket, and he drops the knife. Dean is on his knees, his hands clutching his throat. Graham wonders if anyone is outside to see this bloody display. No, they would've screamed. He doesn't even care if somebody has seen. At least he'll take his brother down with him.

Unable to stop the blood, Dean instead falls face forward. Right onto Graham's boots. Dean groans as the blood pools around him. It stains the ugly brown carpet, turning it nearly black.

Graham is so dazed he doesn't feel two hands wrap around his throat. Before he knows it, he is being pulled inside the house and thrown to the ground. George is on top of him, his face cherry red.

He looks up at his brother and with all the air left in him says, "Do it."

George momentarily loosens his grip on Graham's throat.

"I said do it. I don't care," Graham repeats, coughing.

George makes an agitated sound but releases his brother. He gets off him and kneels next to Dean. Another first. George is crying. In a sick way, it makes Graham happy to see his brother cry. It's like all the times he cried for forgiveness for not being better, and George laughed in his face.

George covers his face with his hands. "Why?"

Graham sits up. "You made me do this."

Graham quickly stands up, grabbing the pocketknife from the floor as he does so. He points it at George, prepared to be attacked again.

"You did this, George! We aren't allowed to get close to anyone. You know the rules. They're the same ones you've been preaching to me your whole life. You think I didn't want someone to hold at night? Someone to love? But no! You and Father instilled in me that killing is all we do. Pain is the only thing we make others feel. I hate you so much."

George sighs before taking one last look down at Dean. He gets to his feet. Graham keeps the tiny knife pointed his way, unsure what George is about to do.

"You're right. Let's get this mess cleaned up," George says calmly.

"Wh-what?"

"Let's clean this up. Close the door. Hopefully no one saw that. If they did, we're both fucked."

George is calm. Calmer then he would be over a spilled glass of whiskey. It doesn't make any sense.

"Aren't you going to . . . kill me, or something?"

George chuckles. "No, not right now."

CHAPTER SIXTY-SIX

June 14th, 2004
1:59 a.m.
Graham

It takes Graham and George over an hour to clean the blood from Dean's house. They roll Dean's body up in the brown living room rug and put it in the van, planning to burn him once back at the farmhouse. Besides the rug, everything in the house is just as it was.

Cleaning homes of blood wasn't something Graham ever had to do. They have never broken into their victims' homes. It causes more hassle than it's worth. George, luckily, seems to know how to clean up a crime scene.

They worked in silence. It reminded Graham of the times George and he had been tasked with cleaning the basement. All silence, no words to be said. Graham has kept the pocketknife on him just in case George does explode and try to kill him. If he does that, it won't be here. If he does, he'll have to explain to Father why he did it. Father may not care about his younger son's life, but he will care about a missing member of the cleanup team.

Graham and George make sure the street is empty of passing cars and neighbors, then haul Dean's body to the van. It has begun raining heavily. Which is probably lucky. Rain keeps people inside.

Once Dean's body is in the back of the van, Graham moves to the passenger seat. Before he can get in, George puts his hand on his shoulder.

"You will never speak of this night again, you hear me?"

"Okay."

George tightens his grip.

"I was going to leave this life. Our life. Now . . . you've taken that from me."

Graham stares at him. George could've saved them both the trouble if he had just been honest. Had not been selfish. *He was going to leave me with Father.*

"Make sure Father doesn't catch you burning the body."

"What do you—"

Before Graham can finish, George punches him. The hit is so powerful, Graham falls to the ground. His nose is gushing blood.

"That was for Dean," George says, turning around and walking away.

Where is he going? He can't leave me!

"George!" Graham yells, rubbing the blood from his nose.

George ignores him and continues walking. Graham stands back up. Before chasing after his brother, he removes his bloodied jacket and tosses it into the van.

"George! Don't go!" Graham calls out, jogging after his brother.

"Graham, I swear to God, leave me alone," George says.

"Where will you go?" Graham asks, stopping in his tracks, not ready to take another powerful hit from his brother.

"Anywhere but here, little brother." George stops momentarily.

"Please, George. Don't go. I'm sorry. I can't do this without you."

George takes a couple steps forward as if afraid Graham will continue to follow him. He keeps his hands in fists, ready to fight him off if needed.

He turns around. "Do as Father says and don't fall in love . . . ever. Because this — this shit fucking hurts."

Before Graham can speak, his brother begins walking again, crossing the street to get away from him.

"Wait . . . George!" Graham calls, taking a step forward.

He only makes it one step before a car appears out of nowhere. It collides with George, who bounces off the hood and the windshield. He drops to the ground like he weighs nothing. Graham feels as though his body has been frozen in time. He is unable to move. Do anything.

The car screeches to a halt. The driver doesn't emerge right away. Graham considers running to them and sticking the knife in their throat. But he's still unable to move. Someone has to have heard that. It's only 2 a.m. Unless the heavy rain silenced the sound of his brother's body being struck by the sedan.

If I go out there right now, someone will see.

They killed my fucking brother. Why do I care?

Graham steps forward to cross the street. Just then, the door of the car opens, and someone emerges from it. He stops again.

Oh my God.

It's a woman. Not just any woman. He'd seen many women, from the beautiful, scared victims of his father to the ones he masturbated to in dirty magazines. None of them compares to this woman. She looks like an angel that has fallen from heaven, floating through the air like a feather in the wind.

She has a heart-shaped face and a tiny nose with a bump. Her long blonde hair is sticking to her face in the rain. She has a sylphic body and large breasts that are partly exposed by her V-neck top.

It can't be real. She can't be real. Graham begins to wonder if maybe he was run over too. The woman he was about to demonically kill is the most stunning thing he has ever laid his eyes on. He can't kill her.

Why, God? Why me?

Why did she have to be the one who just ran over his brother? It could have been anyone else. Anyone else he would have stabbed to death by now. But her . . . He has lost track of time. Doesn't even see his dying brother on the ground. He is transfixed by her.

Graham has always thought the idea of love at first sight was bullshit. Something from a story — princesses and princes, fairy tales, happy endings. Something so impossible it is hopeless to even try to believe in. But maybe it could happen. There isn't any other explanation for the warm feeling Graham has in his heart as he stares at her. He feels poison in his veins, corroding his body and eating away at his brain.

His brother's last words had been to never fall in love. But Graham feels as though he's fallen in love with the very woman who just killed George.

He has to stay hidden. Exposing himself now will cause suspicion. There is a dead man in his van. He can't meet her tonight. But he will someday. Whether she wants it or not, Graham will meet her.

"Who are you?" Graham whispers to himself.

Whoever she is, whatever her name is, it doesn't matter. Graham has to have her.

CHAPTER SIXTY-SEVEN

October 18th, 2009
9:05 a.m.

"The moment — the second — I saw you, I just knew I had to have you, Maxine."

Graham's words ring in my head. He told me the entire story of that fateful night when I had run George over. The last words he said to him. How George had been trying to leave Graham behind. Graham must've been so scared. No wonder he became so fixated on me. The only person he cared about had just been murdered.

It's hard to believe Graham killed an innocent man in cold blood. He let his brother die while being captivated by me, a girl he didn't know. This story brings us closer than ever before. I'm the first person he has told this to.

His father died never knowing his sons' secrets: that George had been in love with another man, and that Graham had killed George's lover in cold blood. Graham says he had told his father they were out hunting for a woman when I ran George over. Graham convinced his father to stay out of the court proceedings, so I would be locked up for less time. That way, Moe would still be alive to take revenge on me.

During the years I was locked up, Graham planned to kill me but found it difficult once I was released from prison and he started stalking me. He thought that the anger he had kept burning for the five years I was locked up would be enough to quell his attraction to me. Then, after I woke up from that dream the night I stayed over, he abandoned the plan altogether. The story of my mother and what she did must have done that. Graham saw what my parents had done to me and felt we were both connected that way. In a sense, we both know we will never find someone so similar and understanding of our dark pasts.

But there is a difference between us. Graham has ended two innocent lives. I have to will myself to understand him. He was far too young to understand what he was doing when he killed his mother. And, after all the years of brainwashing, being told that he was unlovable, perhaps it makes a twisted kind of sense that he couldn't bear to see his brother happy and in love.

"Do you ever feel guilt for killing Dean? For letting your brother die on the street?"

"I regret what I did to both of them, but if I could go back in time and change what I did, I wouldn't."

"Why?"

"Because I never would have met you."

I gulp, unable how to process that. I don't even realize we are back at the farmhouse until Graham stops the van. I don't want to be back here. I wish we could be anywhere else. This house feels haunted. Probably is haunted by all the women who were slain here.

"Come on." Graham pats my knee.

I just nod and get out of the van. The pills Graham gave me have slightly eased the pain. At least enough to get out of the van and begin walking. Walking is almost too much to endure. I take Graham's hand and lace my fingers through his.

We don't say anything as we walk up the stairs. Graham keeps a tight grip on my hand as I use the other to grab ahold of the banister. I go to the bathroom and Graham follows. I need a shower. My skin burns from all the dirt lodged into the open cuts on my legs and arms. He shuts the door and we both get undressed. All my worries dissipate as I feel the hot water run down my body.

Before getting out, we both face each other. I wrap my arms around him and hold him close. We stand there in the hot water for what feels like forever.

I wrap a towel around me, and we go to Graham's bedroom. I lie in his bed and shut my eyes. I've never felt this exhausted in my life. I would fall asleep if it weren't for my wandering thoughts. I shouldn't be lying here so relaxed. I should be with Eva, telling her she's going to be safe. Taking her out of that disgusting basement. But as soon as I do that, my time with Graham will be done. It's selfish, but I just need a few hours with him.

After this is all over, I'll never find someone like Graham. Someone who understands me like he does. Someone who will love me the moment he lays eyes on me. Someone who forgives me for all my wrongdoings.

Once Eva is out, she'll tell everybody what happened all those years ago. And why wouldn't she? The truth deserves to come out. I just know it'll be over for me when it does. Even if I am the one to save her, the world will hate me, and Graham will be gone forever.

Graham gets into bed next to me. He pulls me close. I rest my head on his chest, right above his beating heart. The sound is music to me. It calms my thoughts of the future.

"I don't want to lose you," I whisper.

"I know," he says.

I close my eyes, forcing back tears. I can't cry. It'll ruin this moment.

"Do you think if we met under different circumstances, that things would be different?"

"I know I would've fallen in love with you immediately. But would you have loved me?"

Probably not. I was incapable of love because of my parents' relationship. I didn't want to feel the same pain my mother had. I closed myself off from everybody. Once Graham is gone, I'll have to do the same.

"I'll talk to Eva. I can convince her to . . . to not say anything."

"No, you can't. Eva has endured too much to not say anything about the man that kept her captive."

"I'm going to try. If it means saving you—"

"Shh. Don't worry about it, Maxine. I'll be okay, I promise. Anything that's coming my way, I deserve. I let people die."

"You were brainwashed, Graham."

"It'll all work out the way it's supposed to."

I look up at Graham and see the doubt in his eyes. He doesn't have faith in my plan. I don't blame him; I don't either. But I will try for him.

He puts a hand on my cheek and we both lean into each other for a soft kiss. His kiss gives me a feeling of electricity. Electricity I've never felt in my life. I think I'm going crazy because when I look into this man's eyes, I feel love for him.

"Try to get some sleep," he says.

I nod and rest my head on his chest again. The sound of his heartbeat silences my thoughts, and soon I drift off.

CHAPTER SIXTY-EIGHT

October 18th, 2009
4:24 p.m.
Mikey

The lumberyard closed over twenty minutes ago, but Joey has still not left. Ten minutes ago, the receptionist left with her shirt half unbuttoned and her lipstick smeared. *Good grief*, Mikey thought.

After the receptionist had gone and he knew Joey was the only one left, Mikey moved from his Jeep and over to a bench near the front doors of the building. He wants to be sure he can get right up behind Joey when he comes out. He keeps the gun lodged in his coat pocket just in case. He doesn't want to have to pull it out or use it, but he knows Graham and Joey are hiding something.

You could lose everything doing this.

He's been running through all the consequences if he's wrong in his mind. Holding a man at gunpoint and kidnapping him. He could go to jail, lose his wife and child. But Max's life is on the line. His gut feeling about her being in trouble has yet to fade away, no matter how many times he tries to rationalize it.

No one is left in the building, so there won't be any witnesses. The whole crew left before the receptionist. Joey's beat-up Dodge truck is the only vehicle left in the parking lot. Mikey parked on the other side of the street to keep his distance and not alert Joey.

Mikey hears the door opening and shutting. He quietly stands and creeps over to the three steps leading up to the entrance. Joey's back is to him as he locks both doors. Once Joey has locked the doors, he turns around to face Mikey. He grins and spits a loogie of tobacco on the ground.

"You just don't give up, do you?" He chuckles.

"Where is she?" Mikey moves his hand inside his pocket and takes a tight hold of the revolver's handle.

"Probably with my nephew."

"Why are you protecting him?"

"I don't know what you're talking about." He looks down at Mikey like this is a game and he's having fun.

"Where is Graham, then?"

"He left."

"I know."

"Have you been here all day? Jesus, what is up with you and this chick?"

"If you tell me where she is, I won't say anything about you—"

"Don't try bargaining with me, you little shit."

Mikey is wasting time. He should've known a friendly approach wouldn't make this man budge. He knows she's with Graham and in danger. If she wasn't, Joey wouldn't be so keen on keeping him away.

Mikey pulls the gun from his pocket and points it at Joey. Joey's eyes bulge, but he keeps grinning.

"Come on, man. I just want to go home."

"Get in your truck and keep your hands up."

Joey sighs. Raising his hands above his head, he walks down the steps. Mikey waits for him to pass and begins to follow him. He looks around to make sure no one is nearby. The neighborhood

319

is quiet for now. At five, most people will be getting off work. He needs to hurry.

"Walk faster." He presses the barrel of the revolver into Joey's back.

When they reach the truck, Joey slowly takes his keys out and unlocks the door. Just as he begins opening the door, he reaches into his other pocket and pulls out a pocketknife. Seeing the blade nearing his chest, Mikey strikes him across the face with the revolver as hard as he can. Joey falls to his knees, dropping the knife. Mikey kicks it behind him.

"Anything else?" Mikey asks.

"You motherf—"

Mikey kicks him in the groin. Joey goes completely to the ground, clutching his crotch.

"Get up," Mikey orders, giving him a minute to process the pain and hopefully know not to try anything else.

"You don't know who you're fucking with, son." Joey grabs the door handle of the truck to ease himself off the ground.

Once Joey's inside, Mikey leaves the gun pointed at him and walks across to the passenger side. He climbs in and orders Joey to start the truck.

This man could try to take him anywhere. He could drive him straight to the police station. But if Mikey knows the address, he could at least get an idea as to where they need to go. He opens the glove box, looking for the vehicle's registration.

"What are you—"

"Shut up," Mikey says.

Inside the glove box are some napkins, condoms, and handcuffs. *What the fuck?*

Mikey takes the handcuffs out and looks over at Joey quizzically.

"It's a kink," Joey remarks.

Mikey ignores him and continues shuffling through the contents of the glove box. He finds a plastic bottle filled with clear liquid. The label reads "chloroform." Handcuffs and chloroform right in the glove box of his truck.

"Cops would be interested in why you have handcuffs and fucking chloroform in your truck," Mikey remarks.

"You can't prove anything."

Mikey continues searching and finally finds some crumpled paperwork. He opens it up and sees the vehicle is registered to a Joey Dawson at 21 Franklin Drive. Franklin Drive is a dirt road out of town. Nearly five miles out of town.

"So, as I see it, you've got two options. You can take me to this address, and we can see what sick shit you've got there, or you can take me to your nephew's place."

"And if I do neither?"

"I can shoot you, and you can die for that little dweeb."

"And you'll go to prison for that blonde bitch."

Mikey doesn't hesitate. He strikes Joey across the face with the revolver. The big guy's nose begins to gush blood, and a cut on his cheek is bleeding.

"Keep playing games with me, old man."

"You're making a huge mistake."

"Maybe I'll just kill you now, drive up to your place, and see what's in there myself." Mikey presses his finger on the trigger of the gun.

"Fuck, okay. I'll take you to him."

"Good," Mikey says.

Mikey thinks of the items in Joey's truck and how that could be only the tip of the iceberg when it comes to what he's hiding. Another problem for another time.

What have they done to you, Max?

"If you've hurt her, I'm going to put a bullet in both your and your nephew's heads. This is not a threat. It's a promise."

CHAPTER SIXTY-NINE

October 18th, 2009
4:39 p.m.

I wake up still pressed against Graham. I look up and see he is still asleep. He looks so peaceful. I examine all the bruises and cuts on his face. He looks like a wounded animal who had endured a beating to protect its young. I want to clutch him close and kiss him, but I can't. I can't wake him up just yet.

I slowly inch myself out of bed and away from Graham. He just shifts his body sideways. I stare at him and wish I could stay. Lie with him until we both wake up together. He'll hold me close, and then he'll wake up to shoot his sick uncle.

I'm going down to the basement, alone. I need to talk to Eva. Just her and me. I have to convince her not to say anything about Graham. That me saving her, and Moe and Joey being dead, should be enough in the end. If I fail, I don't know what I'll do.

I grab a pair of Graham's boxers and a T-shirt. Once I'm dressed, I tiptoe out of the room. I pray he forgives me for going behind his back to talk to Eva. I don't want to betray his trust again, but I am going to grab Moe's keys. That way, Eva can have some satisfaction from seeing this is all over, and she is safe. I won't let her out until I hear what she has to say about sparing Graham.

What if she says no? Are you going to let her out anyways, so she can run to the police and make sure you never see him again?

I had similar thoughts the day she showed up on my porch asking for the truth. I wondered what would happen to Dennis. I saw this abused girl begging me to tell her the horrific things she knew deep down happened to her. I knew if I told her the truth she would take Dennis from me. This is different. Graham never hurt her. He deserves a second chance at the life he wasted thanks to his father's twisted ways.

I go to the bathroom and find Graham's jeans on the floor. In the back pocket I find Moe's keys. I head downstairs to the kitchen. I tremble at the sight of the basement door. I turn and go to the sink to grab a glass of water. I'm just thirsty and need water before going down there. Once my glass is empty, I refill it so I can give Eva some. I have no idea the last time anyone's gone down to check on her.

When I open the door to the basement, I smell a disgusting stench wafting through the air and coming up the stairs. *Oh God.* I shouldn't have left her down here this long without knowing she's being cared for. I slept in bed with Graham peacefully while she's been stuck down here in this cesspool.

Eva is lying in the fetal position on her cot, asleep. She has a thin dirty throw blanket wrapped around her. My skin forms goosebumps, either from the sight of her or the chill in the room. I peer over and see her bucket is filled and there are empty plates and water bottles in her cage.

I clear my throat. "Eva?" I say gently.

I spoke so softly, but at the sound of my voice, Eva's eyes widen and she jerks up. When she sees me, she looks around the room.

"Max . . . what . . . what—" She coughs.

I slip the glass between the bars and set it on the ground.

"Take some water."

She gets up and dashes to it. Only a few seconds pass between her grabbing the water and finishing it.

"What are you doing here? I thought you were—"

"Dead?"

"Well, yeah. I saw Moe take you this morning. I thought you were toast."

Why didn't she try to alert me? Say anything to wake me up? I guess that could've gotten her killed. I remember she betrayed those other girls.

I take a deep breath. "Moe's dead," I say coldly.

Eva's mouth widens and she takes more frantic glances around the room. "He's dead? Did you—"

"Kill him? No, Graham did. It's a long story."

"Is Graham dead?"

I shake my head. "He's upstairs, asleep. He doesn't know I'm down here."

Eva spots the item in my left hand.

"Are those the keys? Let me out, please," she urges.

Let her out.

I lift the keys toward the padlock. Then I remember what I need to say. If I let her out, she may not give me that moment.

"You're safe, Eva. It's all over. But I need to talk to you."

Eva's face shifts to confusion, then anger.

"Max, I am not safe until I am out of this fucking box! We can talk when you let me out of here."

"You can't tell the police about Graham."

Eva looks at me in disbelief. Shit, this is going worse than I thought it would. I must look like a lunatic, not immediately unlocking this door. Maybe I am. It's for Graham, though. I can't lose him. I will need him after this is all over.

"Is that a threat?"

"N—"

"Are you going to let me rot in here if I don't?"

"Of course not. Eva, please. I can't lose him."

"Are you kidding me? You're in love with that freak? What changed? I thought you wanted to save us and get him help. Now you want to be with him?"

She's angrier than she was when I told her what happened that night. I can calm her down. I just need to explain.

"I can help him. His whole life he's been brainwashed and abused by his father and brother."

"Spare me the sob story. He let that happen to him because he didn't have the balls to stand up for himself. He let girls die down here!"

She doesn't understand why he let all that happen. That it was because his father was holding something over him: the death of his mother. The fact he saw other girls die. He was too scared to do anything.

"He had his reasons, I promise."

"Fuck his reasons! Girls suffered because of him."

"Girls suffered because of you too."

"Don't you ever compare me to him!"

I left the basement door wide open. Graham will hear Eva's yelling.

"He never hurt any of them," I plead.

"Like you never physically hurt me, right?"

My stomach aches at that. My God, she's right. I'm doing it again. Rationalizing a man's unforgivable actions because I'm in love with him. Maybe I haven't really changed. When I look into Eva's hopeless eyes, eyes that have seen a lifetime of trauma, I just can't get Graham out of my head. He spared me after I killed his brother. He killed his father to save me. He is everything I've ever wanted in my miserable life.

"Please, Max. I know you can do the right thing."

I need to do the right thing for Eva. But that was before I knew she was so dead set on not helping me out. Is that fair? Is it fair I've been risking my life to save her, and she can't even help the only person who will ever love me for me?

"He's all I have left, and I can't let you take him away from me."

"He's a monster! Just like Dennis."

"You're wrong."

I've made up my mind. I am not going to lose Graham.

"You're not thinking clearly. It's just like that night. You're overcome with mixed feelings about some man you barely know."

It's different this time. I'm not drunk and am thinking as clearly as I ever have. I need Graham. I can't fight this. I can change her mind. I have to.

I open my mouth to argue but then behind me I hear his voice. "Maxine."

CHAPTER SEVENTY

October 18th, 2009
4:52 p.m.

Graham's voice calms me. Then I remember I took his keys and came down here without him. I turn around to see him standing at the top of the stairs. He's dressed in dirty jeans and a plain hunter-green T-shirt. I notice something in his hand. It's the shotgun.

"Graham, I just wanted to talk to her," I plead.

"I know," he assures me, walking down the stairs.

"Please don't be angry with me," I beg, running up to him and wrapping my arms around him.

He holds me with his free hand and whispers in my ear soothingly. "It's okay, I know."

The smell of Graham's body wash clings to his skin, and just the feel of him brings me to tears. His warmth, smell, and whole being make me want to melt.

"I love you," I whisper, unable to let him go.

"I love you too."

I release him to stare into his beautiful eyes.

"What are we going to do?"

"That's up to you, Maxine."

"What do you mean?"

Graham takes a deep breath and casts his eyes behind me, at Eva.

"I'm going to support your choice, no matter what it is. You can let her go right now. Let her go to the police. She'll be safe. Or we can end her suffering once and for all."

I gulp. He doesn't mean . . .

He's giving me a choice. I can let Eva go, which would fulfill what I had sought to do this entire time. Or I can let her die and have Graham. I didn't know until now that I couldn't have both. A part of me knew having both was near to impossible.

End her suffering. End all the pain she's gone through and will go through if she survives all this. It sounds harsh, but it is true.

I look behind me to stare at Eva. Her eyes are horror-stricken. As if she already knows what I'm thinking.

"Wait, wait. Look, I won't say anything. I promise," she begs, stepping away from the bars of the cell.

I frown, seeing the lie point blank in her expression.

"I just want you to be happy. I don't care what happens to me anymore. It's you, it's always been you," Graham says.

He leans down and plants a kiss on my forehead.

I think back to that night I let Dennis and those boys rape Eva. Back then, I had done that to be with Dennis. It was wrong, I know that. But this is different. Graham is the love of my life. I feel it so much more intensely than I did for Dennis. I never would've let Dennis kill someone. Graham on the other hand . . . I would burn this world down for him.

"Eva, if I let you go, you're going to have to deal with the trauma your whole life. Do you really want to do that?" I say.

I see tears begin to roll down Eva's face as the realization begins to kick in. It's different this time. She's not under the influence of drugs. She can see the glimmer in my eyes as I protect the man I love.

"Please don't do this. I promise, no, I swear I won't say anything!" she begs, falling to her knees.

I turn away, unable to look at her pain. I can't do this. I can't kill her.

CHAPTER SEVENTY-ONE

October 18th, 2009
4:56 p.m.

"Do it," I whisper to Graham, and when he raises his eyebrows in confusion, I look down at the shotgun in his right hand.

"Are you sure?"

I nod. There is no going back after this. I am once again choosing a man over Eva. Except this time, I am letting her die. I have my reasons, and yes, they are selfish. I am a selfish person, and after all these years of feeling sorrow, guilt, and regret, I feel selfishly free. Free to make my own decision. Dennis pressured me to choose him over Eva. Not Graham, though. He is willing to let me decide what I want to do. And I love him so much for that.

Looking at Graham, I realize I would do anything to keep him.

I hand the keys to Graham, and before he can walk away, I lean over and kiss him on the lips. His lips feel soft and like home to me. Like a home where I'm wanted. I'm not the daughter of a betrayed wife who destroyed her family. I'm not the girl who loved a boy only to be chosen because she knew a horrible thing he did.

When this is over, when all of it is over, we are going to wait for Joey to get here and then kill him. Then I am going to make love to Graham. I'm going to go home and make sure everyone knows I'm safe, if anyone noticed I was gone to begin with. I will go to the hospital and say I was in a wreck. Then, after that, I will follow Graham. We are going to be free, together. No longer chained to our pasts, families, and mistakes. Maybe he can become a famous artist. He'll at least have more time to pursue drawing. Whatever it is he wants to do, I'll support him.

Graham walks toward Eva's cell. I keep my back turned, unable to watch.

"You're a coward, Max Masterson!" Eva screams at me.

"It's all going to be over soon, Eva," Graham says calmly.

"Don't turn your back on me again, Max!"

I glance over to see Graham is at Eva's cell with the key nearing the lock. She is at the wall of her cell. There isn't as much fear in her eyes as I expected there to be. Just anger. She was always full of anger. It was one of the reasons I let Dennis do what he did. Before they went up to that room, she had been so rude to me, saying I was a drunk. It made it so much easier to ignore her. And now it's happening again.

"All the pain you've ever felt will be gone," I assure her.

I drown out what she says next. It's a lot of screaming. I don't blame her for being angry. I just wish she would understand I am doing this not only for Graham, but for her as well. If I did decide to let her go, what life would she even have to return to? She barely managed to survive what happened at the party. How would she ever survive what she's been subjected to this past year? It would take years of therapy, and she would never be able to trust another person again. What kind of life would that be? It's like running over an animal and deciding to let the thing live instead of shooting it and ending its suffering.

"This is the hardest decision I've ever made, but I promise it's for the best," I say, not even to Eva but to myself.

When the door to the cage is open, Graham raises the shotgun to point directly at Eva. He glances at me with those shimmering green eyes I'll be gazing at for the rest of my life. He doesn't say anything, but I understand that look. He is once again making sure this is what I want. I nod.

I can't bear to watch it. To see all the blood and Eva's corpse lying on the cold cement ground of the basement. I shut my eyes, keeping the image of Graham in my mind. I begin to count down from five. Five seconds and our new life can start.

Five, four, three, two—

Before I make it to one, the gun fires. Then I hear the sound of a body hitting the ground.

CHAPTER SEVENTY-TWO

October 18th, 2009
5:02 p.m.

My eyes are still closed when I am pulled into a tight hug. At first, I believe it's Graham, but when I wrap my arms around his body, it feels too large. Was he wearing heavy clothing? No, he was wearing a T-shirt, much like the one I'm wearing right now. It doesn't smell like Graham, either. The smell is familiar, like cedar.

My eyes shoot open. The person embracing me is not Graham. His dark auburn hair is the first thing I see. It's Mikey. My arms drop from him, and my eyes shift from Mikey's face to the sight in front of me.

Eva is still standing in her cage, alive. She wasn't shot. I must be having a nightmare. I try to force myself not to look down at the ground because I know who will be lying there. It's too late. As soon as I see Eva still alive, I look near her. In a pool of blood on that ugly gray cement is . . . Graham.

I freeze, and I feel as though I am having an out-of-body experience. I see Mikey holding me up, stopping me from tumbling to the ground next to Graham. I want to scream and scratch him away. The bastard shot Graham. Tears fill my eyes, and my heart shatters to pieces, but that's it, I can't do anything else.

Our future, gone. Our love, gone. It's all gone. My Graham, my sweet Graham.

I can hear Mikey's voice in my ear as he continues to cradle me in his arms. Along with not being able to move, I also can no longer hear. My vision blurs and Mikey finally lets me go. At first, I'm grateful to have his hands off me, until I see the petrified look on his face. What is he scared of? The so-called bad guy was just shot and killed.

I look over at what he's staring at. Eva. She's no longer in her cell. She's about a foot from the threshold right next to Graham's body. And in her hands is . . . Graham's shotgun.

I barely have time to raise my hands before there is another loud shot that echoes from the walls of the basement.

I go limp and land on the ground. I feel an unnatural pressure in my stomach. I look down and, damn — I've just been shot.

CHAPTER SEVENTY-THREE

October 18th, 2009
5:04 p.m.

Eva appears straight out of a cheesy western flick. The crazed gunslinger who's gone through hell and back and has just taken out the antagonist — me. Eva's eyes are bloodshot and tears stream down her pale face.

"What are you doing?" I hear Mikey yell. He's down on the ground next to me.

Mikey has, at some point, dropped the revolver he used to shoot Graham. I see him eye it and move his hand in the direction of where it lays.

"I wish you no harm, but I will fucking shoot you," Eva screams, cocking the shotgun and pointing it at Mikey.

Mikey lifts his shaky hands in the air.

"Get her in the cage," she orders.

Mikey looks down at me and back at Eva. I can't even imagine what's going through his head right now. Does he know I was seconds from letting her get shot? Probably not. Mikey never did see the bad in me.

Mikey grabs me under my armpits and slowly drags me into Eva's cage. Graham's lifeless body grazes my legs as we pass. I don't care that my fate has been sealed. All I see is Graham. I wanted to save him from this so bad.

Eva slams the door shut as soon as we are completely inside. During all that, she grabbed Moe's keys; she swiftly locks the gate. Now she goes to Mikey's revolver and picks it up off the floor.

"Please don't do this," Mikey pleads.

"I'll call the cops for you, I promise. I just have some errands to run."

"But—"

"Maxine Masterson, you almost got away with it, didn't you? I've thought of this moment for a long time, you know. Thought of killing you all. About what I'd say. Mostly it had been him. I hated what you did for so long, but I hated him more. But now, I think you're the worst of them all."

"This is the easiest decision I've ever made."

I recall my last words to her. *This is the hardest decision I've ever made.* That was a lie. Choosing Dennis over her had been harder. I had said that to myself to calm my guilt.

"Please, don't do this," Mikey repeats. I can hear his confusion.

Eva backs away from us. I see no regret in her eyes. This really is the easiest decision she's ever made. I don't need to ponder long on what errands she needs to run. She's going for *him*.

She walks backward all the way up the staircase, her eyes never leaving mine.

"All the pain you've ever felt will be gone soon. Goodbye, Max," she says coldly, and then she's gone, just like that — forever.

As a child I always wondered what it would be like to get shot. It's said people feel one of two feelings. Some feel extreme pain. Others don't feel much at all. I'm the latter. I don't feel much. In fact, the blood streaming from my abdomen is the only thing that lets me know this is real.

I wonder if Billy felt much pain when he drowned. I hope he didn't. I know my mother didn't. She deserved pain. Maybe I do as well. I was going to let Eva die for a man. It was wrong on so many levels, and the sick thing is . . . I'd do it again in a heartbeat.

My mother probably would too. I guess we aren't too different after all. I tried to resist becoming her. We were both selfish. After twenty-seven years, I understand my mother. I don't hate her anymore.

Be brave, Maxine.

I was brave, Mom. You would be proud. I did it all for love, just like you.

CHAPTER SEVENTY-FOUR

October 18th, 2009
5:07 p.m.
Eva

Eva has dreamed of the day she would escape this hell. In some dreams she leaves the house with her arms raised in the air in victory. It is a downpour and the rain is washing her of all her pain and suffering. In others she is covered in blood after fighting Moe, Graham, and Joey to the death and leaving victorious. Then, in the more realistic dreams, she walks out with her eyes soaked in happy tears.

None of these things happen as she leaves the basement to the sound of Mikey Connolly pleading with her to come back. She doesn't even cry. She used up all her tears begging Max to let her go. Instead, she goes to the kitchen sink and turns on the hot water. She sets both guns down on a counter nearby, runs her hands through the water, and washes her face free of all the dirt and grime.

If anything could make her cry, it's the feel of hot water. She hasn't felt warmth in a year. She savors the hot water for over a minute, before turning it off and switching to cold. She grabs a dirty glass from the sink and fills it. As she is about to take a seat at the dining room table in the other room, there is a loud scream outside.

She walks over to the window by the front door and pulls the curtain aside to look out. Parked at an angle beside the van is an unfamiliar shitty-looking Dodge truck. Perhaps it is Mikey's. Dismissing the sound for nothing, Eva turns to walk away when she hears the sound again.

She looks back and, squinting at the truck, spots someone inside. The windows are too dirty to properly see through. She quickly fetches the shotgun from the counter and walks to the front door. Before opening the door, she checks to make sure the shotgun is still loaded. Inside the barrel is a single shell. Thankfully she still has the revolver for protection. She cocks the shotgun, ready to drop anyone else who interferes with her freedom.

The door is unlocked when she turns the handle. She opens it, seeing the front door is painted dark red. She shivers, remembering the very same red door from that party. She wonders if Max had felt the same uneasy feeling seeing the door and remembering that night. She walks off the porch, the steps creaking under her. It is her first time outside in over a year. The sun is preparing to set, and there is a windy chill in the air. She barely feels it through her thin white T-shirt because her nerves are on fire.

Once off the porch steps, she aims the shotgun in the direction of the truck. She smiles when she sees who's inside. It must be Christmas. Joey is handcuffed to the truck's assist grip. His face goes cold when he sees her, as if he sees a ghost.

She didn't get the honor of killing Moe or Graham, but this will do. Other than Graham, Joey is the one she despises the most. Max thought Eva was cruel for the way she treated Graham. Max thought he was so innocent. She didn't know what he did — or didn't do.

Two weeks after Eva was kidnapped, Moe set up a garden hose in her cell. He gave her five minutes to shower. He left, leaving Graham. At that point she was still attempting to be friendly with him. She knew he was nowhere near as vile as his father and uncle. Then, in the span of a couple seconds, that all changed.

Just as she started to undress and Graham turned his back and headed up the stairs, another figure appeared. Up until that point, none of these men had attempted to force themselves on her. After being kidnapped, that was the first thing she assumed would happen. But Moe seemed repulsed by her, and Graham seemed too naïve and sweet to do so.

The figure at the top of the stairs was that disgusting leach, Joey. Eva waited for Graham to stop him from coming farther in. To stop him and force him back out. Instead, the two made eye contact for a moment and with one glance back at Eva, Graham lowered his head and left. He didn't even attempt to stop Joey. He let that disgusting man in. Eva stopped taking her clothes off. Then Joey took a hunting knife out and threatened her with it.

She stripped off her clothes and showered. She never stopped crying. After that, she vowed to never let her guard down around Graham again. He was a coward, just like Maxine.

* * *

5:57 p.m.

After blasting a shotgun shell into Joey's face, Eva sat and stared at his corpse. She smiled and took the moment in. All of them were dead. Sure, she didn't kill the other two, but Joey would do.

She was covered in Joey's blood after shooting him, so she took an actual shower. She considered taking a nap before heading out but thought better of it. She had things to do and didn't want to keep Mikey down there long. He could have a family waiting for him at home. They would call the police when he didn't return.

By then Max had to have bled out. She pondered going down there to stare at her dead corpse. But Mikey would be down there and might persuade her to let him go. She couldn't risk it. The knowledge that Max died by her hand would have to do. In a way, leaving her fate unanswered was calming.

Now that she has showered and is in some women's clothing she found in a suitcase in Graham's room, she heads back downstairs. She has one small task before leaving this godawful place. She finds a notepad and pen in a drawer in the kitchen. She sits at the dining table and writes down the names of eight individuals.

She admires her list when it is complete: the names of all the people who have wronged her. The ones who ruined her life. The ones who, once they get theirs, will be crossed off.

She has written similar lists, many times. Thinking of ways she could exact her revenge. Back then, she never had the will to do it. She thought of prison and how horrible it would be to be caged up for slaying those evil fuckers. It wouldn't be fair. Now she doesn't care. She has lived through hell. Prison will be nothing.

A song from her childhood begins to play in her head. "Born Free" by Andy Williams. Her mother used to play the song to her when she was a child. They would sing it together, and her mother would tell her how life can truly be a beautiful thing. That everyone is born free. Born free to live the life they dreamed of. Of course, Eva's life has been anything but that. Since that night at that party, Eva has been locked in a cage with demons. But she plans to rid herself of her demons, one by one.

She takes her pen and crosses through a select few names, before leaving the farmhouse for the last time.

"See you soon," she says, looking down at the remaining names written on the piece of paper.

~~Moe~~
~~Graham~~
~~Joey~~
~~Max~~
David
Red
Reece
Dennis

THE END

ACKNOWLEDGMENTS

I'd like to give a sincere and heartfelt thanks to my publisher, Joffe Books, for fulfilling the dream of a lifetime and publishing my work.

I'd also like to extend my thanks to my friends, family, and husband for all the support. Thanks to you, I had confidence to continue following my dream of being an author.

And, lastly, thanks to those who have either read my novels or are first-time readers. Just you reading my work means the absolute world to me.

THE JOFFE BOOKS STORY

We began in 2014 when Jasper agreed to publish his mum's much-rejected romance novel and it became a bestseller.

Since then we've grown into the largest independent publisher in the UK. We're extremely proud to publish some of the very best writers in the world, including Joy Ellis, Faith Martin, Caro Ramsay, Helen Forrester, Simon Brett and Robert Goddard. Everyone at Joffe Books loves reading and we never forget that it all begins with the magic of an author telling a story.

We are proud to publish talented first-time authors, as well as established writers whose books we love introducing to a new generation of readers.

We won Trade Publisher of the Year at the Independent Publishing Awards in 2023 and Best Publisher Award in 2024 at the People's Book Prize. We have been shortlisted for Independent Publisher of the Year at the British Book Awards for the last five years, and were shortlisted for the Diversity and Inclusivity Award at the 2022 Independent Publishing Awards. In 2023 we were shortlisted for Publisher of the Year at the RNA Industry Awards, and in 2024 we were shortlisted at the CWA Daggers for the Best Crime and Mystery Publisher.

We built this company with your help, and we love to hear from you, so please email us about absolutely anything bookish at feedback@joffebooks.com.

If you want to receive free books every Friday and hear about all our new releases, join our mailing list here: www.joffebooks.com/freebooks.

And when you tell your friends about us, just remember: it's pronounced Joffe as in coffee or toffee!